To A
Thank ... in
Support — Enjoy the
read — All the best,
Allen

THE UNCONVENTIONAL GUIDE TO
JOSEPH FINE

A NOVEL

Allen Danzig

Rendezvous Publishing
Naples, Florida

Dedication

To my parents, Elaine and Leonard Danzig.

ACKNOWLEDGEMENTS

I've been blessed with great support from some very good folks. Thank you to Melissa Glossup, my editor, who guided me to publication. Her advice and enthusiasm got me to the finish line. Thanks to her husband, Tedi Zohar, who designed the book art and my web site. And thanks to Robyn Holmes who provided edits and suggestions on earlier drafts.

The idea for this novel was floating in my head for some time. I thought I had something to say. I'm grateful to my wife Lynn who encouraged me to sit still and write it. I didn't realize how satisfying it was to engage in the creative process.

As I wrote this book, I was brought back in time to teachers who had a significant impact. Two of them at Lawrenceville School. Joel Greenberg gave me an appreciation of literature in an English class called the American Hero, that included books like Kerouac's *On the Road*. Bob Lester, my biology teacher, taught me to challenge conventional thinking. This is what I set out to do in *The Unconventional Guide* … And Nancy Sweeten, my English professor at Penn, told the class that to do well, you had to show her something she hadn't seen before. See if you think I did.

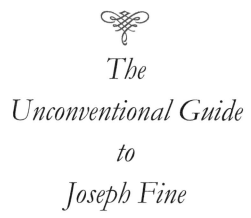

The

Unconventional Guide

to

Joseph Fine

CHAPTER ONE

... Babs thought he was terrific, she really did, but the height thing. Something wasn't right.

I left a promising career and the States to write a book and find the right woman. Are you kidding me?

After all of the soul searching and cerebral machinations, I took an indeterminate leave, and four weeks later, left New York for Venice on a Friday evening in late April right before a rainstorm hit the area. Venice is always busy, and this gave me a small jump on the tourist season. I packed lightly and brought my mermaid-patterned shirt and cowboy boots for good luck.

It was a mad rush to JFK after slogging through cone-laden streets to the airport. What a relief to be up in the air. For me, an admittedly excitable type, it was almost a moment of calm. I sat back, took a deep breath, sipped my first Dewar's, and hoped for a smooth ride. So far, so good, right? Well, until a few more minutes passed, and I thought about Babs, and what might have been. Got to stop doing this. That was almost a decade ago.

She was an old flame (that's a bit of an overstatement) who needed to be air dropped far away. I promise to stay calm while I tell you what happened.

A few weeks after college graduation, Joseph Fine (me, of course) returned from a trip out West with his old friend Jack. He ran into a woman from college named Carrie. Carrie and Joe used to sit and have coffee after one of his classes. Carrie told her girlfriend Barbara, who she called Babs, that she should meet him. She said he's cute in an animated, quirky way. A cross between a youthful Dustin Hoffman and Al Pacino. He wears tortoiseshell horn-rimmed glasses which make him also look intelligent. A little bit like the schoolmaster in *Goodbye, Mr. Chips.* Babs was excited about meeting him.

Carrie didn't tell Babs that Joe is five-feet-three and one-half. And he is closer to five-three. Or less. Carrie thought it might be a non-starter if she told her. Babs assumed, based on upbringing and hard wiring, that the right guy for her was about six feet or within a couple of inches. Joe did not know Babs was five-feet-five and one-half. He was shy with women in general and especially women who were taller.

Babs meets Joe. She tries to hide her surprise. He is surprised too but finds her worldly and attractive with a sunny personality. Early into the date, Babs doesn't think she can take Joe seriously. He acts like he is trying too hard. But he's funny, and she hasn't laughed so hard in a long time. She thinks about two short guys she knew in elementary school. They were loud and silly and craved attention. She thinks Joe might be different. Babs listens as he tells her about his goals. He's going to law school to be an environmental lawyer. He wants to make a difference in his career. Little by little she is more interested. Joe becomes more relaxed and self-confident.

The next morning, Babs meets four friends at Starbucks. They want to hear about the date. After they learn about the height part, they're concerned. One of them asks how she could go out with a guy who is five-three. If that. The others nod. They don't get it either. Babs pushes back, says she will decide for herself. Yes, there's his stature, but there is more to him than other dopey guys she's known. He's studious but not nerdy, well-traveled, and wants to protect the environment. And, by the way, she reminds two of her friends that they haven't had much success with guys lately.

These were guys who were tall, affable, young banker types who went to pedigree schools. The girls had to agree with Babs.

Babs goes on three more dates with Joe and has a great time. She is surprised by how happy she feels. But something is not right. She thinks about what the wedding pictures would look like. They look awkward together. When she leans toward Joe as girls do in photographs, she still hovers over him.

Babs has to do something. She tells Joe she is not ready for a serious relationship. There's too much going on now between her family vacation this summer and graduate school in the fall. Joe learned the real story months later when he ran into one of Babs' friends. She said Babs thought he was terrific, she really did, but the height thing. Something wasn't right.

In college, there were extended periods when I couldn't get a date. Things got a little better in law school. Consciously or not, I limited the potential dating pool to women under five-two. Less risk of rejection. It was hard enough meeting women my own height or less. They also had expectations. It was about time that I had some too. So much for Babs. I am pleased to note that I stayed calm on the plane, and the flight was happily uneventful.

So, I am flying to Venice. It means I'm going somewhere. Maybe even getting somewhere. But I'm getting ahead of myself. What lead to this point?

CHAPTER TWO

"

... they're so risk averse they don't answer the door on

Halloween...

The early career stuff means a lot to me. That's where I'll start. I am an adult by most conventional definitions, and I want to be taken seriously. That was never a problem in the workplace. It has been in my social life, and I'll get to that. Anyway … I got a law degree, which was a means to an end. I got my dream job at the Environmental Protection Agency. Alas, Mr. Fine goes to Washington D.C. It was exciting to stand outside the EPA building, and stare at the Agency sign. When I think about it, I wish someone were there to take my picture. They were paying me to protect the environment, right?

It helped that I looked intelligent. Especially in a town like Washington D.C., where looks and presence carry you to a great extent. I knew the uniform. A heavily starched button-down shirt, short, cropped hair, and horn-rimmed tortoiseshell glasses. A suit or sport jacket. I was smart, not brilliant, but instinct and balls are two traits that make a great lawyer. My boss was a great guy who put me on enforcement cases with big dollar potential. In the first two years, I obtained a few multimillion-dollar settlements against big companies. And I took a couple of stale files, found some nuggets, and turned them into settlements.

Within months after I started, I noticed that women took me incrementally more seriously, and I went out here and there. Sometimes, I even got a little action (emphasis on "a little"). Still, most of my social life consisted of non-threatening happy hours with groups of colleagues at a restaurant near work called Casa Rosita.

After three years, I thought about leaving the feds. You can get stale and lose some of your cachet and marketability if you stay too long. After six more months, I was increasingly restless. I realized I could advance my career in the private sector, help companies do the right thing, and make more money at the same time.

My timing was good. Environmental protection entered the corporate boardroom in the 1980s. The laws required companies to put in pollution controls and clean up contaminated properties. It all cost a lot of money. Companies wanted to do the right thing without giving the government a blank check. They needed lawyers like me to guide them through the regulations. I applied to corporate legal departments and got an offer with a national chemical and paint company called StarColor with headquarters in northern New Jersey.

I liked working at StarColor because the management had my back when I told the business folks what to do, or when I told them what they couldn't do. Sure, sometimes a government order is impossible to meet, and you have to discuss it or even challenge it. As I told StarColor's General Counsel Richard Martin when he interviewed me, "Richard, the government is not always right." I think he appreciated that.

The compensation included stock options, and I received more each year. After two years, I was promoted. Each year, StarColor had healthy increases in revenue and profits. The company grew more with acquisitions, and the stock went up and up. After I was at StarColor for three years, the company was bought by a bigger chemical company named Stanley Walker Corporation. It paid a healthy premium for StarColor's stock, and the stock tripled in those three years.

I made more money than I could imagine in three and a half years. I sold half of my options and took stock of my life in general. The work was going well, and I felt good about it. I was thirty-one years old and well-heeled financially, with no girlfriend or the prospect of one. In fact, I hadn't gone out much in the last year and a half.

For the first time, I thought about leaving the practice of law for a few months or even permanently. I had enough savings for a year or two. The thought of writing a book occurred to me. It had been percolating for a while. Sure, you'll say, another lawyer, another book. But how to do it with a demanding job? Maybe it meant leaving the company for some undefined period. I knew the boss wouldn't like the idea. My value as a lawyer could also diminish over time. Without a regular day job, women might not take me seriously. Well, it wasn't like they were now. A change could help, right?

I talked to two colleagues who thought I was nuts. Of course, they're so risk-averse they don't answer the door on Halloween. I patiently ignored friends who told me to stay in the workplace. I didn't tell my mom since I expected her to say the same thing.

Richard Martin, my boss and good friend, didn't like it one bit. He said he wouldn't take me back after a month. Well, maybe a little longer. Richard took it personally too. He left the Justice Department about a year before I left EPA, and he felt we were a great team. He was right about that. We worked on major matters and got good results. "Why would you leave when the Company's prospects are so exciting, and the opportunity to make a difference is so big?" The lawyer in him said it would be a bad precedent. After talking to him, I was confused and had a headache.

Richard stopped by my office the next day, and his mood changed. He smiled. "I talked to Carol in HR. They're not that concerned. If you seriously want to leave, I won't try to persuade you to stay. The two lawyers who work part-time are women, so

HR says this would show that we accommodate men too. "But Joe, look, point-blank. We can't give you any guarantee that you'll be able to come back after a month, six weeks max."

"I get it. Thanks for checking."

It was time for bold action. I consulted the Inner Voice, who sits in the back corner of my brain rent-free and occasionally gives me feedback. Most of it's helpful. Her perspective was, "If you don't do it now, when will you do it?" Good point. I decided to take an undetermined absence with no guarantee that they would take me back. I was ready to leave the relatively stable and secure halls of one of the best chemical and paint companies in America.

Three weeks later, I left the company. I initially planned to stay put in the New York area. It was the first day of April. A time for Spring and rebirth. And uncertainty. I said a handful of goodbyes. There wasn't much fanfare. I felt bad for Tara, my legal assistant, who did great work and liked to tell me about her social life.

About this book. I jotted down a few ideas the last couple months. One subject was the history of the environmental movement, from Aldo Leopold and Rachel Carson to climate change and the present. Another was a thriller about a big chemical spill, bureaucratic bungling, and corporate corruption. Interesting topics, tough to make readable.

I pivoted to a subject where I had something to say but didn't know very much: male and female relationships. A subject that has intrigued the human species for a long time. I know a lot has been written on the subject. So, I took a different perspective. I had to.

I came up with *The Unconventional Guide to Relationships*. What's the idea? How men and women perceive each other. More to the point - and please don't laugh or dismiss this out of hand - how do we change conventional thinking, so women are willing to date, be seen with, and even have meaningful relationships with shorter guys? A book to change perceptions and knock down barriers. A timeless American theme, right? Sure, it's one thing to be tolerant toward your fellow human beings. It's another thing to act on it in your personal life. And the flip side was to make women aware of a bigger universe of guys and vice versa. It's bold stuff if I can sit still long enough to write it.

I thought the words would spill out. It's easy to make excuses that you don't have the time based on work demand. For the last two years, I scribbled random thoughts most mornings before work. Julia Cameron calls these "morning pages" in her book, *The Artist's Way*. Writing, rambling, to start the day with a positive mindset. I suspected writing a book would be a much bigger enterprise. Could I transition to the writer's world?

The best advice I got was to keep to a schedule. Find a comfortable place to write. Set a daily goal. Write at the same time each day. All easy to say. Distractions are anywhere you want them to be. Without the corporate business-day discipline, it would be tough to stay focused.

I gave myself the weekend off and set up a routine for the first week after I left StarColor. The first four days, I started the morning with friends at the Starbucks near my apartment in Hoboken. Starbucks was a great social news and gossip center. I called my friends the Sweat Hogs in honor of the students on the 1970s TV show, *Welcome Back Kotter*. They were closer to a bunch of yentas. We yakked for about an hour. Then I went to the gym. By the time I worked out and ate something, eleven a.m. rolled around without any writing. Nothing to show.

For the rest of the first week, I tried an incentive system. If I produced at least three pages in a day, I was allowed to go out for a drink. That almost worked for a day. I still couldn't get off the ground. Nervous energy, writer's block, and any little distraction caused additional delay. I spent more time at Starbucks. The hour became ninety minutes, or more.

I stopped going to Starbucks but missed the camaraderie. The second week, I started an hour earlier at nine a.m. and took a break at eleven, which extended until early afternoon. Then mid-afternoon. This went on for four days with diminishing results. I went back to Starbucks with my head down. My friends rebuked me for leaving them, then warmly received me back. I stayed less time at Starbucks and worked by nine. This lasted three days.

All I had to show for two weeks were six pages of an outline and three pages of writing that didn't make sense. The Inner Voice suggested that I start work by nine-thirty and write for one and a half hours. Then go to the gym, and back to work promptly at one p.m. for at least two and a half hours. I did this for three or four days with minimal progress.

After almost three weeks, I was lost and wondering why I left. Something more dramatic was needed. How to light a fire under my seat? Perhaps, a change in scenery was required for a serious writer. Somewhere far away. It sounded like the great American escape strategy. I looked at the Kerouac model, which included a cross-country trek through the great West, the Pacific Coast and Mexico, and the European model, led by a cast of characters like Hemingway, Fitzgerald, and Henry Miller. One way or the other, I had to leave North Jersey. I just had to figure out where.

Something else sat in the back of my mind. My social life was going nowhere, and something had to change for the better. Somehow, I needed better luck with women. A change in setting could help. It certainly couldn't hurt. It's easier to chat when you're away, right?

But going away wasn't enough. For too long, I didn't pursue women who were over five-two. Or five-three at most. I assumed they weren't interested, and I needed to preempt rejection. Create a protective shield. Women my height or less were enough of a challenge. And yet ... the available pool of prospective women could increase if I included taller women. More possibilities could mean better results, even if it meant more rejections.

So, effective immediately, I will consider women taller than me as dating prospects. A taller woman should have the opportunity to go out with someone like me. What was I after? A girlfriend? Marriage? Yes, a relationship with a taller woman could result in marriage, but that wasn't necessary.

First, I needed to feel accepted. Then, I wanted something meaningful. A relationship that goes to a deeper level. You know it when you have it. I wasn't looking for a specific period of time, like two or four months, or a particular number of sleepovers. And to still be meaningful after a breakup, the breakup can't be based on the height factor. It has to be something like a personality trait, money, or communication. For the right women, my new approach could also be viewed as a mutual opportunity. All I wanted was a fair shot.

CHAPTER THREE

"

Nice to meet you too.

I was determined to leave, but where to go? I made a list of locations within a ten-hour plane ride of the East Coast. A simple, subjective list. I narrowed it down to cities in England, France, and Italy, countries where I had a basic familiarity. London is great fun but wasn't intriguing enough. I loved the literary heritage, the village greens, and of course, the pubs. Paris was overused as a literary escape, no offense to the Lost Generation and the legacy of enlightened souls and debauchery.

Then, there was Italy. Two places came to mind. I went to Venice and Siena after law school and loved both cities. Venice was timeless, mysterious, decadent, and most importantly, it was above water. I imagined a pilgrimage to Harry's Bar in San Marco Square, talking to an exotic woman. A great place to get the literary juices flowing. Siena was extraordinarily beautiful in a more classical way. I read James Boswell's eighteenth-century diary in which he described Siena as a magical place to optimize his love life. That made it tempting, but it likely had changed since then. I settled on Venice. I didn't expect to spend two or three months there, given the high cost, but I wanted to start there. Hopefully, this was the venue to jumpstart a book and meet women under my broader criteria.

The next question was where to stay. While it's a spectacular public square, the hyper-busy Piazza San Marco didn't make sense.

I wanted an area that was central but slightly removed from the limelight. I checked out the area known as Rialto di Mercato, which has an ancient fruit and vegetable market. It's close to the fifteenth-century Rialto Bridge, but away from the crowds that fill the bridge each day. I reserved a room at a two-star hotel named Pensione Guerrato. According to my guidebook, it was formerly a convent for hundreds of years going back to the fourteenth century. The pensione should add mystery and inspiration. I would give myself a few days to sightsee before tackling the writing life.

So, it was off to Venice. I arrived at Marco Polo Airport the next morning after three Dewar's on the rocks, a scary meal of pasta and meat sauce, and two hours of sleep. When I stepped outside the terminal, the sunshine felt great. Ready to go with my Indians baseball hat and tortoiseshell sunglasses. I took the airport boat express from the dock outside Marco Polo to Rialto Bridge, entering the bustling Grand Canal along the way. From Rialto Bridge, it was one short stop on the local water bus, the Vaporctto, to the dock at Mercato Rialto on the other side of the canal. Between the Vaporettos, water taxis, and gondolas, traffic on the Grand Canal made Midtown Manhattan look almost orderly.

It was a two-minute walk from the dock to my hotel. I rang the bell of the imposing six-inch-thick, brown wooden door. The pensione is on a narrow alley that doesn't get much light during the day. I walked up to the reception desk one floor up and checked in with a friendly old man. I was too tired to look at the map he put in front of me.

The room was big and sparse with a double bed, an old desk with no outlet, and a small chandelier that provided little light. When I opened the heavy wood shutter, a burst of light entered the room. Fortunately, I looked out over the market stalls and not the dark alley. About fifty yards farther were the Grand Canal and the Rialto Mercato Vaporetto stop.

I tried to take a nap but was too excited and restless. I left the room and walked down the alley in the direction away from the Grand Canal into the charming San Polo neighborhood. On the way back, I stopped in a small square at an outdoor café called Bussola Cocktail Lab, which was around the corner from the market stalls and my hotel. The café table was barely big enough to hold my sunglasses and baseball hat. I ordered a Dewar's on the rocks and a bowl of large olives.

I must have dozed off. The bartender tapped me. I paid the tab, went back to the room, and slept for a couple hours. It was midafternoon when I returned to the café for a stirato with cheese and cucumbers, and a Dewar's with soda and lemon twist. Two tables over, I heard a woman say, "This is your fourth drink. Maybe you should stop. I'm still on my first." The guy was in a daze, his head moving back and forth. I couldn't tell if they were related, married, friends or colleagues. She looked intelligent and affluent. She could be a Junior Leaguer or a soccer mom.

From a distance, the woman was maybe five-five, which is a half-inch taller than the average American woman. I guessed she was in her late twenties. She had a plain, but pretty face, like a classic Jane Austen character, and looked fit, but not overly muscular. Her eyes were dark and pretty, but when she stared out, she seemed serious and businesslike. Long, strawberry blonde hair with light highlights. The humidity made it curlier, and it shined in the afternoon light. Small lips, no readily discernible Botox, or other fillers, and slightly pale. She wore a moderately tight-fitting cotton dress with purple and pink floral prints. The dress gave her a festive air.

Oh, yes, she appeared to have good-sized boobs, just not big enough to get comments from construction guys. And given her somewhat stilted demeanor, you would not use crass language to describe them. The guy she was with perked up and seemed like an affable chap. He had a round face, short brown hair and an oversized Tommy Bahama beach shirt with little umbrellas. He looked like the guy in the *Preppy Handbook* with a genetically attached beer can.

One of them said something I couldn't hear. Then they couldn't stop laughing. The guy said, "That was the fucking funniest thing I ever saw." They were sipping a reddish drink. It was fun watching her curls blow around in the wind. I wanted to enter the conversation.

I looked their way and asked what they're drinking. The woman answered. "It's an Aperol Spritz."

"I never heard of it. What's in it?"

She seemed friendly but reserved. "It includes Aperol, which is an Italian aperitif. Then you add Prosecco and club soda and top it off with an orange slice." This sounded delicious, and I wanted to try it, especially if it helps the conversation. I am appreciative, even grateful, when an attractive woman pays attention to me. We'll see if something happens.

She told me the guy with her is a friend. Which probably means he's not a boyfriend. He looked about thirty and had a British accent. The woman talked American; I'm guessing South Carolina. She ran her hand through the curly hair. He's had too much sun and too much to drink. Reminded me of a windblown English chap I met at a seaside bar in St. Ives last year. The guy was happy and trashed, swaying from side to side.

I ordered an Aperol Spritz. It looks like the local favorite. I love the fizz and the floating slice. "So, what brings you two here?"

She looked at me, smiled, and looked at the guy. She seemed hesitant. He started to talk, but he slurred his words, and I couldn't follow him. She took over and said, "We work for a pharmaceutical company in Basel. We had a conference in Verona and had an extra couple of days off. So, here we are."

"I'm on an extended break." I was trying to get her attention. Her hair kept blowing. She attempted to hold it down. "I worked as an attorney. I took an extended break to start a book. I thought if I don't do it now, I won't for a long time. Venice looked like a good choice to start. It's inspirational everywhere you go around here. The narrow streets, the little piazzas, the churches. I got writer's block sitting in North Jersey. I got as far as a few poems on bar napkins." I was trying too hard to impress her, or at least, get her to laugh.

Luckily, she loosened up. "Everybody's writing a book … What's yours about? Don't tell me. A single guy is tired of working, and unlike Kerouac, he will not be crossing America. He goes to Italy to write, but he's conflicted. He left a career with great potential. The real reason he left is to meet a classy woman. She wears a summer cotton print dress. Funny, it looks like mine. She reminds him of the woman in *A Room with a View*. How am I doing?"

I think I'm in love, but she talks too fast. I have to focus. My attention fades sometimes. Before I can say anything, she continued. "And by the way, I read *On the Road* three times, and we went across the country, my girlfriend and I, and did our own route. Pretty deep, huh? Unlike Kerouac, we had no senoritas, well no senors, and no one-night stands. It did have a romantic aura. Well, you and I know he made some of that up."

"You're unbelievable." This woman has quite the intellectual streak. I can't say anything stupid and must stay detached. And don't interrupt her. No interrupting until the relationship is stronger. I again noticed her dress fit well. Simple, close-fitting, without being provocative.

"I think I'm supposed to say thank you. I'm Cindy Green, and this is Nigel Totham."

"Very nice to meet you. I'm Joseph Fine."

Cindy said, "The company has a research facility in Bologna. We're going there in a couple of days. Nigel's got a new job, so he doesn't care." He smiled, then looked away. Within minutes, he fell asleep. He needs to get out of the sun. She looked at me.

"Joe, will you be here for twenty minutes? Nigel needs help getting back to the hotel. He drinks Aperol Spritzes like most people drink water. I'll be back. I'm staying a couple of hundred yards away. Near the San Polo Church. You know there's a Tintoretto in there. We can have a drink when I get back. I bet you're more of a lemon guy than a lime guy."

"Close. Lemon twist. Only for Scotch. And olives. The big Italian olives. OK, I'll wait ..." She talked to me like she knew me.

Cindy got up and stretched, helped Nigel up, and walked away. He waved goodbye like a little kid. Her blonde curly hair stayed put for the moment. I looked around Rialto Mercato. The outdoor market stalls were closing for the day.

It's a perfect day. A lovely afternoon. Still hot, gradually cooling, great for a stroll. One of those days when you feel all's right with the world. So far, so good. Let's see what happens. Is Cindy fun ..., but normal? Is she a wack job? Will she tell me about her ex or discuss our future relationship before we go out? Why do women do that? What matters is she's coming back. Will she? It was about time I started having some expectations.

I waited nervously at Bussola. I could tell myself one hundred times to relax, but it wouldn't work. It especially shouldn't matter now. I have a fresh start, and I'm meeting an old school friend later today, so I have an excuse if I need to leave. Hopefully, I won't need one. I walked up to the bar, but there's no bottle of Dewar's on either shelf. I cursed under my breath. I'll get another spritz. There wasn't enough ice in the drink. The bartender added two cubes like he was doing me a favor.

I sipped the drink, looked at the clear blue sky, and thanked God for a bright, sunny day. I'm not religious, but there are days when I feel a divine presence. I felt blessed when I took off for Italy. And years before in my first year of law school, when a brown-eyed medical assistant named Lauri said in an intimate moment, "Joe, you gave me the best orgasm." Clearly proof of a higher being. By the way, she broke up with me three weeks later. I wasn't "mature enough," whatever that meant. The shoe dropped or God took a break.

Still lost in thought as Cindy returned, but I quickly regained consciousness. She wore white shorts and a sleeveless navy silk blouse. Did she change to get my attention? I don't know, but she got my attention.

"What would you like to drink?" I asked. That was easy enough.

"I'll go with a spritz. Can you ask for an extra orange slice?"

"Aperol Spritz?"

"Yes, excellent. Thank you."

I went back to the bar. No one was waiting tables. The bartender nodded like he approved of Cindy. This guy would be a good wingman. The orange in Cindy's spritz neatly filled the perimeter of the glass. A sight to behold.

When I was halfway back to the table, the front of my sneaker bumped up against a cobblestone that's about two inches higher than the one behind it. I fell and the drink spilled out. I held on to the drink as I was falling, which was stupid, and fell on my right arm near the elbow. The glass broke. I think I blacked out. Don't know how much time passed. I finally looked up and couldn't get up. I saw Cindy but she seemed far away. Then I wondered why I left the USA but quickly removed that thought.

Somehow, I didn't cut myself. Nothing was broken, but I have a welt near my right elbow, which hurt like hell. Cindy was turned around, watching two five-year-old girls kick a soccer ball, and didn't see the accident. She heard my scream, saw the glass, got up, and asked if I'm OK. I was in a lot of pain. But I needed to show her I'm resilient. "Can I get you a drink?" is what I think I mumbled.

She smiled. "No, thanks, let me see what's wrong first." She looked at the mark near the elbow. "Can you get up?"

Dazed. "I think so. Give me a few minutes." It was going to take longer.

I forced a smile and closed my eyes. *In the distance, there was Joseph Fine, the ten-year-old at Silver Point Elementary School. Playing kickball.*

The children in his class called him the kid. He lived in a ranch house on a one-acre lot with his parents and younger brother, five miles from the northern most part of the Jersey Shore. There is a detached garage that he turned into an indoor basketball court with a fruit basket rim six feet high. He also made a baseball field in the backyard with lime base paths. To get to school, the kid only has to walk past four houses and cross Bridge Road with the help of Mr. Jackson, the crossing guard. Then he's there. He has a three-to four-minute walk to school.

It's one minute if he runs. He always runs.

This was the kid's routine. He races home for lunch, eats the peanut butter and jelly sandwich his mom made, then runs back to school, all in less than twelve minutes. This gives him over a half-hour to play kickball before recess is over. He makes sure he is back on the playground before the kids who stay at school for lunch go outside for recess, and more importantly before they pick kickball teams. He loves to play kickball and has moments of pure joy playing the game.

Today it's especially important for him to be on time. If he's late, he loses his place as one of the fifth-grade kickball team captains tomorrow.

He sees his friend Jack Abner bouncing a kickball, and they wait for the others to arrive. Jack also goes home for lunch.

The kid is the shortest boy in the class, but one of the better players. He has short dark brown hair that is parted and was the first child in his class to wear glasses. That was in second grade. Jack is a bushy-haired blond boy and one of the tallest in the class.

There are nine sets of team captains. The order of the captains is based on how good you are and is largely influenced by the top players. So, the first set are the two best players. The captains in the ninth set, well, the least best.

Today, the captains are the third team captains, so they are the fifth and sixth-best players. The kid thinks he's good enough to be one of the third team captains, but he's pleased to be at least one of the fourth team captains.

He has been practicing a lot lately, and he thinks he can kick the ball as far as the two boys who are second-team captains. The first-team captains are really good, and he doubts he can get to their level. They have booming kicks and great throwing arms. They're also a foot taller and weigh more. But the kid can run as fast as anybody, and they respect him for that.

Waiting for the rest of his classmates to show up, the kid bounces the ball as hard as he can to see how high it will go. He stops and holds the ball when everyone is ready to pick teams. One of the boys, a tall, thin kid named Leo Welton, frequently gets in trouble. He comes over to the kid, takes the ball, and kicks it as hard as he can until it stops at the chain-link fence at the back of the playground about two hundred feet away.

The kid doesn't mind getting the ball because he likes to run. He quickly retrieves it and comes back. Leo takes the ball from him, throws it up a couple of feet with his left hand, and bats it with his right fist. He says, "Hey kid, go get it, you little twerp."

This time, the kid ignores Leo and meets with the other boys to pick teams. Leo yells at him again to get the ball. The kid goes up close to Leo and screams, "You motherfucking douchebag." Everyone hears him. He learned to talk this way playing tackle football without pads or a helmet after school with sixth-grade boys. Leo smiles weakly. Most of the boys voice support for the kid, who says to Leo, "Next time I will kick your sorry butt." The kid picked up the phrase from his older cousin Mikey.

Leo looks at the kid and says, "You dick, you don't even know what a douchebag is." The kid only knows that it's something dirty and has something to do with girls. This time, Leo went too far. The kid chases after him, knocks him down, and sits on his back. Leo has a chocolate donut that he saved from the cafeteria. The kid grabs the doughnut and rubs it in Leo's face. He tells Leo, "Don't you ever talk to me like that again."

This turned out to be a good day for Joseph Fine. Jimmy Smith, one of today's captains, picks him on the second round. He is quite surprised. He's never been picked this early. A few girls from his class jump rope nearby. One of them, his friend Trish Silver, likes to watch the boys play. Trish and the kid play Junior Jeopardy after school and do projects like papier-mache maps. She comes over to him. "Wow, you're a tough little guy," she says with a bright smile that shows all of her big new teeth. She has straight, long, light-brown hair, almost blonde, and is four inches taller than him. They are barely aware of the difference, and they have been friends for two years.

The kid tells Trish about girls he likes, and she tells him about boys she thinks are cute. They agree not to tell anyone about these talks. Trish has two nosy friends, but the kid thinks that she won't talk to these girls. He likes one girl in particular who must be five inches taller than him. The other kids will laugh at him if they find out, and he'll deny it.

At the end of fourth grade, the kid was playing baseball after school in John Hartman's backyard with other kids. John was a stocky kid about average height. He lived behind his friend Jack's house a half-mile from school. John's father was the local high school band director. When the second inning was over, John walked over to the kid and called him a dirty Jew. The kid smiled. He grabbed John from behind, pushed him to the ground, and rubbed his face into the dirt next to home plate. John got up and looked like a defeated puppy dog. He didn't bother the kid again.

Jimmy Smith and today's other captain, Bobby Lawson, have finished picking teams, and Jimmy's team takes the field. The kid is in the field at second base. The first two boys on Bobby's team get on base, and Hartman, who the kid calls a dickwad, is up. He misses on the first roll, and then kicks a ball high in the air. It is headed the kid's way. He runs as fast as he can but can't reach it. He is barely able to hit it back in the air. The ball is caught by his teammate, Derrick Kaplan. Hartman is out. Jimmy's team cheers Derrick. The kid is thrilled that Derrick caught the ball.

The kid thinks about saying something to Hartman but doesn't bother. From then on, the kid was picked either second or third. He worked very hard to get better. A few games later, he kicked a line-drive home run. It started as a triple, but turned into a home run. The kid rounded third base and headed for home. All the third baseman had to do was throw the ball at him from about eight feet away, but he missed. The kid scored.

Shaking my head, I opened my eyes, still on the ground. There was another scrape above my right knee. I wondered how that happened. "I think I can get up, but I need a couple more minutes." I welcomed Cindy's attention. We'll see if it was worth the fall. I gingerly got up and carefully walked around the broken glass to our table. If I shuffle along and lead with my left leg, I should be fine. She helped me wipe off the blood. I'll wash at the hotel.

"So, you still need a drink?" I asked. The top two buttons of the silk blouse were unbuttoned, showing the start of a cleavage.

"You're hurt. I'll get it."

"Thanks, and can I please have extra ice."

She smiled, headed to the bar, returned with two drinks. Two Aperol Spritzes with big orange slices.

I felt emboldened. "Thank you ... So, you work for big pharma, you're here for a break, and you're meeting your boyfriend later, who's coming up from Positano?" I can make up stories too.

"Not quite, no boyfriend, that was three months ago."

"He came up from Positano three months ago?"

"No, I broke up with him after we were in Ravenna. It's down the coast. On the Adriatic side. I broke up with him, but not until we saw the mosaics. Just amazing. I didn't want to mess up that part of the trip."

So far so good. A classy woman with no boyfriend. She went into her purse and took out a plastic bag. "This is for the bruise, to hold the ice."

"Thanks, and thanks for the drink. I wanted to buy the drinks."

"Ok, you can pay me later." She smiled again. I noticed that one of her front teeth tilts slightly onto the other one. A perfect imperfection. This could be a sign of charm and character.

Now it's my turn. Most women like breakup stories so I'll tell one.

"I broke up with, I'll call her Nora, but first we toured the Chinese collection at the Metropolitan Museum of Art." This was not quite true unless two dates are enough to support a breakup. I also substituted the museum to provide a setting. "Then she said, 'It's not you, it's me' at lunch in a coffee shop on Madison near the museum. I've been good at fleeting relationships."

"Well, you know, some women ..." And she left it at that.

I felt comfortable and didn't need to rely on an early escape. There's plenty of time to meet my friend Carter at Harry's Bar. I enjoyed talking to her and felt better.

We finished the drinks. I had a good buzz. "Joe, I hate to break up the fun, but I have work to do. I have a presentation with the board on Wednesday. You'll be OK to get back to your hotel? ... I'm here two more days. I bet there's more you want to see. We can hang out tomorrow afternoon. Or dinner, that would be good too."

"Dinner sounds good. I want to see a few churches and a couple palaces. I'm thinking about Padua too. Can you meet at Rialto Bridge? The Vaporetto stop."

"OK, I'm staying close to there. Cocktails start at five, don't they?"

"Cocktails start when you say so."

"You pick a place, and afterward we'll go somewhere else."

"I will. I'll let you know." Sounds grrrrreat. A spirit of adventure. We'll see how long this lasts.

She leaned over, planted a light kiss on my cheek. My eyes opened and I said, "Nice to meet you."

"Of course. Nice to meet you too." And off she went. Cindy Green. Not a bad start.

CHAPTER FOUR

You don't have to like me, but you will.

Carter Weinstein is a classmate from Leicester School days. He has been a good, loyal friend since tenth grade. If you did not know him and you met him, you would think he's pompous and brash. He's simply confident and doesn't doubt himself. He's got boundless energy. And thankfully, some of his self-confidence has rubbed off on me. He doesn't look in the rear-view mirror.

Carter is close to six feet tall, has good-sized teeth, and a shit-eating smile. He has a full head of blondish, reddish hair and slightly darker sideburns that reach the bottom of his ears. You could confuse him with a youthful Robert Redford. I can handle him because he's usually fun to be around, and I don't have to live with him. A few women have for short periods. Then he moves on and doesn't dwell on it. Carter says he will be so ready when the right woman comes along.

After we graduated from Leicester, we flew to Paris. A week later, we started a long bike trip near the Arc de Triomphe. We had two bonding moments. The first was when we were still in Paris and went to a discotheque. I got drunk on an orange-flavored drink and lost it on Boulevard Saint-Germain. We made it back to our one-star hotel and I was still sick. Carter worried and kept asking if I was OK. He acted like he really cared. I felt better by next afternoon and thanked him for his support.

The second moment was during the bike trip. We stopped for the night in Donauworth, a small quaint town at the intersection of the Danube and Wornitz Rivers, between Heidelberg and Munich. We had biked for a week and a half and had three more days to get to Munich. For dinner, we ate some wretched rubbery wurst and warm potato salad. Both of us got major-league upset stomachs. We felt so weak, we stopped the trip, put the bicycles on the train and went to Munich.

Carter lives in New York City on the Upper West Side and typically calls me when I haven't heard from him for months. He says something like, "Hey Joe, come into the city, meet me at King Cole." The King Cole Bar is in the venerable St. Regis Hotel in Midtown Manhattan. Behind the bar is a 1906 wall-length mural painting by Maxfield Parrish which is based on the Old King Cole nursery rhyme. He likes the bar because it attracts beautiful, mixed-up women. I know, they're not all like that. We horse around and try to meet women. Well, Carter does anyway. I tag along. Carter's a lot of fun, at least for two to three days. Then it's time to go.

Carter grew up around 88th Street and Park Avenue. He talks about his ancestors like he was there at the beginning. They were among the first Jews who settled on Manhattan Island in 1654 before England pushed the Dutch out and renamed the colony, New York. His old man was the first Jew to make partner at a big law firm that, for years, didn't hire Jews. Carter has a gorgeous older sister, Karina, a recently divorced supermodel. She vacations on Lake Como with her new beau. Karina considers her brother childish. I would give him more credit and say that he occasionally acts like an adolescent.

Carter or his current lady friend have introduced me to various women. He builds me up to them, which I appreciate, but I've never gotten very far. I called him before I left for Venice and said I was taking an extended time off. He thought about getting away too, at least for a couple of weeks. He's a freelance writer and has a flexible schedule. He arrived in Venice two days before me. We agreed to meet at Harry's Bar, off San Marco Square near the Grand Canal.

Yes, Harry's is the famous bar with overpriced drinks and mediocre food. But it's where the Bellini was created and was one of Hemingway's watering holes. The customers include tourists, older gentlemen, and gold diggers. What I mean are women who use an ATM card, and it doesn't work, which results in "that's so kind of you to buy me a drink." It's the aura of being there and trying to get the bartender's attention in a small, crowded space. Carter made it clear he was buying. I happily went along.

I walked back to Pensione Guerrato from the café, passing the fruit and vegetable stands. The room keys at reception were attached to miniature loggias from the Doges Palace. My arm still hurt so I lay down. Strange to rest in a building where hundreds of nuns lived. I wonder if any of them sneaked out to pursue conjugal relations in this classically mischievous city. I fell asleep and woke up two minutes before I was supposed to meet Carter.

I took a fast shower, put on a pair of off-white denim pants and heavily starched navy and white striped button-down shirt. I need to look like I live near Gatsby when I walk into Harry's Bar. I weaved through the tourists on Rialto Bridge where they waited for sunset. Everyone angles for a good view of the orange sky and glistening blue water. From there, it's an easy walk to San Marco Square and Harry's Bar.

This is the third time I've been to Venice, and I will never get tired of it. I love to wander here, to eat and drink here, and would love to have sex here. That would put me in good company with the likes of Casanova and doges of Venice past. It's almost the end of April, it's a warm late afternoon, and I felt like there was magic in the air.

Most of my pain was gone by the time I arrived at Harry's. I didn't make any wrong turns on the way, and straight lines are rare in Venice. The entrance to Harry's is translucent glass, so you can't see inside. That's part of the bar's mystique. I peeked inside, then entered. Carter was not there, maybe he found a new friend to tell his embellished version of the Grand Tour. Carter wasn't a great student, but he's good with geographical metaphors. He knows that his animal magnetism and mastery of bullshit carry him, at least for a while.

I walked outside and looked around. Where the hell is he? I was the one who was late. Two minutes pass, and I was grabbed from behind with two strong arms. I turned around. There he was with a charming young lady. Jesus, she's thin and gorgeous, and she's shorter than me. She has dark brown hair tied back and blue eyes. With her white polo shirt, she looked like a tennis pro.

Carter had a crushing handshake, and I got a strong slap on the back for no extra charge. Thank God I didn't fall down. "Hello, Joe, my man, welcome to Venice and welcome to Harry's decadent shithole. The ladies here, oh ma' goodness." Carter's a New Yorker, but he has adopted a Southern affectation. I think he got it at Leicester where there were a lot of students from the South.

"And Joe, this is my friend Liza Thompson." We exchanged greetings. "I met Liza on the train from Milano. She's a decorator for the rich and famous. I promised her a Bellini at Harry's. You know they were invented here." I nodded. It's hard to get a word in with Carter. You just roll with it and watch the show.

He kept going. "Well, you are in for a treat my boy, your timing is très bien because Liza has a friend who saw a photograph of Joseph Fine, that would be you, and she is excited to meet Y-O-U. Her name is DD. Not D-E-E. Just DD. DD is short for Deirdre Dawn. And her last name is Schonstein. Do you know what that means Joe? It means beautiful stone." I don't know what photo he's talking about, but it probably doesn't show how tall I am.

"Joe, you will not believe this, but DD is a nice Jewish girl. And a southern nice Jewish girl. You cannot do better than that. These two went to Vanderbilt. Sorority sisters at SDT. Not seldom dated twice. You'll wish you went to Vandy instead of Yale with all of those whiny women." Liza is not bothered by Carter's bantering. It's early. "Liza assures me that she puts out, sorry sweetheart, I'm kidding. Joe," he said with a faux solemnity, "We can only hope."

I turned to Liz and shook my head. "Look, this is the way he is. He means well, he could use a better choice of words." She has a perky smile, and her baby blue eyes blink a lot. She wore stretch red denim pants with the white polo. Good-sized white teeth and pink lipstick. Do you need perfect teeth to be in the sorority? I stared a second too long, and her eyes said, "It's OK, I get it, I'm flattered."

Carter continued. "Anyway, let's take a stroll. Venice is the coolest, smelliest place, it reeks ambiance. DD is arriving from Milan soon. We'll meet her at Santa Lucia, that's the station and go from there. Ok with you?"

"OK with me. Thanks for your support, big guy." I finally got a word in. My mind turned to Cindy and the dress with floral prints. So serious yet possibly an inner playfulness?

Meanwhile, all I know is that DD was in a sorority at a blue-chip Southern school. She could be a social butterfly or a train wreck. Hopefully, Carter has done his due diligence. The fun of it is, I don't know what's ahead. Will it be Cindy or DD, another woman, or none of the above? The adventure has begun.

"Joe, you can throw out the map and guidebook, you can't get lost here. You're never far from the Grand Canal or one of these Vaporetto stops."

"I have a sense of the city. You do what you want, but I need a map, just in case."

"Come on Joe, risk and reward, DD will give you direction. Hehehe." Carter often thinks he is funny when others can't see it.

Liza waded in. "Yeah, Joe, I think you'll like her. She's in markcting. She's lively. Carter told me about you. Sounds good, even if it's half true," she smiled and looked at him. "He says you're intelligent, but you don't pay attention. This might work because DD is a bit of a scatterbrain. You guys could go out, and conversation won't be a problem because half of it will be, 'What did you say, I'm sorry I missed that.' And then you'll both laugh because you're both spaced out. Sometimes she talks so fast, she forgets what she's saying. How'd I do, Carter?" He winked. OK, so this will be good, or it may implode (or is it explode?), and Carter will owe me drinks ad infinitum.

I let Liza get on my nerves. Remember there is no need for tension. I'm blessed. The stock tripled, I sold some, left some on the table, and here I am at Harry's. Just play hard, then work hard. In a few days, I'll work hard, then play hard. Women think I'm cute, which gets tired at my age. Cute means short, and short, dark, and cute cannot normally compete with tall, dark, and handsome. Will DD go beneath or beyond the fateful first impression and see charming and intelligent? Then I have a shot. And as long as I play to my strengths. What are they again?

We boarded the Vaporetto at San Marco for the Santa Lucia train station. The seats were occupied and there wasn't much standing room. A toddler, maybe three years old, was screaming. His mother tried to calm him. I moved away from the boy and lost Carter and Liza. A minute later, I heard someone say, "Where did that douchebag go?" and naturally it was Carter. I waved. Another badly behaved American visitor. Carter came over, saw Liza about five feet away, and said under his breath, "Joe, I need your help." I know this tone of voice. He needs a wingman.

"What's the problem?"

"Look, I met Liza a couple of days ago. Carrie is coming into town tonight, she's my Texas girlfriend. I don't want to mess it up with her. Can you keep Liza and DD occupied? I'm telling Liza I have an assignment with a tight deadline, and I can't see her tonight. Joe, can you take care of this? Pretty please?"

"This is going to cost you, my friend. And how do I keep Liza from coming to your hotel?"

"I will tell her I'm working late. I have to be on the phone a lot and can't be interrupted. Liza and DD are at a hotel in San Marcuola, it's the old Jewish Ghetto area. Anyway, the girls are staying far from the Rialto Bridge area where I am. You're not far from Rialto too, right? Think about it, Joe, two ladies, one on each arm, when is the last time that happened to you?"

"Look, Carter, just throw me under the bus. Don't sugarcoat it, and you want me to stay with them all evening?"

"Well, what else do you have going on, except imaginary conference calls?" One thing's for sure. I will not miss those calls.

I summed it up. "For you, the fucking world."

We exited the Vaporetto. The train station was in front of us. It's a dull-looking, low, wide building, out of place in an area of old, stately, decadent palaces. Carter walked over to Liza, explained the situation. She didn't seem happy. He said to her, "Look, we'll catch up tomorrow morning, there is so much to see here."

Carter realized he should wait a moment. He tried a small distraction. "Liza, Joe, before I go, look across the Grand Canal, you see the Chiesa San Simeone Piccolo, the Church of the Small St. Simon, built in the 18th century. The name of the Church is the same as the original ninth-century church that stood there. The original church was smaller than the nearby Chiesa San Simeone Grande, the Church of the Big St. Simon. The church you're looking at, which kept the name Church of the Small St. Simon, is bigger than Big St. Simon." Liza and I shook our heads. What is he talking about?

I said, "I'm confused. So, Piccolo is Grande? Interesting."

"Yes, kids, give it some thought. On that note, I have to go." Carter quickly exited, like he was relieved to go. Here I am with Carter's sort of girlfriend who I don't know. She smiled and shrugged.

The late afternoon sun felt good. Liza and I lingered outside the train station for a few moments. I felt remarkably awake given my first day in Venice. We went inside. It was much cooler. I got coffee and a biscotti, and Liza had a cappuccino. I love how the Italians dip the cookies in the coffee. When I do it, the biscotti falls in the drink. We walked toward the track platforms. I kept the pressure off my right leg, and it felt better. The schedule board said the Milano train was a half-hour late. I can pretend to go to the bathroom. No, I'll wait. I might pick up more intelligence on DD. Liza faced me with her back to the platforms.

"Joe, how long have you known Carter?"

"On and off for fifteen years. We were good pals in prep school. After that, I saw him every year or so. He calls me or I call him. He could be around the corner or hundreds of miles away, and we get together. Kind of spontaneous."

"Do you think I can trust him?" She shouldn't ask me this. Fortunately, I don't have many details on his romantic pursuits. You know what the lawyer says so he's not accused of lying? "Your honor, I have no present recollection at this time." It gives you some wiggle room. I can't say it like that. "Look, he's a good friend, he's a good guy. I'm not really up on his social life."

"Sorry, I shouldn't ask you that kind of question."

"It's OK." It's really not OK. "Carter has set me up with women. That's been good." Hopefully, this helped answer her character question. I excused myself. Fortunately, the bathroom is at the other end of the station from where DD arrives. I'll be away enough to avoid further questions.

I walked back slowly. Don't be nervous. It's just another day.

The train arrived. A large crowd with big rolling bags headed toward us. From where we're standing, it looked like we could be run over. Everybody wants a piece of Venice. And they want it now.

A woman walked toward us. Liza jumped. It must be DD. "Liza, Liza," she screamed.

Liza screamed back, "DD, DD, you made it." The way these two jump up and down sounded rehearsed, like this must be their greeting ritual. DD is about five-one, maybe a little more, almost as tall as Liza. Carter said she was a dirty blonde. Her hair is more medium brown. It's perfectly straight, shoulder length, and pulled back. They all like it pulled back these days. She has a round, happy face, and wears a red baseball hat with a gold "V" on it. Orthodontically perfect teeth, unlike mine which have an annoying space between the two front ones. She has good-sized lips with bold red lipstick.

DD was nicely proportioned, OK, she's slightly overweight. No, barely. Tight, not super tight, white denim pants, a light blue button-down blouse with two buttons appropriately unbuttoned. Just right. Her top looked like it was starched and pressed. Good for her. And behind the blouse, there was a very healthy pair of boobs that have started to talk to me.

This girl looked more like a member of the First Anglican Church of Nashville, and Carter told me she's Jewish? I see her serving tea, and cucumber and mayonnaise white-bread sandwiches with the crusts cut off. Maybe one of her parents converted. I bet Carter is setting me up, so if I tell her she's a nice Jewish girl, she will say she's not Jewish or she's not that nice. The latter would be fine.

The two girls regained composure. "DD, this is Carter's friend Joseph Fine. Carter had to work. You know he's always working. Hopefully, we'll see him later."

"Very nice to meet you, DD."

"Hello to you." She smiled. She had a strong handshake. Seemed formal. Are there any Jewish daughters of the American Revolution?

"So, you're on the rebound?" This was what Carter told me. Why did I say this?

"Ya know, I'm not looking for a serious relationship at this time. NOT." She laughed. Very clever, mimicking women who make stupid comments, especially after a bad breakup. Me, I just wanted consideration, attention, and the best imperfect relationship. She doesn't meet the taller woman objective. That does not mean I exclude her. The circle is simply bigger.

She went on. "You don't have to like me, but you will." DD is playfully arrogant too. Is she self-confident or a spoiled brat? Forget the arrogance. You gotta like this girl.

Liza went a few steps and called Carter. She couldn't reach him. "Hey, let's just find a little café, get a drink or a spritz."

DD said, "I would love a spritz, with two orange slices. But first, let's go to the hotel. I need to cool off. Liza, where are we staying?"

"We're near San Marcu... something."

I said, "San Marcuola."

Liza said, "It's close. Two stops on the boat. It's not a bad walk, either. Joe is staying a few stops farther on the other side of the canal." I'm glad she got that in.

Just to emphasize the point, I said, "It's a lively area called Rialto Mercato."

"So, let's go there ... no, let's go to our place first." She looked at me, then said seriously, "Liza, Joe passes the preliminary test ... So, I will see you soon, assuming you agree."

I weighed the options and came to an informed decision. "Yes, I agree."

The three of us decided on dinner at La Campiello, a small restaurant five minutes from Rialto Bridge. It's known for Spaghetti alle Vongole. Well, so is every other decent restaurant in Venice. Given Carter's request, I couldn't go with DD alone. And these two seemed inseparable.

I have until tomorrow afternoon to regroup with Cindy. Pretty good, so far. The prospect that two women could be interested in Joseph Fine? Sure, but remember, two is only two away from zero. You can get to zero quickly. My hope is the romantic, yet stagnant, mystical allure of Venice provides the setting for a little romance. It has for many souls before me. I only wanted to be on that continuum.

The anticipation was a bit nerve-wracking, dulled somewhat by the increasing jet lag. Henry David Thoreau said, "Most men live lives of quiet desperation." Well, I do. Will it be Cindy, a lady of poise and grace, or DD, a woman with a flair for the dramatic? Or neither?

CHAPTER FIVE

> **"**
> *You're like a little boy making a mess with his*
> *spaghetti...*

I must have looked on edge when I returned to Pensione Guerrato. The owner, Lucia, a sweet little lady in her sixties, asked me if something was wrong. She acted like a long-lost relative who was happy to help. I told her I am meeting a woman later, and I hope it goes well. She asked if I bought flowers. Something so obvious skipped my mind. I smiled. "Of course, that makes sense."

It just so happened that her younger sister, Gina, has a flower shop on the other side of Rialto Bridge. Lucia said, "I will call her and say you are coming." I put off a shower and headed to Gina's shop. I walked past it before realizing it. The storefronts are so small here.

I walked in, and Gina knew it was me. She wanted to know everything about DD. I can't keep my cards close with this woman. "Gina, we just met. She is excitable." I waved my hands in the air to illustrate. "She wears a lot of lipstick. I think she wants to be in charge. I'm not sure I like that." Needless to say, I did not talk about DD's physical attributes.

"Women are the new bosses." She laughed, a loud, repetitive laugh. "Always ... Right?" Luca, her husband, walked in. I guess he's not part of the family's management team.

Gina showed me a ceramic gondola containing a half-dozen roses and other flowers that I don't know by name. Naturally, it's three times more than a simple bouquet. This was an easy decision when I think of the drinks I have bought for and wasted on chatty women who disappeared after their second Cosmopolitan. Gina put the arrangement in a bag with good handles. The Inner Voice said, "Don't drop it."

Luca took me aside and asked if I have adequate protection since the gondola gift almost guarantees an intimate evening. I acted like I didn't understand. This reminded me of a talk I had with my father before I went on the backpacking trip with Carter. Luca went inside and got a two-ounce square glass container. Gina said it's cologne and Luca likes it. And they've been married for twenty-eight years. Gina added, "If Luca has cologne for mistress, no more Luca." She giggled. I thanked them several times and returned to the pensione.

I know I am overthinking preparation, but my expectations are high. If I base this on experience, it won't matter. That was then. I have to look good, smell good, and put on the right clothes. It starts with boxers that don't cling in the humid weather. I put on dark denim jeans that hid a modest girth. I lay out three shirts. The winner was an off-white button-down twill shirt with red and blue mermaid prints. Light-weight and conversation-worthy.

Lastly, what to wear on my feet? I packed cowboy boots, dark brown ones with a rounded toe. DD might wonder why I'm wearing boots on a warm, humid night. The alternative is brown Oxfords. I went with the boots since they're good for my confidence. The boots give me two inches, not that it mattered. I polished them with saddle soap, and I was ready to go. If DD wears flats, it could mean she wants me to feel taller. Fine with me. I'll take her in heels and a snug top anytime.

I walked out to the alley, which is not more than six feet wide. Barely enough room for a nun to escape the advances of a wealthy trader in the old Mercato. Then it was back over Rialto Bridge toward San Marco and the restaurant. I allowed time to stop at a mask shop. These stores are all over Venice. The shop window was a piece of artwork itself. Clowns, demons, monsters, and even Humpty Dumpty. I settled on two black-metal eye masks with silver glitter. One for DD and one for Liza. Pretty kinky, huh? I also bought a dark-red eye mask for myself.

I got to La Campiello twenty minutes early with a knot in my stomach. DD has a lot of enthusiasm. But is she too intense or a bit of a nutcase? The Inner Voice said, "Shut up and move forward. Put one foot in front of the other and don't make any assumptions. And stay awake."

The restaurant sits on one side of a small square or compo and has a large outdoor seating area. The tables are close together. Like many Venetian squares, there is a small church on one side and an ancient well in the center. A bearded painter worked under an easel light in front of the restaurant. I went next door to a small bar with no stools and ordered Dewar's on the rocks with a lemon twist.

DD appeared with a contagious smile emanating from her bright red lipstick, her beautiful brown hair tied back. She wore a relatively tight-fitting sleeveless blue cotton dress. I was mesmerized by her ample chest and radiant energy. I must be dreaming. Where is Liza?

"It's just you and me," DD said. "Carter came back, and Liza wanted to spend time with him before he leaves. Actually, Joe, that's not true. I asked Liza if she wouldn't mind if I met you myself, and she was OK. I would do the same for her."

"OK, great. Here we are." So, Liza could go to Carter's, and he won't be there, and what if he shows up later with someone when Liza's there? Not my problem.

We sat outside facing each other between two loud couples. At least we were at a table that seats four. DD got up and sat next to me. The lady next to her acted like DD encroached. Best to ignore her. Maybe DD's the faux cuddly type. It's no time for analysis.

The gods were with me so far. She saw the waiter. "Cosmo martini, por favor, and Joe, what do you want?"

"Dewar's is fine. With a twist. Many rocks."

The waiter was confused. DD said, "He means ice and a lemon peel." I'm still not sure he got it.

She said to me, "First things first, you're from New York?"

"No, originally, the Jersey Shore, but I go to New York a lot. For fun mostly, sometimes work."

"I grew up in Astoria, Queens. My dad is Irish and Jewish, does that make sense? Well, the mayor of Dublin was Jewish in the 1960s and my dad's mother was related to him. And my mom's Italian. From the boot part. We were raised Jewish. We changed Santa Claus to Chanukah Charlie. Mom just wanted a Christmas tree. She liked to say she was so poor growing up that they had to wait for grandpa to blow his nose, so they could have tinsel for the tree."

"OMG. I'm Jewish too. Spiritual but not religious." Whatever that means. I tried to be cute, and she ignored me, as she should.

"So, we moved to Louisville. My dad had a business opportunity, that I can't explain. I liked New York, so I moved back after college. I got a marketing job with Procter & Gamble. You know MacDougal Street, where it crosses Bleecker Street? I love it around there. Great coffee shops, pizza joints. The pizza's better in New York than Italy."

"You're right." I was looking for an opportunity to tell her she's right.

We ordered Spaghetti alle Vongole, with a side order of jumbo green olives. She drank pinot noir; my wine of choice was Dewar's. We didn't talk much during dinner, and I looked at her from time to time. She was animated, vibrant. I learned about Sigma Delta Tau, the raucous sorority parties, and their initiation when you're blindfolded, and you think you're eating a worm which is really cold spaghetti. I coughed and got sauce on my shirt. I quickly wiped it off, but she saw it. "You're like a little boy making a mess with his spaghetti." I was embarrassed. She sensed it, and said, "I'm sorry, but it was so cute the way it happened." No need to overreact. She might like you.

"I forgive you this time." It took me a few minutes to get over it. Then I remembered. The flowers and the gondola. "These are for you. And the eye mask."

"I wondered what you had there. Thank you so much. Soooooo sweet." She put the mask on and tried to scare me. We got another look from DD's neighbor, so DD looked at her and said, "Boo." She liked that.

We skipped dessert and went to San Marco Square for a nightcap. DD took my hand. *Stand by Me* was coming from a nearby street. I moved my arms around, going easy on my sore arm, and pretended to sing into a microphone.

"Wow, way to go, Joe."

I bowed and said, "Thank you, thank you." A little early to let my guard down, but it worked. Don't blow it with your Springsteen imitation.

Hand in hand, we carefully walked through the stone arches and dark alleys. We came to a little canal bridge and DD stopped, turned toward me and pressed me against the railing. I'm nervous about the water and turned around to check the railing. She kissed me and kept going. I wasn't ready. It happened so quickly. When she pressed, I felt the proud, projecting boobs that made an immediate impression, if not sooner. "That means, I mean it," she said.

"Wow, you get to the point." I was tongue-tied. Please save this moment.

By this time, I was just about sleepwalking. We sat outside Caffe Lavena on San Marco and watched a lovely woman in a long black gown play piano accompanied by a cellist and a singer, both in tuxedos. She played *Something About Love* by Gershwin. "DD, what else do I need to know? You're in marketing, and you're a sorority sister ..."

"OK, my boss is fundamentally an asshole. And she's a woman. What a bitch. I'm a very good marketing manager. I'm leaving and I'll make more money." I won't engage her on this one.

"And Joe, I know about you, it's online. You're a big shot? You worked for EPA, you left, you didn't go to the dark side, you helped the company comply, and you feel good about that. Sounds fulfilling, and I could be falling in love. As long as you don't spill anything else. Kidding! Let's see, do you have more room to be fulfilled? There's nothing dark and scary in your past?" She put on the mask and made scary sounds.

"Not at all."

DD is very direct, it's easy to pay attention. Liza gave me the impression she doesn't focus. I haven't seen it. She kept going. "I want you to know that I separate trash for recycling. Carter told Liza that you were a pioneer in the environmental movement. You were ahead of your time?" She thought she was funny.

"I'm a pioneer? Carter embellishes. That's what friends are supposed to do, right? We had a recycling program at school. Before it went mainstream. Carter taunted me when he threw his cans in the trash. Then he stopped, and he even helped load the truck."

"Carter sounds like the embellishing type."

"Yes. But he's a good friend at heart."

I walked her back to the hotel. She said she didn't want a late night, it was great to meet me, and she wants to see me in New York. Another kiss and that was that. I was wiped out. Lingering jet lag the end of the first full day here. Tired but pleased, I started to jog. I hit an elevated stone, fell on my butt, and scraped the side of my leg. I was sore, but I could get up. This city is one continuing health hazard.

I called DD. She can't be very far. I'll call Carter if she doesn't pick up. I didn't want to wake him up. She picked up. "DD, I'm sorry to bother you. My shoe caught on a cobblestone. I need help getting up. I'm only a couple of streets away from your hotel. I'm near the Vaporetto stop at San Marcuola."

"Joe, give me a few minutes, I'll find you."

I sat on a nearby step. I'm sore, but I can easily get up myself. I can't tell her that. Should I tell her not to bother? No, see what happens.

DD appeared and seemed winded. Must have been concerned. How about that? "Joe, what's going on?"

"A little sore, I was a lot sore, doing better."

She bent down. She changed since I saw her and wore a V-neck T-shirt and gym shorts. She bent over me, and forgive me, the T-shirt was loose around her neck. I looked inside, which took little effort, and the view was spectacular. I couldn't help laughing. I'm lucky she didn't slap me.

"You know, Joe, I think you're full of beans. You don't look hurt, but I'm glad you called. I wanted to hang out longer, but I was afraid something bad would happen, and you wouldn't want to see me again."

I smiled meekly. "No, I do. Listen, it's OK." I put my arm around her. "Where do you want to go now?"

"I don't want to go anywhere." I got up slowly for effect. We walked a few steps toward a narrow alley. I wonder how people lived in such close quarters. DD put her right index finger over my mouth. "Be quiet." Like adolescents with an opportunity, we got somewhere between second and third base. I felt up and down and all around. She had a couple of moves herself. "Imagine, these could be yours." She sounded like she was running a game show. Her chest would be difficult to leave.

She laughed. I think it's sincere. "Joe, like I said, let's call it a night. Again." I was giddy. I wrapped my arms around her, lifted her and squeezed, and let go. Funny, all the pain was gone. I walked back to the hotel, and the stagnant air felt good. Any air would have felt good. What made me think this? After all that, I wasn't sure I wanted to get back together.

The Inner Voice scratched her head. "What is your problem?"

Next morning, Sunday, I woke up quite content. Why not lie still a few minutes and savor last evening? All in all, it was a very good night, almost too good. I was flattered. I felt relaxed most of the night. Unusual for me. Could she have been persuaded to have a sleepover? She's right. This is likely to last longer if we save some extracurriculars for later.

Another thing. DD wore flats last night. Did she wear them so I would look taller? To make me feel good? Hopefully, she didn't have a reason. No need to compensate. For the record, I like cowboy boots because they are cool and give me swagger, not because they add a couple of inches. I am not a cowboy, I'm not from Texas, I don't eat beef jerky, I've only been to one rodeo, but cowboy boots are the coolest thing I own. What else mattered? Hopefully, she thought I was intelligent and even charming.

Later that morning, DD and I went to a café near her hotel on Nuova Strada. By Venice's standards, it would be considered a main thoroughfare. Something tells me, it's too early to go this well. It will peak and whimper out, and I will be run out of town and ride off into the sunset in my cowboy boots. Does she act this way with other guys? Does she flirt, jump in, and exit?

DD tried to get my attention. "Joe, are you there?"

"Oh, sorry, I was in my own world. I do that sometimes."

"What?"

"I daydream. If it looks like I'm bored, I'm not. I enjoy your company and want to keep it going." I already said too much.

"Well, that is so nice of you. It would be fun to stay here longer or go somewhere like Lake Como, and on and on ... Joe, when Liza and I were back in the room, I got a message. I have to fly to

London tonight, the Company is wrapping up a big sale. It covers my products. The other company has a female executive coming. My folks think another woman will help. I think it's bullshit to think like that. But I am the right person."

This will work out well. I planned to say I couldn't meet tonight because I was going to Ravenna. The city has incredible mosaics. I am going to Ravenna, just not today. Tonight is for Cindy.

All of a sudden, DD looked harried. "I think I know you, but I can't figure you out, Joseph Fine. Maybe that's alright. Can we meet in New York? You're close by in New Jersey?"

"Yes, I am."

"Carter told Liza you like King Cole Bar. Let's go there, or somewhere?"

"Absolutely. Love the place."

She paused like she had to choose her words carefully. "Joe, your buddy Carter messed up. Liza saw him last night with a woman. She thinks the woman is a girlfriend. Well, that's it for a double date."

"I doubt it's a girlfriend. Maybe he hasn't known her very long."

"So, you knew about this?"

I needed to stay vague, but credible. "Look, I'm not up on his social life. Don't make me a character witness."

"I think I believe you."

I asked her about a gondola ride. "I'm afraid. We would have to stay on the side canals."

"You're afraid?"

"Yes, but you know why? Ten years ago, I did a semester abroad. I was on a crowded Vaporetto with a friend, and the driver hit a gondola on the Grand Canal. There were three tourists on it, one got badly injured. You're a sitting duck."

So much for that. Then I thought, the stuff about her old man sounded strange. Probably overthinking again. Clear your head, old boy. She led me to a narrow side street off Nuova Strada to make out. She must have checked this out in advance. We went at it for two minutes when she stopped, stood back, and looked at me. What is going on? If this relationship continues, I will be concerned about coitus interruptus.

"Joe?"

"Yes? What happened?"

"Joe, we're here in Venice. It's mysterious. It's the perfect place to find love, right?" I nodded to show I was listening. "So here we are, and what's going to happen when I'm back in New York and you're where you are, and we won't have palaces and canals, and what's that drink, apple?"

"Aperol Spritz."

"OK, well that too. Do you think you'll like me in the States? It feels like nothing can go wrong here like we're protected, like we're in fantasyland."

"DD, this is real, we're having fun. I won't be back in the US for a while. We'll have more fun when I'm back. I'm not clairvoyant. We'll see what happens." I put my arm around her and squeezed. Jesus, this is getting too emotional. She cares, and I'm touched, but she thinks too much. Oh, that sounds like moi. I wouldn't say it, but why can't we have this talk in six months? We said goodbye, and I wished her luck in London in my best British accent.

CHAPTER SIX

> **"**
> *I have to give her a fair shot. I want a fair shot.*

Sunday afternoon. DD's gone, and I took a deep breath. I walked to Campo San Polo. Just a short walk inland from the Grand Canal and Rialto Mercato. I got an espresso macchiato and an almond biscotti at an outdoor café covered by green, white, and red umbrellas. I can now dunk my biscotti without losing it in the coffee. I moved my table to sit in the sun. My view was an ancient well in the center of the square lined by three small steps filled with students and tourists.

There's something this unabashed woman is not telling me. I'm not looking for a deep, dark secret, but if there's material information, as the lawyers call it, then I need to know before the deal progresses. Yes, I am seeking a meaningful relationship with a taller woman. But I am not looking for a problem with DD just because she's an inch or two shorter than me. Well, I don't think I am. I can't be biased. What would that say about me? I appreciate her attention. I have to give her a fair shot. I want a fair shot.

As far as Carter is concerned, you can't take any woman too seriously. For him, that's the key to a stable, continuing relationship. I think he says this because he hasn't been in one. What is true, you can't take yourself too seriously.

Later that afternoon, I went to his hotel. He sat out front with a broad smile, wearing the Cleveland Indians baseball cap he bought at a Tribe/Yankees game with his Shaker Heights cousin.

"Carter, DD said Liza saw you with that other woman. I didn't say anything."

"Joe, my good man, I took care of that. Carrie's just a pal, nothing serious. It's casual in a healthy, safe-sex sense. Say that three times fast. That's what I tried to convey to Liza. I mean the casual friend part. Hey, my sister is in Lake Como. We're meeting in Bellagio, and you should come … Are you on a sabbatical or extended absence, and you're telling people you're a writer?"

"Yep, all of those with no guarantee of returning."

"It adds to your aura if you stay in Lake Como. Let's go. Liza has to go home in a couple of days, I'm staying longer. What's going on with your new girlfriend?"

"I don't know about girlfriend. She wanted to add a couple of days so we could spend more time, but then she had to go to London. She said, 'I don't want it to end.' How about that? Hey Carter, she's too short for me … Just kidding!"

He looked at me like I was insane. "How full of shit can one person be? Joe, what are we going to do with you? You have more hang-ups, more mishigas, my grandma taught me that word. DD likes you. She has nice glands. What is the problem?" Two more days with Carter could be a problem.

"Carter, no problem for now. Thanks for the Lake Como invite. I want to go south to Ravenna, then I have to buckle down with the writing."

"I think she made up the trip to London. Just a hunch."

"An old boyfriend's there? No, you're busting my balls." He shook his head.

I left without mentioning Cindy. I'm supposed to meet her early this evening. We decided on a café near the Accademia. There's art all over Venice, much of it in churches like the one in Campo San Polo, but Galleria dell' Accademia is the city's main art museum and a good place to start. If you don't believe Venice is more or less the same as five hundred years ago, take a look at the paintings of Piazza San Marco and other Venetian scenes at the museum. The grand palazzo hasn't changed, except for fewer priests, fewer notables, and fewer processions. OK, clothes styles and drink menus have also changed.

I have to make the mental transition to Cindy. Right now, I have two teams. Cindy is on the refinement and grace, yet stilted, team, with a latent sexual charge. DD is on the Mediterranean emotional and fired-up team, where the sexual vibes percolate near the surface. I like excitable. But too excitable borders on volatility. That can work in the short term, but get ready to bolt when the shit hits the fan.

A composite sketch of the two women could provide a nice balance. Of course, that's not reality, you can't pick and choose personality traits. Which takes me back to the concept that perfection doesn't exist. And it probably shouldn't.

I sat on the steps of a small church opposite Bussola Cocktail Lab, the bar where I met Cindy, and wrote for several hours. I was oblivious to the outside world except for the occasional laugh or cry of a child. Back at the hotel, I put on a clean shirt and my cowboy boots. Yes, they're not the right shoes for Venetian stones, but I told you why I need to wear them.

What should I do with Cindy? Maybe take a tour of the Ghetto, the former Jewish quarter. The Jews had to build their synagogues inside buildings, so you couldn't see them. Imagine a woman where you cannot see behind her façade and get to her essence. Since I am not superficial, I will go behind her façade. Will she look behind mine?

Cindy was waiting for me at the Accademia Café. I'm relieved she showed up. She wore stretch white denim and a loose-fitting navy twill top. Each outfit gets better. This one was incrementally more provocative than the print dress. I didn't want to look, but I think she wore flats. Again, did she wear them to appear shorter or simply to go with her outfit? Cindy was pleasant, albeit businesslike. She needs to lighten it up.

"How's the pharma lady?"

"Very funny." She did seem to let her guard down. "No, not bad. And how is my favorite environmental lawyer?"

"How did you know …?"

"You said something. And I looked you up. There's a wealth of information on you. It's good, don't worry. I guess you know that."

"I think I do." I didn't want to boast. We started with cocktails. Aperol Spritzes, of course, which keep the symbolism of our initial chance meeting. This was followed by crostinis with mozzarella and tomato.

Cindy looked at her watch. Not a good sign. She was preoccupied with something. "I'm sorry, Joe, I have to finish something for a presentation tomorrow. Let's have a drink and take it from there. I fly back to Basel tomorrow morning." She sounded sincere. We had a second round of spritzes. She occasionally glanced at her phone which I didn't like. It's not fair because I am making a concerted effort to focus. I don't need a phone in front of me to lack attention.

"I thought it would be fun to see the Jewish quarter. The tours run until six. Would you like to go?"

"I would, and I want to go, let's sit and relax. Between the drinks and the sun, I can't move. Oh, what the hell. Joe, you're a smart guy. What do you think about …?"

"Think about what?" The drinks and the sun were slowing me down.

"Me. About me?"

"You're smart, focused." I lied on the last one. "I think you would make a great soccer mom. I say that in a good way." Now, I have to say it. Right now. "Gorgeous too."

"That's so kind … I like you. You're … different. Look, enjoy the day. See what happens. You're …"

"Impressive? Shorter? Great looking?"

"You are, but it's not so important."

"The height one?"

"Yes, but it's not a big factor. Good looking too. For me, the guy has to be smart. No exceptions. I can't handle stupid guys or women."

We talked longer, and then ... "Would you like to see my place?"

She laughed. "Very good. You're luring me back?"

"I didn't mean it that way. It's a pensione with a unique history. It was a convent. And it has a dungeon-like front door."

"Thanks, but ... I should go in a few minutes." I think the second Spritz helped. I ordered a third. We talked more about her work and Basel. It sounded like she missed the USA. She moved her chair closer to me. I thought the tea leaves were easy to read. I planted a real kiss. Then I wondered if it was too soon. "Wow, I wasn't expecting that," she said. "We'll see, right?"

CHAPTER SEVEN

> *"Where am I with these three women?*

It's Monday noon. Like any bright spring day in Venice. People move in all directions at the busy Santa Lucia Station. They walk by each other. They come close but normally do not touch. There's an occasional bump, and then "mi perdoni" or "excuse me." A man stops to look at the departure board. A woman ten feet away also looks. They walk past each other. Lost interactions. Missed opportunities. Romances and breakups that will never occur.

I normally do not have the nerve to randomly stop a woman and start a conversation. Will the right woman stop me? She did once when I stopped at a street corner outside the Yale English Department. She had seen me riding my bike around campus and wanted to meet me. We went out for four weeks. It was worth it, and then it was over. But it was worth it.

I was confident the right woman was out there, but she could be hard to find. One way to make it easier or increase the odds was to increase the pool. A year ago, I would not have considered Cindy. I would have looked, possibly said hello, made some gratuitous comments, and left. No follow-up. Now, I started a conversation and it led to some … Well, we shall see.

I boarded the train for Bologna, with a connection to Ravenna. Ravenna is ninety miles south of Venice near the Adriatic Coast. After I read about the exquisite Byzantine mosaics there, I had to see them. The train ride, itself, was a great way to clear my head. I had a backpack with a change of clothes, laptop, legal pad, note cards, pens, and an entertaining book called *Piccadilly Jim* by the irrepressible humorist P.G. Wodehouse. Wodehouse is a constant reminder not to take yourself too seriously. I also brought some bar napkins in case I write poetry.

The train cars had individual compartments with two rows of three cushioned seats that faced each other and a narrow table separating the rows. I walked through two cars, and most of a third, before I consciously settled on one with two women, late twenties or early thirties, and an elderly Italian man.

The man had a full head of nicely combed white wavy hair. He wore a dark wrinkled suit, a white shirt, and thick, dark-framed glasses. He smiled sheepishly and said he didn't speak English. He reminded me of an older version of Spencer Tracy in *Father of the Bride*. He fell asleep soon after departure. The women wore white shorts and dark tank tops, one was prettier than the other. I wondered if that created resentment or jealousy. The less pretty one had a quirky bohemian look with braided, red-dyed hair, and thin silver tree of life earrings. She was outwardly the more interesting one. She smiled when I entered, which I viewed as a good sign. The other one had straight blonde hair and a blank stare. She was listless or bored.

My perception was that the bohemian one had to work harder to get a guy's attention. Or maybe not, if she had a naturally great personality. I bet she does not think about it. I'm rooting for her. First thing was to start a conversation. I had to warm up and read for a few minutes. I looked up at the bohemian. She asked, "Where are you going?"

An easy question I could honestly answer. "I'm going to Ravenna to see the mosaics."

"Oh my God," she called out. "You'll love it. What a collection."

"That is great to hear. I don't know anyone who has visited."

"You know, it's spread over five churches. You sound like you know what to do. We're going to Bologna." She has a thick New York or Long Island accent. Once a New Yorker, always a New Yorker. Yes, but I grew up in New Jersey and first worked in Washington D.C. I adopted a slight Southern accent when I was there.

I looked at her again. The long bright-red hair. Candy-cane red. What a dye job. I wondered what color it was naturally. She had a content, almost pretty face with round cheeks. I love her accent. She sounds like the ghost of Joan Rivers. I think she was about five-six, but I won't know until she stands up. Would a bohemian type be attracted to an interesting, short-statured guy? So far, I see a friendly human being.

"I'm Leslie Lipsitz." She pointed to her blonde friend who read something on her phone and got annoyed.

"This is Jocelyn." She lifted her head like it's a lot of effort and said a weak "Hi."

I said to Leslie, "Hi, I'm Joseph Fine ... Did you spend much time in Venice?"

"Just a day and a half. I want to go back, it's soooooo interesting. Know what? I was on a gondola, and I almost got clipped by a Vaporetto."

"Interesting." Then an extended silence. She could be fun to talk to, this woman with bright red hair. My hunch is she sees her hair as a statement and doesn't care what somebody thinks.

"I'm in art school in Bologna, and Jocelyn is visiting for a week."

Now the hair makes sense. The artist's presentation of herself. Some of the great artists are just good artists who know marketing.

"So, you know about the Ravenna mosaics? I've seen the floor mosaics from Pompeii. Then I learned about Ravenna. I got so excited."

"Yes, the mosaics. My thing is sculpture." She smiled. "Mostly human busts, heads, and shoulders." She smiled again. She has a good set of teeth, almost too big, and lipstick that is a faint pink. Nothing overpowers her hair. "Have you been to Florence? Most think Michelangelo's *David* is memorable. And his *Moses* in St. Peter's. Personally, I like Donatello's *David* in the Museo Bargello. Did you know it was a former prison? Funny about the Catholics. They love King David, Moses too, but they don't like his people. Well, I think that's changing." Is this her way of telling me she's Jewish?

She went on. "No, I'm not Jewish, but I have a lot of ..." I nodded. I get it. "A lot of Jewish artsy friends in New York. I know a couple of MOMA curators. So, my bona fides are pretty good, right?"

She thinks I'm smart enough to know what bona fides are. Another good sign. I said, "Yes, good bona fides." OK, she's an artist. I never went out with an artist. I have been with emotional cases. In fact, to the extent women have been attracted to me, they were emotional types.

"And what's after art school ..., more art?"

"I'm not sure. I've sold a few pieces, hopefully, I can sell more."

I saw Jocelyn reading the book, *Fear of Flying*. She doesn't strike me as the fearless type. More like the "not tonight, honey" type. "Leslie, I need a nap before we get to Bologna. Do you mind waking me up, so I don't miss the connection?"

"I might fall asleep too. Don't worry, the last stop is Bologna, and the train guy will get you up."

"Thanks." I shouldn't lie but what the hell. "I like your hair, and the outfit, that too."

"Thanks, some of my friends think it's too strong. This is me. Period." So, I see. She smiled, which became a laugh. The old man opened his eyes, looked around. He smiled too. A front tooth is missing. He said something like "buon giorno" and "good Americans."

"Sì, sì," Leslie responded. I perked up. She turned to me. "I like this guy. He'd be a good subject for my work." I nodded and closed my eyes again.

The train slowed down. Jocelyn was on her phone. Leslie put down her book and looked at me. She smiled. "You're cute when you're sleeping. Like a little boy. Are you married? Girlfriend?"

"No and no." I appreciated the comment, although I am touchy about the little boy part. I know she said it in jest. Still, if I were a foot taller, would she have said that? I don't know the type of guy she's attracted to, and I don't feel an immediate connection. I have read too much about artists and unstable relationships.

I got off the train and waited for Leslie and Jocelyn. Jocelyn walked ahead. Leslie said, "Joe, enjoy Ravenna. I would love to go again, but I have school. Hey, can I have your contact information? I'll send you mine. We can meet. Have you been to Bologna? It has so many mysterious porticoes, and the food is terrific. It's not Florence, but there is plenty of art to keep you going." Or enough Leslie to keep me going. Jocelyn was impatient. Too bad.

"Sounds good. Give me a couple of days in Ravenna, I'll be in touch."

"Sure." I gave her an awkward hug. I need to work on that.

"What are you nervous about? Look where you are. The world is right here ... Call me."

I waved, and they headed for the street exit. A few seconds later, Leslie came back, kissed me on the right cheek. Like an aunt at a family dinner. "That's for, I don't know. Hey, you're more Al Pacino, no, Rick Moranis, you know the guy in *Ghostbusters*?" I stood dumbfounded. When it rains, it pours.

A good train ride, for sure. Before connecting, I found the closest bar to the platform and got a Dewar's on the rocks. The bartender gave me a separate glass of ice. This guy knows what he's doing. That will get him an extra euro. There's a bowl of big meaty green olives on the bar. So, a kiss and an olive. Sounds like a good movie.

I got into Ravenna late afternoon and taxied to Casa Masoli, my hotel. I was so excited. The City has world-class art, but it is quiet, charming, and under the radar. I can't explain why I'm intrigued with mosaics. It's mind-boggling to think artists and artisans spent their lives making huge mural-size designs from thousands and thousands of tiny, colorful pieces of stone and glass.

My self-guiding tour started next morning at the sixth-century San Vitale octagonal-shaped church. It has a massive dome and walls of intricate mosaics. Throughout the vast church are mosaics of Jesus, the apostles, other biblical figures, many saints, as well as animals, trees, flowers, and fruit. Around the altar is a mosaic of Emperor Justinian and his court on one wall, and Empress Theodora and her court ladies on the opposite wall. They ruled a vast empire from Constantinople. He looks bored; she is covered in jewelry. This is what you need to know. Theodora was a former prostitute. Justinian gave her a chance, fell in love with her, and bought her nice stuff. There's a message here.

I loved the sightseeing but missed the excitement of my first few days in Venice. There were three more churches with mosaics to see. Then, I found the nearest wine bar, ordered a glass of Lambrusco and took a cat nap. As much as I enjoyed Ravenna, it would have been fun going with a free spirit like Leslie.

I couldn't work on the train going back to Venice, so I had plenty of time to reflect. Where am I with these three women? Cindy is the most conservative, demeanor-wise. DD is a fully charged battery. And Leslie acts like all's right with the world. That's a great way to be when you're traveling. Will I get beyond the camaraderie of fortuitous meetings or dates with any of them? The field is open. My gut says Cindy and Leslie could say goodbye anytime. DD thinks she is here to stay. When I returned to Venice and Pensione Guerrato, there were two messages. One from DD and one from Cindy.

This was from the sorority girl:

> Dear Joseph,
>   I had so much fun with you in Venice, and
> I hope you are enjoying the next part of your journey.
> I would like to see you before I leave Venice. I'm back
> from London and here three more days, and then
> Liza and I are going to Florence, and from there
> to Paris. I liked the story about your school's
> recycling program. See, I was paying attention.
> You were ahead of your time. It must be the glasses.
> Anyway, please let me know if you'll be back, and I
> promise I have a surprise for you.
>   XO XO DD

And the message from Cindy:

> Hi Joe,
>   When you have the next Aperol Spritz,
> remember the woman who showed you the drink.
> And by the way, when I got back to Basel, I had one,
> and it wasn't as good as the ones we had in Venice.
> It must be the atmosphere and the company. Please
> stay in touch. If your plans take you to Basel or
> somewhere close, please let me know. Nigel says hi.
> He has become more coherent since you saw him!
>   Best, Cindy
> PS, I looked you up. Are you the Joseph Fine
> who's a professor at a New York law school or the
> one who is environmental counsel at some big
> chemical company that sells paint? You're the paint
> guy, right? Well, I would like to know you better,
> so stay in touch.

Between the two, DD seemed more interested, and she's the one close by, for now. And she wore that T-shirt when she "rescued" me Saturday night. Her boobs are driving me crazy. I hear Springsteen bellow, "I want to know if love is wild. I want to know if love is real." Make no mistake, DD's are real. Now for the love part?... I said I appreciated her note and will be in touch.

I want to progress with Leslie and Cindy. Not because they are taller than me, but because I like them, AND they are taller. I told Cindy I would meet halfway. She liked that. Unfortunately, Basel is not around the corner.

And Leslie. I texted her, and she said she needed to finish a piece in the next two days. If I am still around, we can meet. She suggested Padua, where there is a small chapel with exquisite mural paintings by Giotto. I gave her a tentative yes. Leslie was fun, but is she playing with a full deck? She mentioned she read Henry Miller and Charles Bukowski and said they changed her life, but so what? Well, she is expressing herself, and that's all there is to it. Her attitude is either accept me for what I am, or I don't care. But the hair? The Inner Voice said to get over it. Look, I want women to accept me for what I am. Whatever that is.

One good thing about a true artist is that she is not afraid to challenge conventional wisdom or accepted practice. So, a taller artist should be more receptive to a shorter guy. It doesn't seem to be an issue with Cindy. I can't tell with Leslie.

CHAPTER EIGHT

> ❝
> *Is this what you're looking for?*

I wanted to surprise DD when I got back to Venice. She said she had a surprise for me. What if she latched onto a sleazy guy while I was gone? I called her from Santa Lucia Station. She didn't answer. I called again when I got to Rialto Mercato. I didn't recognize the voice.

"Hello, this doesn't sound like DD."

"It's not DD. This is Anita Simon. Who is DD, is this her phone?"

"Yes, I think you have her phone. It wasn't locked? Where was it?"

"And who are you?"

"I'm a friend. I'm Joseph. Can I meet you and pick up the phone for her? I know where she's staying."

"I want to be sure you are who you say you are. Tell me how you know her." I told Ms. Simon that I met DD through my friend Carter.

She said, "I'm near the Accademia. Do you know where that is? Can you meet me there?"

"Yes. I'm five-three and a half, and I have short dark hair with glasses."

"I'll meet you at the Vaporetto stop."

"Thank you so much. Give me twenty minutes ... Wait a minute. Where was the phone?"

"Oh, the phone. It was in the breakfast room in the hotel."

"What hotel?"

"I'm not sure I should tell you that."

"OK." I didn't press the issue. Maybe I don't want to know. I just wanted to get the phone.

I walked quickly, watching for uneven stones given my prior mishaps. In front of the Accademia, I saw a thin woman, average height, with gray hair pulled back into a bun. A middle-aged, attractive curmudgeon. She looked around suspiciously. "Ms. Simon is that you? I'm Joseph Fine."

"Yes, dear, it's me. And nice to meet you. Can't you kids hold onto anything?"

"Oh, I agree, she should be more responsible. She hasn't been out of school very long. She has some growing up to do. Please take this." I handed her a twenty-euro bill.

"No, no, I can't." She smiled. The suspicious look became a more curious one. "I did my good deed." I think we made an immediate connection. "You seem like a charming young man. Isn't this city fascinating? I never tire of it. I give English-speaking tours starting in San Marco. We go all over Venice. Places you would never think of visiting. I would love to include you and any friends. Here's my card. We specialize in singles tours for older folks. But all ages are welcome."

She talked like she knew me. Almost too familiar. "I just got divorced. My husband met a guy at Harry's. Did you know that guys meet guys there too? I pushed him in the canal when I found out. One of the small canals off the Grand Canal. The police were sympathetic. It happens more than you think."

"That is ... interesting. Thank you for the tour offer. I'm not the tour type, but I'll keep your card. I need to go. Bye, bye."

"Bye. Oh, but wait. Joseph, right? My company is sponsoring a costume party tomorrow night. You know, it was just carnival season in Venice. You and a friend can be my guests. It's at the top of a beautiful palace called Ca' d'Oro. Please let me know if you can make it. You have my card."

I said thank you and walked away. It's curious that she invited me so quickly to this party. With DD's phone in my right zippered pocket, I went to her hotel. Fortunately, I remembered the name, Hotel New York. They like American cities for hotel names here. I stopped on the way at Basilica dei Frari, a church on my list, with paintings by Titian and Donatello. Titian made naked women look so innocent or untouchable. Donatello is all about feeling and passion.

When I see DD, I'll say I came back a day earlier to Venice to surprise her. I can drop off the phone, leave her a note and go on my way. Then get to work. No, I'll take two Tylenol, go to her hotel, and hope for the best. I know I am already dealing with a live wire. I stopped at a mask shop in San Polo and bought her another eye mask. This one was black and pointed up over each eye, like cat eyes, with red and silver glitter around the perimeter.

I walked into the small reception area of DD's hotel. The young man at the small reception desk was arguing with a customer. I'm glad they spoke Italian, so I can't understand. Each one waved his hands. They finished up and shook hands, so I guess it wasn't that bad. The customer walked away, and the man made a sign to me that said he's crazy. I asked the man, "I'm trying to reach DD Schonstein. Do you know if she's here?"

"Joseph Fine, you're not supposed to be here until tomorrow." DD was behind me. She gave me a tight hug from behind. I could feel you know what. I turned around and gave her a hug with my right arm. She said, "Did you have fun on your little trip? You missed me, and you wanted to come back early, right?"

I was about to say yes, but she kept going. "You don't have to answer that. And Joe, I have a surprise for you. I know you're on a sabbatical and you're writing a book. My folks are arriving in Paris tomorrow. Would you like to go? Daddy said he would pay. So, what do you think? You don't have to tell me now ... Oh my God, I forgot to tell you I lost my phone and I have looked everywhere. Liza and I had a couple of drinks before she left, and I think it fell out of my pocket or fell out in the bathroom. I retraced my steps. No luck."

I paused for dramatic effect. "Is this what you're looking for?" I took the phone out of my pocket.

"Oh ... Where did you get this?" She threw her arms around me, and I felt fleshy lips and lipstick. I told her about the lady who found the phone. It wasn't the time to lecture DD. It might get me disinvited to Paris. Actually, that would be OK.

I don't know what hit me. I wanted to crawl under a table, or go away, have a drink, and find a place to write. Of course, there was no table in the reception area. I came to Venice to write a few chapters, not to be whisked away to meet somebody's parents. I just met her; how can we do this? And what's after Paris? Casablanca? Rick's Café? When will I finish Chapter One? I'm feeling too many distractions. I stood there, thinking. She stared at me.

I took the gentlemanly approach. "DD, that's very kind of you, and thank you, but I think it's too early for that." The less said the better. "When are you going to Paris?"

She frowned. "About three days. I go home in a week and a half, back to work. I thought it would be fun. How about we go for a couple of days ourselves, and then we meet up with my parents?"

"I think it's too early. Let's have fun here. I need to work." She gave me a blank stare. "The lady that found your phone is charming. A bit of an odd duck. A pleasant, odd duck. She runs a tour company and she invited us to a costume party tomorrow night. The party is for her tour group." I took the mask out of the bag. "You'll look very mysterious and Venetian when you wear this."

"Joe, you are really into these masks. It's so weird. I like it." She put on the mask and snarled like a cat. Nice job. I think this did the trick. No more Paris discussion.

"You're so devious."

She was very excited. "We have to get costumes. Tomorrow night? Not much time. You need to work, right? You've got this secret book you're writing. So, you do that, and I'll buy costumes. You'll like what I get." She thought for a moment. "Ooh, I know who I want to be. Contessina de something. She was Cosimo de Medici's wife. You can be Cosimo. Are there Medici costumes? I'll find something."

"Yes, you do that. Oh, and the party is mostly Brits and Americans. A lot of older singles."

"So, it's an older woman you're after?"

"No, you're old enough, or no, young enough. I don't know how old you are. Don't tell me. I'm thirty-one."

"How old do you think I am?"

The Inner Voice warned me to be careful. The last time I got this question, I really messed it up. I guessed thirty-five and the woman was twenty-eight. She was a smoker and spent too much time in the sun, so it wasn't a bad guess. Still, I need to be careful. "You're … twenty-eight?"

"Close enough, I'm thirty-two. You know, Joe, or as you may know, when you're shorter, you age more gracefully."

"Somebody told me that a long time ago."

"Is there a problem with my age?" I don't know why she's touchy.

"No, you have young genes. Good for you."

"If it's a problem, you should tell me now."

"No, it's OK." It's not an issue for me. Life's not fair. I know that. I will be fair to some extent. I want her to be fair.

"Hey, Joe, you're not six feet tall, but you're big as far as I'm concerned, and I'm good with that. So, there you go. Where were we?"

"You're going shopping. I'm playing Philip Roth."

"Yes. I'll see you in about three hours. Is that enough time?"

"Give me three and a half."

"Joe, do you know who Anita Simon is? Don't you think this is a little strange? She finds my phone, and just like that, she invites you to a party? Maybe she took my phone and pretended she found it. Maybe I should be worried that one of her friends will steal you away."

"I think you think too much." Anita Simon did seem odd, maybe she's just quirky. I couldn't put my finger on it.

"OK, enough of this."

"Good. See you." She came closer, kissed me. She pointed to a dark, narrow street, more like an alley, near the hotel. What is it with DD and alleys? It was wide enough for her to press me against the outside wall of a resident's flat while a teenage boy ran by with a wheelbarrow of fish. She reeled me in, and the lip-locking proceeded.

I didn't know what to say, so I said, "Thank you," and then, "OK, I gotta go. To work." I smiled; I was blushing. The other time I was against a wall was years ago at a sorority party, but that didn't count because my date was drunk, and I'm not sure she knew it was me.

CHAPTER NINE

"

Live your life, my boy.

I left DD feeling wanted and liked, possibly loved. She encouraged the creative juices. I needed that. But with DD, I saw us taking the kids to the psychologist because she micromanaged and yelled too much. And she couldn't understand how it happened.

I was also eager to see Cindy. She could be the real deal. The grounded soccer mom. The woman with poise. I also want a vibrant, enthusiastic personality. Is Cindy exciting enough? Too much enthusiasm could be a bipolar sign. I don't want that either.

Oh, one more thing about DD. Her breasts. They are beautiful, maybe spectacular. Enough to keep me interested in the near term. Like millions of males who will never grow up, I gravitate to ample boobs that look at you. And talk to you. To be clear, there has to be a lot more to keep a relationship going.

Some of this predilection stemmed from a two-foot pile of old Playboys in my older cousin Mickey's bedroom closet. I was twelve and studied the centerfolds. After a while, I knew them well. Now that I'm older and arguably wiser, I know this distorts how men look at women. For the record, if the relationship otherwise works, I can overlook smaller boobs. As I said, I have to be fair if I want to be treated fairly.

Enough on that delicate subject. I stopped for a double espresso and a chocolate almond biscotti in the small square where I met

Cindy. Around the corner from the pensione, two little boys kicked a soccer ball to each other. They saw me and kicked it to me. I kicked it back. Then they kicked it past me. They were good young players. I saw Joseph Fine, the kid, running on the playground.

When I returned to the pensione, I ran up to my room, sat at the wobbly table, and wrote a verse that was in my head:

> Little boy runs to school
> To get in on the game
> Kicks the ball, scores a run
> Basks in all the fame

A burst of energy. A good start. On to the book. Sit still and write. I did not get up, except to wipe off DD's lipstick. The words came out, slowly at first, then more and more. I kept at it. I took a break from the book and finished the verse.

> Glory comes to the kid
> He hears the cheers so deep
> The world is now
> The world is here
> The world is at his feet

Ah, to have the world at your feet. The writing produced a rush. Time to be amused, so I called Carter. Late evening in New York.

"Hello, Joe, I am glad you called. I got back to New York last night. Early enough to go to the King Cole. I'm done with Liza. She would drink, then complain about something. She got sloppy drunk the last night I saw her in Venice. I felt like a chaperone. We squeezed in a boat ride to Murano, and she lost it on the boat. The boat was full. Holy shit. Joe, Carrie's the real deal. She has deeper values.

"I meant to tell you. Liza said something about DD and told me not to tell you. I said OK, but I have permission from a higher authority. No, she's not a former lesbian, she doesn't do threesomes, she doesn't make a lot of noise when she climaxes, so you don't need to close your window over the fruit and vegetable market. Well, that's up to you. DD's old man is loaded or was loaded. He owns a bunch of businesses, real estate too, and he's going to jail for tax evasion. The Justice Department went after him. His underlings ratted him out. So, I don't know what DD is thinking, but she's got to be rattled."

"Carter, she asked me to go to Paris and meet her parents. If he's going to jail, how did they let him out of the country? Maybe this is a stepfather? Anyway, I'm not going."

"You're a wise man, Joe. You can go to Paris any time. If you get writer's block again, go there. Sit at Café du Dome or Les Deux Magots and look inspired with your laptop and twelve-euro café au lait."

"This daddy thing sounds messy. I can't ask her about that. She's a good kid. Beaucoup energy. Beaucoup body. What about her mom?"

"They're separated, so I don't know, I guess you would have seen her mom and a new guy. I think daddy is in the USA. Supposedly, Mother Schonstein helped take daddy down. Pretty intense stuff."

"I'm getting a headache. What happens if DD thinks I didn't treat her right? Will the goons come and get me?"

"Joe, Joe, go get a drink, don't worry about this. Live your life, my boy. It's springtime in New York, and the ladies are ready to bloom."

"Liza, what's with Liza? I thought she was a nice kid, a little needy, but you liked that."

"No, I messed that up. I fast-tracked Carrie. Maybe I have to focus on one woman at a time." There is no point in giving Carter advice.

Jail time for daddy, huh? I wrote three more pages and walked along the Grand Canal to a tiny corner bar for a shot of French whiskey. At the top of Rialto Bridge, I saw the Ca' d'Oro palace to the left about a quarter of a mile on the other side of the Grand Canal. I wanted to see it before the party. The palace has the same distinctive loggia windows as the Doges Palace and beautiful mosaic floors in the courtyard entrance. I ran two flights to the top and saw Rialto Mercato and the fish market on the other side of the Canal. The back of the palace is on Strada Nuova, one of Venice's main thoroughfares. I stopped there at a small bar called Montelvini with three outdoor tables. It was perfectly stocked with a bottle of Dewar's and a bottle of Aperol. Sadly, the waiter couldn't provide a lemon twist.

I sat outside and started talking with a middle-aged French couple, Rene and Sylvie. They drank grappa. I was afraid to drink it. Years ago, a bartender told me it was strong, bitter, terrible. I thought people drank grappa if they were Hemingway sycophants or if they wanted to punish themselves. Rene said the grappa here was better than cheap grappa that tasted like kerosene. He asked me to try a shot. I declined, then gave in.

They bought the drink and proceeded to tell me their disdain for American culture. I sipped the grappa and let them vent. I kept it positive and said that the French contributed great food and the mistress culture to the world. Rene and Sylvie were university professors and complained that they didn't make much in France. Rather than piss and moan, they should find something else to do. I suggested they write a book on American culture. They liked that.

The grappa burned in my throat but was followed by a jolt of good feeling. I looked up and said to my new friends, "Oh, mon Dieu, there is a God up there." We laughed, and I bought the next round. We talked up a storm.

Rene said, "Why not one more?" I grimaced but gave in. Sylvie said she liked me because I reminded her of young Benjamin Braddock in *The Graduate*.

"OK, but I'm better looking than him."

They liked that and wanted to set me up with a French girl. I said, "My goal is to fall in love with a tall woman like your president's wife."

Sylvie looked at Rene. "What about my sister Elisabet? She would like Joseph."

Rene said, "I don't know. She's quite bossy. Joseph will not like it." I didn't say anything.

The grappa was good for camaraderie but nothing else. I drank plenty of water but felt like I had a hole in my stomach. I was getting plastered and asked for a cup of tea. The bartender was a wise-ass. "This is a bar, not a tea house."

"Hey, I drank your shitty grappa, and I need some relief." I took the risk that he did not speak English. We laughed.

Sylvie said, "Please visit us when you're in France. If your lady friend doesn't work, I will ask my sister." I thanked them for their thoughtfulness and said I hoped the Americans and French would be close friends for a long time. They happily agreed.

I felt a little better after I left but asked DD if she could stop over later than we planned. I said I was in a good writing groove. A small lie, since I needed time to get over the grappa.

She was fine. "Joe, you're going to love the costumes I bought ... No Medici costumes. You're Casanova and I'm your high-class bitch. You know, Casanova had high-class bitches and low-class ones. I assumed you wanted me to be a high-class one, given your fancy education. We must present ourselves in a proper manner."

"Yes, we must."

CHAPTER TEN

❝

You little guys have it all figured out.

Have I made progress toward a meaningful relationship? It's too early to say. There are three women, two are taller and one is slightly shorter. I want to move ahead with Cindy and Leslie, even if it means slowing a budding relationship with DD. I've spent more time with DD, but I also have more questions. I need to ask her about her old man. I can't imagine having a parent who goes to jail. If she has too much baggage, it could be time to bolt. Wait, I have to cut her some slack. How can I ignore a woman who pressed me against a wall twice? God, that was good. She was sober, and she consciously did it. I went back to the pensione to get ready for Ms. Schonstein. I still had a headache from the grappa.

Corporate life seemed far away, but I had lingering withdrawal symptoms. After all, it paid the bills and made it possible for me to leave. Grinding out a few pages a day was a good reason to stay away from the chaotic world of corporate legal practice. I was surprised the company didn't delete my email account. I couldn't help myself and quickly skimmed them.

It was early evening and the cool air felt good. I waited outside the pensione, guessing what DD would wear. Something loose or tight-fitting? And heels? I hadn't seen her in heels yet. That would make her more exciting. A shot would help, but I didn't want to chance it after the grappa. I sat at the café and read *A Moveable Feast*. The Lost Generation. The backrooms and brothels of Paris.

I saw DD cross the fruit and vegetable market. Five-feet-one never looked so good. Tight jeans. Semi-tight burgundy sleeveless top. Lipstick. Heels. Yes.

I was elated. "Well, well, you look, oh my goodness, great."

"And I like your shirt with, what are those things? Mermaids?"

"Yes. It's my good luck shirt. Gets a lot of buzz ... Should we take a walk? Something to eat? I know a place on this side of the canal."

"How about let's go to your hotel. I need to use the bathroom, well, not really, I need to use your room, and so do you."

"Oh, OK ..." We went up and I opened the window to let the nuns' ghosts out. I quickly straightened up the room.

"Joe, you're nervous. It's just me." DD took charge. She's agile. She's vocal. Indeed, she took good communication during sex a little too seriously. A memorable event, nonetheless. I laughed and whispered, asked her to whisper. She ignored me. Good thing I closed the window before we started.

Yes, there they were. Beautiful globes of the world. Too big? No, not too big. And originally installed. Thank you, God for the natural world.

I was sweating after the maneuvering and the sound effects. How did this happen? Seemed like everything was progressing. At some point, I heard three of the most feared words. "What about me?"

"Oh, yes, yes, right away. I thought ..." I was forgiven but put on notice. Equality reigns in the bedroom with DD, as it should. No issue with that. I addressed the situation, and minutes later, fell asleep. An hour later, she woke me. And jumped on me. I thought the earth moved. Use your imagination for the details. Just make them good.

It was a great evening, until about halfway through dinner. When the intimacy is still fresh, don't segue into a potentially volatile subject. I should have shut my mouth, especially while we enjoyed Spaghetti alle Vongole, and forget everything else.

"I read about a Harold Schonstein. That's your father?"

She nodded. "Yes."

"I don't know how to say it. I read that he went to jail. It was in the Times. Is that so?"

"Can we talk about something else?"

"OK, I just wondered ..."

"No, not now."

"OK."

"Not now, Joe, that chapter is over. Daddy messed up. Mommy left. Daddy took his mistress, girlfriend, fiancée to Paris. The first thing he did when he got out of jail. I wanted to go to Paris with you. I was looking for a reason to go. What else do you want to know?"

"Nothing. You don't need a reason to go to Paris. Sorry, I can't go."

"You told me."

"Yes, now tell me about the costume. Do you have it?"

"Mine is being fixed. It was snug on top. I didn't want to be spilling out of it."

"That's very thoughtful." Now stay serious. "And Casanova's?"

"I said I would pick it up when I get my costume. The store man was a little guy like you. He was fine with that. You little guys have it all figured out ... Sorry, did I offend you?"

"It's OK, I have a tough skin." It still pissed me off. I was uneasy. She could tell. I said, "Let's get out of here."

We walked to Caffe Florian on San Marco Square. It's touted as the oldest coffeehouse in the world. The 1720 café reeks of decadent Art Nouveau architecture, with fanciful wall paintings of men, women, and floating angels. It puts you in a time warp. We sat outside the coffeehouse, where four guys in black tuxedos played Sinatra and other soppy songs, while the ghosts of bishops, cardinals, wealthy merchants, and aristocratic bullshit artists marched across San Marco Square.

DD ordered two Aperol Spritzes with extra orange slices. There was no need to talk. It was enough to sit in this strange, exotic square. Then my thoughts bubbled. Deep down, it can't last with DD. Should I leave her sooner than later? Maybe she has a boyfriend. But, what's the rush? She's here. For now, it's one more round with DD and her assets. And the costume party is tomorrow.

She said, "You're so easy to read, Joseph Fine. No, I don't have a boyfriend. We broke up before this trip. Want to hear something funny? I went out with a guy about five years ago. I invited him to dinner with my parents. He was nervous like you. I thought, oh my God, his shirt isn't tucked in. He's such a nebbish. Liza told me that word. It's Yiddish. Not flattering. Anyway, Daddy wore dark brown pants and a brown polo shirt. I said 'Daddy, you look like a candy bar.' My boyfriend laughed. Daddy didn't think it was funny."

I didn't ask her what happened after that. "How will this play out? You and me?" I mumbled to myself.

"What did you say?"

"I said it's been a great day."

"What did you really say?"

"I said it's a nice night."

"You're lying. But it is a beautiful night. "

I was in San Marco Square with a woman next to me. No matter what happens, I will remember this day, this place. Everywhere I looked, people were content. I looked at her and said, "Thanks for everything." She could see I was grateful.

After a couple of Broadway tunes, I put my arm around her and felt her soft, long brown hair. I didn't want to move and eventually fell asleep. She squeezed my cheeks, and I woke up. I'm not used to this amount of attention. I tried but was not as skilled at pressing her against a wall. After a good laugh, we retired to our respective hotels. A good time for a break? It felt like the right thing to do.

CHAPTER ELEVEN

She smiled like she knew something. I felt positive

energy.

Somehow, I missed an email that Leslie sent late yesterday. Not clear why it's in the junk file. Leslie wondered where I was, and why she hadn't heard from me. I thought I was supposed to hear from her. She was excited about a bust she finished of a famous citizen of Bologna. Her professor thought it was good enough to enter in a local show. She felt bad about canceling Bologna, but she wanted me to know she had been productive. That sounded legitimate. She still couldn't leave because of school but wrote, "I can squeeze you in for a drink!"

Leslie wanted to meet in Padua to see the Scrovegni Chapel, a small church with wall-to-wall biblical frescoes by the early Renaissance artist Giotto. I liked that. Padua was an easy train ride from Venice or Bologna.

The sky was dark and scary-looking. I stood at the top of Rialto Bridge and watched it pour on the Grand Canal. My only protection was a baseball hat. The wind blew it off, and it landed gracefully on a passing water taxi. I waved and yelled to the driver to keep the hat. "My gift to you." I was soaked, but the wind felt good. The heat and stickiness from last night were gone.

By early afternoon, the rain stopped. The sun appeared. The bright light hit the wet stones and canals. Glistens, sparkles, it's a new beginning. To me, it's emotional. Times change, society advances and regresses, but a Venetian in a 275-year-old Canaletto painting appreciated this bright moment as much as I do today.

I thought about the party tonight. What if DD picked a silly costume? No, it's impossible to be embarrassed at a costume party. I won't know anyone there except her and Ms. Simon. For now, it's back to the writing life. Three hours of work or no costume party for you, Joseph Fine. To play hard, I need to work hard.

Lo and behold, by the grace of God, five pages were completed. I don't like to get specific, but it covered one of the tongue-in-cheek concepts in the *Unconventional Guide*: listen about half the time and don't listen or listen carefully the rest of the time. Some women will be horrified by the thought. It sounds contrarian. How many times has a woman said, "You're not listening to me?" What's the upside? Is there an upside? Yes, you reduce the risk of an unpleasant reaction if you don't listen to a statement or thought in the first place. But, if you're going to do this, make sure you listen well and be responsive the rest of the time. Very responsive. See if it works. The advice should be taken with a grain of salt. And you may not want to try it if the person doesn't have a sense of humor. Then again, why would you go out with someone who doesn't have a sense of humor?

It was late afternoon and two hours before party time. To reward my progress, I went to a wine bar not far from Rialto Bridge, a tiny dimly lit place called Osteria Allegro. The wine bar is close to the bridge but tucked away down a narrow street that felt like a world away. I found it by chance when I walked down the wrong street two days ago on the way to San Marco. What a great find. Eight bar stools and two small round tables. The padding was ripped on a few of the stools. There were two tables outside. That's it. The walls were filled with colorful scribbling by freelance graffiti artists. I fit in with a T-shirt that said, "Drink More Coffee. Do Stupid Things Faster."

The disheveled bartender had an indifferent expression. Once I greeted him, he showed signs of life. I sat there with my notebook and book light on the corner bar stool, jotting down new ideas for another chapter. The other stools were vacant. There was a man and woman at one of the outside tables.

I saw a small pile of white cocktail napkins at the end of the bar. The napkins are perfect for poetry. A shot of Maker's Mark in hand, I wrote a verse on a napkin. I kept my head down and went to work. To a passerby, it could look like I was upset. What I produced were a few words about memorable bar snacks served at a Manhattan bar across the street from the Met, in the Stanhope Park Hyatt Hotel. Here goes:

> Olives and almonds
> And cranberries dried
> No better bar tray
> Ever been tried

I guess it was my optimistic outlook on women, but I added a verse on libations.

> Cosmopolitan
> Sex on the Beach
> No time to dawdle
> All within reach

Imagination is a wonderful thing. I've never had either drink. Or sex on the beach. I laughed. There was no one around, or so I thought.

"What are you working on?" It was a lady's voice. There was a proud dignity to it. She startled me. I jumped but acted like no one was there. I looked up. She had a comical expression. She was anywhere from her late twenties to late thirties. It was too dark in here to tell.

"Oh, two short poems. Just something fun."

"Can I see them?" She moved closer and stood behind the bar stool next to me.

"It's not much, but here, please don't laugh."

She read from the napkin. "It's pithy, almost heartfelt. You care about the snacks. And what do you mean, 'Sex on the Beach?'"

"It's a drink."

"I know that." She winked. "You have more?"

"I have a few others, nothing very long. I'd rather fix them before I show them to anybody."

"You think I'm just anybody? Just kidding, darling." My new friend was a proper English woman or an American with an affectation. I saw friendly hazel eyes and an informal aura which I immediately liked. She had mid-length blonde hair that touched her shoulders, with lighter highlights. It looked like she just cut it. She was five-five, maybe add a half- inch. Almost thin and certainly fit. It was too dark to see if she wore heels. I loved her dark jeans and French long-sleeved white sailor jersey with navy stripes.

Her inquisitive eyes moved around. She smiled like she knew something. I felt positive energy. What is she thinking? I must remember this is Venice, where it's one big fantasy.

I said, "I'm sure you're talented in your own way." Yes, each one of us is unique and has something to contribute. I gagged on my own BS.

She nodded. She looked at me like she knew me. Then I remembered. She was nearby when Anita Simon gave me DD's phone. Does Ms. Simon know her? Interesting. "Well, thank you for letting me take a peek at your work. I'm meeting my soon-to-be ex-husband at the Rialto Bridge stop, and we're going to Murano. Have you been? They make exquisite glass objects. Are you Jewish? My Jewish friend taught me the word tchotchke. I love it. I want to buy a colorful glass fish tchotchke. You know what that is?"

"Yes, I don't think you're pronouncing it right, but it's a knick-knack, a decorative piece."

"Yes, thank you ... I wanted to meet you. I've heard ... Sorry, I have to go. I noticed you on a bench next to the canal. You know, where people sit at night and look out on the canal. You were writing and looked up to figure out the next step. Deep in thought. It was so cute. Like a little, I mean a young boy, taking a test." I didn't like the little boy reference, but she caught herself in time.

She looked at my T-shirt and laughed. A big throaty wholesome laugh. Nice white teeth. Not quite straight. In other words, perfect, "The coffee T-shirt, that's not you," she said. "You do smart things in a deliberate manner. I can tell you reflect. Here's my card. I'm Jennifer Trotter. I go by Jen." She lowered her voice. "My husband goes back to London in two days, so call me at 3:30 the day after tomorrow. I'll be here three more days. I can show you a couple places I'll bet you've never been before. So, call me. Bye, bye."

She left quickly. I waved timidly. Just like that. She liked the poems that took a few minutes to write. Was that innocent flirting or something else? I didn't smell alcohol on her breath, so she appeared to be fully cognizant. Still, I don't know what she's thinking. It could be awkward, but I wanted to know. I told the bartender I would be back and ran outside. Jen was almost at the Vaporetto stop. "Jen, can I ask you something?"

"Yes, dear, what is it?"

"I was wondering ..."

"What were you wondering?"

"I'm having trouble asking."

"Here, sit down and calm yourself."

"Jen, you said to call, you wanted to get together?"

"I think that's what I said."

"For a drink?"

"Well, what do you do when you get together in Venice? We can start with a couple of palaces. I'll go to more churches if you insist.

And then a drink, a boat ride? Look, you're a smart chap. And I'm bored to tears. And your next question. My husband? He's history ... I need a diversion. So, Joseph, your job is to help me out."

"I get it." Whatever that means.

"That's it, darling, now I really have to go. We'll chat."

CHAPTER TWELVE

> **"**
> *I know my track record with men doesn't make me an*
> *expert, but get off the height thing.*

Late afternoon. It rains, pours, and stops. The ancient stones dry. The sun appears. Some things don't change. Then again, when is the last time someone called me 'darling?' Did she reserve that for me? If nothing else, I'm curious.

I can't dwell on that now. Time to get ready for the costume party. I feel like I'm further along with DD, and possibly getting further behind. But she has provided the most comfort food. Well, tonight could be amazing. It's one evening, nothing more. Remember, DD is the only woman in the room. Don't think about Cindy, Leslie, or Jen, especially Jen. The situation with her husband sounds odd. Forget it and take a nap. I sat on the soft sunken chair in my room and fell asleep.

I had a dream, which was a nightmare. Cindy and then Leslie jumped in the Grand Canal. Before jumping, each one said, "You could have had me. See, I'm not that tall." And then they disappeared. DD showed up, knocked me over, and she disappeared too. She cried, but I could not see her. I looked around, lost my balance, and fell down a steep hill. DD was at the bottom of the hill wearing an eye mask with a painted face. She had a deep, mean laugh which scared me. Someone appeared with a cape and mask which scared me even more. It was Carter. He took his mask off. "Joe, this height thing, for God's sake, you've got two arms and two legs, and a fucking brain so shut the f... up. They like you." I opened a door which led to another door, which was the door to my office. Someone else's name was on it. A loudspeaker said, "Get the fuck out of here" but I knew this was my office. Jen walked by.

Then I woke up. I was rattled, and within seconds, greatly relieved. I washed my face and looked out the window. I saw orange sky and sunset. A moment of calm. A few minutes later, three loud knocks on the door. There was DD in her Casanova mistress costume, a tight black dress with a corset tied in the back. A blue scarf around her neck. I couldn't figure out how she fit into the dress. With the eye mask and all of the red and blue makeup, I would not have recognized her. When I looked below her neck, I knew for sure it was her.

"Joe, what have you been doing? We're late. I tried to reach you. We gotta go, you need to put on your costume." She paused to catch her breath. "Oh, fuck it, we can be a few minutes late ... Take me in your arms." Which I did, and the sea parted. Well, something parted.

"I'm going to create a spell over you, my Casanova man ... What do you think of your costume?"

"Interesting." That's the best I could do. I know it's from the 18th century, but it's a little girly. A frilly white shirt, a frilly long red coat. At best, I am a fine young prince.

"DD, we could just stay here."

She glared at me. "No, no, what's wrong with you? Let's go. I want to see what everybody is wearing."

Hand in hand, we walked to Ca' d'Oro. DD was eye-catching in her sleazy outfit, while I was a model of aristocratic charm and sophistication. When we arrived at the once gold-leafed palace, I expected a butler to announce us. I also imagined a well-appointed maiden waving from the top-level balcony. I almost waved back.

DD and I were greeted by a plain clothes security man and a lady dressed as a flapper at a 1920s Supper Club. She had layers of makeup and wore an ornate lavender multi-level brimmed hat like the ones ladies wear at the Royal Ascot Races. A couple dressed as court jesters stood behind us. We exchanged greetings. I thought about Old King Cole, who is flanked by jesters in the mural painting that bears his name.

We were directed to the top level and the large reception room. There was a big poster with the name of Anita's company, Simon Adventures. A crowd of about forty people was milling around. I saw Ms. Simon from a distance greeting guests. The women and most of the men had wads of makeup. A lot of blue and green and red faces, and tight period dresses. Several guys had wigs that you see in an English courtroom. I looked at some of the women and breathed in and out several times.

DD and I walked out to the balcony and looked out over the Grand Canal. A perfectly still and enchanting view. A woman dressed as Anne Boleyn circled the room serving champagne. I picked up two spritzes and someone tapped me on the shoulder. It was Anita Simon.

She said, "I'm so glad you came. Please enjoy yourself. And you're so close by."

"Thank you for having us." I introduced her to DD, who was very gracious.

"Me too." It was Carter. He snuck up behind me. I thought he was in New York. "Yes, here I am, I never left Italy. Some minor social issues kept me here. You met Anita Simon. She's my aunt." Carter looked at me and lowered his voice. "Anita is flighty. Married three times. She's forty-seven, but she's childish even by my standards."

"Carter, this continues your tradition of spontaneity and wonder." He grinned.

"I'm a New Yorker too," Anita announced. "I'm a spinster tonight. You know Jane Marple, the Agatha Christie detective. Normally, I'm a well-appointed lady."

"My oh my, this must be DD," Carter said with a shit-eating smile. "You two look like you've been together forEVER." He's as obnoxious as ever.

I introduced DD to Carter. "Carter is Anita's nephew. By the way, she is the one who found your phone." DD looked at her. I know she figured this was too much of a coincidence. Anita condescendingly looked at DD. Fortunately, DD did not make any comments.

"Hi Carter. And oh my God, yourself," DD said, a bit flippant. She waited until she had his attention. "Do you know how pissed Liza is at you?"

"Well, DD, does Joe know where Aunt Anita said you lost your phone?" Things were getting a little tense.

"At a hotel. That's what Joe told me."

"OK, which hotel?"

"What do you mean?"

Anita intervened. "Hey, we're at a party, get out there and dance."

"I agree," said DD. "Rock me, Casanova." DD didn't say anything else about the phone.

We strolled around the spacious reception area. There were colorful costumes, including a king and queen, aristocrats, nuns, and a priest with a gold cross half the size of his chest. That was Pope Julius. I think he was the pope when the Medicis ruled Florence. The one with illegitimate children. And look out, a guy walked by who looked like Michelangelo's *David*, with fig leaves covering his pecker. He waved hello to us. I stood back. DD talked to the pope. She said, "Joe, this is Robert. He's Pope Julius."

He said, "Yes, my child, and this is my girlfriend Simone the nun. We are from the south of France." DD sized up the pope. I think she was flirting. Ok, for an event like this. And Simone. She wasn't your typical sister with a skintight tunic and dark eye shadow. I took a deep breath. What do the Brits say? Keep calm and carry on.

DD asked Robert, "Do you know who Joseph is? He's Casanova, and I'm his high-class mistress. Do you know Anita?"

"Simone works with Anita. She has a travel agency in Provence." I fantasized about spending two weeks with Simone in Nice. With all of the masks, it was hard to tell who was looking at who, but I felt Simone staring at me.

Carter saw me eyeball her and tapped me on the right shoulder. "I need to tell you something." We walked to the bar like we were getting a drink.

"Joe, don't even think about it. Simone is crazier than my aunt. Yes, I suspect she's a real banger. When she's pissed, stuff flies around the room. I don't know anything about Robert. So, listen. About DD's phone ... I knew where Liza and DD were staying, and I told Anita. She took the phone from DD's table in the hotel breakfast room when DD walked away for a moment. Anita wanted you to think the phone was at another hotel. She doesn't think DD's right for you. Not sure why. Liza told me DD is a loose cannon. I think Anita wanted to talk to you, but she didn't have the nerve."

I watched DD go to the bar. The bartender wore a white shirt, black bow tie, and red vest. He served a drink to King Henry VIII, who was complete with frills, buttons, velvet, the famous feather hat, and a glaring expression that said, "I am the boss." She came back with two vodkas, lime, and olives. Carter was talking to an Andy Warhol lookalike. I was with Simone and Aunt Anita. DD handed me a drink and walked away. I said to Anita, "Thank you again for having us. Great venue. I love the front of Ca' d'Oro. Such a striking design."

Simone said, "Anita told me about your ... I guess it's like a sabbatical."

"Actually more of an undetermined absence. I probably won't get my job back. I'm fine for now." She nodded approval, laughed like I was making this up. Still, I saw sunshine and warmth and eyeshadow that started to melt, making her even hotter.

"Well, if you come to Provence, Robert and I would love to have you. We're near Avignon in a village called Aramon. It is a peaceful little village, but it is hard to find. The only sign to the village is blocked by a fruit tree, so call first for directions. How exciting! We could have a writer in residence."

"I don't have much done yet. So far, I'm a doodler in residence."

"If you can't write in Venice, where can you? Then again, Provence is even more inspiring. It's wonderful for the creative type. The sea and air are magical."

"Of course."

Anita jumped in. "The only thing that holds Joe back is DD."

"Now, Ms. Simon, give me some credit. She's a nice girl. You didn't have to take her phone."

"Yes, I did. Carter is highly complimentary of you. Joe, you are quirky and charming, and you have trouble stringing sentences together, but you should go high up the food chain. You can do better than DD."

"Carter exaggerates. And the speech thing is only when I'm around women. And leave DD alone."

Anita was not satisfied. "One more thing. I know my track record with men doesn't make me an expert, but get off the height thing. Carter mentioned it. Look, I used to want straighter hair and straighter teeth. Simone, you wanted bigger boobs, but you're glad you didn't get them. You like what you have?"

Simone must be used to Anita's joie de vivre. "Well, yes, I do." I would have loved to interject, "Me too."

Simone said, "How do you say in English, vite, vite? Joseph, we want a book from you. Anita and I will have a book party. We will have all of our crazy friends from Marseilles to Portofino."

"I will try to meet your expectations."

DD came over, and thankfully, Anita and Simone were quiet. I still couldn't get over DD's provocative outfit. She gave them a blank stare and took my hand. "Shall we dance?" The band played *Satisfaction*. We went to the center of the reception hall and started to move around the floor. Most of the other guests were dancing. I worked my way over to two women who danced together and got between them. DD did not appreciate this, so I returned. We moved around too much and bumped into another couple. I said, "Excuse me," moved closer to DD, and accidentally stepped on her dress, which touched the floor with a few inches to spare. I slipped and fell on a lady dressed as Wonder Woman and plowed into one of the bars, knocking over bottles, glasses, and a bowl of large olives.

The security guard came over. I said I was very sorry, but he waved his hands in the air, grabbed me with his left hand, and motioned with his right hand to leave the party. DD stood there and held her head in her hands as I left. She was not happy and said she didn't want to leave. I waved to Aunt Anita and said I was sorry. She wasn't sympathetic. The security guard worked for the Ca' d'Oro, so Anita could not do anything. Simone could not stop laughing. Carter smiled and affably said, "What a douchebag. I'll catch up with you later." I went down the two flights of steps to the ground floor entrance and the empty courtyard, where I found a long bench, laid down and fell asleep.

A couple of hours later, DD tapped me and woke me up. She slurred her words and sounded drunk. "I know you were having fun. I've done some dumb things in my life too." I didn't bother to say her costume dragged on the floor and was an accident waiting to happen. She did bend over and kissed me on the head like I was a little boy.

"Sorry, I just got too wound up and slipped." She looked at me with a blank expression.

I saw Carter run down the steps. Behind him was a young lady who looked in her early twenties. "Joe, my boy, you are a star. This will go down in Venetian party history."

"Thanks," I mumbled.

We waited for Aunt Anita, Simone, and her Renaissance Pope to come down. Anita wanted to go to Harry's. "Come on Joe, get up."

I stood up slowly. I took one more look at the ornate mosaic floor designs. DD was anxious to get away from Aunt Anita. With everyone downstairs, we said goodbye. It was a short distance to Pensione Guerrato but with a cranky DD, it felt like an hour.

CHAPTER THIRTEEN

" Wow, you are a respectable guy. You're unusual.

The next morning, DD was bright and cheerful. She didn't mention Anita or my early ejection from the party. So far, so good. We had the perfect Venetian breakfast, chocolate biscotti, and cappuccino. I took one more of each. I sat for a moment, then got up to look outside. She grabbed my arm. "Come here. Can't you sit still? ... You better call me," she said, with lots of charm. "We look good together, don't we?"

"Sure." She looked at me. I didn't say it with enough enthusiasm. Back in the room, we had one more kiss and I peeked inside her silky blouse into the Grand Tetons. I made a mental picture and stored it. Late morning, I walked her to the Rialto Vaporetto stop for the airport boat express. As soon as she left, I was relieved but missed her. I don't know if any woman cared about me like that. All this within the space of a week.

Leslie texted about Padua. We agreed to meet the following day at Scrovegni Chapel, which was a short walk from the Padua train station. Was this a date or a friendly get-together? The best advice is not to assume any romantic intentions on Leslie's part. The Inner Voice agreed. Some women like to talk and pal around, nothing deeper. They're friendly, and you have to get used to it. What mattered is that Leslie agreed to meet. As long as she doesn't tell me I'm cute, as in "cute little guy." If she means cute as in handsome, then it's OK.

It's cooler than yesterday and perfect for touring. Early afternoon, I went to the train station. There were no seats on the Vaporetto and barely a place to stand. I found space next to a young mother with a baby girl who was crying. I know girls cry a lot, but this was pretty spectacular. Yes, I know baby boys cry too.

Two college-aged women next to me looked happy and green to the world. I'm guessing they were from Minnesota or Sweden. Both blonde. They were from Manhattan. So much for perceptions. One of them said they were going to Verona, the city of the tragic lovers Romeo and Juliet. I said I prefer happy endings. They liked that. I wished them good luck and darted into the station to the train platform. My plan was to arrive early and mentally prepare.

Padua is a pleasant low-key contrast to Venice. The city has a calm, quiet air, which makes it feel older. It's ancient like Venice but doesn't have the Disney World crowds. I passed few people on the short walk from the station to the Scrovegni Chapel. I stopped near the chapel at a tiny corner bar for a shot of Dewar's and a small bowl of green olives. I asked for the drink in a plastic cup and sat in a small park next to the bar. I had a half-hour to ease any nervousness. The best preparation? I leaned back and closed my eyes a little.

Leslie appeared. "Joe, here I am. I looked around. I didn't see you at the entrance." I got up slowly. Leslie looked almost mainstream in white shorts and a loose-fitting, silky red sleeveless top. She wore purple Converse high tops. Her hair was the same bright red and no longer braided. By letting it out, she sent sexual energy my way. I remembered her large front teeth. She gave me a platonic hug from the side, which avoided any inadvertent feel. I wore Adidas sneakers, not cowboy boots or Swedish clogs. No heels. Comfortable in my own skin.

"Yes, hi, and sorry. I didn't mean to fall asleep." Which was not true.

A woman walked toward us. "Joe, this is Samantha. She's in art school with me. We have wanted to see the frescoes since we started school." Samantha was cordial but reserved. She looked younger than Leslie, and a tad heavy-set with long dirty-blonde hair, indigo jeans, and a yellow V-neck top.

Leslie hadn't mentioned Samantha. I decided to treat it as a non-issue. I asked Samantha about her artwork. She showed me photographs of her sculptures. The one I liked best had two figures, a woman and man standing and embracing, almost merging into each other. The sculpture was about a foot high and a half foot wide.

We walked to the chapel entrance. Inside, it is close to thirty feet wide and close to seventy feet long. The security people allow a small group to enter every fifteen minutes. Leslie and Samantha didn't mind the wait. Leslie was beaming. "This is a big deal coming here. I am so excited."

"Me too," echoed Samantha. I nodded.

Leslie took me aside. "Joe, Samantha just broke up with her boyfriend, and I wanted to cheer her up. I didn't think you would mind if she came." She quietly added, "We can talk later. Samantha said she'll go ahead to the Cathedral after we're finished here."

"No, no problem." Wow, Leslie seems so considerate.

She got excited as the line shortened. I love enthusiasm when it's about something creative. As we entered, one of the guards reminded us not to talk. I tried to be engaging as we wandered through scenes from the Old Testament and then the lives of Mary and Jesus. I whispered to Leslie, "Do you think Giotto realized how great he was, a Renaissance painter ahead of his time?" Two guards glared at me and pointed to the "Silence" sign.

Leslie whispered, "We'll talk later."

I enjoyed the artwork, and for a moment, I was not preoccupied with Leslie's sexual energy. We took a final look at the frescoes at the lower part of the two walls called Virtues and Vices. It's where

Giotto painted figures to symbolize opposing human qualities of foolishness and prudence, uncertainty and fortitude, wrath and temperance, injustice and justice, infidelity and faith, envy and charity, and last but not least, desperation and hope. I was full of hope as we exited the chapel into the midday heat.

When we got outside, I tried to act informed. I asked, "Who are the innovators today like Giotto was then?"

Leslie picked Diego Rivera based on the simplicity and raw humanity of his native subjects. "The woman holding flowers on her back is so moving."

Samantha chose Auguste Rodin. "I love *The Burghers of Calais*. They're as real as it gets."

I took the easy way out and went with Picasso. "You know, the cubist designs."

We sat in the shade and talked. Samantha put a couple of fingers to her ear signaling for Leslie to call her. She took off. Leslie said, "I discovered a new drink. Sex on the Beach."

"You mean the drink?"

"Yes, I just said that. But I'm a Bellini girl. What do you like?"

"I'm a creature of habit. Dewar's and a twist of lemon, with ice, lots of ice. They think two cubes is a lot here. The drink has to be soooooo cold. And the twist makes a difference. You want a Bellini?"

"No, Dewar's, I'll get what you're getting."

"Have you had Scotch?"

"No, but I'll try it."

I like that. Leslie is open to new ideas. That's good. I mean, I won't drink a Bellini, or a Cosmopolitan, or one of those creamy martinis. We went to Canenero, a little bar in the medieval Jewish ghetto. A maze of narrow, winding streets.

I liked Leslie but wanted to learn more. She went to college and at twenty-seven, she was still in school, albeit art school. She first painted at the New School in New York, then started to sculpt. She worked part-time jobs, including a French bistro called Balthazar on Spring Street in Soho. I went there once and sat in the bar area where I kept getting bumped by people waiting for a table. Anyway, Leslie flirted with Buddhism, loved Taos, and all the crazy rich lost souls who seek a spiritual path to go with their three-martini lunches.

Leslie's folks gave her money to study art in Bologna. She didn't have specific plans after art school other than to continue sculpting. Does she have growing-up issues? Is she grounded? I thought about asking, "Where do you see yourself in a few years?" I have growing-up issues, but I saved some money. For all I know, she's a trust fund kid.

I could see she had something on her mind. "What is it?" I asked.

"I have to tell you something. I broke up with Antonio last week. I thought it was coming." She said it like this guy was my friend. Why do I need to know this? She doesn't owe me an explanation.

"Antonio?"

"My full-of-shit Italian tight-jeans, tight-ass boyfriend. I caught him with a senorita."

"Oh." I don't like breakup stories, but if there's a benefit for me, I'll listen.

She smoothed her hair back. The color can't get on her hands, right? "It was great to leave Bologna, even for a short trip … Joe, what do you think of me?"

I told myself to be careful. The right words could make a difference. "Let's see, interesting, cute, kind of bohemian, you seem like a free spirit. I think you're a decent artist. You're searching for something." That sounded good and it could mean anything. Everybody's searching for something.

"Well, I am once and for all advancing my art career. I think I have something to say. Are you going to ask me what I think of you?"

"No, but OK. What do you think?" I squirmed.

"Start with cool. Pacino. You look smart. Sometimes you act so serious. Relax. You're funny, kind of goofy. You have an odd side but in a good way. Maybe?"

"Thank you. I think that was complimentary."

"Yes, but what I was getting to is that I have a break. I'm free for a week. My father sent me a birthday present. We're going to the Riviera, near Nice. St. Paul de Vence. It's a better place than Venice for a writer."

"Who is going? You and your father? Samantha?"

"You and Samantha ... The three of us." She thought that was funny. A threesome, huh? No, strike that. This woman is loosening my grip on reality. "I'm kidding. I mean you and me. Separate rooms of course." She smiled.

After the initial shock, I thought maybe I should consider. It's funny because I was thinking about a quiet and cheaper place to write. Venice was the starting point. Perhaps another home base would be helpful. I had two thoughts. Run as fast as possible, or take a flyer and go with her. I can always bolt when I get there. "Leslie, I need to think about this."

"Tell you what. I'll take a walk around the old town hall and you think all you want. Don't let it rattle you."

"Sounds good. Take your time."

I don't know if she's stable or a budding artist with at least one foot on the ground. She did say her old man is paying. Paying for what? Leslie doesn't feel like home, at least yet. DD feels like home, although it could be a chaotic one. Leslie seems relaxed enough to be a good travel partner. This was a part of France beloved by talented artists and writers. And the book cover could read,

"Joseph Fine got the inspiration for writing *The Unconventional Guide to Relationships* during his travels to Italy and the French Riviera."

Wait a minute. At some point, I need to see Cindy. I haven't been in touch for two days. In geological time, that's nothing. In human time, she'll forget about me. She is attractive, upbeat, albeit stilted, and has a very good job. I love the way she ties her dirty blonde hair back as long as she doesn't make a bun like the creepy old lady who was my babysitter when I was six. She would be the perfect soccer mom and perform well at social events. I imagined Cindy talking to a friend, a fellow Junior Leaguer about me. "Yea, I met this guy, he was funny in an odd, obsessive way. He was nervous when it was time to do it. First, he checked the doors to make sure nobody was around. He got in bed and moved around in a circle. He says when you're shorter, you're more agile. He makes sure you're satisfied during the big event. Then he says, 'It's great to be alive.'" Yes, I'll see if Cindy and I can meet in two weeks.

Leslie returned an hour later. I was asleep after two Dewar's. She poked me. She was excited. "I had a wonderful walk. I took my time like you said and walked around the old town hall. It goes back to the thirteenth century. There are markets on either side. One for fruit, one for vegetables ... So, do you have an answer?"

"Let's go. I'll pay my share. I'll go for a few days. Maybe I'll stay longer if the work goes well."

"Yes sir." She was all smiles. "Of course, you will write. You'll be in good company with many artists and writers." Leslie moved her hands up and down like a happy child. "Now that that's settled, we'll celebrate."

I looked around. The waiter was occupied. I caught his eye. "Signore, a Bellini and a Dewar's, with ice and lemon twist. And bread and cheese?"

She said, "We should get champagne. It's more festive."

"Thanks, I need to stay in my comfort zone. I like champagne, but I want to stick with Dewar's."

"I see …" Then out of the blue, she asked, "Am I hot enough?" That was easy. "Yes, you are." I held her left hand and nodded.

"Let's find a room. After the drink." I must be dreaming. That's the kind of thing a guy would say to see if it sticks. It may sound stupid, but I have mixed feelings. The Inner Voice said, "Cut the shit." No, I think there are times when it's good to slow down.

"I planned to go back to Venice tonight."

"Is this outside your comfort zone?"

"No, no, no. I'm in. I'm flattered." I was going to say I was honored or grateful, but this isn't an awards ceremony. I walked up to the bar, found the waiter, and asked him to make it a double. Then I changed my mind. That's enough. I took a few olives from the counter.

"What did you say to him?"

"I asked him for a twist."

"You did before."

"I wanted two. I really like a twist." Leslie was puzzled. I smiled, I went over to her, looked at her, kissed her. "Thanks. Nice work."

"You mean about the room? I couldn't have done it without you."

Where is this going to end up? An offbeat woman, a lady who likes our man in Padua, and I'd say she's about five-six. When I look back at the trip to Padua, it's one reason I believe there's a God out there. The Dewar's also helped.

Leslie found a two-star hotel in the piazza of the old town hall, not far from the bar and the Basilica of St. Anthony. I waited in a soft padded chair while she checked in. I offered to pay for the hotel, but she insisted. We took the tiny elevator to the fourth floor. The room was modest but clean with two twin beds, a sink, and a lamp that didn't work. I sat on one of the beds and the mattress was soft. She sat next to me. A ray of light came through the lone window and lit up her hair. We still had some of the afternoon left and I asked her about other sightseeing. She seemed indifferent. "I saw the Scrovegni Chapel. Incredible. That's all I came to see. And you."

She leaned on me enough to fall on the bed. She smothered me with her crazy hair and whispered, "Good things come in small packages." I think she was describing me, not a particular body part. You wouldn't know it from her loose blouse, but her boobs were bold and assertive, not as big and round like DD's, but more than adequate. I lost count on how many places she put her tongue. It makes sense, she's an artist. We had fun rolling around. I was careful not to fall off the bed.

Is Leslie ready for the big event? I'm not sure. I am confident in my ability to amaze and delight, but I wasn't ready. If this is a one-night stand in the late afternoon, and I don't see her again, I can't consider it a meaningful relationship. That's my goal, right? So, I should defer the opportunity to get to the top of the mountain. For now. I lay still.

"Is something wrong? You're doing great."

"So are you, believe me ... I don't want to go further. At least right now."

"Oh?"

"If this is going to last, I thought the sex part should wait." I couldn't bring myself to just say sex.

"You gave this a lot of thought. That's impressive. It's not me?"

"Absolutely not."

"Wow, you are a respectable guy. You're unusual. That's good."

"Yes."

"I think I like you more now."

Up to now, I never pictured myself with someone like this. She handled the situation graciously and added bench strength as a practical matter.

I fell asleep. She woke me up minutes later with her chest dangling over me. She asked, "This doesn't go too far, does it?" I tried to shake my head, but it kept glazing her boobs. She laughed hysterically. I finally just put my head between them and made various noises.

I got free and answered. "No, it was fine. I had to get some air."

"Thank God. Do you still want to see St. Anthony at the Basilica?"

"If you don't mind."

"Not at all."

Before I went to sleep that night, I sent Cindy a note that I'm in a good writing groove and asked if we can tentatively plan to get together in two weeks. Who knows? By that time, the playing field could look very different.

CHAPTER FOURTEEN

❝
I appreciate being part of the adult community.

Leslie and I lucked out and got a cheap fare on a morning flight from Venice to Nice. Before we left Venice, she reserved a room in St. Paul de Vence, a charming village about ten miles from Nice.

We sat in aisle seats next to each other. I was dozing before takeoff, and Leslie said, "Joe, pay attention. I talked to my friend Henri a couple of days ago. He is the main curator at Fondation Maeght. It's the modern art museum in St. Paul. They have Chagall, Giacometti, Joan Miro."

"I've heard of it. And you know him how?"

"From New York. He worked at MOMA. He's from Nice, returned home, and got the position here. A good guy, a little pretentious, a bit of an art snob. He said I must spend time in Italy. Oh, and he's gay. We went out a few times, and then he made the big announcement. We stayed friends."

I'm not sure how to respond. "This happened right after you went out with him?"

She acted like she didn't hear my question. "I mentioned you. He wants to get together for a drink. We tentatively planned for later this afternoon."

"That's good. How about you have drinks while I sit at the pool and work?"

"I thought you'd get a kick out of meeting him, but OK."

"Thanks."

I sat next to an elderly Italian couple who clearly enjoyed each other's company. They were dressed for a wedding. Both were about five-one, and "cute" is the best description I can use. I would add "sweet" for the lady. I violated my own rule on describing short people as cute, but this is a couple. If they were four inches taller, I would still say cute. I asked them how long they've been married. The man, his name was Bruno, was next to me. He grinned, "No, not married. She's my girlfriend."

Through broken English, he said he was divorced, and she's a widow. He leaned over to me and said his ex-wife was a bad person. She had an affair, such nerve. He had two affairs, but men are different, right?

He pointed to Bella, then looked at me, and said "Fantastico." I could tell he loved her. Bruno asked if Leslie was my wife. I squirmed and said she's my friend. Leslie winked. Bruno and Bella laughed and said, "'Bueno" in unison.

I asked if I could buy them a drink, maybe grappa? Bruno moved his index finger back and forth to say no, Grazie. We chatted away. Bruno had family near Nice in Ventimiglia, one of the first towns on the Italian Riviera. I joked that the pizza in New York was better than in Italy. He didn't buy it. We wished each other good luck.

Leslie and I arrived around noon and ubered the ten miles to the hotel. It was a lovely ride through winding roads and villages. There were great views of the Mediterranean as we climbed the hills leading to St. Paul de Vence. We entered Hotel Le Hameau through a red cobblestone path which was covered by a lattice with dense vines. Flashes of light came through the vines and dotted the cobblestones. The hotel has two long whitewashed buildings with bright red-tiled roofs and a pool in the middle. From the pool, you could see the old walled village of St. Paul de Vence about a mile away.

Leslie walked ahead and approached the reception desk. She wore jeans with bleach spots, a loose flowery top, her signature purple Converse high top sneakers, and thick-frame blue sunglasses shaped like Buddy Holly's glasses outside the Buddy Holly Museum in Lubbock, Texas. I went there three years ago for a friend's wedding.

She mentioned the reservation. The desk clerk said, "Bonjour," which confused Leslie. As a culturally sensitive traveler, I told Leslie to say "Bonjour" first and then conduct her business. She complied. The clerk winked in appreciation of my facilitator role. Leslie blew me a kiss. "I'll get you for this," she whispered.

"Can't wait." I smiled.

I was surprised she asked for two rooms. What I didn't hear was it was a two-room suite. That provides flexibility. The suite had a rustic feel, with a dark brown hardwood floor, white walls, dark wood-beamed ceiling, a queen-sized bed with high spindle posts, two armchairs, and two old French Champagne posters. The second room had a desk and a sofa bed. The mid-day sun poured through the two large windows in the bedroom. We had a great view of the medieval walled village. "What room do you want?" I asked.

"You're in the adult room with me. If you approve the arrangement, and you're a good boy, of course."

"I appreciate being part of the adult community." Not to be touchy, but she sounded like she was talking to a good little boy who gets a cookie on vacation. A veiled reference to stature? I let it go.

I sat on the bed. A light blue and white striped fluffy comforter. "Leslie, this is a beautiful area. The sea. Calm, scenic villages. I wasn't sure about going. I'm glad I did."

"You think too much ... Joe, can you close the blinds? I know you love the view, but we have an hour before I meet Henri. And then you can write to your heart's content."

Maybe I was getting too relaxed. "Leslie, one thing, give me a heads up if you think you're becoming a lesbian." That was a bad joke.

Leslie got playful and threw pillows at me. That led to an all-out pillow fight. I didn't plan on playing before foreplay. It was almost as much fun as kickball. I held my ground as well as I could. She declared victory, wrapped her arms around me, and fell on top of me. Loud breathing, panting, and moaning ensued. I couldn't defer the big event with Leslie any longer. She was in very good shape, and I was worn out when it was over. I was pleased. And felt accepted.

The reverie did not last long. Leslie got ready to meet Henri and left. I took my laptop and found a table at one end of the pool area. There were blue and white striped lounge chairs and umbrellas and a few tables surrounding the pool. What a pleasant place to work. My concentration was good until a forty-something lady turned over on her back without a top. Not to be shallow and immature, but it would have been better if she stayed on her stomach.

I'm surprised I have not heard from DD. Presumably, she is in Paris, and hopefully not getting boned by a Frenchman. I liked the break from DD, but now I miss the old girl. I miss the hills that are alive and undulating with the sound of heavy breathing.

I bore down and worked for more than two hours, enough time to earn a drink. Plenty of warm sunlight. A couple arrived in the pool area and sat at a table at the middle of the pool. Neither one was much taller than me and both were stocky. The guy had black hair with a very bad comb-over. They talked loudly with a Brooklyn accent. The guy was pissed about the jewelry she bought. He was not very discreet. At first, it was entertaining to listen to. Then it got stale. I felt sorry for the two of them.

I was almost done working, but still needed to concentrate. I said, "Hi folks, can you keep it down just a bit? ... Maybe you two should get a room." His wife ignored me and said, "Bye Harry" and stormed out. Harry walked over to me. He asked who I was, and then with a big smile, he told me to fuck off. I could tell he was having fun.

I played along. "Harry, it's too scenic for that kind of language." He smiled again. I saw a big space between his front teeth. Harry was heavy, not as heavy as his wife, and had a hairy chest and back. He gazed at an attractive woman who was on her back without a top. He couldn't believe it. I told him this is relatively common in the Riviera. He looked at me like a long-lost friend. "You see that woman over there. Jee-zus H. That's not real, is it? What the fuck, right?"

I shouldn't start trouble, but I couldn't help it. "Hey, Harry, ask her if she wants a drink." He thought it over and shook his head.

"No, I can't." He sounded defeated. "My wife wanted to come here. I'm happy on the Jersey Shore. There aren't any fucking rocks on the Jersey beaches. Hey, where's the nearest topless beach?"

"I don't know. Go ahead, buy her a drink."

"Look, I can't do that, I'm in enough trouble."

"So, you might as well."

"Not worth the fallout."

I said I was taking a walk to the old village. He wanted to come along. I said, "Sure," and hoped I didn't make a mistake. His wife returned. He asked her if it was OK to go with me. I could hear her shrieky voice. She told him to have fun and don't play in the road. She has a funny streak.

The two amigos started up the hill into town. Harry must think I'm a psychologist. He will get what he pays for. He said, "I have a fucking headache. I came here to relax, and she wants to run all over the place. How many Picasso museums can you go to? And there's another exhibit she wants to see. All the artist does is put streaky lines on a canvas. And how many shitty beaches with stones do I have to walk on? They call that a beach? Nice is one big rock pile. So is Cagnes-sur-Mer. Well, fuck that. Hey, let's get a drink."

"I wanted to explore the town, look around, maybe in a little while."

"Sure, OK, I needed to get away. Thanks. We're here with our two daughters. All they do is piss and moan. Their cell phones, I'm ready to throw them into the Mediterranean. Can't they read a fucking book? I think I'm successful because I read a lot."

"You're on vacation, have fun, forget it. They have time to read." I felt like his wife hired me to babysit.

"You're probably single, so you don't have anybody crawling up your asshole, well, maybe you do." I assured him that was not the case. The metaphor did make me slightly uncomfortable.

We approached the village gate of St. Paul de Vence. The compact medieval village is on a hill and partially enclosed by a high wall. It's charming and fairytale-like. During the day, droves of tourists fill the village and wander through its art galleries and shops. Harry was pleased that his wife had not discovered the shopping.

Just outside the village gate, there was a bar and restaurant called Café de la Place. The café had an inside bar and two rows of tables on a patio. Outside the restaurant, there was a packed dirt area where four guys played boules. Harry was pissed because the café didn't have Fireball, the cinnamon whiskey that my contemporaries like. I tried to sensitize my new friend. "You know, Harry, if you went to your favorite restaurant in North Jersey, they wouldn't have Pastis 51. It's a strong French drink, like grappa. Try it out."

He looked at me like I spoke Chinese. He shrugged, didn't want it. "Ok, then ask monsieur if they have absinthe. It has an extra kind of kick. It will put you out of your misery." He liked that idea. Harry ordered absinthe, and I got vodka with soda, lime, and extra olives.

Two nearby tables were occupied. At the closer table, two women drank martinis, and one of them was very loud. They were platinum blondes in their mid-thirties with big round dark-frame sunglasses. Both wore white shorts, sleeveless black tops, and white sandals with four-inch fuck-me heels. I love that look. Monaco chic. I took a big sip and walked to their table. I took a chance they spoke English. "Let me guess, you're in school and doing a semester abroad, and you've got time to explore." They laughed easily. That's a good sign. I continued. "Would you like to sit with us?"

The one named Tammy said, "Well, thank you," like I just bought her a drink. Tammy was on a work trip for a French cosmetics company in Nice. Her friend Brie owned a women's clothing store on the Upper East Side. They were going back to New York in a few days.

Tammy was originally from New York City but adopted a slight drawl. Brie was a Lone Star State native. She was full-figured, brash, and had a seductive smile. With Brie, it was "honey" this or "honey" that. Guys on the piggish side would simply call her a banger. Tammy was a bit shorter and more slender. She was reserved, but once she warmed up, she had plenty of spunk. Tammy liked to talk about her sales team but didn't act like a big shot. I liked that.

"Would you like a drink? Harry got absinthe. Good, Harry?" He nodded. I could tell he was uncomfortable with the women.

Brie responded. "No absinthe, thank you, a couple of martinis would be lovely. Light on the vermouth. It's fine if the bartender can't understand the vermouth part. And mucho olives, please."

"No problem. No vermouth in the martini." The waiter was impressed. Two guys with women, and they're not the tall, dark, and handsome type.

Harry relaxed. He was so happy to be here. He told the ladies about his business, which was manufacturing ladies lingerie. It was actually his father in law's business, but, of course, he ran the business. He went on about how the industry has changed. Costs rise but there's less to cover. Harry thought he was funny. Tammy and Brie forced smiles. I was now in for two martinis each. Well, I offered and was glad to do it.

My phone kept buzzing. I finally put it on silent mode. Brie said, "Honey, there's somebody who really wants your attention. I'd shut it off. I'll bet it's his wife."

I whispered, "No, I'm not married."

There were five text messages from DD. "Excuse me, Harry, can you keep the ladies entertained?" He smiled like a baby. I left the café and walked toward the village gate.

I looked at the first text. "Joe, I'm in Paris, and I miss you. No sun for the last two days. Is there any way you can come to Paris? I go home soon. It's tense with my dad here." Then she texted "Call me" three times. The last one simply said, "Please." I wrote that I was in transit and will call later. Should the white knight go and free the fair maiden from her daddy? No, that will not happen. Still, I better call DD tonight. Now, what to say?

Back to the fun and games. Tammy asked, "Everything alright?"

I was in a dramatic mood and said, "I broke up with my girlfriend, and she keeps calling me. I'm trying to move on."

Brie said, "Honey, I've been there, I just got rid of my husband. He was a pig, pig, pig. Now, he won't leave me alone. Begs me to come back. I would rather find him a mistress. He was with another woman for years, had a kid with her. I didn't know anything. Well, it's refreshing to sit down with two gentlemen like yourselves. You two are so normal." I let that one pass. I guess there are times when I want women to look at me superficially.

Tammy said to Brie, "The boys are expecting us for a couple of hours." She turned to Harry and me. "We met guys in Nice, they think they're going out with us tonight. Brie, let's cancel it. We'll find another bar with these two. You guys have humility, that's a good trait for a man," she said, her voice slurred by the libations. She looked at Harry. "If you miss work, and you want to talk business, we can talk business."

Harry was startled. Brie said, "No, honey, not that kind of business. We are high-quality ladies." Harry was happy again. We agreed that another bar was a good idea. I sent Leslie a message that I might not be back for a while.

Tammy found a bar about halfway inside the village of St. Paul and just outside the city wall called Chez Moi. It was a short uphill walk and Harry started to pant. Fortunately, he stopped, and I got him some water. He took a couple of deep breaths and said he felt better.

We sat at an outside wood table and had a great view of the village of Cagnes-sur-Mer and the Mediterranean a few miles away. It was a kick to hang out with these women. With heels, they were at least five-eight. No one talked about height. They wore a subtler shade of red lipstick than DD. Harry couldn't believe it when Tammy said she and Brie would buy the next round. I accepted with thanks and humility.

Tammy and Brie were staying at La Colombe d'Or Hotel, which stands on a lovely hilltop outside the village. They knew the area from prior trips and preferred it to Nice. Tammy wondered if we could get together tomorrow. Harry stuttered and said he was leaving in the morning for Bordeaux and a wine tasting tour. "But I really don't want to go." The women were touched.

Tammy said to me, "You can come over. We have a beautiful pool."

"Thank you. I have to work, but we'll see."

Our waiter, Jean, brought martinis for the ladies and me, and absinthe for Harry. Three absinthes will send you into space. After a few sips, Harry did not make it into space. He tilted his chair back and fell on a piece of freshly cut grass. He was groggy for a few seconds and gradually picked his head up. I got him a glass of water. Brie told him she knew CPR. That got his attention. I threw some cold water on his face, and he felt better.

We also ordered crêpes. Harry took a few bites and said he needed to go. We were enjoying the day. I hated to leave but decided to go with him in case he falls on the way back. Tammy gave me her business card. I hoped I could meet them tomorrow.

We walked back to Le Hameau. Harry's balance was shaky at times. He garbled, "Thank you, Joe," and then, "I never had women like that pay attention to me." He asked me to pick up a bottle of absinthe. I told him gently that was a bad idea. It was hard to get mad at the guy. I did a good deed getting him away for the afternoon. We returned to the hotel without any mishaps. I gave him two Tylenol. He said, "Thanks, and what was her name, Brandy?"

"Brie, like the cheese. You need to forget about her when you see your wife."

Harry left, and I went to the hotel bar for coffee. The clerk kindly brought it to the pool. I dozed off, waking up with a sunburned forehead and two burnt feet. I had lotion in the room. Leslie wasn't back yet. I saw an old-fashioned handwritten note on the bed. Wow, people still do this? That's so sweet. The note said, "Joe, so sorry, I needed to leave after I saw Henri. Explain later. Keep the room. I had fun. Leslie."

Strange. She could have called me. No, maybe that would not have gone well. She reserved the hotel for three days. I went over to reception and learned that the bill was paid. It feels funny staying here now. I'll stay tonight and go from there. My curiosity increased, and I called Leslie. No answer. I knew it. Is Henri straight again? That can't be. Maybe she had a good reason to split. I texted. No response. I worked a few hours. It was midnight. A delightful evening, but for the drama. My phone rang. The alcohol wore off, so talking would be more difficult. I warned myself to take the high road. "Hello, Leslie, are you alright?"

"I'm good Joe, I'm sorry I took off like that."

"You're OK, that's the main thing."

"Joe, I messed up, this isn't going to make any sense." I thought, why me? And why the drama? Note to self - the big picture is very good. Stay calm. This Leslie thing. It's about a guy. It has to be.

She said, "Please don't be mad. I know I dragged you to St. Paul. I had a nice visit with Henri. What a glorious day. Joe, I was going to say I got a call from the Art Institute and won a prize for a painting of an old city portico, and I left to accept the award." She paused. I took a deep breath, held it for several seconds, and breathed out. "I really messed up. I met this guy Salvatore in Bologna. Salli, he's about fifty years old, he has a business in Milan. He makes very expensive shoes. Well, we went out a few times. He started buying me things. There was a necklace, I think it was expensive. Then he paid my rent.

"Salli called when I was with Henri. He was in Bologna and wanted to see me. He was adamant. He said he would cut me off and get his money back. I got my things, taxied to Nice, got a train ticket to Bologna, and believe it or not, I was about halfway there. Then I thought, enough of him. I'm coming back to St. Paul. Screw him with the threats, the conniving little shit. I fell for the cologne. It's Tom Ford. You melt when you smell it. Good judgment goes out the window.

"The guy's nuts. Last time I saw him, he said his wife ripped a pair of his pants and a shirt. Crazy. So, Joe, oh, it's after midnight, I will be back by the middle of the day. I might just fly to Nice if I can get a flight from Milan." Leslie was crying. I wanted to run. She kept going. "I know you think I'm crazy, and you should, but I was starting to like you, you don't beat to anybody's drum, something like that."

"Leslie, thanks, I don't know, I'm glad you're alright. I'm really tired." That was it for the time being. I thought about a piece of advice Leslie could have used. I learned it from an executive coach at StarColor. "Be aware of the unintended consequences of your actions." And I would add to that, "including sleeping with an older guy who's a pig, in exchange for a short-lived bump in your standard of living." Of course, I didn't say anything. Is it time to back out?

CHAPTER FIFTEEN

> *She has my attention.*

To stay or not to stay? Should I leave before Leslie's back? It's two o'clock in the morning. I was restless enough to go to the pool and work, only interrupted by the crickets and cicadas.

Where am I with Leslie? Yes, she gave me a chance. And yes, I gave her a chance. As far as I know, she accepted me for what I was, this woman who is at least three inches taller. We have spent quality time together. Biblically, he hath lain with her. Does all of this rise to something meaningful? No, but it seemed headed in the right direction.

The relationship was tainted by Leslie's bad judgment with a bully named Salvatore. She let him control her. As far as I know, she's coming back. I have plenty of reason to leave sooner than later. I guess she was prone to unconventional behavior when I met her. I viewed that in a positive way. It meant she's open-minded. You can't get to meaningful without a little craziness.

Our plane ride to Nice had gone well. We talked, napped, played Scrabble. I could tell she was intelligent. She knew the Renaissance artists, but asked a deeper question - "How do you explain a burst of creativity within such a concentrated period of time?" She answered there was a convergence of factors, like most major historical events. "And yet, someone could tell me all day long about the Renaissance," she said as we were about to land, "but it remains hard to comprehend. There has to be something magical at work." I liked that.

So, what to do? I have part of the new day before she gets back. I put down the laptop, sat back, took a cat nap, and planned to wake up in ten minutes. Three hours later, I woke up to sunrise. The laptop was about to fall off the lounge chair, and what do you know? My friend and aspiring wingman Harry was sitting on the next lounge chair. What's he doing here so early? I wonder if his wife kicked him out of the room. I nudged him, he looked up and wiped his eyes. "Joe, she's pissed off. Hope she cools off ... Let's get some breakfast. I think I've been here an hour. Were you here all night?"

I was irritable. "Harry, I have my own issues. I fell asleep after midnight. I'm tired. But I'll get a cup of coffee. Don't ask me any questions. Just deal with your wife. She married you, didn't she? She made a free and uncoerced decision. She loves you. Or she tolerates you. You married her because she had redeeming qualities. Now then, after we get coffee, go back and tell her you're sorry, give her a kiss, and tell her, yea, it would be good if you could lose a few pounds. No, no, leave off the last part. Tell her you want to try a new position. Keep it fresh. No, don't do that either."

He laughed so loudly you could hear him outside in the lobby. "You motherfucker. I look to you for support, and you get me more confused ... No, you're right."

"Just having fun with you, old boy." I'm starting to talk like Carter. "My girlfriend, my supposed girlfriend, took off for Italy while you and I were in St. Paul de Vence with the New York ladies. It was something about another guy. She's on her way back. Don't try to understand this. I need to decide whether to leave before she gets here. Tell your wife you want to go to that museum up the hill, Foundation Maggot? That's how it's pronounced. But we'll go to the village and find those women. Brie, I think she liked you ... Oh, I forgot, you guys are checking out today."

He shook his head. "Let's get some coffee." It's comical, watching Harry work through the marital jungle. I must be careful; he might listen to me. We sat in the breakfast room. The coffee was strong and delicious. "Joe, it's serious, she found out I was having fun with one of the company's models. It's her cousin. She's a ho and it's her fault. The kids don't know, thank you, God."

"That does change things. Just be sweet. You want to stay with her, right? And strike all the previous advice." He looked very unhappy.

The breakfast room opened. There was a newlywed couple, you could tell. She's excited, he's paying attention, no one is throwing anything. Harry's wife walked in a few minutes later with a plate of food from the buffet. Harry said, "There she is. Joanne." She came to our table, and I said hello. She had an omelet, potatoes, lots of bacon, and a gorgeous-looking baguette with Nutella on the edge of the plate. Oy vey. What an appetite. She was very friendly. Maybe it's the breakfast. And she's attractive, but for expansion in certain areas.

She said, "Joe, do you know anything about the Picasso Museum in Antibes? We want to go today."

"I know Picasso went through various phases, and I know the museum overlooks the Mediterranean. Sorry, I haven't been there."

"Harry would rather look at the boobs at the pool and the beach." This could be fun.

I attempted to bring them together. "A lot of nice people go to the beach."

Harry broke in. "I would love to go to the Picasso Museum, maybe Joe would like to go too."

"I appreciate it, but I have work to do. You guys go. Years ago, I had a chocolate crêpe in Antibes. It was incredible."

I went to the buffet and grabbed a baguette, apricot jam, and coffee. Give me a piece of fresh bread and a strong cup of coffee, and I'm content. Add a bright, warm day, and nirvana is here.

Joanne was eager to leave and get to the museum when it opened. I think she freaks out about time schedules. I gave each one a strong handshake and patted Harry on the shoulder.

Weeks later, Harry called and said that his wife forgave him, partly because she knew her cousin was a major league tease. Poor Harry was seduced. He acted very contrite. He also told me she was unbelievable.

Now, what do I do? Find another room with a view? Or keep the door open with Leslie? A few years from now Leslie will have an exhibit at MOMA and all the savants will fawn over her. She'll have wealth and fame, and I won't be there. Or will I? Leslie left a note on the bed, so should I leave one? A call is easier. When you talk, you can adapt what you say to the conversation. If you are paying attention.

So where is she? She missed her connection in Genoa. She should be in Nice in an hour or so. I called and pretended it was another day at the beach. "Hi, Joe, we're playing Scrabble, is 'irregardless' a word? I said it isn't. These kids say it is."

I thought a moment. "They're technically correct. It's a word, but it's bad English. You can use it for Scrabble, but don't say it. It sounds uneducated. Listen, Leslie."

"I know. You're leaving. I heard you talking on the phone after the call dropped the first time. You didn't hang up. I'll be there about three this afternoon. Don't go. I need a proper goodbye."

"I don't know, Leslie. You make me nervous. Something's not right. I'm glad I came. I love it here. You were good to me. And the sex ... You know you're talented. I know I will see your stuff in a big gallery one of these days. I'll tell the clerk that you'll be back this afternoon. Oh, breakfast is incredible. Great coffee and a beautiful baguette with fresh preserves. I have to go. Ciao."

"See you."

I dialed DD's number. No, I didn't finish with Leslie. I called her back.

"Joe, I thought that was it, forever and ever, and here you are. You didn't give me a chance to say goodbye." The happy bohemian. She laughed. "Hold on, the game's almost over. I won twenty dollars; I'll buy you something."

"Leslie, I wanted you to know." I was stumbling. This was difficult. "I wanted you to know. You took me seriously. Most women wouldn't. I appreciate that."

"Joe, listen." Leslie turned serious. "I'm not sure what you're talking about. I don't give a shit about what most women think. They're all phony. It's all junk and there's a word ... hubris. I went to Nice with you because I liked you. That's all you need to know, now cut it out ... I have an idea. You do what you're doing for a week or so, get moving on that chapter on how climate change affects relationships. Work like you're on a mission. Call me if you want to get back together. What did you say? Make the best imperfect decision. I like that. Jesus Christ, I miss you already, you little jerk." Overall, I liked what she said, so I didn't complain about her use of "little." Not only that, I teared up. I felt weak.

"Leslie, that's a good plan ... Hey, with Salvatore, that's done?"

"Done, done ... Done."

"Let me ask you something. Not that it matters."

"Then why do you want to know how tall Salvatore is? He's six-two."

"I knew it."

"No, he's five-two. He's a dapper guy with silver hair. Don't worry, he's full of shit, in a bad way, and you're better looking. See, I'm an artist. I think big and small, and I like people who are alive. Got it?"

"Yes, thanks. Wow."

It was late morning, and I felt good enough to have a celebratory drink. I had a small bottle of Dewar's. A woman in a cook's apron came out the kitchen door smoking a cigarette. I asked for a lemon twist. She reappeared with a lemon slice. I took out two euros. "Pas de charge. No charge young man."

"Many thanks." I handed the coins to her anyway. I carefully separated the peel from the lemon, dropped it in the drink, and sipped it. Then I ran outside, did a cartwheel, and fell down on the grass. No soreness.

I went back to the room, packed, and left. I took a bus to Vence, the next town up the road about four miles, and found a tiny hotel near the town cathedral, named Hotel Simple. While St. Paul is a storybook village that closes up at night, Vence is a bigger, bustling town that stays open. It also has a medieval quarter with plenty of ambience.

Time to check with Tammy and Brie. Then DD. Then touch base with Junior League Cindy. Jen wanted me to call like it was urgent. What's her marital status? Talk about potential trouble. My head is spinning. Dive right in.

Tammy had a calming voice compared to her raspy sidekick Brie, who bubbled over with energy. "Hello, Joe, there you are. That was fun with you guys. I think your friend doesn't get out enough."

"He'll be OK, he's under a lot of pressure." That's always a good excuse. "He left this morning. Hey, any interest in the beach or sightseeing?"

"Joe, Brie needed to make some calls. Work-related. Remember those days when you were on vacation, and you took a conference call. Not good."

"Yes, I do. You're supposed to feel loved and needed and important. I didn't feel it."

"Like I said, it sucks. Go write your book and we'll drink later."

"Yes. You're a good influence. I changed hotels. Up the road a few miles in Vence. I found a cool place called Henry's Bar."

"I know the town. Let's go later. Joe, just so you know, I have a boyfriend."

"Sure, that's good ... Takes the pressure off."

"Takes the pressure off, huh?"

"Yes." It was a relief. I can act normally around Tammy. She's soft-spoken and takes me seriously. I don't have designs on her, so if I space out for a moment, not a big deal. Paying attention is overrated. When a woman says, "Did you hear what I said?" or "What did I say?" she should know the answer is no or I don't know. Well, at least some of the time …

We had afternoon drinks at Henry's Bar. Henry's has a perfect location on a lively street corner at the edge of Vence's medieval quarter, with plenty of outdoor seating to watch the flow of humanity. After a couple martinis and a small bowl of olives, Tammy talked nonstop. I learned about her current boyfriend, her former boyfriend and the one before that. She kept talking, and I kept nodding. And, oh my God, she told me the sex was good with her current boyfriend, but the relationship was hollow beyond that. He was good looking and sociable, but he had an oversized ego, in relation to what he brought to the table.

"Don't get me wrong," she said, "I need a guy who stands tall and stands up to bullshit, but this guy?"

I guess I have to fill in the blank. "Tammy, don't you deserve someone deeper? You want somebody you can talk to all night, until you're so tired and so happy."

"And then what happens?" She put her elbows on the table, her chin on her hands, and looked at me like a little girl waiting for grandma to finish the story.

"You found him, oh sorry, but it was a dream. But wait, you met an unbelievable guy. He looks like me, he'll talk with you all night and fall into your arms."

"And that's how it goes?"

"I wanted to give you a happy ending. It's not reality, but I want you to feel good."

"Joe, I feel very good. You're a good listener." Carter would piss in his pants if he heard this. "Now please get me another martini." No one else was around. She leaned over and whispered, "I'm breaking up with him. He told me he could do better."

I whispered back. "That's mean. He shouldn't have said that. No one should say that."

She looked around, then at me. "First question. Do you have a girlfriend? Second question, what's the cologne you're wearing?"

"I go out, no regular GF." I think that's accurate. How do you define regular? "The cologne is Tom Ford."

"That stuff is unbelievable. Your cologne, the sun, the soft breeze. Touch my arm. Am I dreaming?" No, it's the three-martini effect. I didn't want to spoil her fun, so I shook my head.

"Hey, Joe, just hold me. I'm a big girl. You're a big boy." She put her hand on my right leg. I liked Tammy but as we say in the corporate jungle, I did not see a path forward. I think you can have the best talks with women that you aren't pursuing.

All that said, I needed a break. My phone rang. It was Tara, my legal assistant from StarColor. I told Tammy I had to take a call.

It was a mistake to answer. "Joe, we miss you. Billy has his hands full, and Richard hasn't backfilled." Billy's a litigation attorney who took over some of my work. "Richard thinks you're coming back. He said he'll give you a month to get back before he closes the door on you. This merger is causing a shitload of work. I must say, your timing was perfect."

Tara is a great legal assistant. I understood the sentiment, but ... "Look, Tara, I wanted to do this. I had to."

"Joe, we know what you're made of. Brains and bullshit. It's a race to see which one's ahead. I'm sorry, we just miss you. It's boring without you. Nobody says, 'What the fuck' with the same feeling you do."

"I miss you too, and I miss the place." That was a slight overstatement. I missed her and some of the work. "I need a couple of months to see what I can get done. Things are fluid. Please don't say anything. I know there's no guarantee of returning. I'm a bad precedent."

"Yes, you are. Peter is leaving the end of next week." Peter is one of the senior attorneys. "But he's been here more than ten years. He's got more money than you. Hey, the stock's up about ten percent since you left. Maybe you should stay away."

"Wish him the best. I'll call him."

"You know who misses you? Sandra. This place is her life. I'm not supposed to tell you, but she's sick. The C-word. She'll be OK, but she's weak now."

"Oh dear, Sandra. As long as she's getting better." Sandra was my paralegal at StarColor. Early on, she wanted to see me outside of work, but I wasn't interested. Also, not a good idea. Certain office romances are too risky. Look how many male lawyers wrecked their careers by putting their third leg where it shouldn't be.

"And Joe, Richard is having a hard time keeping his head above water."

"He knows he can call," I said, biting my tongue. I didn't want to encourage him. "You know, now I feel bad ... No, I will not feel bad. Say hi to everybody."

I returned to the table with Tammy. She looked at me with a blank stare. "I'm sorry, it was my office or my former office. I thought I should take the call. It would have been better not to."

"No problem. Where were we? Joe, you know what would be fun? you and me and Brie and Harry on a double date. Wouldn't that be hysterical? He's such a nebbish, but he's likable, and she will take charge. You know the movie *Sideways*. Miles and Jack go out for dinner with Maya and her friend Stephanie. Miles is awkward and Jack, he's just mixed up. He goes out with Stephanie a week before he's supposed to get married to another woman. You're like Miles, but more confident, you've got direction."

"That's a compliment? Thanks." I helped Tammy up.

"You work and maybe we'll catch up tomorrow."

Tammy left. I returned to the hotel and sat on the back patio. The words spilled out like a pounding waterfall after the snow melts. Late in the day, another call.

"Hello."

"Where are you?" a female voice asked.

"Who is this?" A few more seconds and I'm hanging up.

"It's Jen. So, where are you? I went to your hotel. The one with the nuns. They said you left." I didn't want to tell her where I was.

"I left Venice three days ago. How did you know where I stayed in Venice?" This better be good.

"I ... I asked Anita. She thought you were still there. You know how I know Anita?"

"I didn't know you knew her."

"I'll tell you. She's a dear friend from college. She went to college in her late twenties, and we overlapped one year when I was a sophomore. We stayed friends through bad husbands and boyfriends. I thought if I told you I knew her, especially after she took DD's phone, you would hold it against me. And by the way, you didn't call me." I let that go.

"So, that makes you?"

It was quiet for a couple of seconds. "Thirty-nine ..."

"Oh."

So, Anita takes the phone and stirs the pot against DD, thinking this will help Jen? Did Jen know before she took the phone? It doesn't matter. "You two are characters, and I have work to do."

"Well, where are you?"

"Southern France. That's it ... I need to go. I have your contact info."

"Can I call you in a week? And Joe, are there other women offering themselves to you?"

"I don't like talking about this."

"That means none."

"That's unfair but OK. You're right. I got to go. And tell Anita I loved the party, but her goodwill is wearing off. No, don't say that. You guys are quite the tag team. How long are you in Italy?"

"How long are you in France? Never mind, I'll call you."

"You will? And the height thing?"

"What's the height thing?"

"My height."

"Oh, I see. You're short and so what? Maybe, you're too tall for me. Be happy you have a mature fine wine. Joe, if you give me the opportunity, we'll have martinis, and I will drink your little ass under the table. And then if you're a good boy ... Now, aren't you glad I called? And one more thing. My grandfather, who was from Marseilles, I think he was less than five-three, so I'm used to guys like you. What do you say? Oy vey. My Jewish friend taught me that."

"Yes. And what about the husband?"

"Oh, he will soon be out of the picture."

"Jeez, it sounds like you hired someone to finish him off."

"It's a figure of speech."

"Sounds creepy. You mean it's over?"

"Just about. Separation papers in a couple of weeks."

That does not sound definite. I didn't want to quibble. She has my attention.

CHAPTER SIXTEEN

> *When your fingers move and the words flow, it's a*
> *great rush, a creative high.*

I spoke with DD the next morning. She didn't sound as panicky as her messages. I promised to meet her in New York when I'm back, at an old haunt like McSorley's or Chumley's, and maybe we'll make out in an alley off one of the old Manhattan streets. She liked the last part. She couldn't wait for a New York rendezvous and threatened to get sick on olives if I didn't see her.

DD said Carter is back in the Big Apple and can't stop talking about the Venice party. When she talked too fast, I quickly said 'uh-huh, uh-huh,' so she didn't ask me what she said. She'll catch me eventually. I heard the last thing she said. "I don't trust Carter's Aunt Anita. The woman is devious." She's right about that. I was curious about her old man's status but didn't ask.

Vence was a good place to work. I had peace and quiet, strong coffee with almond and chocolate biscotti each morning. The old city was all around me. Hills and scattered houses in the distance. Sunny skies, lots of walking, lots of writing. When your fingers move and the words flow, it's a great rush, a creative high. I was getting somewhere. As well as good fortune with women. Sure, fate played a part, it always does. That's why you take advantage of what's in front of you. You have to. Is there a spiritual force at work? Yes, it's something that follows "God helps those who help themselves."

I took an early morning walk in Vence's circular old town, down lanes and alleys, and under arches, and stopped at its cathedral, the smallest in France. There was a room of fifteenth century polychrome wood statues that were almost life size. In the back of the sanctuary, there was a Chagall mosaic showing Moses being saved from the River Nile. An inspiring piece of artwork for any creative pursuit. I went back to Henry's Bar and cranked out the words. If I make enough progress, Henry's could be a literary café just like La Dome or La Closerie des Lilas, where Papa Hemingway sat and wrote and drank.

Mid-afternoon, I texted Tammy about possible beach plans. She responded, "Joe, I can't get away, but my company is sponsoring an event tomorrow evening in Cagnes-sur-Mer. At one of the small beachfront hotels. It's for the French and American sales teams. Nothing fancy. Would you like to go? As friends, of course. Brie can't make it. You take the bus from Vence to Cagnes-sur-Mer. Get off at the beach stop. I'll send you the address. You will have more to write about."

The invitation sounded like an afterthought, but who cares? I'm not in her sales group, and I'm not a big cosmetics customer, so this is a gracious offer. "Yes. Thanks, Tammy. I'll see you there."

"Good, just yourself, no girlfriends. It's really a corporate event."

"Of course not. The last one left anyway." That was more or less true.

"One more thing. These are mostly women in the cosmetics and perfume industry. A freewheeling crowd. You need to have an open mind. No comments about the outfits or makeup."

"I will be tolerant. I want women to tolerate me, right?"

"Yes, that makes sense."

Tammy is a legitimate female friend. I have no agenda. So, no potential for drama or saying the wrong thing. I still want to look good. To be noticed. The presence thing. For the party, I'll wear the twill shirt with the mermaid prints. No, stick with a starched shirt.

The next day, I had a shot of Jameson's and a cheese plate at Henry's Bar before hopping on the No. 9 bus to Cagnes-sur-Mer. My security blanket? Two shot bottles of French whiskey from the Tabac near the bus stop and a bottle of water mit gas.

The bus passed St. Paul de Vence at sunset. I stared to the left at the walled village for the seconds it stayed in view. A mythical, timeless place. If the party disappoints, the ride there was worth it. Twenty minutes later, the bus dropped me off at Cros-de-Cagnes, a beach area and former fisherman's village. From there, it was a short walk to Hotel Chagall, the party location.

Cagnes-sur-Mer has a low-key beachfront with small hotels, shops, and cafés. There's an enchanting inlet and a long jetty, but Harry was right about the stones and rocks they call a beach. I was surprised there were still a handful of people sitting under an umbrella or lying down. It made me appreciate growing up near the sandy beaches of the Jersey Shore.

I walked through the hotel lobby to a courtyard in the back with an oval pool. The approaching evening remained warm with a light breeze. Calm and peaceful on the Riviera. In the pool area, I saw great complexions, good teeth, and colorful outfits. At the last minute, I changed my mind and went with the mermaid shirt before putting on the Tom Ford cologne. As Tammy said, it was mostly women and a few guys. The guys looked like models. I guess some of the women did too. There was a table with blank name tags. A dozen or so people lingered at the pool bar. I didn't see Tammy.

"Bonjour," I said to a young lady. She looked mid-thirties. "I'm Joseph Fine. I'm looking for Tammy."

"Je suis Cecille," she smiled. "You're Tammy's friend. I think she's on the phone. You're the writer." Sounds like the staff was briefed. Cecille introduced me to a few of her colleagues. The rest were scattered around the pool. Most had enough makeup for a

Halloween party. Cecille did not wear makeup and was dressed in a dark pants suit. She must be a financial type. A few folks looked at me like I was a novelty. The way they talked about Tammy, she must be the big boss. They said how much they loved working for her. I was ready to gag.

The bartender laughed when I asked for Pastis 51. "C'est terrible. Rien." I laughed and called him a douche under my breath. An apt use of the popular French word. I walked across the street to the beach. Small numbers of people walked along the concrete esplanade. I looked back at the hotel and heard laughter interrupted by noisy seagulls.

Someone screamed from the hotel. I saw Tammy with her arms in the air. "We got it. We got it. We'll be in more than one hundred stores in Provence and the Riviera." I walked back to join the party. She was with about ten people, mostly women. Most wore blinding lipstick and not-so-subtle face paint. A lively, animated group.

Tammy turned to me. "Joe, you made it, did you meet the group? This is my team. We just landed a big account. Cha-ching. They worked their butts off." She told me this like I was part of the senior management team.

I smiled my approval. "That is just great." I tried to fit in. The chatter got louder; the drinks poured freely. The bartender heard someone say my name. He said to me, "Bonjour, Joseph, faites attention." He pointed to a woman. "She's American. She wondered who you are." He cupped his hands in front of him and moved them up and down in a provocative manner.

What the hell, I introduced myself. The woman wore a maroon pantsuit with a red and white striped blouse. The first three buttons were unbuttoned. I was careful not to stare. Tammy came over and introduced me. She beamed that Marie was one of her top salespeople. I guessed she was twenty-five or twenty-six.

Marie Lavitz had short-cropped dark brown hair in a bob. What hit me was her intimidating big emerald eyes and dark eyeshadow.

I almost didn't notice the subtle pink lipstick on her full lips. She was at least three inches taller than me even with the clogs I wore. We started to chat. She had a slight French accent but was fluent in English. She was born in France but lived and worked in Chicago since she was much younger. Her black-framed rectangular glasses gave her a serious look, like a TV newscaster. She projected poise and exuded sexual charm.

Tammy said Marie would be the product manager for a new cosmetics line. I acted impressed. Marie asked me how I knew Tammy. I spaced out for a moment trying to picture what was behind the buttons on her blouse. Marie touched my right arm to get my attention. "I'm sorry, I get distracted. We were in St. Paul de Vence and started to talk."

"You're a lawyer, but you don't work?" She was confused.

"Who told you that? Don't believe everything you hear. If she said I have a great personality, that part is true." I might have stared too long, so I excused myself and went to get a shot of Dewar's. I settled for cheap French whiskey.

I thought about DD. Her last text said she went to a Vanderbilt alumni event in New York City. Hopefully, she hasn't met a tall, dark, and handsome Southern transplant. She wouldn't offer her chest to anybody, right? I'll text her later. The Inner Voice thinks I'm too concerned. DD should have fun while I'm away. If she cares, another month or two won't matter.

I returned to Marie and Tammy at the party. Tammy left to talk with a few others. Marie said, "When Tammy comes to France, she makes big speeches and takes the credit, and we do all the work." Yes, according to Corporate Life 101, you're supposed to make the boss look good. That was always my mantra.

I simply said, "You look very smart ... and attractive." What the heck, let the bullshit fly. I think I've become incrementally nicer and more liberal with compliments since I left the States. Yes, it's self-serving. My father told me you get more with sugar than salt. I'm not sure this is what he had in mind.

"You're too kind."

"Thank you. I mean it."

It was time to go after a couple of hours. I was surrounded by makeup and didn't want to drink too much. I found Tammy and thanked her, and then said goodbye to Marie. I told her it might be fun to get a drink sometime. She smiled in a noncommittal way. I said, "You know, it's so pleasant tonight, I think I'll take a walk on the promenade."

"I'm bored here. Can I go with you?"

I was hesitant and uncomfortable, then nodded yes. "Sure, come on."

We walked for about a mile up and down the beachfront. The night was cooler, and it felt good. The street was quiet except for an occasional car or scooter and there were few walkers. It was strange to walk with this striking woman. Maybe she liked the law part of my resume.

Marie was more than cropped hair and power eye makeup. I learned she left Chicago after graduating from DePaul and went to New York City for a job in cosmetics retailing. She didn't like the Big Apple. Too much of a status culture. She hated bars. "Guys are the biggest liars. What's with their wives? Come on ladies, put out. Guys aren't complicated. Some of them are even nice, right?" She's so young and so skeptical.

I agreed that New York could be a tough place for socializing. "You strike me as someone who can hold her own in the big city."

She nodded. "You're right."

After New York, she went back to Chicago to manage the cosmetics department at Macy's in the Loop. Tammy found her and offered her a job. She made good money for a woman in her mid-twenties.

We walked by a café that looked like it was about to close. I asked the lone waiter for two shots of Pastis 51. He made it clear he was doing us a favor. I told Marie I thought she would like it. "It's the liqueur of Provence."

She took a sip, and nearly spit it out. "I'm sorry. This is disgusting. You like it?"

"Not sure, I thought it would be fun to try it. There must be better French libations." She took my arm. I noticed that she buttoned the third button. I was now with a respectable woman.

"You know, there are better ways to get me trashed than Pastis 51."

"That's an excellent point."

We returned to the Hotel Chagall. Almost everyone from the party had left. A makeshift bar behind the reception desk had eleven bottles. I noticed the absinthe and asked the clerk for two shots. We took them and crossed the street, sat close to the surf, and got wet. Marie thought it was very funny. We sat there for a few minutes until our pants were drenched. She moved closer to me. I said, "Marie, I just met you."

She giggled. "We're all wet. So, maybe a wet kiss?" I obliged. We rolled around until we were a sandy mess. Fortunately, there was a shower in the hotel's pool area. We went back to the reception desk and the clerk graciously handed us towels. I gave him a good tip. He also ordered a taxi for us.

I nodded off almost immediately after getting in the taxi. She put something in my pocket, which made me jump. She said, "It's OK, you're OK," like she was comforting a child who had a nightmare. "Good night."

"Marie, thanks for ... everything." I dropped her off and taxied to Vence. I slept great. No dreams. No nightmare.

CHAPTER SEVENTEEN

I bet you know what you want.

Another glorious morning on the Cote D'Azur. Another opportunity and adventure. I got up at sunrise to express my gratitude. If I do my part, the Almighty will do hers.

I checked my pockets from last night. There it was, Marie's contact information. She said something about going to the beach at Juan-les-Pins before she left the taxi. Did she ask me to go or tell me her plans?

Tammy and I met for coffee at a little café near my hotel. I thanked her again for the party. She hugged me. I think she would have hugged a tree. That sounds insincere, but she was sky-high about the order she announced at the party. I very much appreciated her friendship. "The least I can do is buy you breakfast." We ordered scrambled eggs, potatoes, baguettes, apricot preserves, and double espressos with milk. I know, not the routine. The waiter acted like he never heard of scrambled oeufs. I thought my pronunciation was quite adequate.

Tammy said, "I talked to Brie late last night. She got a kick out of you and Harry. That's a real compliment because she doesn't trust men in general. You know she got burned by her ex. When we're all in New York, she wants to meet. She thinks you're cute with those studious glasses, and I should go out with you. I told her, 'He's fun, but he's too short.' And you know what? She's loud to begin with, but she got louder. 'Don't underestimate a short guy.'

Maybe she's right. I married early, got divorced, and by the way he was six-three. He was so boring, especially in bed. You have to keep it fresh, right?" I did not need to know this. Maybe she was part of the problem?

There was more. "He was the late-forties CEO who walks into a room and the rest of the Board goes gaga. Jared had neatly combed salt and pepper hair, and big confident teeth. When he smiled, he won you over. The board was impressed with his gravitas bullshit. A board member later asked me how he became CEO. He said they should have canned him after he sold two profitable businesses. Amazing how guys get by on some phony aura. Sad to say, women do the same thing."

"So, Tammy, maybe you'll go from tall, dark, and handsome to short, dark, and really handsome?" I enjoyed this. My gut said don't go out. Not a good idea with Marie working for Tammy. I hesitated, then went on. "I don't know about going out."

"I don't know either."

"Great, that's settled. Let's do drinks at Minetta Tavern when we're in New York. I'll find Harry and we'll all meet."

"Great."

I took a deep breath and we both laughed.

My brief stint on the Riviera was going well. The work was advancing. I stepped it up. It was an exciting week, watching the words spring to life. On my third day in Vence, I took an Uber and met Marie late afternoon at the beach esplanade in Juan-les-Pins. It's a busy beach town next to Antibes with, yes, a real sandy beach. F. Scott Fitzgerald and wife Zelda lived here in the 1920s when it was more primitive. I imagine the Fitzgeralds picking up Marie and me in their convertible and driving around Cap d'Antibes. We enjoy cocktails on the veranda of their house. I ask F. Scott about Gatsby. With this kind of karma in the air, I knew I could write a great book.

We sat on the Grande Plage near a jetty that was also close to cafés. Marie wore a white bikini with red polka dots that left little room for the imagination. Between the bikini, which was more like a thongtini, her round, white-framed sunglasses, and broad-brimmed straw hat, she could be in a 1960s Italian beach movie. "That's quite a bathing suit," I said in the most dignified manner.

"That's all you can say?" She sounded like Leslie without the accent. They were both free spirits, but Marie had another layer of substance. She could take care of herself. She was certainly playful, but more grown-up.

"No. It fits well too." I was tempted to say it fits so well I can't move easily, which was true. "I hope you have sunscreen; you need it." She shrugged. I put some on her shoulders.

"What's going on? No, it's good." She eventually sat up. "Joe, I want to be a character in your book. I am more than eyeshadow and face cream. A character with a great body and a great mind."

"Yes. There's no question."

Putting on the sunscreen got me excited. I needed to calm down before I stood up. She eventually rose, wiped the sand off her bottom, and put on short shorts and a T-shirt. We walked along the esplanade and stopped at a thatched-roof beach café that reminded me of a tiki bar in Key West. The cool sand felt great on my feet. I already like Juan-les-Pins better than Cagnes. We grabbed a table in a prime viewing area.

A waiter showed up fifteen minutes later. Normally I'd be pissed about the wait, but I greeted him with my best bonjour. I was in such a good mood that I didn't care when he reappeared another fifteen minutes later and unabashedly checked out Marie's cleavage while he put two Aperol Spritzes on the table. As long as he doesn't touch the artwork. After the spritzes, I ordered shots of absinthe which sent us to Shangri-La. It was an "all is right with the world" moment. I said, "I love it here. People are so content. Can't somebody spill a drink and get upset?"

She moved toward me and whispered in the kindest voice, "Would you please shut the fuck up? Now, let's get some lunch."

We ordered crêpes. The absinthe provided abundant food for thought. We started with favorite cartoon characters. Hers was Tweety Bird. I liked Elmer Fudd. Then we moved on to the Little Rascals. I liked Spanky for his leadership skills. Marie liked Darla for her female mystique, and Porky because he was just happy to be there. Then a philosophical moment. "You know why I have hope for the world?" I asked. "Shows like *The Simpsons* and *Family Guy*. Bart Simpson hasn't gotten older in thirty years."

"Joe, they're not real people," she said loudly. She looked at the couple next to us. "Tell my friend Joseph that the Simpsons are not real." They stared at us and froze.

We were sleepy from the sun and drinks by the time the waiter brought the crêpes. We shared one sweet and one savory. I had café au lait, and despite my objection, Marie had vodka on the rocks, which meant a single ice cube that melts in two minutes.

It was hard to get up after that. We ubered back to Vence. She didn't want to go to Cagnes. We fell asleep shortly after we got to the hotel. I woke up after midnight, and Marie wasn't there. She wrote me a note that she was short on cash but didn't want to wake me. She took 150 euros from my wallet and said she was very thankful and would of course pay me back. Nothing else was missing. I guess I paid a premium for a thong suit and colorful conversation. She should have gotten me up.

That precipitated some sadness. For the first time since I left the States, I missed the good old USA. I missed cheesesteaks and Taco Tuesday, baseball, and peanut butter pie. I could not go back until I made significant progress. True, I started to find my voice. I had done well, juggling a book with a decent social life. The potential for both was limitless.

Then a potential opportunity came up.

A few days ago, my friend Bill Santos called me. Bill and I were attorneys at the EPA during my Washington days. We worked on cases together and negotiated big fines against companies for major chemical spills. We liked to say we collected many times more money than we earned while working for Uncle Sam. Bill left D.C. to go to a white-shoe law firm in Manhattan, and I got an opportunity as the in-house environmental counsel with StarColor, which had a much better reputation than the companies we prosecuted.

Bill told me about an opening for a partner track attorney in his firm's Environmental and Government Relations Department. He talked to the senior partner in the department about my credentials. The partner, Ray Winston, wanted to talk to me. I could become a partner within a year if I brought in enough work. So, I was looking at a lucrative situation at a law firm with a kick-ass reputation.

I knew I could do the job. While my skills with women are a work in progress, my skills as a legal eagle are very good. The downside was real. If I took the position, the book writing would go to the back burner. It's all or nothing with these law firms. You give them your life, and they pay you a lot, but you give them your life.

My gut said to stay put. The work was going well. Then I figured, no harm, no foul, it doesn't hurt to talk. Did I want to be a big shit in a big firm? What's the benefit besides money? Professional growth? More attention from women? Those didn't add up. Time would slip away that could be used to pursue the literary life. Long work hours could strain the social life. The only rationale was it did not hurt to talk.

I decided to go to New York in a couple of days on Thursday and stay for a long weekend. Putting on a suit could be difficult. I think my neck expanded, and it would be hard to button the top button, let alone put on a dress shirt. And I would have to be careful not to get coffee stains on my shirt.

I texted Cindy and Leslie that I was going to America but said that, like the Terminator, I would be back. Marie was sorry she left, apologized again about the money, and was upset about my plans to leave. She didn't come out and say it, but if we were in different locales, there was no point in becoming emotionally engaged. I was leery about the future, but I promised to call if we were in the same area. She was positive but noncommittal.

I had mixed feelings about contacting Jen on the upcoming trip. She was back in Boston, her home base. I loved how she said darling, but maybe that's how she talks. Her energy and excitement held my interest. I kept a warm seat for her on my bench. By the way, I do not say bench in a condescending way. It's my way of building a security blanket around my social life until one woman goes to the front of the line. As for DD, I was drifting away from her and decided not to give her a heads up about my trip. If I see her, it can be a surprise.

No matter what, I left southern France feeling good about my time there. The plane was almost full, but my frequent traveler status got me an aisle seat. No one was next to me. Once airborne, I stretched to look out the window and saw figures and faces in the majestic cloud layers.

An hour passed before the snack cart arrived. A short flight attendant with blonde highlights, sparkling white teeth, and puffy lips stopped and smiled. I asked for a Dewar's on ice but settled for Johnnie Walker Black. She gave me a second bottle and said softly, "This is because we didn't have what you wanted." That felt good. I had a burst of energy and wrote eight pages without stopping. I wasn't even distracted by the guy behind me who kept clearing his throat.

I chatted later with the same flight attendant in the back while I waited for a bathroom. She asked, "What's going on in New York?"

"A law firm wants to talk to me about a position. It could be a great opportunity." I made it sound important. "I have mixed feelings. What should I do? Stay with the creative route or return to the big bad corporate world?"

"I bet you know what you want." I liked her answer.

You never know when you've tossed enough S-H-I-T against the wall for a woman to take an interest. We talked later, and she smiled and whispered. "I'm not supposed to do this, but here's my card. I live an hour north of New York City, near Poughkeepsie, and ... just a minute, someone is pressing the button. I have to go." She returned in a couple of minutes. I noticed a necklace with a Star of David. She said, "The lady pressed the button by mistake."

Thankfully, I paid attention. "Poughkeepsie. I've been there. My brother went to Vassar."

"Do you like craft fairs? There's one Saturday. Music too. I'm off. You're probably busy with the law firm."

"My interview is Friday." I told her this before. Maybe she is a poor listener, like me. "I have your card. You're Lily. Lily Lambert. I'm Joseph Fine. I'll let you know about the farmers market."

"The craft fair."

"Yes, that's what I meant. Can I trouble you for a Johnnie Walker, lots of ice?" I felt good. "God, you're very attractive." I'm getting good at this.

"Thank you. Really, I'm just trying to find my way." Sounds like something I would say. She turned and left. See ya later?

CHAPTER EIGHTEEN

❝

Joe, come on, you're backpedaling.

We landed at JFK in a big thunderstorm early Thursday afternoon. It was a mess getting into Manhattan.

After checking in at The Algonquin Hotel and dropping everything off except my laptop, I beelined to Fifty-Fifth Street and Fifth Avenue and the venerable St. Regis Hotel. My New York ritual starts at the King Cole Bar. I love to stare at the mural painting of the old smiling king surrounded by whimsical assistants and, of course, the court jesters. There is a row of bar stools, followed by a row of rectangular high-top tables. Small round café tables line the bar's perimeter. If you want an intimate conversation, sit at one of those.

I know two of the bartenders, Felix and Victor. Both have been here more than ten years; both are from El Salvador. Victor does a better job topping off drinks, but they are both good fellows. Bowls of salty, baked parmesan crisps sit on the bar. The drinks are appropriately overpriced, the crowd is a mix of businesspeople, wannabees, and tourists, and I love the place.

The bar stools were occupied. So were the high-tops and the little round tables. An elderly couple paid their tab. They left the bar, and I put my hand on one of the stools, only to hear a big, muscular, bald guy say he was there first and planned to sit with his girlfriend. She had high black hair and a long red dress with rows of sparkles running up and down each side. She looked skanky, but he must have seen something deeper. I graciously moved without fact-checking his claim.

I wanted to make the best of the trip, which includes my New York City lady friends. Harry had an event with the kids and couldn't meet. I waited for Tammy and Brie in the lounge area outside the bar where a young red-haired lady in a black cocktail dress played the harp. Vivaldi's Four Seasons was a serene contrast to the noisy bar. I still like the bar better.

I went back to the bar a second and third time to look for a table. Four suits got up from a high-top table after slapping each other on the back. I quickly grabbed an end seat at the table. Two women and a guy took the other seats. The ladies, Eva and Carrie, were tall, five-nine or five-ten, in their mid-thirties, and wore sleeveless charcoal cocktail dresses. I looked down and I saw at least three-inch black heels They had high cheekbones, long black silky hair, and dark eye shadow. They must be twins.

Carrie was married to Ray, who was at least six-four and had a round, shaved head. He wore a navy suit. Eva met them for a drink. They were very friendly. Carrie and Ray were on their way to the Metropolitan Opera to see *Rigoletto*. So, fitting for them to start at the King Cole Bar, because Rigoletto was a court jester.

Eva said to me, "And what are you doing here?"

"I came from France for an interview. I always stop here first."

"I would have stayed there. What town?"

"Nice. The French Riviera."

"Even more reason to stay. The coast is gorgeous. My ex and I were there, well, why bring him into this, right?"

"Up to you," I said. "Some women can't help themselves." Ray liked that. "And yes, it's beautiful and charming and all those things. But when there's an opportunity ..."

"You're right," said Carrie.

Jumpin' Jack Flash came over the speakers. Tammy and Brie were supposed to be here a half-hour ago. Carrie and Ray left. I was alone with Eva.

I want to be accepted and loved by a taller woman. At five-nine or ten, Eva was too much of a mental leap, even for me. I know, it doesn't matter when you're lying down. Can a tall woman have issues being accepted in the social arena? That's not fair either. I offered Eva a drink, which she did not expect given the platonic nature of our impromptu meeting. She got a Lemontini. I switched off and ordered a Tito's martini, extra olives. She was effusive in thanking me for the drink. I appreciated her sincerity.

Eva talked about her young daughter and then her ex, which is when I tuned out but nodded, so she thought I was listening. She discovered his bad behavior on West Coast business trips. I was rescued by a vibrating phone and a message from, OMG, Jen. I excused myself and ran out of the bar. Of course, that's when the ladies walked in. I waved to them and said I'd be right back.

I looked at the message. "Joe, I'll be in NYC in a couple of hours, down from Boston. Anita told me you were coming in. I'm going to an exhibit tomorrow at MOMA. I know the curator. Let's go to Bemelmans tonight. It's in the Carlyle Hotel, if you didn't know. They have a jazz trio. Usually a bass player, pianist, and singer. My treat. You'll love it. Jen." Interesting. She came down from Boston. Just like that. Anita is Jen's eyes and ears. It didn't occur to me to ask her to come here from Beantown.

Bemelmans is at Seventy-Seventh and Madison Avenue on the Upper East Side. I've walked by it, but never went in. I wanted time to horse around with Tammy and Brie, so I suggested nine-thirty. Back at the King Cole, the ladies waited at a little table against the back wall. I waved them over to my high-top table with Eva. Everybody was introduced. I told my St. Paul de Vence pals why I was in New York. Tammy was not happy to hear it. "Joe, come on, you're backpedaling. This is not what you want. You get back to France or wherever else you can work ... Now, get moving."

Eva chimed in. "I don't know you, but instinct tells me the same thing."

"I appreciate the thoughts. Look, I'm just talking to the firm. Nothing's settled."

We had a great visit. Brie was on her game with all the "honey" talk. She was flying to Miami for a fashion show. I warned her about the smooth talkers in South Beach. She wasn't worried. "They're like little, lost boys who never grow up. The biggest talkers are the smallest producers." She must be a handful in bed, but for the right guy, it has to be something cosmic.

Tammy had a trip to southern France scheduled in two weeks. "That's not why I said you should go back to France. I would call you anyway."

"Of course." Something held Tammy back and I don't know what it was. We had another round of drinks. The ladies weren't in any rush. It was almost nine o'clock. I told them I needed to prepare for my interview tomorrow, which was not true. I paid for their drinks without going through mental exercises over whether it was fair from a societal perspective. When I'm having fun with friends, it's worth it. I hated to leave. We exchanged air kisses and promised to get together.

On to the Carlyle. Everything is happening so fast. I didn't tell anyone I was coming to New York, except Carter and my brother Ronnie, who also lives in the city. All I have to do with Jen is relax and keep all my cards in front of me. Was this the right thing to do? I taxied the twenty-three blocks to the Carlyle. Jen seemed carefree with a persistent side. I never gave her a serious thought. I thought she was someone who popped in and popped out of my life. Just treat it as fun or fantasy with an older woman. She said she's thirty-nine. She seems younger.

The Carlyle is an elegant old hotel that has maintained its charm and pretentiousness. You enter the small but ornate hotel lobby and take an immediate left to Bemelmans Bar. It's dimly lit inside. Built-in burgundy velvet sofas and round cocktail tables line three sides of the perimeter of the bar, so you can sit together against the wall and see the band. A Steinway grand piano and an upright bass on a stand sit in the middle of the room. The musicians were on a break. All of this is conducive to romantic pursuits.

I looked around and didn't see Jen. I got up and walked by the crowded bar. At one end of the bar, two ladies of the night in ultra-tight red push-up skanky dresses and high heels winked at the bartender who had a very bad brown toupee. At the other end, there was a door that led down three steps to a decadent lounge with soft cushy chairs and a wallpaper design that evoked the Ancien Regime. Jen was not in there either.

I headed back to the host stand. The hostess, who wore a low-cut dark cocktail dress, took me to a table where the view of the musicians was obscured by a square column. I ordered Dewar's on ice and munched on nuts and potato crisps. Jen texted she was delayed. Can I believe what she said about her marital status? I need to leave quickly if there's a problem. I finished the drink and paid for it. We can start fresh when she gets here.

As expected, Jen made a dramatic entrance. "Joe, I am so relieved to see you." She wrapped herself and her long navy coat around me. I went to kiss her, and she kissed me somewhere between my right cheek and my lips. The signature alluring and devious smile. We sat next to each other.

"I think I'm done with the motherfucker. He's out. He and his little pecker. Well, that wasn't the issue. It's what he did with it. He's at the Roosevelt Hotel. The same place that Don Draper, you know the main guy in *Mad Men* went when he left his wife. What a pig he was." She needed time to catch her breath. I offered her a glass of water.

"No thank you, Joe, I'm fine, I can wait for the server. I'll have a martini up, up, up, with a piece of lemon. Lots, I mean lots of olives. Can you help me with my coat?" She wore a striking sleeveless navy cocktail dress that was three inches above the knees. Her blonde hair glowed in the dim light. She wore long silver leaf earrings. Elemental and elegant with little makeup and subtle pinkish red lipstick. Perfume that held me hostage. That, and penetrating hazel eyes that studied me. Maybe she saw something. She said, "I was at a charity auction, and I couldn't get out of there. I'm sorry. I stopped at the hotel. And now, let's talk about you."

Before I opened my mouth, I saw an open table against the wall with a clear view of the musicians. I asked the hostess if we could move, and she graciously obliged. We had two seats next to each other. I said, "It's funny, if you had been on time, we might not have a good table like this. And this is quite the surprise."

"I like the way you think. You connect dots. You appreciate random events. I wouldn't have met you in Venice an hour later ... Oh my God, imagine that." I guess that was quite the veiled compliment. We ordered the martinis and two appetizers of smoked salmon, capers, and crème fraiche. "So, you were about to tell me why you're here?"

"I came in to talk with a law firm. They have an opening for an environmental counsel. A good partner track position. Someone who can serve their existing business clients. You know, most companies want to do the right thing, and I'm here to help."

"You sound like Mr. Clean."

"Jen, seriously, I'm not sure I want to change course again and go back to the corporate world. I felt good about my writing. But the law firm could be lucrative." Her eyes glazed over. When I said "lucrative," she focused again.

"I have full confidence in you. Now let's toast. To you ... And me."

The jazz trio played Gershwin tunes to honor Bobby Short, who sang at Bemelmans for many years and had a warm, welcoming voice. The crowd loved it. The pianist, bass player, and singer enjoyed themselves. When the woman sang *Someone to Watch Over Me*, I teared up. I quickly turned my face and wiped off the tears. I didn't want Jen to see me. Most of us want to be loved and protected. Is there anything as important? Yes, to love and protect someone else. For a moment, I felt connected to everyone in the room. I moved toward Jen, put my arm around her and whispered, "This music is so moving, unbelievable."

She whispered, "Yes, I'm touched. This is the beginning of our extended mating ritual. Step by step until ... Do you agree? Joe, darling, you are in for a treat. Let's sit for one more set and get a cab. I'm in midtown, not far away. Be right back." She left for the restroom. I took care of the tab. I wanted to stay and enjoy the music.

We heard a few more songs and I got a text from Bill Santos that read, "Please call me right away." I should have shut my phone off. I looked at Jen. "I'm sorry. My friend from the firm messaged. I need to talk to him."

"Please come back." She sounded like she was worried I would split.

"I absolutely will."

Bill picked up. "Joe, I'm glad I reached you." His breathing was heavy.

"What's up? You're ok?"

"What's up is, I just learned Fenster and Banks filed for bankruptcy late this afternoon. It's a mess. I talked to two guys in the firm. The firm owes millions of dollars. They lateraled in lawyer superstars from other firms, they agreed to pay them wads of money, and they can't pay. My advice is don't come in tomorrow. Ray might not even know yet. I can tell him. I'm waiting for another message, but I think the office will be closed. Forget it. They won't bring on anyone. You don't want to be here. The place could liquidate. So sorry I got you into this. I talked to my friend Jeremy, he's a junior partner. He was blindsided too. Sounds like most of the partners were in the dark on the finances. Jesus Christ."

I felt sorry for Bill. I know he'll find work, he's a great lawyer, but the financial mess, the disruption ... "Bill, I'm so sorry to hear that. Unbelievable." Jen came out to the hotel lobby, tugged on my sleeve, wanted to know who I was talking to. I asked her to wait.

"Nothing more to say for now," he said. "You know, we're alive and we have our minds, so we should make it."

The whole trip made me laugh. "They probably won't reimburse my travel? Never mind. Thanks for telling me, Bill. You still good for breakfast tomorrow?"

"Sure, but I'm sleeping in. It's party time now. Hey, how were the hookers at Bemelmans?"

"I'm on a date if you don't mind." We laughed.

"See you then."

I turned to Jen. "Sorry I had to make a call. Unbelievable."

"What?"

"I'll tell you in the cab."

We walked outside. A light misty rain. If it's going to rain, this is the best kind. A light, happy rain. A yellow cab sat in front of the Carlyle. We got in, and I told Jen what happened. She understood. "I feel bad for all the secretaries, the paralegals, it's worse for them. Most of the lawyers can transition, well, the ones with a book of business. I thought it would be fun with you working in New York. Maybe you'll still end up here. I'm upset. Maybe it's a sign."

"If you mean you and me, it's not a sign. I'm here through Monday. So, I'll hide in the bowels of the New York Public Library and write. I'll see you before I go back."

She perked up. "It all makes sense. You came to New York so we could get together. By the way, young man, I was in court today, or rather my lawyer was. He filed the divorce papers against that colossal dickweed. I want to celebrate. I'll buy you a nightcap at the minibar. Driver, excuse me, the hotel is up there on the left." Jen was at the Waldorf Astoria. This was months before it closed to become condominiums. So sad, the well-dressed prostitutes would lose their office space at the hotel's Bull and Bear bar. We walked past the ornate lobby. The architecture and aura of the Gilded Age. One crazy night in Gotham.

A female harpist played in the lobby bar. We stopped to listen. The music was soothing. The harpist, in her long silver dress and long wavy blonde hair, blended into the instrument. Jen wanted to go upstairs. She left, and I stayed to listen. The harpist played Pachelbel's *Canon in D Major.*

Jen's room had a fading elegance. There were velvet burgundy drapes and a flowery bedspread. Two beige Queen Anne armchairs. Wallpaper with horses, dogs, and guys in tricorn hats. I was very tired and fell asleep in one of the chairs. Jen nudged me a few times and didn't waste time. I woke up. She must be releasing months of pent-up sexual frustration. She stared at me and said it was our obligation to stay in the moment. So, this was more spiritual than sexual? I watched my life whiz by. I did my best to keep up with her. At one point, I thought she didn't care if I was the guy in the bed. It became clear this was not the case. Jen was here at this moment to take care of me. A beam of light leading me down the true path. My primal sense said we were here for a reason.

I said, "I can't believe you. How did you learn that?" I will not be graphic. I'll only say we applied a silverware metaphor.

"Are we good or what? I think we used most of the bed." She took a deep breath and let it out. "I feel like I can breathe. Good thing you didn't start that law firm job two weeks ago. Your timing was good. Now you have a clean slate. Tabula rasa. Well, except for me."

"You used the whole bed. Well, that's why it's here, right?" I wrapped myself around her again and let go. Within minutes, I fell asleep. I assume she did too.

Sometime in the middle of the night, Jen shook me, woke me up. "Joe, Joe, can you hold onto me?" She started to cry. Did she have a nightmare? I wasn't prepared for this. "Joe, I'm done with the bastard. You know what? I had a miscarriage a year ago. He gave up on me. He changed his mind. Stopped trying. Bastard. Now, I'm a fucking mess." She kept crying. I tried to comfort her.

One thing I know. I don't have sympathy for guys who string their wives along when they're trying to get pregnant. You've got to go for it or get out of the way. I have friends who had a hard time getting pregnant. It's emotionally draining. You need a lot of support to get to the finish line. I was understanding. And she was drawing me in.

She continued. "With all the baby stuff going on, he thought I should get a boob job. Not big enough? Are you kidding me? Joe, they're OK, what do you think?"

The Inner Voice warned me to be careful. "You're fine. More than fine. Really good. Great." I studied them, and nodded approval. I was emboldened. "What's his problem? It's all good with your boobs and the rest of you. I like all of it." The truth is, in my distorted perfect world, they might be slightly bigger. Physically, the rest of her makes up for it.

"Thank you. At one time, I felt so alive, anything was possible. A little rest and we can go at it again. If you're up to it."

At this point, I actually thought about leaving. I did my best, but this was very intense. There was no question that she got to me. She was unique, a fighter, and good for my confidence. So, I stayed, opened my laptop, and used a reservoir of nervous energy to rattle off a few pages. I finally fell asleep facing the other end of the bed.

Late next morning. Jen woke me up by brushing me with a pillow. I got dressed and told her everything would work out. "No, I know it will work out," she said.

I asked her to meet me after breakfast with Bill. She was visiting a friend on the Upper West Side. "It's a guy, he's gay, it's OK." I was relieved. Then she asked if I could "squeeze in one more for the road."

"I'm honored and humbled, but I gotta go. Look if you're in town tomorrow, we can go to the Morgan Library. There's a new exhibit on Thoreau's writing. Charles Dickens too. Then more fun after that."

"Joe, darling, I can't, I have another charity event tomorrow night in Boston, so we'll figure something else out."

I considered asking her not to say anything to Anita. Forget it. That might encourage her. So, where did I stand with Jen? Not sure, but I was all in for now. She accepted me. No, it was more than that, and my height didn't come up. Did we reach something meaningful? Not yet, but on the right trajectory. Another difference. Normally, a woman's volatility isn't a good thing. But I liked her version.

CHAPTER NINETEEN

Don't tell me everybody is the same size in bed.

The kid's second to last day of first grade was unseasonably warm. The young students can't wait for summer vacation. They can't sit still. The classroom windows are open, but there is no breeze. Fortunately, there is a water fountain in the back of the classroom.

Today, the children use crayons to draw pictures of the American flag. The teacher, Ms. Lipson, has given this assignment on this day for the last twenty-three years. If they don't already know, the children will learn the number of stars and stripes on the flag. The kid likes this assignment.

Ms. Lipson has one more year to teach before she retires. She's a tall, large woman with gray hair and beady eyes, and wears a loose-fitting, beige, print dress. When she looks you in the eye, she's scary. Most of the children do what she says, even the ones who get in trouble on the playground.

The kid sits in the front row. He is the shortest student in the class. He does well in school and has never been in trouble. Ms. Lipson gives him an extra assignment when he finishes his work early, so he doesn't get fidgety. She also likes to call on him when no one else knows the answer.

The children draw the flag with red, white, and blue crayons. The kid uses these colors too but adds a purple line between each stripe. Because of this, he needs extra time to finish his flag after most of the children are done. The kid hurries to finish. Ms. Lipson approaches his desk and looks at his flag, notices that he outlined the stripes. She looks at him quizzically with her beady eyes and says, "Joseph, you can't do that."

He thinks the lines make the flag look neat. The art teacher likes when the kid draws something differently. The kid doesn't understand why there is a problem. He says, "So what?"

Ms. Lipson grabs him. He kicks his feet in the air as she puts him out in the hall. The kid must stand there ten minutes until gym class. He doesn't know what he did wrong. When he goes home, he tells his mom what happened. "You talked back to her, that's why she put you out in the hall. You have to do what the teacher says." His mom, Ellen, is an artist and finds the story amusing. She likes her son's creative streak but will not say anything to him that will undercut the teacher. "Tomorrow, tell Ms. Lipson you're sorry."

"Yes, Mom. I still don't understand."

Fortunately, tomorrow is the last day of school, and the kid is thinking about day camp. Before he goes to bed, he puts the shorts and polo shirt on his bed that he will wear in a few days on the first day of camp.

I thought about that day while I sat outside the Red Flame Diner on West 44th Street and waited for Bill to arrive. Maybe it's the perils of the unconventional life. I hope he isn't a basket case. It's not unusual anymore to lose a job at a law firm. You have to watch your back wherever you are.

Bill is my tallest friend at six-five. I have never held it against him. He also is probably my smartest friend. Bill played basketball at Williams, which is a Division III college. He taught prep school in Connecticut for two years, went to law school at NYU, and worked for the Securities and Exchange Commission on high-profile fraud cases. He was at the SEC while I was at EPA. He left the SEC for the purportedly lucrative pastures of private practice.

Bill and I had mutual friends in D.C. who met for happy hour at Casa Rosita on the Potomac waterfront. We became good friends. Even double-dated once. His date was the same height as my date, at five-two. Afterward, he said he felt like the group leader on a field trip. I asked him how the height difference affected sex. "How do you do it? You're six-five. She's five-two. Don't tell me everybody is the same size in bed."

He said, "It's really not complicated. The rest of the relationship, that's all falling apart."

When he finally arrived at the diner, he was unusually edgy. Getting trashed last night didn't help. He showed up in a frazzled state, in jeans with a big hole in the knees and a black T-shirt. The former white-shoe lawyer in a Silicon Valley costume. Tall, handsome, a full head of uncombed reddish-blond hair. I tried to be supportive. "Billy, boy, I'm very sorry about the firm bullshit. Did you learn anything else?"

"I reached one of the senior partners. He was sorry about the lack of information. Sorry? What a schmuck. The managing directors could be in deep doo-doo. The shit hit all at once. No more money to pay the big shot laterals. Those guys will want their money. Everybody wants their money. Meanwhile, I have to find a job. I don't know if I want the law firm life. Maybe I'll go in-house."

Breakfast couldn't arrive soon enough. Bill had oatmeal with almonds and walnuts. He told me this was very nutritious. I had the all-American: two eggs over easy, home fries, extra crispy turkey bacon, wheat toast with butter on the side, two packets of orange marmalade, and two strong cups of coffee. I love this diner because they plant American flags in the entrees. You won't get this breakfast in Venice. I wondered if Ms. Lipson ever ate here.

Bill thought I was misguided to break from legal practice. "You work for a great company, they're well managed, the stock rocketed. Why would you hurt your greatest asset, which is yourself. What is wrong with you?"

I said politely, "Everyone's entitled to his opinion."

"You'll figure it out. I have an idea. We'll get on a freight train to nowhere like Sal and Dean. You know …"

"I know. *On the Road*. I don't see you as a modern-day Kerouac. I could be ..."

"I thought about taking a trip to find myself. That lasted five minutes. I have to make real money, Joe. How long will you pretend you're F. Scott on the French Riviera or a well-heeled Sal Paradise with airplane upgrades? How can a woman be serious with you if you don't have a day job?" He has a point. "I guess I'm cautious ... And don't bullshit me." He laughed. He had a hearty, raspy laugh. "I know why you're doing this. You tell women you're a writer, and they gaze at you. Joe, you're not going to bed women as easily as Sal or Dean. And this thing you have about taller women, forget it."

"You do what works for you. You'll run the SEC someday. I'll be there when they swear you in. Think about it this way. If the Mets could beat the Orioles in the 1969 World Series, and Joe Willie and the Jets could beat the Colts in the 1969 Super Bowl, then I can make it in the literary world."

"You should play to your strengths ... Tell me what they are again?" I loved the friendly abuse.

"I will go to you if I need help with a publishing contract."

"Now, you're talking."

I enjoyed Bill's company. You need good friends to keep everything in front of you. In law school, his friends thought he would become a judge after he made a few million practicing law. If I get too close to the edge, Bill will bring me back. For now, I'm OK as a qualified risk-taker.

CHAPTER TWENTY

> **❝**
> *Thinking over the past month, I thanked God for the*
> *women I met and the words I produced.*

Charles Pong was a five-two Chinese American bartender at the Algonquin Hotel's Blue Bar for more than forty years. The last time I saw him, he worked New Year's Eve six years ago. He was ninety-three and impeccably dressed in a powder-blue short double-breasted jacket and a black bowtie. The other bartenders adored this modest, good-natured gentleman with neatly parted gray hair and a sweet smile. Bartending, when done well, is a true and honorable profession, and Charles was a master. I was in New York three years later at the Blue Bar and learned that he died. I cried and said a prayer for him.

After breakfast with Bill and several hours at the New York Public Library, I went to the Blue Bar for old times' sake. I gazed at the painting in the back of the Algonquin lobby called The Algonquin Roundtable, a group of literary snobs in caricature form, including Dorothy Parker and Robert Benchley, who wrote for the New Yorker in the 1920s. The pinnacle of highbrows and pretense.

My plan was to meet Carter at the Algonquin and go to Yankee Stadium to see the Red Sox/Yankees game. Carter has an office nearby at 48th and Sixth Avenue. He got two tickets from a friend who works in the Yankees front office. The question, as always, was who would be with him.

I called Carter, and he didn't answer. He left me a message he was busy and said to meet at the Stadium's Gate 4. The Inner Voice warned me about a Carter surprise. For all I know, he could show up with DD or Anita or ... OMG, even Jen? If Carter does this, I expect free drinks for a long, long time.

I left the Blue Bar, walked down West Forty-Fourth Street toward Fifth Avenue, and stopped at Kellari Taverna, which has a bar with a lively happy hour. I had a Tito's on the rocks with lime and olives. The bartender also gave me a small bowl of Greek olives and slices of stinky salty yellowish cheese with toasted baguette pieces. Absolutely delicious. This is why I love the place.

Next to me, two women faced each other as women often do in a bar. This tells you they are talking to each other and not to you. Otherwise, one of the women could feel left out if the other one starts to talk to a guy. And who knows what might happen after that? True, the reason could be one or both women have a boyfriend or husband, so please do not bother us. When I boldly asked the women what they were drinking, one of them acted like I drove into her rosebush. With much effort, the other one said a Cosmopolitan and a pomegranate martini.

I didn't engage them after that. I sipped the Tito's, ordered grape leaves, and jotted notes for my next chapter. I thought out loud about my book, "If they do this, will they work it out and stay together, or break it off?"

A female voice behind me said, "I think they're going to work it out. I feel good about it." I guess I didn't talk quietly enough. I didn't recognize the voice. It had to be DD or Aunt Anita or Jen. I turned around. It was a woman I didn't know, late twenties with a slight build. She smiled.

"Alright," I said to her, "what should I do next?"

She thought for a moment. "I would say that the guy has been away for six months. They used to go out, they never really broke up, and he runs into her at a bar on West 44th Street. They start talking, they get something to eat, and it's going well. Sex is in the back of their minds, and neither one wants to screw it up. There's a kiss, and wow, then a long drawn-out kiss. They want to get together the next day and plan on a walk. She suggests the High Line, it just opened, and maybe coffee after that. How am I doing?"

"Not bad. Do you mind if I ask? How tall is she?"

She looked at me, confused. "I have no idea, how tall is the guy?"

"I'll buy you a drink and we'll figure it out. The woman should be taller than the guy."

"And smarter."

"Yes, smarter too. That's a given. You sound pretty smart."

"That's what my boyfriend tells me." She pointed to a guy coming toward us from the back of the restaurant. He got closer, and WTF.

He put his hand out. "I'm Jack. Jack Flash. Nice to meet you."

"Carter, you are the biggest D-I-C-K." I turned to his lady friend. "Sorry about the language."

"No, it's fine. I expected something like that."

"Rosemary Tucker, this is Joseph Fine. Joe is a close friend from Leicester. Rosemary does standup comedy."

She looked at Carter. "Do I know you?" Rosemary is very good.

I said, "Hello. Now, Carter, somehow you left work earlier. You douche. We were supposed to meet at the Stadium."

"I understand how you feel. Take a breath. Your problem, Joe, is you are predictable. When you're near the Yale Club, you go to two bars, the Blue Bar and the bar at Kellari. You're a creature of habit. Oh, and King Cole Bar, but that's not around the corner from here, so I figured you were at Kellari ... It's going to be a good game."

"Both teams are prima donnas."

"By the way, I met Rosemary at a fundraising event a couple weeks ago. She looks like a sweet Iowa farm girl, right? Look at these cheeks. Wrong. Joe, she's a nice Jewish girl."

Rosemary jumped in. "My mother converted. She's more religious than my dad."

"OK." I don't know what to believe.

Carter continued. "I took her to see Grandma Ruthie at the nursing home. I had to convince Grandma she was Jewish. At that age, she says what she wants. She said to Rosemary, 'All my grandson does is go out with shiksas. Most of them are nice, but ... You must be very special.' I assured her she was. And Joe, Grandma wanted to know when my friend Joseph is going to settle down."

"Ok, Carter, any more surprises for tonight?"

He reflected. "Well, your favorite aunt or rather my favorite aunt is meeting us. She's a big Yankees fan. She went out with one of the players ten years ago."

"That figures. And that's it?"

"That's it, so act surprised when you see Anita. You know, she's one of your fans." He gave me the signature toothy smile. He has more charm than Robert Redford. Carter knows how to reel women in. And how to reel them back out.

"Joe, let's get a quick drink. I'm buying."

"I've had a couple. You two go ahead." We sat there with our drinks. Rosemary had a wine spritzer which made me think about Cindy in Venice. Carter had an Old Fashioned.

I took him aside on our way out. "Carter, is there a woman named Jen coming too?"

"No, but I heard about Bemelmans Bar, and Auntie thought it was cute."

"Don't bring it up, please."

It was a pleasant Spring evening, early May in New York, a clear night, light breeze, mid-60s and a full moon. I wore an Indians baseball hat that I bought in Cleveland on a work trip. Tonight was my first trip to Yankee Stadium in years. Last time I went with my father on a Rotary Club bus trip. One of the Rotarians, Vince DeGennaro, made veal and pepper sandwiches. They were delicious.

We got off the subway and walked to Gate 4, the gate for seats behind home plate. After waiting a few minutes at the will call window, I noticed Aunt Anita trying on hats. Carter called out to her. She saw us.

Carter poked me. "Joe, I forgot. I have a birthday present for you."

"My birthday is in February." Must be a gag gift.

"Then, I'm a few months late."

I opened it. "This is great. Thank you so much." It was a biography of Wee Willie Keeler, the baseball player for the New York Highlanders. The Highlanders became the Yankees in 1913. Wee Willie was five feet, four and a half, and one of the greatest hitters of all time. Carter knew Wee Willie was one of my heroes. I didn't like the nickname, but his fellow players respected him.

"You're welcome, big fella.'"

"Hi everybody," Aunt Anita announced. She wore a Yankees pinstripe jersey with Derek Jeter's No. 2. "Auntie, this is Rosemary. She's in the corporate development office at NYU. She does stand up too. She's the female Rodney Dangerfield, but she gets much more respect."

Anita said, "Hello, yes, very good. I was in fundraising. Nonprofits are interesting. Some are well run. Some, well, not so much." She turned to me with a big smile. I saw her stained teeth. "Hi, Joe, don't worry, we're not going to talk about it. My lips are zipped up." She touched her lips and grinned. I didn't believe her. She wanted to be my friend. I worried she could derail my social life. She thought she was trying to help.

Carter had four great seats behind home plate in the lower level, twelve rows up. I sat between Anita and Carter, and Rosemary was to the left of Carter. I figured Anita wanted to sit next to me for maximum gossip value.

We had a good old time. On a sliding scale, Rosemary was more impressive than most women I've seen with Carter. She headlined at Dangerfield's and performed there once a week for the last month. Anita wanted to know when I was going back to Venice as if I planned to go. I was noncommittal. She had a twenty-four-person tour group going to Italy in late June.

The Yankees were way ahead after three innings. I started to zone out. Anita saw an opportunity. She whispered to me, "You know I've been friends for a long time with Jen. She's like a younger sister. She's a lot of fun, but she is also fragile and between us girls, can get excitable. She likes you, she really likes you. If that's not where you're headed …" I waited. She didn't finish the sentence.

I was gracious because it was Carter's aunt, and he was next to me. "Anita, I appreciate your interest, but honestly, I don't need an intermediary. Yes, I like her too. Very much. You know the ELO song, *Do Ya?* It's the line, 'But I never seen nothing like you?'" This is how I see Jen. If this gets back to her, fine.

Anita was warming up. "Now, don't you want to ask me about my social life? It's pretty quiet, except for this guy Sergei who lives in Queens, but I think he mostly uses me. OK, I use him too. I have to get beyond a boy toy. A man of substance, and some means, of course."

"Thank you for the update."

Next, Anita wanted to know about DD. I have to avoid this minefield. Anything you say can and will be used against you. "Have you heard from her?"

"Really Anita, we haven't talked much. And anyway, I'm going back to France. I don't expect to see her there." Hopefully, that was vague enough.

"Well, I don't need to tell you again what ... I think." I think she wanted to say "we," to include Jen.

"You're right, you don't." I had to smile.

Carter asked, "What are you two chatting about?"

"We talked about you and agreed Rosemary is a step above." Rosemary stood, then bowed to accept the compliment. She said she gets so much respect, she has to store some of it.

We left the game in the eighth inning with the Yanks way ahead. I had a stomachache from too many kosher hot dogs. We returned to Manhattan and got out at 57th Street and Sixth Avenue. Carter and Rosemary went on their way. Anita and I walked a few blocks to Benoit, a French wine bar on 55th Street near Sixth Avenue down the street from the King Cole. Anita insisted on buying me a nightcap. I said I was done, then gave in and we had two Fireball shots. Not the first drink you think of at a wine bar, but who cares. I thought we were done with DD. Anita said, "Jen and I were talking. We think you have so much potential. DD is in New York and you're going to see her, right? I think it's a mistake."

I bit my lip. "Anita, I appreciate your concern, but please, that's enough. Don't worry." She sure is a busy body, but she might have my back.

Later that night, Jen texted me. The timing was curious. "I'm an emotional basket case. Maybe we can get together when I calm down. Anita's a good friend, but she overprotects me." This sounded like a good cop, bad cop routine. I'm not good at relaxing, myself, but I suggested that she do just that.

Maybe it was the Jen effect, but I slept great and woke up content. Thinking over the past month, I thanked God for the women I met and the words I produced. And I hoped that the magical ride continued on the path to what's meaningful.

CHAPTER TWENTY-ONE

> **ĺĺ**
>
> *Look at it this way. If you're little or small, you're more*
>
> *alive per foot.*

I left DD a message before the game that I was in New York through the weekend. Three sunny days ahead. At least for the weather. DD said she had plans Friday night and was busy this weekend with friends and a family function. She could see me for an hour tomorrow morning. It looked like she didn't want to meet. I called and expected the worst. That way, it won't be as bad. Someone else answered her phone. Funny, this happened before.

"Hello, is this DD's phone?"

"Joe, it's Liza. How are you? DD's in the shower. Can she call you back? Joe, she's on edge. She's pissed, but she misses you."

"Hi, Liza. And how are you? Thanks for the heads up."

"Hey, Joe listen, DD is going to the Strand. Why don't you wait there for her? Go in a half-hour. And tell your buddy Carter to fuck off."

"I'll meet her. And please call Carter and tell him what you want."

"I have. He hangs up on me. The next guy I really like, it's going to be a lot of revenge sex."

"OK, nice to talk with you."

Late afternoon and still a gorgeous day. I waited for DD at the coffee shop next to the Strand. The Strand is the largest used and new bookstore in New York City. It's the ideal place for a curmudgeon to spend hours poring through books. And some of the employees look like they hide in the woodwork at night. Ah, the smell of people, books, and old wooden shelves.

Liza called and said DD was late. Another twenty minutes passed. Two minutes later, I saw her walk by. I called out. She saw me, ran up, and gave me a big hug. I missed her physical comfort food. We crossed the street and sat on a bench. I could tell she spent time getting ready. She had a pretty red and blue striped sweater to go with her smile and bright red lipstick. The sun shined on us for a few more minutes.

"Joe, Liza told me you'd be here. I'm supposed to be surprised. Who cares? You know, since Carter, she's turned into a tramp."

"Don't say that."

We chatted before the predictable shoe drop. "OK, now what's wrong with you? You came to New York and waited to call." She had a motherly way of scolding me. "I am very upset with you, Joseph Fine." This was followed by a motherly hug. "I missed you, you big bullshitter." I couldn't make an excuse that this was an impromptu trip. It was, but I could have called.

She took a breath. "Joe, if it doesn't work out, I'll be OK. We're good together, right?" She said the same thing in Venice. I don't know why women get ahead of themselves in relationships. They want to know how the story ends before it's over.

"DD, I'm glad to see you. Can you go easy on me?"

She was thinking. "Joe, my daddy went to jail for six months. I'm a mess. My mom is a basket case. My sister is conveniently in California. That's how she deals with it."

"I'm sorry, I didn't know." I knew he was sentenced. From what I read, he was lucky to get only six months. I didn't know the jail term started. "DD, I know you're rushed. How about Monday?"

"The truth is, I didn't have weekend plans. You upset me. But I need to see my mother. She's in Brooklyn. Is Sunday good?"

"Good." I told her I was flying back to Southern France Monday night. She wasn't interested. I said I would probably be back in a few months. She didn't like that either. So much for positive reinforcement. She started to cry and said she wanted to come to France. I didn't respond. Sure, DD could take good care of me. She could also smother me.

We got up and stood in a small area of the street blocked from car traffic. How to distract her? "DD, come on, let's dance." I wore cowboy boots, I was ready. Perfect. She had flip-flops. I can't step on her feet. "Ready?"

We heard the song *Wagon Wheel* coming from a nearby bar. I imagined an undiscovered band from West Texas playing the song. I set the song on my phone, raised the volume. "Hey, momma rock me." DD and I danced. A few folks stopped to watch, and others joined us on the asphalt dance floor. Here we were, dancing on a little piece of Gotham.

I'm not a fan of public displays of affection, but I planted a kiss on her painted lips. For some reason, *Fire and Rain* played in my head, and it almost made me cry. I wasn't sure I would see her after tomorrow. We transitioned to a slow dance. It went well until I stepped on her left foot. She shrieked. I apologized. The crowd applauded. I bowed and DD sheepishly waved to the crowd.

We crossed the street back to the Strand. What's the attraction? Going here is a cerebral adventure. I like the feel of a book. It's a comfort thing. For the few books that are a part of me, I have multiple copies. Three copies of *On the Road* - one from an English class at Leicester called The American Hero, one from a used bookstore in Cleveland, and the third from a Florida flea market. I also have three copies of *Catcher in the Rye* and *A Prayer for Owen Meany*. If I lose one copy and loan another, I still have one left. It makes me feel more secure. As for movies, I have multiple copies of *Tin Men*, *Sideways* and *Five Easy Pieces*.

DD went upstairs to the Art section and came back with a book about William Hogarth, the eighteenth-century painter and engraver. Also, a satirist and caricaturist. "Didn't you tell me you liked him?"

"I love his stuff." I opened to the center of the book. It's what I was looking for. There was a group of eight paintings called *A Rake's Progress*, which shows the decline and fall of a rich young man from womanizing, drinking, and throwing money away. All fiction, of course.

"I got it for you. Joe, I have to run. My mom's expecting me. See you tomorrow night." A kiss and she was off. I purchased books by Nelson DeMille and Elmore Leonard, two guys who bring you into their world. From there, I walked and walked, first down to the Battery, where I waved at the Statue of Liberty, and then back up Lower Broadway to stop for a chocolate chip cookie at Dean & Deluca. Then I returned to the ghosts of the Algonquin Roundtable for inspiration and writing.

I wasn't ready for the call I got from Jen that evening. She started with, "What's wrong with you?" Maybe it's me, but this seems to be a common phrase in the female toolbox.

"Hello to you, too."

"Joe, your writing. Who are these women you're writing about? One of them is a spiraling out-of-control sex goddess. The character that sounds like you can't decide who or what he wants. The shorter woman has big boobs, right? Your character loves those things. Her old man ran a gambling ring. Yes, a little bird told me she's trouble."

I must have left the laptop on at the Waldorf. I wondered why she hadn't mentioned this before. Stay calm, it will pass. "Jen, it's fiction, the characters aren't real. The guy is a composite sketch. The women are made up. I'm using fictionalized characters to illustrate my points."

"The hell you are. I think the goddess is me. And her friend, the gossipy pain in the ass, what do you call her, a yenta? That must be Anita." She sounded like a teacher scolding her student.

"Wrong again. I like Carter's aunt. She's eccentric, but that's a good thing. And she's your biggest fan and I dare say, your defender."

"Well, if you tell me the truth, I forgive you." I mostly told the truth. "And when is the last time someone used the words sexual intercourse? What are you, the sixth-grade health teacher?"

"OK, one of the characters is loosely based on you. Very loosely... She doesn't look like you, she's not as smart as you. Not as good in bed, either." Might as well dig a deeper hole. "The guy in the book gets more women than I ever did. Isn't that always the case?"

"See, I know you're full of shit. Just keep us out of the book. Now, can we change the subject? I just read about a new position in Cosmo by a sex therapist. I know, you're probably like her boyfriend who wanted two at once. That is not going to happen, darling."

"Agree, you're plenty." At least she said 'darling.' And she segued to a better topic. I should be fine.

"Damn straight, I'm the best. And I don't give a flying fandango that you're five-three and a half or whatever you are. And yes, we have a meaningful relationship, you wondered about that too. When I see you again, we will proceed in a meaningful way, of course." She paused. Seconds passed. "Now, I'm starting to think it was sweet what you wrote about me, you little dirt bag."

"Jen, I don't like it when you say 'little.'"

"Well, I'm sorry. Little is better than small. Well, not always. Belittle is not a nice word."

"And small has a meaning that goes beyond size, like 'He made me feel small' or 'He's small-minded.' Hey, why isn't it demeaning to say, 'He made me feel big?' or 'he's big-minded?'"

"I've known enough big oafs. Big boring dopes. They think all they need to do is show up. Mr. Fine, if you're tracking the rise and fall of companies, somebody should look at the oafs, the CEOs who got there by being there." Almost sounds like Tammy.

"Yes, but don't lump them all together."

"You're too fair. Look at it this way. If you're little or small, you're more alive per foot."

"I like that. Why isn't that part of the definition? You're logical and crazy. How can that be?"

"I'm multi-talented? Hey, you're sure you can't find a quiet place in all of these United States to write your opus?"

"I'm sure."

"Joe, I only called because I care."

"I know."

I was overwhelmed, which made me sad. Well, if I'm going to be sad, there better be a good reason. Otherwise, get out of my head. I chased the sadness away.

Jen called back minutes later. I held my breath and picked up. She spoke quietly. "Hi, I'm so sorry."

"No, I'm sorry."

"I'm more sorry."

"Ok." We talked for an hour. She tried again to get me to stay in the US. I didn't budge. I planned another two months in France, my apartment in Hoboken was sublet, and she was welcome to visit.

I told Jen my imaginary Cosmo story. "On the cover was a frizzy-haired psychologist who said an increasing number of taller women were dating shorter guys. These women felt liberated from outdated dating norms. They no longer dismissed a shorter guy out of hand. And there were more affluent short guys now. With technological advances, a crop of new CEOs at successful startups didn't have the traditional presence or height of a taller executive. Short guys in button-down shirts or dark T-shirts were making their mark, and bit by bit, women took notice."

"That may be, but I took notice all by myself. I'm not part of a trend or any of that nonsense."

"Good for you."

After that, I took a long walk. It got me thinking. Something I blocked out but had to wonder about ... at some point. Jen's age. A few years difference is one thing. Eight years with the bio-time ticking is another.

CHAPTER TWENTY-TWO

''

To be fair, she took me for what I am.

I stopped to see my mom and younger brother Ronnie at his apartment on West 96th Street. My mom came in from Montclair. My parents divorced about six years ago, and my dad lives in Newport Beach, California. Since you might wonder, mom's about my height. Dad's close to five-seven. Ronnie is five-eight. His wife Marcy is barely five feet. Their one-year-old Nelson is average height and weight, and adorable, of course.

Ronnie works at Goldman Sachs in currency trading. Marcy teaches first grade and runs the house. She tells him what to buy, where to go out, what movies to see, and where to vacation. When she states an opinion, it's in the plural form, as in 'we like this' or 'we like that.' Ronnie seems very happy. I could never be married to someone like that. I want someone who takes care of me but lets me think for myself. Lets me say what I like.

This morning Marcy made mushroom quiche, crispy potato squares, and French press coffee. She is a terrific cook. It's starting to show on both of them.

Marcy set me up with her friend Fran last year. She was a short, intelligent, moderately attractive woman. Marcy claimed she had down-to-earth qualities. We got along well, and after a couple of dates, Fran and I went to Cape Cod for a long weekend. On Saturday morning, she said she felt guilty for leaving her boyfriend three weeks ago. She mentioned it again that afternoon. I felt stupid for going to Cape Cod. It was a long, awkward ride back to New York. Fran later told Marcy I should call. I told her, nicely of course, that she must have meant a different Joseph.

When I returned after brunch to the Algonquin, I attacked a mild writer's block and outlined the next steps. Then a late lunch of chicken and rice from a Halal Guys cart on Sixth Avenue, and a walk on the High Line to prepare for DD. There were happy children everywhere and babies in strollers with truck-sized wheels. A guy with a shaved head was on a business call. He was loud and upset, and anyone near him knew it. Something about an asshole in Zurich who is holding up a shipment. I thought, can't you save it for Monday? A skateboarder headed toward me and veered away just in time. He's an asshole, too.

Other than that, it was a great day to be out and about. Was I destined to go with DD into the sunset? She was ready to take care of me and squash me if I didn't toe her line. I thought about backing out of dinner. That would end it for good. I told myself to treat dinner like a timeshare sales presentation. Enjoy the meal, and when the pressure keeps building, always remember there is no obligation.

I sat on a bench on the High Line at 22nd Street surrounded by lush vegetation and called Carter. He wasn't happy. "Fucking women. I spent two hundred dollars on Rosemary, and then she said I'm so much fun, but she needs time. It slowly came out that she met a guy. He's your height, Joe. I wondered if it was you. Well, that wouldn't make sense."

"It's not me. I wouldn't do something like that. I thought you two were good together."

"Imagine, the little douchebag."

"Well, maybe we're seeing women go for shorter guys."

"No, we're not. The dickweed is loaded. I googled him. He has lingerie retail stores. Good perks if you're a crossdresser. I liked Rosemary. She's hot, she's smart, she's from Iowa, her name is

Rosemary, and … we started to be something. What is going on here?"

Sounded at first like he was talking about Harry, but it couldn't be. He makes the stuff. No way he would do something like this. "I don't know, Carter. I can't predict women's behavior."

"Well, Joe, you suggested the Tom Ford cologne. At first, she couldn't keep her hands off me. She'll come back, and I'll say, 'Let me think about it for a few months.' And then I'll say, 'Come on, let's get a drink.' Hey Joe, do you have time for a drink?"

"I'm on the High Line around 22nd Street. Let's go. I have plans later … with DD."

"Joe, far be it for me to say, but you can do better."

"In the meantime, I'm meeting her. Look, DD is like Oreos and milk, basil and tomato. She's like coming home."

"Coming home to a mess."

"I was about to get to the hurricane part."

"Home for her old man is the big house. You can do better. Let's go to Chumley's. Do you have your to-do list for the date?"

"Yes. I'm stuck on the flowers."

"See you then."

Chumley's has been a fixture in the Village for a long time. The bar top is oak-colored wood with carved names, initials, and hearts. The tables are also carved up. Minus the modern plumbing and liquid soap, this bar could be an eighteenth-century London pub. Carter was still miffed, so I bought him a drink. We ordered Dewar's on ice with lemon twists. The twists were a half-foot long and expertly carved by the bartender, who was gorgeous except for snake tattoos up and down both arms.

"Joe, we should go into business together. A high-end matchmaking service. You and I pick the best ones."

"You get enough women. You just can't hold on to them. You think someone better is always around the corner."

"Hey, I helped you meet most of the quality women you've known. And who gave you the bench concept? Don't blame me if DD draws you in."

"I won't. You and I might have to return to Venice and start all over."

"That's what I like about you. Think ahead, with no steps in between. You're an enigma, but I love you."

I didn't bother to argue. The bartender approached us. Her tight black sleeveless top was a tipping machine. I could outline her nipples with pastel crayons, if permitted, of course. She looked at me and said, "I love your shirt. Where'd you get it?"

It was the short-sleeved twill shirt with the mermaid prints. "I think it was a flea market in Florida."

"Well, it is very cool. I'm Tiffany."

"I'm Joe, and this is my friend Carter."

She looked at Carter. "I think I've seen you before."

"Makes sense."

"The woman you were with last week, if you don't mind me saying, she was tough on you. She should have a spat somewhere else."

"Totally agree."

"Well, let me know if you need anything else. And you," she looked at me, "don't let that shirt go to your head."

"Yes ma'am."

Carter said, "She's nervy. I like that. And while we're all being critical, Joe, you need to improve your vocabulary. All you say is douchebag, dickweed and fucknuts."

"I can't argue with that. Thanks for the prep session." We had one more, and it was time to split.

So, what has fate delivered? Cindy and Leslie. I was still attracted to them. Not sure what they thought of me. I don't know them very well. But I need to keep them in the game. They're attractive, taller, intelligent, and at least Cindy is grounded, if not slightly on the dull side. Leslie could have a reliability issue. Jen and Marie are lively, fun, and hot in their own way. We have a mutual attraction. Each one provides good entertainment value and prowess in the bedroom. Are they realistic for the long term? Marie probably isn't. Jen? Not there yet.

While DD is the shortest at five-one, most women that height also seek out taller guys. To be fair, she took me for what I am. They all did. So, I appreciate each one. None have raised concerns about how short the kids would be. Of course, I don't know if any of them have thought about it. I know a lot of women are hard-wired that way.

I went to Macy's and bought a red and white striped button-down shirt. Combined with my stone-washed jeans and round-toed dark brown cowboy boots from a vintage store in Salida, Colorado, I should be ready for prime time. What if DD wants to visit France? I'm not sure. I need to concentrate on my work. A lot of writers have brought significant others with them. Don't I have to be a writer before someone comes along?

For dinner, DD chose Balthazar, the buzzy Parisian bistro on Spring Street in Soho. It's on a cool, quirky street with restaurants, boutiques, and street vendors with fruit, flowers, books, jewelry, New York City photographs, paintings, and even movie screenplays. I stopped and bought a dozen red roses. Within a block of the restaurant, four Black gentlemen in tuxedos stood on apartment steps and sang Motown songs. They did *Buttercup*, which was an apt description of my dinner guest's upper body.

Balthazar could be bad luck. Not because Leslie worked here at one time. Three years ago, the wall-length mirror behind the bar came unhinged at the top and started to fall. An alert French diplomat kept the mirror from crashing on the bar and hurting anyone. The mirror was reinstalled, but it made me nervous. The sides opposite the bar, as well as the back wall, were also covered by smoky mirrors.

It was very crowded inside. The bar was full, and patrons formed a row behind it. Next to the bar against the front window was a group of round café tables, each barely big enough to hold two plates. People waiting to be seated hovered over folks at these tables. I lucked out and got a seat at the bar just as a hipster in tight indigo jeans and black T-shirt and his lady friend in a tight black cocktail dress, four-inch stilettos, and long curly black hair, got up. A heavy-set strawberry blonde woman quickly sat next to me before I could save the seat. I smiled politely.

DD walked in and looked around. God, she looked good. I imagined a band leader's voice, "Ladies and gentlemen, Mr. and Mrs. Joseph Fine," as the crowd stood and applauded. I called out to her. I didn't walk over to her lest an opportunist takes my seat. I cupped my hands over my mouth and raised my voice. She turned and saw me.

She had red khaki pants and a white silk blouse with red trim faux pockets covering her gorgeous chest. Red Swedish clogs. Complemented by sparkling teeth and bright red lipstick. Spring has sprung. She walked over and we kissed. I handed her the roses, which got me another kiss. I offered her my bar stool and she whispered, "Joe, I love you and I'm mad at you." At least the love part came first. With DD, I expect something good to be followed by a big but.

"DD, you look great. Love the outfit. Red is my favorite color. Now, it's a beautiful day, don't be mad, or at least, can you wait? What should we drink?" I pointed to the bartender, ordered an Aperol Spritz for DD and Tito's with lime and extra olives for me. I looked into her big brown eyes and saw the sky open up. Outside, a thunderstorm was brewing.

DD started to cry. It's too early for this, although she is cute when she cries. "Joe, I'm sorry. My mom is a wreck with my dad away. I don't know what he did or didn't do, but it's not fair to her.

I won't see him for months." I had no choice. I leaned over and put my arm around her.

"Hopefully, it will be OK at some point." I was out of my element. She calmed down. She blew her nose, which could be heard at the opposite end of the restaurant. DD finished her spritz and ordered another. She seemed better after that.

The host called us. We were seated in a row of rectangular tables for two, with no more than a foot between each table. Compared to the café tables near the bar, this area was roomy. We were at least thirty feet from the mirror behind the bar, so I felt secure. I ordered another Tito's and DD got a third spritz. I asked her if she was going too fast. She said she was not driving and ever since Venice, drinking a spritz put her in a good mood. "Just saying the word is fun, don't you think?"

We enjoyed a delicious meal. DD had steak frites with a little green salad, and I opted for sautéed trout with capers and lentils. Soft crusty baguettes. Her shoestring fries were almost as good as McDonald's. We had water with no ice. It's a French bistro, after all. And another spritz and Tito's.

So far, so good, no talk about my plans. I know she wanted to stay near her mom. At some point, I thought the conversation could go south.

"Joe, dear, you know what I don't understand?" I was nervous. "I don't get it, you're doing well, you're a young guy. I googled you up and down, you're a talented attorney, why leave it so early? Don't you do work that's useful? A lot of lawyers make people miserable. They call them bottom feeders, right? Can't you do both?"

"You mean be a bottom feeder and a good lawyer?"

"No, please focus. Work during the day, write your book at night. And you have to go to France? Don't you like it here? It's way better in the USA."

"Thanks for the support, but I'm going. I can't multitask."

"You can do your lawyer stuff, you make good bucks, you buy a house with a picket fence. Actually, I want an open yard. And you will live happily ever after ... with me." A big smile. She is trying to reel me in. But Joseph Fine is not easy bait.

"Look, DD, I need to prove something. I can always go back to practicing law if I'm not AWOL for more than a few years. I'll know, say, in less than a year if the writer's life is worth continuing. Meanwhile, I have a cushion, a financial cushion."

"I think you're escaping. You go away to write; you think that will make a difference. You know what?" Damn it, she started to cry. "I don't know if I can go out with you if you go back." This is too complicated. She's thirty-two. Not fair to make her wait? "By the way, what are you writing about?"

If I tell her I am writing a book on relationships, she might throw something at me. "I don't like to give much detail. It's bad luck. I started writing a thriller about an FBI agent who goes after companies for dumping bad chemicals. I couldn't make it interesting. So, I went with a new perspective on the age-old subject of men and women. I don't know how it ends yet."

"Joseph Fine, now I know you're full of it." She laughed. What a relief. But her throaty laugh made me uncomfortable. "Are you looking for sympathy?"

"No, I am not looking for sympathy. Look, I'm going back to France and you can visit. I'll pay for you. You have to let me work during the day. Come out in a month or so." The tears returned. I looked to see if anyone was watching. She's not the first person to cry in a restaurant. "DD, I'm making the best decision I can at this point in time. The best imperfect decision. That's all I can do."

"I don't know if I can leave just like that. My mom needs me, and my sister isn't helpful." I looked down. My phone was vibrating. Text message from Cindy Green. The couple next to us left. I moved next to DD.

"It's OK. I'll call you. We'll talk." I don't think she believed me. I don't want her to walk out on me. But it could be a couple of months or more before I see her. I excused myself and went down the narrow worn-down wood stairway to the bathroom.

I opened the message from Cindy. I should have been in touch. She wanted to know if I was still in Europe. She has a meeting in a week and a half in Lugano, Switzerland. She knows it's far from Nice, but it's a lovely city and asked if I could meet. I couldn't tell if this was a romantic overture. No emotion, except at the end when she said, "Thinking of you," with one "O" and one "X." Pretty good. I quickly wrote back that I was in New York and returning to southern France tomorrow night, so it was possible. Maybe there's a way to fly from Nice to Lugano.

I was excited and ran up the steps two at a time. I fell forward on the last step, barely grabbing onto the railing. My phone fell and landed three steps down. I scratched my right arm. I also had a scratch with a line of blood on my right cheek. I reached for the phone. It hurt to get up. I stopped at the bar and grabbed some cocktail napkins to wipe off the blood. This is what I get for reading Cindy's message. I cannot multitask. I headed slowly to the table.

"You OK?" I couldn't hide the discomfort.

"I'm OK, just slipped."

"Let me see. Your face has a bad scratch. You didn't hit your head?"

"A little bit, but my brain is intact." My right knee buckled, and I fell again.

I slowly got up. The server asked if I needed help. "I'm fine, thank you. That's very kind of you." I turned to DD. "Let's celebrate. Dessert?"

"Look, you better take it easy. Are you going to be alright on a plane?"

"Of course."

"Well, I'm not convinced. And we're celebrating?"

"I met you a month ago. Liza was excited about introducing you to me."

"Joe, maybe you are a romantic."

"Maybe." I felt like saying 'Don't push it.' You can't win in these situations.

"We'll sit longer, so you can relax."

"I'm telling you. I'm fine."

"We'll see." She didn't believe me.

It's funny, I fell twice in Venice. Is somebody trying to tell me something? No, if I pay attention, this should not happen.

I felt stifled with DD. I wanted to excuse myself, come back and start fresh. It was difficult to talk. As the night progressed, the less I thought we would spend it together. I called the server and asked for two glasses of champagne. "The house brand," I whispered.

"What did you say to Horace?"

"I told him it was a great evening."

"You're full of shit, but I love you."

I couldn't do it. I couldn't say "I love you too." She looked at me, then looked away and thought for a moment.

"Let's go to my place. I want to show you my artwork."

"You're an artist too?"

"No."

DD's studio apartment was at 75th and Broadway. Small but neat and clean. White stucco walls, dark wood trim around the ceiling. The queen-sized bed took up a quarter of the main room. Next to her laptop were two family pictures, including one with her father. Harold Schonstein. The photograph showed him with a shit-eating grin. I cringed.

We started to kiss, and we kept going. She gently but firmly pushed me away. It was a sad moment. She knew I couldn't reciprocate her feelings. I said something flimsy like "It's late, and you have to work tomorrow." I blew a kiss, held her for a moment, and then uttered a weak "goodbye." She sat there and stared ahead. I hurried out the door.

Waiting for the elevator, I heard her scream, "You know where I stand." I was exhausted by the time I stumbled into the Algonquin. I wish Charles Pong were there to talk about it.

Chapter Twenty-Three

... the next step was to join a morning coffee group.

I left New York late afternoon Monday for Nice. A beautiful day to be up in the air. We soared through blue skies and layer after layer of thick, puffy, white clouds. I imagined a magic carpet and genie surfing the top layer. The flight itself was uneventful. I needed to catch my breath after my adventures in the Big Apple. I was excited to continue the writing life.

I arrived in Nice late morning Tuesday and taxied to Antibes, ten miles away. It's a lovely, bustling town on the Cote d'Azur, with natural beauty all around the coast. I rented a large room en suite for two months in a nineteenth-century two-story townhouse in Vieil Antibes, the old section of Antibes. The owners had great reviews and made the choice easy. The townhouse had a nondescript pinkish beige façade with a simple wooden door and two outside windows covered with metal grates. It stood in the middle of a quiet, tree-lined, one-way street of mostly attached beige and gold townhouses.

The room itself had a large bed, an old writing desk, and a 1950s Air France travel poster of Nice's Promenade des Anglais and Hotel Negresco. There was a small kitchenette in one corner of the room, and a separate entrance along a five-foot alley that extended the length of the house. There was also a large patio connected to the main kitchen in the back of the townhouse, followed by a small yard and garden. I was free to use the kitchen if I kept it clean. The patio had a textured glass table and four purple tulip chairs. My favorite kind of chair. It looked like a great place to sit and write.

The townhouse's location near the train station and the Mediterranean was ideal. It was less than a ten-minute walk to the station and five minutes to the sea. Cours Masséna is the main commercial street in Vieil Antibes, and a stone's throw from the sea. The Marché Provençal, the fruit and vegetable market, occupies the large median area on Cours Masséna. I loved to weave my way through the morning market crowds and walk the narrow, inviting streets of the old town.

The owners of the townhouse, Bernard and Lisette Manteaux, were a gracious, reserved couple. I worked out the details with Lisette, a modest, slight woman in her late forties, who liked to wear cotton print dresses. She was British and grew up in Cornwall with a French father and an English mother. Bernard was a Frenchman from Lyon. She met him on holiday in Antibes thirteen years ago. They bought the house after they got married.

Lisette was quiet to the point where I thought she was bothered by something. My relationship with her was cordial but distant. Bernard was a distinguished-looking gray-haired chap who seemed overly formal. After I met him, I barely talked to him. He was away most of the time, and Lisette seemed to take little interest in what he did. I occasionally chatted with her, and she perked up.

The first thing I did after I dropped off my bags was walk to La Crêperie, considered the best crêpe shop in town. I watched closely as the crêpe maker spread the batter over a twelve-inch round, flat grill, added bananas, strawberries, and Nutella, and then turned the crêpe over and folded it into a delicious treat. It was as much fun to watch him make it as it was to eat it. I texted Cindy that Lugano sounded good. I said I needed to establish a solid work routine before going, but in two weeks I thought I could make the trip. We had a good time in Venice, but most travelers are upbeat just by being there. So, I might have gained a false sense of reality. It's going on a month since I met her. I didn't know what to expect.

A few days later, on Sunday, she sent a cute text. It looked like she gave it a lot of thought. "Writers have their own quirks, and I am sensitive about distracting your creative mind. I suspect you were out with a smart, pretty woman, just not as smart and pretty as I. I think you butt-dialed me. It sounded like you were in a loud restaurant. You were chatting with someone. Not a problem. I hope you're fully healed from your slip in Venice. X and O, Cindy." She must have meant Balthazar. I need better phone discipline.

Yes, it has been a while, but I can't act surprised to see her. Will she be blonde, dirty blonde, or strawberry blonde? I recalled a physically fit and potentially hot soccer mom, Junior League style. She was smart and self-confident, but as I had observed, a bit stilted. The X factor? One of her front teeth encroached on the other, leaving an imperfection that made her seem vulnerable but more appealing.

Which brings me to Marie. It's hard to think straight because the first image I have is a practically painted on string bikini and tan lines. She could play a movie superhero with her great body, dark brown bob, and blazing pink lipstick. Add a cape, and she would be indestructible. Still, I had mixed feelings about contacting her. What attracted her to me? Yes, the question reflected a lack of self-confidence that is ridiculous. Somehow, I viewed her as unreachable. The Inner Voice barged in and almost railed, "Get over it!" Another round with Marie and this could be a meaningful relationship. I sat back, reflected. I am doing what I set out to do. I am breaking the height barrier in baby steps, one woman at a time.

With surging confidence, I called Marie on Tuesday. She acted surprised. She was at a trade show at McCormack Place Convention Center in Chicago and had gone to the basement bar at the Drake Hotel the night before to hear a sultry female singer and a pianist play and sing jazz. I decided not to bring up the 150 Euros.

"Joe, you'll like this, I have to be quick. There was an older guy in a dark suit at the Drake. I shouldn't have let him buy me a drink. He had expectations, like most guys. I hated his furry mustache and got chills thinking about him rubbing it against my face. He got too close, and I threw a glass of pinot noir at him. He stormed out. I thought about you. You wouldn't do that. You would approach the situation with grace and humor."

"I agree. I would ... I have to say ... honestly. I miss you."

"You too, got to run ... Oh, a check is in the mail."

"Thanks, you didn't have to." Yes, she did.

Marie called back the next day. I took a deep breath, held it in, and blew out. Her group was preparing a new product launch for the following Thursday in Nice. She had to work day and night but was free on Saturday and Sunday. I told her Sunday should work.

Back to the writing, which was the primary reason I came back to France. It was critical to have a routine and stick to it. I'll call the first week in Venice and St. Paul a warm-up, and I actually had a good start there and New York. For the routine, I needed a neighborhood coffee shop to stir the morning creative juices. I discovered Bacchus, a bar café with outside tables that were shaded by a weeping willow tree on the other side of Cours Masséna, about fifty yards from Marché Provençal. There was no sign with the bar's name, only a small blackboard with coffee and wine suggestions. The board was next to an open wood door that led inside to a bar and more seating.

My day typically started with a walk along the seafront, then a stop at Bacchus. It was a great place to sit and write random thoughts before the real work began. Each morning, I had a double espresso with two ounces of hot milk and a baguette with marmalade or strawberry preserves. Once a week, I bought a chocolate croissant and dipped it in the double espresso. I became friendly with the owner, Charlotte, who said I dipped too long. "One quick in and out is all it takes." Without asking if this was a sexual innuendo, I got better at it. Charlotte was a free spirit who sat with customers when she wasn't serving.

I made sure I left Bacchus early enough to stay on schedule. I went back to the townhouse or found a quiet spot to work by mid-morning. The routine worked. I simply had to treat it like a real job with a real deadline. I worked until twelve-thirty, had a snack, and worked for at least another two and a half hours. Then it was time for a walk or a quick train ride to the beach in Juan-les-Pins. On some late afternoons, I went to Café Clemenceau in Vieil Antibes to get a shot of whiskey and watch children play in Place Nationale.

After I found a café I liked, the next step was to join a morning coffee group. I noticed three guys who sat at the same outside table at Bacchus most mornings. One was a fifty-ish Englishman named Jack. He had a deep tan and dyed his hair blond. He loved to make suggestive comments about women who walked by and puffed about his womanizing.

I heard Jack say two words that I learned were not complimentary to women: slag and minger. At least minger could also apply to guys. I sat nearby scribbling. He looked at me and was intrigued, like I was a zoo animal. "What are you doing, mate? You look like you're writing your life story."

"No, I'm writing your life story. See, it only took two pages."

He laughed a raspy, smoker's laugh and said, "I'm looking for someone to write my biography. I'm Jack. I come here for two or three months a year." He had a booming laugh. We shook hands, and he almost crushed mine. He took a small flask and poured a drop into his coffee.

One of Jack's café buddies was a forty-something guy named Bruce. He had a grayish toupee that you could see from the Mediterranean. He said, "Don't write about him. He's nuts. All he does is yak about women. No, I'm a much better subject."

"I'm Joseph. Thanks, but I am already working on something."

"What's it about?"

"Loosely speaking, men and women ... Relationships." Jack exploded with laughter like this had to be a joke.

He said to his friends, "This guy is writing a book. He's a tight-ass like you two," he said to Bruce and the third guy, who was Dennis. Jack laughed after just about everything he said while the others waited until he stopped.

Bruce asked me to sit with them, which I appreciated. My chair hit the table, knocked over my coffee, and spilled it across the table. Some of it spilled on my pants. Fortunately, only the bottom of my notebook was soaked. "I'm very sorry. Pardon, pardon." All three guys thoroughly enjoyed my misfortune. I became an immediate group member. I went to the bar inside and asked for towels. Charlotte said, "Five euros." Then she laughed deviously and said, "Non, non, it's OK." She was a ballsy lady, but good fun. The four of us stood while an employee, a cute young woman in an apron, cleaned the table. She asked who made the mess. The three of them shook their head in unison, then pointed at me. Anyway, my morning coffee group was in place, and it was occasionally informative.

This was not informative. According to Jack, women could be divided into two categories, tight-asses, and bangers. I said this was unfair and simplistic, given the variety of women's personalities. Jack was adamant. Bruce and Dennis were glad to see someone challenge him. They normally got nowhere. I talked in terms of shades of gray and nuances. Jack wasn't persuaded and wondered why I would use a French word like "nuance."

He claimed four or five girlfriends at a time and liked the drama that ensued when one woman learned about another. Bruce took me aside and told me one of the women threw his clothes in the trash when this happened to her. Jack claimed he was the victim. This time, Bruce and Dennis weren't persuaded.

Bruce has been coming to Antibes in May for a month for the last three years. He's on vacation for three more weeks. He has a big boat he docks in Fort Lauderdale and takes groups of up to ten people on charter trips to the Caribbean in the winter. His wife, Terry, is the chef. She is in Paris teaching a two-week cooking class. He loves to talk about her cooking. He is also happy she is in Paris.

Dennis is our resident Frenchman from Marseilles, who owns hair salons in Nice, Cannes, and Antibes. He met the other two last May. Dennis has brown hair that he pulls back into a man bun. I had a creepy old babysitter with a bun. Since then, I have never liked buns, whether they are on a woman or a man. Of course, I didn't say anything. This was how he expressed himself. Dennis is eagerly anticipating signed divorce papers any day. "C'est impossible," he said, when I asked how to stay married on the Cote d'Azur. So many smart and lovely women in Provence and the Riviera. He nodded but wasn't smug about it. As a salon owner, it's even worse.

So, I had coffee each morning with these three. We met at eight o'clock. I started my morning walk early enough to make it to Bacchus for showtime and keep to that all-important routine.

I made the mistake of telling the guys about the party in Cagnes and Marie. Jack asked if Marie had a single friend or even a distressed married friend. I said I wasn't sure. Bruce was sadly counting down the days until he meets Terry in Paris. He moaned that all he wanted was a woman to give him attention. He would consider sex, but only if it made sense, which I interpreted as if he could get away with it. Meanwhile, Terry kept a great household, and Bruce wasn't going anywhere. "I'm a big baby," he said. "Somebody has to take care of me." I think he loved her and didn't want to admit it.

Dennis thought Bruce was all talk. He said, "If you're not happy, go find someone else." With all the drama, it was great fun hanging out with these guys.

Toward the end of my first week in Antibes, I got up at sunrise to walk around Cap d'Antibes, a scenic peninsula that extends south from Vieil Antibes. I took a small notebook to capture thoughts and ideas. Within minutes, the sky went from bright to dark. I stopped to find cover under an arch in the old city wall that led to the small downtown beach. The wind roared and the rain poured. I looked down the rocky coast and watched the pounding surf. The rain promptly stopped minutes later. The sun came out with a vengeance. Bright, hot sunlight. I found a bench and sat down. The peninsula walk would have to wait.

A short, stocky lady in her seventies with straight black hair, dark-rimmed round glasses, and a youthful spark approached. She wore jeans and a blue V-neck polo shirt and carried a large umbrella. "Un belle jour, maintenant," she said.

"Oui, oui. Now." We laughed. She had a space between her grayish front teeth.

"Anglais?"

"Non, Americain." I reached the limit of my French.

"Ah good, the best." She winked at me.

I can't wink, so I smiled. "Please sit," I said, and used the end of my yellow polo shirt to wipe off the bench.

"My husband, he was fifteen years older, he died, he was in Resistance. Very good. I say bless America."

"Yes. I agree." I turned my head away and waited a few seconds. This kind of story gets to me. I fought to keep tears back. "My grandfather. He was in Normandy, at D-Day, 149th Engineering Division. I don't know how they did it."

"Bon, bon, bon." She smiled. I was ready to adopt a grandmother.

"You're so young. You have girlfriend?"

I laughed. "I'm not sure. Maybe one or two. Maybe none."

She thought a second. "No, you have many. You know when it is right."

"I hope you're right."

"Oui, les premières femmes. The first ones, just for practice." She was so understanding. I didn't deserve this much rope. "I have three grandchildren." She opened her purse and took out a photograph of three adorable little girls. They each wore a blue and white striped sailor dress.

"Très bien. Belle jeune filles." I think I said it right.

"C'est curieux," she said. "Why some women, they don't want children. Incomprehensible."

"Yes, I agree. I want children. At least three." She nodded her approval.

She put her hands together. "Please come to my house." She took a piece of paper out of her purse and wrote Marguerite Chanson, her address and phone number. She handed it to me and pointed down the coast toward Juan-les-Pins. "I live over there."

"Merci, I will come."

"My daughter will visit soon. These are her children. I know other ladies you can meet. So, I will go. Au revoir."

"Au revoir." Sweet people like this make the world better. I didn't make it very far around Cap d'Antibes that morning, or even south to Plage de la Garoupe, but I felt great as I walked to Bacchus for morning coffee with time to spare.

CHAPTER TWENTY-FOUR

"
What am I going to do with you?

I got enough done to green-light a weekend trip to Lugano, the end of my second week in Antibes. In the past few days, I changed my morning writing venue from the townhouse patio to the back of the bar at Le Vieil Antibes on Rue Thuret. Mix it up and keep it going. To celebrate steady progress, I stopped at the Absinthe Bar on Rue Sade, donned hats with the other customers, and sipped the once prohibited drink while others sang Provençal ballads. The basement bar prides itself on its collection of diverse hats that customers are welcome to try.

Cindy called and I said I would call back. The timing wasn't great after two absinthe shots. I got lost on the way back to the townhouse although it was only blocks away. It was getting dark, which also didn't help. Fortunately, the third person I asked directed me, by telling me to turn around and look at the street sign. I finally got back and called.

After the pleasantries, Cindy sounded businesslike and distant. Not like the fun, upbeat woman I met in Venice. I thought she would be excited to hear I was coming. She was focused on logistics. She's concerned that I didn't have a plane ticket or hotel room yet. That didn't faze me. There's always a seat, there's always a room. She asked me my shoe size, which I thought was odd until I understood she planned on buying me hiking boots to descend a mountain. This sounded like overkill, but maybe she was in the Girl Scouts and prepared for everything.

Now the part that required attention. Cindy asked, "What are your expectations for the trip?"

I said in clear and vanilla English, "I'm looking forward to the trip and seeing you. Lugano looks like a beautiful city. And whatever happens, happens." That was non-threatening enough.

"OK, yeah, you're right. That's how I feel too." Funny, usually I'm the one who acts skittish. I don't know if she was relieved or unsure.

"How's this, Cindy? You liked me enough to invite me. So, something's there?"

"Yes, we'll have fun." Vague, but OK for now. I think she felt less pressure.

We spoke again the next day. I have been coherent so far. Just need to avoid the soppy stuff. "Are you up for an Aperol Spritz?" I was looking to disarm her.

"Sure. That was fun, wasn't it?" I still didn't feel warm and fuzzy.

I thought this before - why some women need to know what will happen before it happens. I like spontaneity. Let the adventure begin. Let the story unfold. I don't want to know if it will go well or exceed expectations. OK, there are times when I would have canceled a date if I only knew ... But here, how about a pleasant surprise? Thankfully, the question-and-answer part was done, and Cindy did not set any ground rules. I survived the call and went out for coffee to reduce the absinthe effect.

I flew to Lugano early Friday morning on one of the new discount airlines. It was a short one-hour flight, way better than eight hours by train. I taxied to Hotel San Carlo, on Via Nassa, the main commercial street in the city, and a five-minute walk to Lake Lugano. Cindy is staying at a business hotel down the street. She was at her conference until mid-afternoon, so I had time to wander.

I took a delightful walk along Lake Lugano to the main city pier. It was a great day to explore. The sweeping lakefront forms an arc and gives the city an airy, wide-open feel. A lovely city park with trails and a string of beautiful gardens named Parco Civico covers much of the Lugano waterfront. The City Hall sits in the middle of the park. Lake Lugano goes for miles and merges with Lake Como in Italy. Surrounding the lakes are majestic mountain ranges.

I needed to buy flowers. There was a beautiful multi-color rose garden in front of City Hall. When I thought no one was around, I removed three roses. I should have walked back to Via Nassa to a market. An elderly lady walked by and scolded me. I said I was sorry, I needed them for my lady friend. She wasn't satisfied and yelled "Polizia!" I said I was sorry again, and she stormed off.

It was a cool, crisp, bright mid-May afternoon. Perfect for the hike Cindy had in mind. It's so calm and peaceful. I sat at the pier for a half hour and daydreamed. Nearby, two men played chess on a cement game board about eight square feet with two-foot-high chess pieces. Six other men stood around the board and watched. I walked up and watched too.

Cindy caught me off guard. At first glance, I didn't recognize her. She added blonde highlights and cut her hair shoulder length. I liked the lighter hair color. It gave her a younger vibe. Hair color is great, as long as it looks natural. I know I'm not consistent because I liked Leslie despite her otherworldly red hair. Let's just say it worked for her.

Everything else about Cindy looked good and right. White stretch jeans, blue silky top, and a jean jacket. Blue and white flats. Made me think of vanilla ice cream and blueberries. I couldn't compete in my indigo jeans and heavily starched red and white striped button-down shirt. And Swedish clogs. She must have changed after the conference. The coup de grace was her tortoiseshell horn-rimmed sunglasses. I didn't remember them in Venice. They were just like the ones I wore except hers were tinted and had more yellow specks in the tortoiseshell frame. Was this a veiled compliment?

"Hi, Joseph, I'm sorry I just got here, two of the speakers couldn't stop talking." She took off the sunglasses. Deep blue, inquisitive eyes.

"For you." I gave her the tainted roses.

"Thank you, and how's my writer?" A more girly girl would have said, "Oh, that's so sweet." Cindy was upbeat and relaxed. Not like last night on the phone. We quickly kissed but weren't in sync. It was a happy, friendly kiss. She smiled, opened the bag she was carrying, and took out two pairs of hiking shoes. I started to feel more comfortable. "Here they are. Size eight. They should fit." They felt big, but I'll break them in. "We're going to take a short boat ride to a place called Paradiso, and then we take a funicular to Monte San Salvatore. It's drop-dead scenic up there. You're not afraid of heights?"

"Only when I'm on top of a skyscraper. I got squeamish on top of the Empire State Building. You've been here before?"

No, I read about it. Thought you'd like it." She loosened up. "You're adventurous, I can tell. Here's a cinnamon roll. There's an incredible bakery next to my hotel. We'll eat when we get to the top. You'll like it." Great, the tour comes with a late lunch. We left the city pier and walked along the lake to the dock in Paradiso. I wondered where the name Paradiso came from. Any symbolic meaning for the weekend?

We boarded a small motorboat which took us to the funicular. The boat driver showed no expression. There were six other passengers. One couple and four kids, all with khaki shorts, safari hats, walking shoes, and binoculars. I hate it when people are so prepared. Cindy told me to put on my life jacket. My gut reaction was, "I'm a big boy, and don't tell me what to do." I said, "Sure."

The funicular building looked like Geppetto's fairy-tale cottage. It was a two-story brown rustic building with white stucco on the first floor, red wood paneling on the second floor, and bright red shutters on both floors. We got in, and the funicular started with a small jolt. We started to climb, and the view was spectacular. Miles of lakes and multiple mountain ranges.

We reached Monte San Salvatore. We walked up the concrete stairs and stopped to look out one level from the top. The metal railing protected us against a precipitous drop. Clouds, like flowing royal robes, rose against the great light blue sky and the seemingly endless blue lakes. Great expanses of light and dark green vegetation covered mountain ranges, near and distant. I felt like hugging the first person I met. I took a deep breath, held it, and blew out. I know it's the wrong mountain range, but I hummed a few lines from John Denver's *Rocky Mountain High*.

He left yesterday behind him
You might say he was born again
You might say he found a key for every door

It inspired me on the quest for "meaningful."

As happy as I was, it was too early to put the moves on. On the other hand, there isn't one set of rules for these situations. I went toward her, got on my toes. I have to be in sync this time. She smiled and said, "What are you doing?"

"I was so moved by the scenery and being here with you and so …"

"But there are a lot of people around." She hesitated. "Oh, fuck it." She put her hand over her mouth, embarrassed by the expletive. This was followed by a three-second kiss along the railing. We were still awkward, but it was cute. And that was a good use of the word. I got the feeling she doesn't make out with just anybody.

I felt pretty good, although the hiking boots hurt. The wind beat up, and my Indians baseball cap blew off, dropping over fifty feet. It was too steep a drop to retrieve it. A bad omen? We walked up the steps to the terrace restaurant. Thankfully, we were inside and protected from the strong wind. We could see for miles to the end of Lake Lugano and the beginning of Lake Como. Cindy ordered two Aperol Spritzes. "This is how I remember you when we met at that café," she said. "You looked around like you were lost. You were so serious."

I nodded. "It's hard for me to sit still." She laughed, and the waiter came by. We ordered grilled piadinas, which are Italian flatbread sandwiches. They were filled with brie, prawns, lettuce, and mushrooms. The sandwiches tasted better with a second spritz. "Thanks for bringing me up here."

"Sure, but wait until we walk down. More great views. Don't worry, it's a well-marked path."

"Hey, so what have you been doing?"

"Working, mostly. I'm taking a poetry class. The poetry is a great diversion. The problem is I don't have time for it. And I was waiting to tell you, I got a new job. Sales director at an eight-year pharmaceutical startup in northern New Jersey. I've been in Basel two years, and I missed the States. This company has two drugs that were approved by the FDA, and they're working on a few more. If they get the approvals and go public, I'll make some real money. Then I'll meet Prince Charming. Are you that guy? After I met you, I thought, 'What about Joseph? He's different, he's outside the box.' Most guys I meet, they're good looking, intelligent. They want it, boom, boom, boom." She pounded her fist three times. "Most of them are boring. The Swiss guys are looking for a Swiss hottie. They're boring too. My poetry class. It has eight expats. Two are talented. The others don't have a clue. They like the camaraderie. I thought you wrote poetry?"

"I did for a time. I like writing on bar napkins."

"Ok, now what's going on with you?" She sounded serious. This could be a tough interview.

"Well, I think I'm outside the box ... Let's see. Work is going well. I hang out each morning at a local café with a few guys. It's good for my work routine. I'm here for two months, maybe longer. After that, I can stay longer, or go back to the States and write, or return to corporate life and write when I can. I don't know if that's doable. Well, and I met you and here we are."

"So, we're outside the box. Well, you are, anyway. I never met anyone like you."

"That's a good thing, right?"

"I think. You give me a lot to digest. Oh, and Joe, can't you be a writer without being in France?"

"Fitzgerald spent time in the Riviera. Look what happened. *The Great Gatsby.*"

"OK, he had Zelda, you're on your own. You need a crazy companion to follow you. Not sure I'm the woman for that. I know you, you're easy to figure out, Joseph Fine, you thought you would meet a French woman and la-di-da. You like bars and boobs; you like to travel and write. You don't sit still. What did I miss?"

"I'm an environmental lawyer. That meant a lot to me. It still does. Can you list that first in the bio?"

"That's a fair comment." She gave me a reassuring look.

"I haven't worked as a lawyer for over a month, but the environmental stuff is important to me. It's part of me. It's hard to cut the cord completely."

I ate my piadina quickly, then wandered around while Cindy finished. The wind slowed; the heavenly cloud cover gave way to a mostly blue sky. I was excited about the hike to the bottom. I hope she isn't a fast hiker. I could see she's in better shape.

I said, "I need one more look from the top. The sky is now almost as blue as the lake."

I don't think she was listening. She stared down, looking at emails. "Sorry, I had to answer someone's question. What did you say?"

"Oh, nothing. Just, it's gorgeous all around ... and gorgeous, as in you."

She walked over and lightly pinched my cheeks. "What am I going to do with you?" I didn't answer. Was she being positive? Regardless, I could have sat here for hours. On top of the world. At least, on top of Monte San Salvatore. "Come on, let's go. It's well marked."

I looked at Cindy. I loved the way one front tooth leaned over on the other. A perfect imperfection. We looked toward Lake Como, saw the scattered towns on each side of Lake Lugano and the mountain ranges of the Swiss and Savoy Alps. A sign at the top said two miles to Paradiso. It wasn't a steep walk down. We took our time, and several groups passed us. Many happy hikers. About halfway down, we came to a stretch of old rail tracks. When we arrived at the Paradiso dock, Cindy said she needed to make calls. I waited. It was late Friday afternoon. She couldn't wait? I know it's hard to say no to a work call when you're loved and needed. Sometimes, enough is enough. She read my mind and whispered, "They think you're supposed to be available twenty-four seven."

I whispered back. "I agree, it's the worst."

I made a call too. It was time to catch up with Carter. Only late morning in Gotham. I found a bench near the boat dock. Typical no response. He called me back in a few minutes.

"Boy, Joe, I don't hear from you for a year, and here we go again. That's good. It means you want to tell me your social life is going well."

"Carter, I don't know who else to talk to. I'm visiting a woman I met in Venice, we're in Lugano. By the way, it's incredibly scenic. I like her a lot. I'm not calling because she's two and a half inches taller. Could be three. She's smart and focused, I think she's a waspy Jew like you but a tad stilted or is it rigid? Or both? She acts a little like my mom. The way she plans this and tells me that. She does have poise, and she's not crazy out of the gate like DD."

"You know what it sounds like? She's boring. Or she's too grown-up for you. That's why I thought DD might work out. Now, Joe, I have to tell you something. Don't be pissed. I know Marie. I did some business with her company."

I screamed, "Carter. WTF." Cindy ran over. "Are you alright?"

"Yes, my brother got in a spat with my mom. I told him to knock it off."

"You're sure?"

I nodded, and she walked back to finish her call. "Carter, are you still there?"

"Joe, Marie's a friend, not a friend with benefits. She really likes you. How about that, big fella? Please, I am often full of shit, and you don't have to believe me, but she does. By the way, she is a moderately big shit at that cosmetics company. She made a ton on commissions last year."

"Carter, was this all by chance?"

"Don't get pissed. Maybe half and half. You must have spoken highly of me and Marie figured out the connection."

"I didn't talk about you. She found my phone at a party. I dropped it and she found it on the grounds. I guess she scrolled through past calls."

"Joe, so you're with who?"

I didn't answer.

"Marie told me she's seeing you Sunday."

"Late in the day." Cindy walked toward me. "Carter, I have to go. Please don't talk to Marie."

"Joe, I saw a picture. She's a banger."

"Don't talk like that."

Cindy asked, "Somebody said banger?"

"It's a friend. He has bad judgment. He was bragging."

"Oh."

We took the last boat back to the Lugano pier. I was distracted. Cindy dropped me off at Hotel San Carlo. We regrouped later for drinks and pizza near the pier. Things started to feel awkward like I was here, and she had to spend time with me. We walked back to her hotel, sat on the floor of her room, and watched a comical Italian movie from the 1950s. Lots of sex, they just didn't show it then. Here, no fooling around, but Cindy liked it when I put my arm around her.

We acted like a seasoned couple and fell asleep. I had a dream. It wasn't a nightmare, but close enough. I was in the courtroom with my friend Bill Santos who acted as my attorney. The court was reviewing my application to date a woman who looked like Cindy. She was at least five-five. I think Carter, Marie, and The Inner Voice were in the courtroom. Marguerite, my friend from the Antibes walk, waved from the gallery. The other lawyer glared at me and started his questioning.

"How tall are you?

"Five-three. OK, and maybe a half."

How tall is your father?"

"He's five-seven."

"And your mother?"

"Five-two."

"Ok, your siblings?"

"My sister is two inches taller than me. My brother is an inch taller than her."

"Is that it?"

My father's father was five-three. And my grandma was five feet tall. I would also like to state that my art teacher liked my work, and I went steady with a girl in seventh grade. She was four inches taller than me. Your honor, may I ask the opposing attorney a question?"

The judge nodded, but he didn't like me. "You may proceed."

I fumed at the opposing lawyer. "You're big and pathetic." The judge banged the gavel.

Marie yelled out, "Leave him alone, judge, he's my big guy." Now she's in trouble with the judge.

I think more happened, but I woke up. It was past three o'clock in the morning. Cindy leaned on me, sleeping. Hopefully, I didn't talk in my sleep. I better go. I whispered I was leaving; it was just a short walk. She smiled. She was groggy. "Don't go. What happened? Were we making out? That's OK, right?"

For the first time on the trip, I was completely relaxed. I went to the bathroom, closed the door, washed my face, and bawled. I don't know why. I thanked God for two arms, two legs, and a brain. Then I gave Cindy a kiss and left. The walk down the silent, empty street to my hotel energized me.

I barely fell back to sleep and woke before sunrise. I jumped out of bed, grabbed the laptop, and left. I wanted Cindy to join me but let her sleep. In three minutes, I was at the lake. I found a table and worked in the dim park light. Then sunrise and daylight. Two men showed up and started a chess game.

Marie was fresh in my mind. Then Jen sprang out of her cubbyhole in the back of my brain. I told them to stay put. They didn't pay rent to sit there, and I would get back to them. I was set to leave Lugano on Sunday morning, and that was that. For all I know, Carter will show up in Antibes, and Marie will set him up with one of her friends. The Inner Voice said, "Don't be paranoid." She's right again.

Cindy planned a trip to Lake Como Saturday morning. It's a short bus ride from Lugano. She did not set a departure time. I sat near the lake, wrote and napped, and went to her hotel before ten. The clerk, a guy in his twenties with a ponytail, served coffee. I sat outside. A lovely morning that could only get better. The tea leaves told me to keep my room another night. She may need space after another day with me.

Cindy came outside the hotel. She wasn't happy. "Joseph," she said like a stern schoolteacher, "Joseph, where were you?"

"I left your room around three in the morning. I got up very early, was at the lake, wrote a bit."

"I know, but we're late. You have a few minutes before breakfast is over."

"I'm good. I stopped and had a baguette and coffee."

"What about me?" Uh, oh. Not that again. Now, I had to be proactive.

"I'm sorry, I just thought ..."

"Well, you didn't."

"I'm sorry." Cindy was big on schedules. Even apparently when she did not set one. I guess clairvoyance was needed.

I don't hear the phrase "What about me?" much, but it makes me squirm. It has nothing to do with Cindy. When I was a senior at Yale, I was fortunate to have a graduate student in my room who clearly wanted to have sexual relations. She was very bright; I think she was getting a Ph.D. in biochemistry. We were "doing it," but I didn't fully address her needs. She said, "What about me?" Ever since, the phrase gets me unglued. For the record, she came to my room one more time. This is neither here nor there, but I distinctly remember she was also a screamer.

Cindy went on. "Joe, you're only here for today, and you're leaving tomorrow. Then what?"

I acted like this was about spending the day in Lake Como. "I don't know. I thought you might want to sleep late. I needed time to write. If I miss a day, I can lose the flow."

"Well, I'm sorry, I meant what about the two of us?"

I whispered, "OK. We'll see, right?" I looked around and didn't see anyone. We kissed and kept it going a few seconds. What a roller coaster. Was I going to end up on the top or the bottom with Cindy? I mean overall. Where is this going?

She didn't say anything else. On to Lake Como.

I needed a few things for the trip and ran down the street to my hotel. She yelled, "You won't need the room." I liked the positive reinforcement but kept the room. I can say that I didn't hear her.

The clerk at Hotel San Carlo looked at me like I did something unseemly. "Everything alright?"

I was flustered and said, "At this point in time, yes." She burst out laughing. What did I do to prompt this? I ran back.

Cindy was itching to leave. "You want to go, don't you?"

"Absolutely I want to go."

"I made baguette sandwiches with brie, cucumber, and tomato. The kitchen had extra food from breakfast. They are so nice here."

It was less than an hour bus ride from Lugano along a meandering downhill lake road to Menaggio, a village on Lake Como, just south of the Swiss border. I'm glad we didn't drive. We passed the villages we saw from Monte San Salvatore. I loved the wind on my face. Cindy studied the travel guide. She read about a palace called Villa Carlotta in Tremezzo. "Joe, it was originally built in the seventeenth century. Beautiful grounds and gardens. You'll like it. It was a popular stop on the Grand Tour."

I was groggy but I had to say something. "I know. It's what pampered young Brits did rather than work for a living."

"That's unfair."

"Yes, yet a modicum of truth." I was looking for an excuse to use the word modicum. I could have said, "Yes, honey, you're right," but she ignored me anyway.

We arrived in Menaggio close to noon. It's a sleepy town with a handful of tourists milling around. We walked the town's lakeside promenade to its ferry dock. Menaggio is relatively flat. At least near the dock area. Other lake towns, like Bellagio, rise from the lake almost immediately into the hills above. It was foggy and misty, then it started to drizzle. The lake has a dreamy feel. It appears to merge into the sky. The fog adds a mystique like time is suspended. On the other side of the lake, the mountains look like distant shadows.

From Menaggio, we took the lake ferry to Bellagio and on to Tremezzo, where it's a very short walk to the entrance of Villa Carlotta. In front of us stood a delightful, decadent, five-level palace and gardens. At the top of the palace, there is a clock inside a small cupula. We walked through the gate and were greeted by a moss-covered Roman statue in a lily pad-filled fountain. The fountain was surrounded by a bale of big turtles that bumped into each other. We went up two flights of crisscrossing stairways that meet at the official entrance.

There was a statue of Napoleon in the rotunda and other worldly creatures. Cindy stared at a painting on the next level up called *The Last Adieu of Romeo and Juliet*, which was described as a "sensual embrace between the two young lovers of the Shakespearean tragedy."

She said, "They were so young and innocent." She took my hand.

"OK, but it's a story, with too much drama." Too late. I should have shut up.

She was baffled. "There's so much feeling. Don't you see it?"

"I think so. Yes ... I'd like to go upstairs." The main room of the top floor looked out onto a balcony with a majestic view of the lake. Clouds and fog delicately obscured the mountains, which were shades of light gray and blue.

There was an exhibit on botanical drawings adjacent to the main room. I guessed the artist, Livia, was in her mid-thirties. She sat at a large mahogany desk with her book *Passeggiate Estive* or "Summer Walks" for sale. We chatted about her work. Her innocent smile and youthful eyes made me feel optimistic about the world. I loved the colorful fruit and flower drawings. I bought her book. Next time, I'll fall in love with her.

I lingered at the exhibit when Cindy walked into the room. "Cindy, look at these drawings. Flowers and fruit. Lemons and berries. And did you see the lake from the balcony?"

"Joe."

"Yes."

"We need to go."

"What hap…?"

"My uncle Edgar. He's very sick. My mom doesn't think he'll make it. Joe, are you there?"

"I'm sorry."

"He taught me how to ride a bicycle. He bought me my first camera. The bastard, he had a mistress for years before anybody knew. My aunt wouldn't leave him. She loved him."

"Oh, dear."

Cindy started to cry. She quickly calmed down. "Actually, I wouldn't be able to get home before tomorrow night, and my mom said to wait. Joe, can we go outside and sit?"

I waved goodbye to Livia and ran downstairs, stopping for another look at the Romeo and Juliet embrace. Maybe it's the story's tragedy, but I don't know what she sees in the painting. Cindy was near the gate between the fountain and the turtle pond. We walked to the gardens next to the Villa and found a bench along a row of citrus trees that lined a gravel path. No one was around.

"Try to think good thoughts about your uncle," I said.

"He was awfully funny. Joe, you don't try to be funny. You just are. You're a mix of balls and bullshit. Uncle Edgar was bigger on the balls part." She laughed uncontrollably. It's the best antidote.

A little boy, maybe four years old, came running down the path toward us. As he got closer, he started to skip. His mother said, "Luca, Luca." He was a cute kid with perfectly parted wavy brown hair. He said, "Buon giorno" to us with a big smile, and put up four fingers, which we assumed was his age.

I said to Cindy, "Do you remember when you were four years old?"

"Barely. I had a pretty red and white dress. Blonde curls. My older brother liked to hug me, but sometimes he hugged too hard."

"My sister was an infant. I talked to my invisible friends."

"You remember that?"

"I remember Bucky and Joey and their little red sports car."

"My uncle made up crazy stories about princesses and witches. He said 'Akka mazakka' and took quarters out of our ears."

"How do you feel now?"

"Hungry, tired, and well, I know you well enough, a little ... It starts with 'h' and ends in 'y.'"

"I got it. Yes."

"But I want to hold off until we get somewhere." I suspect she means more than somewhere. What does Bob Dylan say in *You're a Big Girl Now*? "A change in the weather is known to be extreme." And then he says, "But what's the sense of changing horses in midstream?"

We returned to Lugano by sundown. Cindy fell asleep on my shoulder in the bus. Back in town, we agreed Lake Como was well worth the visit. She was sorry she said not to bother about a hotel Saturday night. I said I didn't hear her say it. She was tired from last night and wanted to call it a day. I didn't argue and promised to bring breakfast tomorrow morning. I strolled around town and along the lake before landing at a lively bar near my hotel. I talked to an English woman who was at the conference with Cindy. She said Cindy gave a talk and sounded a bit self-righteous.

Next morning, I brought two coffees and two crêpes with Nutella, and we sat on the hotel patio. She was in a light-hearted mood and excited about New Jersey. Her uncle was holding on so far. I said, "I'll pray for your Uncle Edgar."

I talked about seeing Cindy after she moved to New Jersey. She was lukewarm. Maybe I didn't show enough emotion during the weekend. I kept picturing Marie in her thong bikini and remembered Carter said she liked me. "She really did." Time for her later. For the closing ceremony, Cindy and I had an obligatory, polite kiss. Nothing deep or prolonged. She looked like she was trying to solve a puzzle. "I haven't met anyone like you before. You're like a ...?" She paused. "You're a train that keeps moving. Do I want to stay on the train? I think so."

I waited a couple of seconds. "I think so, too." This was too many metaphors, even for an educated person like me.

"That's all you have to say?"

"Cindy, it has to work for you."

"Yes. You need to go. We can both think about it."

"Good luck in Jersey." With a smile, a few skips, and an increasing tension headache, I taxied to the airport.

CHAPTER TWENTY-FIVE

"
*I don't want the night to end. I want to save it, bottle it,
put it on the shelf and open it later.*

I know it's not home, but I felt pretty good when I touched down in Nice. Antibes was my residence, my comfort zone. I had a routine that worked, and what looked like an evolving, if not progressing social life. And there was plenty of Sunday left. I took the express bus from the airport to the Antibes station and called Marie. She said she was on her way to the beach. I should have asked which beach. I confirmed we were on for later today.

"Or earlier if you like." I turned around. There was Marie and a friend.

I said, "Oh, mon Dieu," loud enough for anyone outside the café to hear. Marie stood in white shorts, a black tank top, and Sophia Loren sunglasses. The short dark-brown bob seemed longer than before the Lugano weekend. We did the European kiss routine. She introduced me to her friend Chelsea, who was tall and thin, and worked in the company's Nice office.

Marie said, "You told me your flight got in at 12:15, so I thought you would take the bus. I wanted to surprise you. I lucked out. How was Switzerland? Not as much fun as Antibes, right?"

I took her bait. "Almost, not quite, of course. Striking scenery. Lake Como's near Lugano, so I went there too. The lake is so dreamy." I was ready to tell her I visited a college friend if she asked why I went.

"Looks like you got some sun. Well, you're back, and you want to work, right? Then you'll feel good about seeing me later?"

"Exactly." I liked the positive reinforcement.

Marie and I chatted for a few minutes. She and Chelsea took off for the beach at Juan-les-Pins, on the other side of Cap D'Antibes. While Vieil Antibes has charm and verve during the day, Juan-les-Pins has a long sandy beach with cafés and lots of night buzz.

Lisette and Bernard were in the front of the house when I arrived. Lisette was on her knees in the small garden, while Bernard stood on the sidewalk with his hands in his pockets, like he was lost or didn't belong there. She could take pride in her garden of yellow and white lilies, blue orchids, red roses, and purple irises. A female neighbor with a lovable reddish-brown cavapoo stopped to talk to Lisette. I dumped my bag on the bed and made a sandwich.

I thought it would be fun to wake my friend Bill on the East Coast and congratulate him on his new job. He didn't appreciate the call and asked if he could talk later. Then he gave in and couldn't stop talking. He assured me the new firm was financially viable. It specialized in class-action securities litigation, which is fancy language for a claim that shareholders lost a lot of money when the stock dropped because the company wasn't upfront about its financial status. Lawyers are usually the big winners. It sounded like Billy Boy would be ringing the cash register.

The good news for me was that the firm did not have an environmental practice so there was no possibility of luring me away.

But, I should have known something like this was coming. Later that afternoon, Richard Martin called. I was on the patio working. He thought I wouldn't mind a call on Sunday. I like Richard a lot. He gave me an opportunity to prove myself in the rough and tumble private sector. I showed him that someone with an EPA background could be comfortable in the corporate world as long as the top brass had my back, which they always did.

We caught up on personal stuff. He has a gorgeous wife and two smart, but over-indulged children. Once he asked me how this happened as if I had the magic bullet. I told him he was caught in a wave of societal change, and he shouldn't follow his upper-middle-class peers who weren't allowing their children to grow up.

Then he got down to business. "Joe, I'm calling you discreetly. Jeremy can't keep up with the work." Jeremy was a newer staff attorney. "He needs supervision. I didn't want to backfill your position, but this isn't working. Do you think you would be interested in coming back? We'll make it worth your while. I got a preliminary OK to give you stock options for 3500 shares if you get back here. Can you let me know in a week? I don't give a shit when you actually start, well I do, but you can start in a month. I just want you back on board.

"One other thing. This is very confidential, but we expect to be working on an acquisition soon, I can tell you this because you are still officially with the Company on an extended leave. Kind of like maternity leave. So, the timing would work well if you get back here. Joe, it's so busy, and I can't fill positions fast enough. It's good to be busy, right? I haven't taken a vacation in a year." That kind of talk makes me nervous because I've heard stories about people who snap when they don't take time off.

I have a soft spot for the StarColor legal department. I had a great career in Washington, but North Jersey is where my career took off. "Richard, I appreciate the call. It means a lot to me. As of now, I'm planning to be in France at least another five or six weeks. I'll need to get back to you. You know I'm grateful for what you've done for me."

"Well, you earned it." A little mutual back-scratching. "How are you doing, anyway? When will we see the bestseller?"

I noticed he didn't react when I said six weeks. "I've got a long way to go. It's hard work, a different kind of hard work. It's me, the computer screen and my imagination. And research here and there. That sounds like legal work. Believe me, it's not."

"See, it will be an easy transition. What's that shitty place downtown you liked for happy hour? Lots of women, you said ... I'll tell you one negative. You can't be yourself at work anymore. You have to watch everything you say. A woman comes on to you or flirts, stay the fuck away, don't say 'fuck' in front of her, and, whatever you do, don't fuck her."

"Of course." I could have put it all to bed right now and permanently cut the cord on going back. I didn't. I punted. "Richard, I will get back to you by next Sunday. Please send regards to the crew."

"I will."

I'll wait until the last day to respond. With the demands of legal work, there was no way I could produce my opus too. Spare time would be at the gym or a mad rush to happy hour before it ended. As for meeting Jersey girls, I didn't have much luck in the past year, except for one woman I met at a fundraiser for a state senator. She was five-one, like DD. I think we went out three times, and she pulled the plug. This was before I adopted broader dating criteria and ignited my self-confidence.

The call with Richard rattled me a bit. After struggling most of the afternoon to produce the obligatory three to five pages, I heard from my pals Tammy and Brie. Tammy texted she was returning to Nice for a sales meeting in early June. She said Brie was spilling over with enthusiasm, chasing a special guy who wasn't toxic. He's not yet anyway. Tammy asked about my social life. Did this mean she wanted to keep her foot in my door? Not a good idea with Marie in the picture. I said, "Nothing special." I regarded Tammy and Brie as friends to keep. It's healthy to have women friends who you aren't chasing romantically.

Marie remained an intriguing puzzle. Not to be self-disparaging because I've improved, but it was hard to believe that such a striking woman took an interest in me. We weren't the kind of couple people would say, "Oh, they look so good together." You could say the same about Cindy, although at times we both fit the confident preppy look. One thing I've overcome. I don't care what people think when I walk down the street, whether it's with Marie, Cindy, Jen, or any of them.

I headed out back. Lisette was now in the garden behind the back patio. She picked a few roses and orchids and sat on one of the tulip chairs. "Surely, you must know someone special who would like them." I graciously accepted without going into detail. She seemed particularly happy, which was unusual. I went inside and put on a shirt with little bicycle prints to go with my jeans and cowboy boots. I splashed on the Tom Ford cologne.

When I got close to Marie's hotel, I tucked in my shirt and cleaned my glasses. I met her in the lobby. "Joe, comment ca va?" I handed her the orchids and roses. She gave me a quick kiss. "You're so sweet," she said. Marie looked like a proper schoolgirl. She wore a navy and red plaid skirt with white streaks, a crew-neck red sweater, and navy flats. The dark brown bob was now a bob with a little ponytail. And there were reddish highlights in her hair, which gave her a warmer look. Her dark eyeshadow made it easy for me to focus.

"I can't get over how great you look. You're an innocent high school girl, it's the beginning of your senior year, and you've made a good impression."

"Thanks, Joe ... Is that hair color on your forehead?"

OK, she caught me. "Never mind," I said, blushing. We stepped outside.

"Joe, I see how you look at me. I normally think, if you've got it, flaunt it. With you, I don't want to wear an outfit that says fuck me. You know what I mean?"

"Yes, I do. I'm touched."

"Just so you know," she started to laugh, "The thong bikini is just for the beach. I have short shorts too, but I threw out the pair that has a hole near my tushy."

I laughed. "Good. What a relief."

"I picked a place in Antibes. Vietnamese and French. We'll take a taxi back. I told my mom I would call. I told her about you." Immediately red flags went up. "I said you're part Al Pacino and Michael J. Fox ... Oh, I forgot, I got you something."

She went to her room and returned with a worn hardback. "I found this at the flea market in Old Nice. Cours Saleya." She handed me something wrapped in tissue paper. "It's an old English edition of *Moby Dick* with drawings, published in the 1890s. I heard you mention it at Tammy's party. You said most fiction is shallow compared to this book. I wondered, 'Who is this guy? I need to meet him. Here's a bunch of cosmetics people and he's talking about a crazy sea captain who is obsessed with a whale.' You can leave the book here. We'll come back for it."

"Thank you very, very much."

"Pleasure is mine."

Marie brought me to Le Bon Matin, an unassuming Vietnamese restaurant, which sits on a pretty tree-lined street named Boulevard Marechal Foch. I was curious about the street name. It sounded like a famous Frenchman. Marechal Foch is actually a French wine grape. It's a hybrid grape, which means wine produced from two varieties of grape that work together. If Marie and I were grapes, we would definitely be different varieties. Would we work together?

We were seated at a small table against the wall facing the entrance. The owner of the restaurant, a short-statured gentleman, greeted each customer. He told me his father fled Vietnam in 1975 when the Americans left. A sad and tragic year for so many people. Above us hung a recent color photograph of a busy circle in downtown Saigon with hundreds of scooters and a few cars. We ordered a bottle of pinot noir, which is also a hybrid, and two orders of vegetable spring rolls.

Marie asked official first date stuff. My career with the feds, then corporate life. Then how I left work, left town and started a book.

I said I viewed the book as an extension of myself. Isn't that the appeal of creating something? When you have three glasses of wine and the company is stimulating, it's easy to try out a few phrases. But that didn't capture what I wanted to tell her. "Marie, this is what you need to know. I was a great kickball player, and I didn't take shit from kids who were bigger than me. And I went outside the box in art class. And I have a lot to offer to the right woman."

"Joe, that's … impressive." She took a big sip of wine. "It tells me a lot. I don't want to sell lipstick forever, either." She looked at me closely. "Do you ever wonder what you're doing? Millions of people get up in the morning, go to work and go home, or they get up and work at home. The same thing the next day. You go to a party, and I'm there. You can tell me how it happened, but how did it really happen?" I didn't want this story to end.

It's easy to get deep on a few glasses of pinot. She kept going. "I know why you like me, besides the looks and the smarts. I looked deeper into Joseph Fine. If your mind were measured in inches, you'd be the tallest in the class. If I were pissed at you, I wouldn't say, 'Don't be short with me.' I would use a neutral word like asshole. Most women give a guy's mind short shrift. Sure, most guys are superficial too."

"You're onto something."

"I busted through my comfort zone. My friends wouldn't do that. Guys think I'm gorgeous and stupid. If he's a tall, cute guy, he thinks I'm a pushover. Well, f--- him." I think the wine made her louder. It definitely increased her entertainment value. "I need to see what's inside Joseph Fine. You want the same from me. Joe, how did we get started on this? I'm hungry. They have these soup dishes where you tilt the bowl and slurp it down with your spoon. Try the beef pho."

"I will." I would have complied if she told me to do a cartwheel outside. "I'm flattered that you looked deeper." Thank you, pinot noir, for your facilitator role.

I saw a big toothy smile and the ground shifted. "Of course. Can we order another bottle of wine? I want to talk about *Moby Dick*. Would I like it? It's not scary, is it?"

"No, no. Yes, more wine. Here, you should drink some water too."

"You're telling me what to do?"

"Yes."

"That means you care, right?"

"Yes."

She was thinking. "Joe, you know what I want? Moules Frites. Mussels and fries. With garlic red sauce. I know a good place near the beach."

"What about the pho? If you really want ..."

"And then let's go to Villefranche-sur-Mer. It's the nicest town on the coast.

"You don't mean tonight, do you?" Villefranche is on the other side of Nice.

"I guess not. I got ahead of myself. But we should go."

"Yes, boss." She blew a kiss off her right hand.

When we arrived at the beach restaurant, we ordered a bottle of wine, and she changed her mind again. "How about we get crêpes and sit outside? I'm sorry this is confusing, isn't it?"

"Any more changes?"

"No. Look, the man in the moon is glowing. I don't want the night to end. I want it to go on and on and on. I want to save it, bottle it, put it on the shelf and open it later." An hour later, another bottle of wine consumed, we taxied to her hotel and hobbled inside. Someone forgot about moules frites and crêpes. Good thing we ate the spring rolls. I sat on the sofa in her room, fell asleep. A good, deep sleep.

I woke up with a headache. It was still dark out, and I felt something push against me. I was sandwiched between a naked Marie and the back of the couch. I looked down. She wore the thong part of a bikini. "I wore this just for you. Now, go back to sleep."

"I don't want to."

"I don't either." I thought she might change her mind again, but she didn't.

CHAPTER TWENTY-SIX

Joe's therapist requires him to have company, so we act
as his friends.

Monday morning. I got up after sunrise and returned to Antibes. With Marie's help, the weekend ended in a near-spiritual experience. The best place for me to express gratitude was the beach. I sat on the ledge at the back of the Picasso Museum and looked out to the calm, ancient Mediterranean. I took out my notebook and wrote ten pages of blather, but it felt good.

I walked to Bar Bacchus and found Jack and Bruce at an inside table near the back. All other inside and outside tables were taken. The boys weren't happy. Someone took the outside table they considered theirs. Jack sulked because he didn't see any bangers. Dennis showed up and told them to stop complaining. I talked about the weekend without mentioning Cindy or Marie. Jack didn't understand why I would go to Lugano for a weekend. Bruce was focused on his last week in Antibes before Paris.

Jack smelled a rat. He said to me, "You normally look lost when you come here. You're tired and happy today. Did you meet a French broad? That's it." He clapped his hands, confirming his answer. "You met a French broad."

"No, sorry, not true. Marie has a French-sounding first name. She's an American. She has one set of French grandparents who left before World War II. So there. You're such a gossip."

"So, there is a broad after all."

Fortunately, Jack's inquiry was deferred when he spied two young ladies looking for a table. Both were well dressed in dark pantsuits. One was Marie's friend Camille. She had a white V-neck silky top. Her friend wore a navy and white striped button-down blouse. Both were eye-catching. Ever notice how pretty women hang out with other pretty women? Camille saw me. "Joe, bonjour. How are you?"

"Good, good, would you like to sit with us? I'll get chairs." Hopefully, Jack won't cause any commotion. He winked at me, and Bruce perked up.

Camille said, "Merci, so nice of you. This is my friend Amélie. We work in Nice."

"What do you do?"

Amélie said, "We are attorneys. Avocates."

I said, "Sounds like avocado." Everybody laughed. "You work in a law firm?"

"No, we work for the state prosecutor."

"So, you put les criminels in jail? Hear that, Jack? These are my friends Jack, Bruce and Dennis. They're detectives. Jack and Bruce are searching for French women. Dennis doesn't have to search. He has hair salons."

"Joe is a famous lawyer in the United States," said Jack. "He makes beaucoup de money."

"Don't listen to him," I said. "But I am well known in my field." I normally don't puff like this.

Amélie said, "You look very smart." The ladies laughed.

"It's the glasses," I said. "They fool everybody."

Camille said, "Well, we are on our way to a conference for women business leaders. Marie will be there. Joe, she is a very accomplished woman. And only twenty-seven. She said you are an accomplished writer. Un auteur." The words rolled off her tongue like you could catch them. Jack laughed so hard I thought he would pee in his pants.

"She's too kind," I said, "but I just started." Jack kept laughing. I acted like he wasn't there. Fortunately, a minute later, he got a call from one of his girlfriends and stepped away.

"Ladies, it was a pleasure." He kissed their hands. I thought I'd gag. "Joe, you owe me drinks for not telling us more about Marie. Bruce, talk to Amélie. I'll take Camille."

"Where are we going?" Bruce has a worse attention span than I do.

The ladies stood up. "Sorry gentlemen, we're busy," said Camille.

"So, you know, we start most mornings here," said Bruce. "Joe's therapist requires him to have company, so we act like his friends."

"Leave Joe alone," said Camille. She looked my way with what I thought was a flirtatious glance. Maybe I'm feeling so good, I'm seeing things. "And Joe, you don't need any more advice, but I would keep your job and write the book. You have a professional license. We all have licenses." I nodded and didn't want to discuss it. Just getting attention from these two was gratifying. They didn't stay long.

I didn't think I would hear from Cindy. Things were up in the air when I left Lugano. She texted Tuesday, two days later. I'm glad she went first. She said she enjoyed the weekend and did not appreciate the gardens at Villa Carlotta until we left. Then she surprised me. She said I am such a gentleman, and of course, most men are not. And yes, she wants to see me. Thoughts of an imminent breakup dissipated.

I texted back I had fun too and added something vague about being in touch. The truth is, I'm not sure there's a real connection. I pictured an on-again, off-again relationship that goes on for a few years and gets tougher to end due to inertia and fear of not finding someone else. I have an occasional dark feeling about being left alone. It could happen in a week. Or a day. No point in obsessing. Seeing three or four women at a time gave me a cushion. A deeper bench. The sun emerged through the clouds, and darkness turned to light. Thank God for sunny days and unpleasant thoughts I can put on the back-burner.

A more immediate priority was Bruce, who needed a sendoff before leaving town. He's been more agitated about his upcoming departure. He looked like a lost soul. I suggested an afternoon in Nice and he appreciated the thought. We took the train Tuesday afternoon. I brought along my frayed copy of *Piccadilly Jim*. I considered taking *Tropic of Cancer*, but I wasn't in the mood for Henry Miller's self-absorbed, pathetic short-term relationships.

Bruce and I walked down Boulevard Gambetta toward Promenade des Anglais, the seaside walk named after well-heeled Brits who came to Nice over a century ago. We stopped at Hotel Negresco, the grand lady of Nice, for a drink. Bruce couldn't find any eye candy in the old woody bar, so we continued down the promenade to Old Nice and the crowded outdoor market on Cours Saleya. We discovered a lively restaurant on the beach with ample shade under the red, white, and blue umbrellas.

I found Bruce a well-situated table near two women. He got antsy and complained about the heat, the women, and French politics. "Look, Bruce," I said, "No pissing and moaning. And when you go to Paris, be nice, let her go to the Louvre while you go to one of those pretentious cafés with bad service that Hemingway liked."

"It's all overrated. You know what I want. A good cheesesteak. A Philly cheesesteak. With ketchup and hot sauce."

I was still determined to give the old boy a good sendoff. "Get a drink and shut the fuck up," I said courteously.

"Got it. Hey, Joe, see the woman staring at me?" She was at the table with the other woman. The one looking at Bruce had crutches next to her chair. She was a shorter, stockier version of Marie with a darker complexion and long jet-black hair but didn't exude as much raw sexual energy. Yes, that would be a high bar to reach.

The other woman smiled and walked toward us. She was tall and blonde with an innocent, baby face. I whispered to Bruce to pay attention.

"Do I know you from somewhere?" she asked Bruce. The oldest line in the book. Of course, she didn't have any more details on that somewhere. I smelled someone looking for a free drink. "I'm Patrice, by the way, and this is Margo. We're teachers. She fell off a scooter." It wasn't funny, but it came across that way. We introduced ourselves. They looked mid-thirties. Margo, the shorter one, had a lusty Fanny Hill look. She looked like she had a drink or two before we sat down. She was also a giggler.

Patrice said, "It's OK, she's like a wind-up toy." Patrice acted like her chaperone.

"Would you two like to sit with us?" asked Bruce. I almost fell out of my chair.

Margo said, "Can you two come to our table? It's bigger and I have my foot up." I think Bruce was shocked by the response. I prepped him to think that every event is an opportunity. I asked the ladies what they drink. Bruce squirmed about paying for drinks, and I gave him a look. Something told me Margo was an opportunist. She ordered vodka with lemon. I got the same with olives. Patrice had a spritz. After much deliberating, Bruce ordered a spritz too. A good move for collegiality.

Now we were two pretend couples. It was hard to keep up with Margo. Subtitles would have helped. She said, "I just got divorced and it was nice to get away ... From the little shits at school too." Then a longer giggle. "Of course, it's too early for a new relationship."

"Of course." Why would I disagree?

"Patrice, on the other hand ... is not married and ready to roll," she said loudly and sloppily. Patrice turned beet red.

"Margo, please ..."

I couldn't tell if Margo was about to laugh or cry. She stuttered and said to me, "Hypothetically, would you go out with me, I mean, hypothetically?" She inched over, put her arm around me. "Patrice, do you think he's a keeper?" Patrice politely told Margo she had too much to drink and they should get going. They were meeting their teacher friends for dinner. Margo protested and said that wasn't for a couple of hours. I think Margo also forgot her question.

Bruce perked up. "You know what bothers me? I can't get a cheesesteak or a juicy cheeseburger. A good one."

That's all he needed to say. Patrice showed her righteous indignation. "We live in Kansas City, and I agree. I miss my barbecue." She loosened up ... finally.

I knew about the barbecue culture from work trips, and two ridiculously detailed articles in The New Yorker. This is going to blow them away. "Who do you like better," I asked, "Arthur Bryant's or Gates Bar-B-Q?"

Margo was beside herself. "Arthur Bryant's, of course. When you come to KC, that's where we're going." I don't know about Kansas City, but we went on about food and drinks. Patrice got visibly impatient. She stood up. Margo started to get up on one of her crutches and said meekly, "One more drink?" Patrice wouldn't budge. I think she did this because Margo was enjoying herself. Sad when that happens. Women can be tough on each other.

"Joe, take this. You never know." Margo passed her business card to me. Bruce and I waved to our transient friends. I felt like I was saying goodbye to people leaving on a cruise ship. I guess we're paying the bill too.

They said goodbye and left. Bruce said, "You're welcome."

I didn't think the women heard him. Patrice turned and said, "Oh, thanks for the drinks." No embarrassment there.

Another event in the books. Bruce appreciated my support. I reminded him that, if he were interested in Patrice, I could probably get her information from Margo. "Of course," he said, "that would be for purposes of a nice conversation, nothing more."

"Of course."

The late afternoon. Intermittent light and shadows on the rocky beach. To me, it's the most hopeful part of the day. A quiet charm spreads over the Riviera. Boat masts blowing gently in the calm dark-blue water. Minutes away, crowds of people on Cours Saleya eating, drinking, walking, talking, laughing, crying, living.

Bruce was back to his grumpy self on the way back. I did my good deed for the day. I was waiting for something like this. He asked, "Do you think Patrice would go out with me? I mean, hypothetically?"

I took a while to answer. This could come back to bite me. "Yes, but ... You could call and say hi. No, do your best with Terry in Paris. Maybe there's a part of her you don't know, something you couldn't see before."

"Like what?"

CHAPTER TWENTY-SEVEN

「「

Look, these women could all disappear overnight.

I dreamt that Marie walked down my street in Antibes. She wore a tight long-sleeved black ballet top. God, she looked good. A tall, bearded guy in a tuxedo accompanied her. Who was he? Was she married to him? That didn't make sense. I walked past her, and she ignored me. I kept walking, and there was DD with a big, nasty dog. She talked to Liza like I wasn't there. "Wow, he was something, now he's gone, he went to France, well, fuck him sideways." Cindy was asleep on a bench in Central Park. That made no sense either.

I woke up confused. The sun came through cracks in the blinds, and I felt better. Lisette knocked on the door. "Come in."

"Joseph, good morning." I looked up. "Would you like to go to Marché Provençal with me?" This was unusual; she never asked me to go before. We normally didn't interact much, especially in the morning.

"No, thank you. That's nice of you to ask. Maybe next time."

"That's fine. Would you like anything?"

"No, thanks. Thanks for asking."

I called Carter. He didn't find my dream amusing. What didn't I understand? "You think a woman will take you seriously if you don't have a day job. Most won't take a flyer on you. How will you get laid for an extended period without long-term stability? The smart ones want financial strength. Even when they make a good buck. You didn't mention Jen. I suspect she is a sugar mommy. My aunt says she's loaded, but I don't know if she's the direction you're going in."

"Carter, please don't call her a sugar mommy, and you're assuming I can't have stability if I change course. I can't agree."

"Do I detect a soft spot for Ms. Trotter? Hmmm."

"Jen encourages me, but I'm doing this on my own."

"Well, Joe, you're lucky, it doesn't matter, you have an option C. You do your writing until the last day Richard will take you back. Then go back. You'll write in the evening and on weekends, then go to California with Jen. You know she's getting divorced."

"I know."

"So, every time she fucks you, she thinks she's fucking over her ex."

"Please don't talk about her like that. She's a good influence. I like her enthusiasm."

"Whatever you do, don't get on her bad side. By the way, DD texted and asked why Joe doesn't respond. She thinks you found somebody. Can you say something to her so I don't have to be your spokesman? And what's with Marie?"

I ignored the Marie part. "I'll call DD. Carter, option C is just recasting option B. I think it's between A and B. I have to stay with A. Stay the course here. If I have to return to the work world, I will. I can earn a buck if I need to."

"I don't know, Joe. How are you going to afford drinks at the King Cole?" He got me there. I never want to be in that position. Still, I'm OK for now. I have to hold my ground.

"This is the time to take a risk. If I reach that point, I'll reevaluate."

"Now, Marie?"

"Carter, you can't say anything to DD. Or anybody.'"

"Of course, I'm now your confidential secretary."

"She's gorgeous, very smart, has a great job, and I can't figure this out, she likes me ... a lot."

"She meets your height criteria?"

"She's five-six, no closer to five-seven. Her boss, Tammy, invited me to an office party for her sales group. I met Tammy in France last time. They work for a French cosmetics company, so they travel to Nice periodically. I had no expectations. Maybe that's the key. You wouldn't believe the perfume smell at that party."

"What happened to the other one you met in Venice?"

"Cindy? She's very accomplished. I thought it was over, but apparently not. We met in Lugano last weekend. Something wasn't right. I thought she'd say I'm a decent guy and other happy horse shit, and I thought the 'but' was coming. Not so. She was up in the air, then said she wants to see me. Different day, different opinion? She's fun, she had the weekend organized, maybe too organized ... When she made no plans, it felt like there was nothing to do."

"I told you she sounds boring. Meanwhile, all the women stay in the picture. It is the golden age of Joseph Fine."

"I have been fortunate. Look, these women could all disappear overnight. That's what scares me. DD, she acted like it was predestined, you know, what's supposed to happen. That's the problem I have with her. I'm not clear what the attraction is for Marie. She is hot to trot and intelligent. She gets me. Carter, you would be impressed. And Jen, she came out of nowhere. She acts like my biggest fan. She gets me too. But she's eight years older. She doesn't look it."

"Ask them what they want or what they're looking for. I forgot. Most of them don't know."

"Not sure that's fair, Carter. I think these two know."

"Well, if it all comes crashing down, you'll go back to work, and we'll meet at Minetta Tavern to plan Joseph Fine's next chapter. We'll call it 'Four New Women in Forty Days.'" Minetta is a charming circa 1937, intimate bar and restaurant on MacDougal

Street in Soho. It's always crowded. The liquor is behind stained glass leaded casement windows. I like Minetta almost as much as the King Cole. Carter and I had a double date there five years ago. It went well for him.

I called DD later that day. I made mental notes like "Sorry I'm late, I've been busy." She won't buy it, so I'll keep it simple, stupid. I didn't need to prepare. "Hello, is this Joe?" she said abruptly.

"DD, how are you?" There was a pause. She took a breath, then hung up. She'll feel bad and call back. An hour later, she did.

"Joe, you better break up with that woman. Now get back to New York." I didn't ask her who she meant. Maybe Carter and Anita had a role in this. It didn't matter. I missed the lips, the lungs, and the lipstick. But not the controlling personality. I thought about ending the call on a high note, a soft departure. I didn't bother.

CHAPTER TWENTY-EIGHT

How did she fall into my lap? It was still a mystery to me.

"*You're the inexorable one.*" *Mr. Kramer, the art teacher said to the kid who was in third grade. Mr. Kramer was close to three hundred pounds with a roundish face and a full head of black greasy hair that he combed back. The kid didn't know what inexorable meant but knew it must be something good. Mr. Kramer liked his imagination and the way he thought big.*

Mr. Kramer asked the class to paint a picture that included the American flag. Another flag assignment. The kid painted an astronaut placing an American flag on Mars. Just like Neil Armstrong walked on the moon, someday someone would step foot on the Red Planet. Mr. Kramer liked the painting and held it up for the class to see.

He also threw erasers at kids who talked in class or didn't pay attention. He threw them mostly at two tall stocky boys who were in the lowest reading group. The kid thought maybe tall kids weren't as smart as shorter kids, but there were clearly exceptions like his best friend Jack who was tall and very smart. So, he didn't pigeonhole his classmates. One day, one of the moms called the principal's office and complained about Mr. Kramer. He had thrown the eraser at her son's mouth. The boy had a coughing fit from the chalk dust. Mr. Kramer had to stop throwing erasers. Then he started to grab kids. He had to stop that too. The kid felt sorry for the two boys but did not avoid them or any other kids unless they were complete and incorrigible asswipes.

Another time, the kid was the last one to leave the classroom. Mr. Kramer let him finish a drawing. The teacher said, "Joseph, most of these kids will amount to a bunch of nothing. You keep working hard, you'll do fine."

It was fun telling this story to Marie. Better than the one with Ms. Lipson.

"Did you make that up?" Marie asked. We laughed so hard we rolled off the bed in my room. I was on my back and her top half rested neatly on me. I looked into her dark green eyes, which opened up to fields of fruit trees and lavender.

"Of course not."

"When I was in fifth grade, we were coming into the classroom. I went to sit, and one of the taller boys pulled out the seat from under me. I fell on the floor. I almost cried. The teacher took recess away from him. He couldn't play kickball for a month. "

"So, your views on taller boys were formed at an early age?"

"Not really, but it's a good story. For a while, I thought that most of them were stupid. I should say all of them." Marie put her arms in the air like a maiden in distress. I helped her get up. Marie was returning to Chicago in three days. She added a couple of days for my benefit. When she leaves, I have to make sure the door is open. Marie, please don't close the door on me.

I was excited about a mid-afternoon trip we planned to Villefranche-sur-Mer. It's a small coastal town tucked away just east of Nice with an ancient harbor and beach. On the train, Marie was reading *A Tale of Two Cities* in French. I brought Elmore Leonard's *Glitz* and a little blue notebook. She fell asleep. Her straw hat gave her a classic elegance and made her seem unapproachable. How did she fall into my lap? It was still a mystery to me.

We walked from the train station in Villefranche to the well-preserved medieval section until we came to a fortress. Along the way, we passed several streets with arches going back to the fourteenth century. The old town had a mysterious, isolated feel to it. I bought a chocolate croissant and got chocolate on my upper lip. Marie wiped it off. "Comme un jeune fil," she said like I was a naughty boy.

We left the semi-darkness of the old quarter and sat on the terrace of the Welcome Hotel with a great view of the ancient harbor. The café tables were mostly occupied by single women or couples. We ordered Aperol Spritzes, followed by mussels in garlic wine sauce. There were plenty of toasted baguette pieces to mop up the sauce.

Marie and I talked about family trees. She was French from her mom's parents and Russian on her father's side. The Russians were Jews who left a village near Minsk in the 1910s during the last major wave of immigration through Ellis Island. I told her my great-grandfather came from Odessa. I felt like a kindred spirit to Marie. My mom's side were English Jews and my parents randomly met outside a soda shop on West Third Street in Greenwich Village.

"When I hear these stories, all I can say is God bless America," I said, with my arm around her. Marie liked my plan to stay in France until real progress was made. We ordered more mussels and another spritz. When we were ready to leave, she promptly excused herself. After three more trips to the restroom, I ordered her ginger ale. We stayed put and lost track of time. It was early evening and the streetlights that dotted the harbor created pillars of golden light in the calm green water. Haunting, beautiful, perfectly still. Villefranche-sur-Mer at dusk is the mystery of life, what you think you understand but don't.

We returned to Antibes without any more gastro issues. Marie rested against me on the train. There was fatigue and sadness in her eyes. I didn't want her to get emotional. Was this the last hurrah? I asked her if something was wrong. She shook her head. A few minutes later she said, "I don't want to leave. I want to stay with you."

"But your work? You have a great job."

"I know. And so do you or you did. Well then, when you get back to the USA, will you come to Chicago? Or I'll see you in New York? You should chase your dream, but it would help if we were in the same place. There is very good writing karma in Chicago. Saul Bellow and Studs Terkel. And others. Plenty of inspiration."

"Great writers, for sure. Look, I don't know what to say. I know you more now. I like everything I see." What I liked was her fluid mind and her awesome body. Like me, she wanted her life to evolve in ways she couldn't predict now. A creative, rambling mind, a type of controlled chaos. The way we left it, we'll see each other, sometime in the not-too-distant future. It wasn't enough certainty. She looked like she was going to cry. What am I doing? She cares that much? Now, I was upset too.

She whispered, "Joe, I meet all of your criteria and … I am a great f-u-c…"

"Please don't say it like that."

"OK, well you think about it." It's easy to like someone when they like you. She didn't care about stature or breaking barriers or challenging conventional thought. Like Jen, kind of. I couldn't believe she liked being with me just because … Just because. I couldn't let her get away.

A few minutes passed. Out of the blue, she said, "I'm even the right religion and you didn't even know it." I was hesitant to get into this subject. She brought it up, so it's OK. She was definitely talking relationship.

I said, "So you're Jewish?"

"I was raised Jewish. I went to Hebrew School. I didn't like it. Doesn't that make me Jewish? I went to Taos with an old boyfriend, nice guy, not too stable. We went to a conference on meditation and Buddhism. I kept the Jewish part and added the Buddhist part." Imagine that. She's a Jewish Buddhist. A Ju Bu.

"You don't see many Jews with the name Marie."

"My father liked the name, my mom went along, she likes it now, and they couldn't call me Marcus. He was my mom's grandfather ... Joe, sorry about the F-bomb. I didn't startle you?"

"That is total hypocrisy on my part. You expect it from guys. Women are supposed to be too good to talk like that. If it helps you express yourself, go right ahead."

"Fucking great. Anything you say, Joe."

So, what's the key to contentment? Keep it simple, right? What to do? Spend time with people you want to be with. Do things you like to do. Sure, that should include useful things. I read this in *The Artist's Way*, and it makes guttural sense. I would add, act responsibly when needed.

We got back to Antibes, and I called Richard. It was late evening on the last day he asked for an answer. Late afternoon in New Jersey. I wasn't sure what to say. Make the best imperfect decision, right? Easier to give good advice than to take it. Whatever happens, don't burn any bridges. Can I work and write? Can I multitask? I don't know. Other than making excuses, I've never really tried to do both. Before, all I did was say I couldn't. Interesting. All I did before with women was avoid the taller ones. Is there a pattern here? Have I talked myself into believing anything is possible?

So here goes. Richard picked up after the first ring, which means he was waiting for the call. I heard screaming and barking. He asked me to wait while he found a quiet room. He came back on and said he ran into Samantha, a woman I went out with two years ago. I took her to a party at Richard's house after we finished a deal. She got drunk and irritable and said I mostly cared about getting laid. Not fair. With Samantha, it was the only thing I cared about. Richard properly feigned ignorance when she asked about me.

That was the disarming part of the conversation. "Now for the good part," he said. "What do you think? Hold on, Joe. I need a percussion lead-in." He thought he was funny imitating a drumbeat.

"Richard, I'm grateful and I appreciate everything you've done for me ... I'm staying with the writing life ... For now."

"So full-time is out of the question?"

"Yes. This was tough for me. Very tough."

"Joe, I was ready for this. I should leave it at that. But, for you, Joseph Fine, I'll go to the well one more time. I have another option ... Joe, you know we don't want lawyers to work part-time. It doesn't work. That's what the thinking was. Well, we changed the policy after two female attorneys asked to work part-time. We didn't want to lose them, and we made it clear that we didn't like it and it was a case-by-case decision, and blah, blah, blah. So, the point is ..."

"You're asking me to work part-time?"

"As a fallback, yes, and if it doesn't work for you, I'm done asking. I'm tapped out. You can let me know by the end of the work week. That's it. Carl is breathing down my back to have the legal department fully staffed." Carl Crenshaw is the CEO. "Here's the deal. We're growing like crazy, the stock's rocking, it even went up since you left. You know the mentality, the better we do, the more paranoid we get. Only thing is, you can't get a bonus if you're not full-time. That's a corporate-wide thing."

I had to clear the deck, stop the internal machinations. At some point, this might work. And it's not a forever thing. "I'll do it." As soon as I said it, I thought about reeling it back. No, that's it, I went with my gut, at this hour, at this moment. Part of me wanted to come home. Except for four or five days in Gotham, I have been overseas for over two months. If I can broaden my social life, I can figure out how to work and write. Especially on the terms offered. Damn it, those options looked good. And if I made a mistake, I'll know soon enough. Funny, I benefited from a change that was designed to accommodate female lawyers.

"Great." I couldn't see him, but I could tell he was relieved.

"I need at least a couple of months."

"That won't work. A month."

"A month and a half."

"OK. You're pushing it. I can do that. Don't take it to the bank yet." I know a straw man when I see one. "Oh, and Joe, sorry to throw this out again, but when you get back, go easy on the expletives. Two women, paralegals, complained the other day about a male attorney. I don't need to say who."

"Jesus fucknuts, Richard. They think they run the fucking place ... Of course, I will maintain all appropriate corporate decorum. And Richard, thanks for everything. I know I'm a PITA."

"If I didn't like you so much ... And Carl knows you were amazing on the Stanley Walker acquisition."

My thinking was relatively simple. Like I said, this wasn't a forever decision. I could revisit in a year or two and see what progress I'm making.

With that behind me for now, I stopped at Marie's hotel Monday night. Thankfully, her stomach was better. She sat at the desk finishing work. We talked while I sat on the sofa a few feet away. I didn't mention my conversation with Richard. I nodded off. Marie tapped me. She looked tired. She had an early Tuesday morning flight, and I thought I should go. I decided to tell her about my conversation with Richard. She was glad I made a decision.

"Over here," she said.

"What?"

"Right here. See, on the floor." She pointed to the carpet at the other end of the room. I thought she saw a mouse or a cockroach. Please don't ask me to deal with it. I walked over and looked down. The thick red carpet felt good on my feet. I didn't see anything. She took off her Blackhawks jersey. Unbelievable. "You're supposed to get on the floor."

"What? I thought I was leaving."

"You're a lawyer, Joe. You know the concept of a reservation of rights. I reserved the right to change my mind. Capeesh? Didn't you just change your mind about work? Looks like a good move. You gave it some thought. I gave this some thought. Oh, and could you get the little table out of the way?"

"Yes. Anything else?"

"You can help me out of my shorts. Oh, and take the top sheet off the bed and put it on the floor. The carpet could be itchy."

"Got it."

And Joe and Marie lived happily ever after. Well, for that magical moment.

CHAPTER TWENTY-NINE

"

The landscape has changed.

Every morning is special. Every day is a gift. I'll never get tired of going to Marché Provençal, looking out to sea from the Picasso Museum, or walking around Cap d'Antibes. Or morning coffee at Bacchus and watching women pass by.

I didn't plan to call DD after my last conversation with her. It didn't take much last time to upset her. I'm supposed to view a human being as multi-layered and nuanced. With her, it was difficult. She was still on the bench, but barely. Two days after Marie left, DD called. It was before midnight in the Cote d'Azur, late afternoon in New York. I pictured DD. Her little girl eyes drew me in. Her lips and boobs kept me there. Of course, there is much more to her. I was just having a hard time finding it.

I said hello and heard a meek, soft voice. She sounded restrained. If the conversation goes south, I'm ready.

"Joe, honey, hello, it's me, DD. Joe, I'm so sorry about the last call."

"Hi DD, what do you mean?" I knew full well what she meant.

"Well, I thought about coming to France. I have a week of vacation. I always wanted to see Monaco. Would you like me to visit?" I should have practiced a response. Marie was fresh in my mind. Very fresh. I was ambiguous at best.

So why did I say this? "I think it's a good idea. My work routine is better, but I need to be further along with a first draft first."

Translation: "I can't concentrate if you come so maybe you shouldn't."

"Oh, maybe you're not sure because you have a wench running around with you in Antibes." That didn't take long. Get ready to tune out.

"What are you talking about?"

"You know what I'm talking about."

"No, really?"

"You must have been texting Carter. My friend, Liza, you remember Liza? We went to his apartment. He was in the bathroom, and he said to come in. His phone was on the coffee table, and you texted him about a Marie, and there was another one too."

"She's a friend."

"I'm not going to respond to that. What do you fucking lawyers say? It doesn't pass the smell test? Everybody's mad at you. My mom, my dad, my sister, and Liza blames Carter for encouraging you. I don't blame Carter …

"Joe, you had me. I was ready to make you soooooo happy. I'm an old-fashioned girl. I have a good job, but I believe in making my guy's life easy." I almost choked. "And now it's gone. My father is trying to start his life again fresh. If he sees you, he could end up in jail again." That's a good selling point. I stared at the wall. Carter will owe me drinks for the rest of his life. She continued. "Now, what are we going to do?"

She gave me the opening I needed. "I guess that's it."

"That's it?"

"Sounds like there's not much point."

"I want to get together. I can let it go if you're good."

I was trapped. "I don't know. I …" That's all she needed. Any evidence of equivocation. She hung up. It took longer than I thought.

The landscape has changed. Jesus Christ, I'm down to two women. If I don't count Jen. I don't know how to count her. Let's just say she's the X factor. We'll put her in a special category. And I can't include Leslie. That train left. It's amazing. I don't think anyone cared about me as much as DD. Those eyes. Sweet, big, and innocent to the world. Will I regret this someday? Thankfully, there's no storage room in my brain for regrets, and yet ... her two beautiful globes will stay in a guarded vault in the dark recesses of my mind.

I pretended the call with DD was like practicing law. Of course, it wasn't. With legal work, you win some, you lose some. You get a great result, the judge takes your position, you're vindicated, you saved the company millions of dollars. Then you lose a motion, the mediation goes nowhere, or the deal falls apart. It happens, you can't take it personally. With DD, there isn't a multi-million-dollar claim to defend. It's not about money or corporate reputation. It's worse. It's personal.

With DD, the deal I thought was a good fit, wasn't. With too much risk, it's time to move on. I gave myself credit for good judgment. Which meant not deferring to her judgment. I reluctantly placed DD in the outbox for relationships that didn't make it. Was my action influenced by the goal of a meaningful relationship with a taller woman? Was it an unconscious factor? I hope not, I don't think so, but ... At some point, I would narrow the field of women or have it narrowed for me. The question was when.

I was up early the next morning to see the sunrise. The yellow, orange, and blue sky appeared with no clouds in sight. I ran into Marguerite again. She couldn't have been friendlier although I never followed up on her invitation. I told her about my plans, and she was excited. She said, "Now, hurry and find the right lady before she marries an imbecile."

What an inspiration. After that, I took the ritual walk to Bacchus. I joined Dennis who was talking to another salon owner. She was a blonde version of a youthful Susan Sarandon. OMG. I splurged and got a piece of broccoli quiche to go with the double espresso and milk. Absolutely delicious and arguably healthy. It looked like a great day ahead. Until the evil demon showed his face, and I started to second-guess myself. I considered calling Richard back to say I made a mistake. My better judgment said, don't you dare. Let the dust settle. Get through some good workdays.

I was pleasantly distracted by twin blond curly-haired boys about five years old who kicked a soccer ball to each other outside Bacchus. They walked up to me and said their names, Jean and Louis. They asked me to kick the ball with them. I looked around and didn't see a parent or adult. Someone must be nearby. I took a sip of coffee and got up. The twins told me where to stand to make a triangle. We kicked the ball to each other. Then, each boy kicked the ball by me and cheered like he scored a goal. I gestured that I kicked the ball very far when I was in school.

Two women approached from the other side of Cours Masséna. I guessed they were the boys' mother and grandmother. The boys yelled, "Ma Ma."

The mother said, "Vous avez un ami." She told them it was time to go to the market. She looked at me. "Bonjour. Are you Joseph?"

"Yes."

"You know Marie. I am her sister, Nancie, and this is our mother, Sophie. I am visiting. She lives in Villefranche-sur-Mer." I saw the resemblance. Nancie was older, shorter, and heavier than Marie, and had long jet-black hair and sharp features like her sister. Sophie was an older version of Nancie. Both women wore print dresses. Sophie probably turned heads in her day.

I said, "Bonjour."

Nancie said, "Nice to meet you. Marie talked about you. We got together a few nights ago. I live in the Chicago area too."

"So, you knew it was me? This is not a joke?"

"No, not a joke. Marie knows the café you like. She wanted us to meet you. Ah, too bad she had to go back to Chicago so soon."

I said to Sophie, "Your daughter is quite a woman ... The boys are adorable." Always helps to mention the kids.

"She said you will be a famous writer."

"She's too kind. We'll see." Nancie and Sophie were down-to-earth and very polite. We talked while I kicked the ball with the boys for a few more minutes. I high-fived the twins and waved goodbye. "Au revoir, Jean et Louis." The boys asked me to go to the market. I said thank you, but I needed to go and do my work. I said "work" loud enough to make it sound important. I assumed the mom or sister would debrief Marie. Que sera, sera. I didn't want to be sabotaged by female family members. It happened before.

I called Marie later in the day to tell her. She said she told them about me. She didn't suggest they stop by. She paused. "Joe."

"Yes."

"They loved the way you played with the boys ... My mom said she's not sure ..."

"Not sure about what?"

"Not sure about you. I told them that they don't know you, and this is my business."

"Thanks, I appreciate that." I was simmering.

"It was silly, my mother wondered if you're old enough or have your feet on the ground." That made no sense. I was four years older than Marie.

"Anything else?"

"I didn't like this. She thought I should go out with someone who is more mature."

"I played with your nephews. Cute kids. I love to kick the ball around."

"I don't think that's it. I know what she meant. Joe, I got angry. My sister has beautiful boys, her husband is six-two, a big talker, and a deadbeat. When I told my mom more about you, she backed off. She was impressed. Naturally, I agreed."

I was more upset than angry. The tears surfaced and I squashed them. Fortunately, she couldn't see me. I waited a few seconds. Women are so easily influenced. I think Marie stands on her own.

"Joe, are you there?"

"I wish you were here, or I was there." I considered saying the three magic words, but I couldn't do it.

"As soon as you're back." She sounded upbeat.

This exchange brought me back. Toward the end of law school, I dated a nursing student named Sandra, or Sandy, for four weeks. I remember the time frame because I took the bar exam two days after she broke it off. She had a warm, beautiful smile and eyes that opened to the sky. Eyes that carried me. At first, she liked me. Well, that's how she acted. She helped me advance on the physical front and always complimented my moves.

Sandy invited me to her parents' house for dinner two weeks after I met her. I went against my better judgment. During dinner, I was fidgety. Her mom couldn't stop asking me questions. Her father didn't have much to say all evening and sat there with a blank expression. Sandy seemed comfortable. At some point, I realized my shirt wasn't tucked in. I got up to fix it. Her mom was staring, wondering. Sandy was particularly quiet on our way back to her apartment. Three weeks later it was over. When we broke up, or when Sandy broke it off, she said her mom thought she needed someone more grown-up, more mature. A code word for something else? The Inner Voice thought so. "Yes, short."

I was upset about that fateful evening, but the five weeks were well worth it. I also passed two bar exams that summer, which was worth a lot more than another month or two of a relationship that might have run its course when my attention faded. I think about Sandy once in a while. And I wonder what might have been if she wasn't easily influenced.

CHAPTER THIRTY

▐▐

... don't forget the rain check. I haven't.

Not bad, not bad at all. I increased the work time for the next two weeks. It was a steep uphill climb. Not easy, but the output was gratifying. I was determined to finish strong. Raw pride says I needed something to show for my time here.

Assuming I continue to advance, how about a dramatic ending, like a raucous party, before I leave? Lisette has become more sociable in the last two weeks. Maybe she would let me host an event. No point in talking to Bernard.

The idea quickly fizzled when I thought about who would not make it. Carter is in New York, Marie is across the Atlantic in Chicago, Cindy is in Basel on the way to New Jersey, Leslie is sculpting models in Bologna, Bruce is back in the USA, and Jack is on his way to the annual Berkshire Hathaway annual meeting in Omaha, where they serve hot dogs and French fries. Jen shuttles between Boston, where she lives, and New York, where she plays. Yes, Dennis is close by and his salon friend was interesting. There are Marie's friends Camille and Amélie. Margo and Patrice? Ok, I don't know many locals. So much for a raucous party.

The next morning, I was about to leave the house as usual. Lisette was on her knees in the patio garden. She wore faded jeans and a navy V-neck T-shirt. She asked if I have a moment. We sat at the glass table on the patio. Another bright sunny day. I wish I could save the sunshine.

"How are you?" She acted surprised that I asked.

"Jolly well. I'll tell you why. And you?"

"Doing well, but it's tough, I'm leaving in four weeks."

"That, Joseph, is too bad. Now, Bernard is traveling to Lyon next weekend to see his children. I thought it was a good excuse to have a banging fun time. I'm inviting the ex-pats for a Summer Soirée. My bezzies." I suspected something was up with her and Bernard.

"Bezzies?"

"Bezzies, my dear local friends. Mostly my lady mates. You're welcome to come, invite a friend or two. You've been a good tenant, so this is for you too."

"Thanks, that's so kind. My invitee list will be sparse. Almost everyone I know is somewhere else. I'll help you."

She shrugged. "No, not necessary."

"No, I insist, and thank you, this is a great idea." She smiled warmly. I love to prepare for a party. It's almost as fun as the event itself. I viewed the party as a last hurrah, a grand finale with all of the suspects present. Friends of Lisette's? Probably too old, but no point in speculating.

Last night, Carter's Aunt Anita conveniently told me that her next tour group to Venice was the last week in June. She wanted to stop first in Antibes. So, there's a possible invitee. It dawned on me that Jen could show up too. She's a mere 3795 miles from here. I called Anita later in the day. The gist of it was, "Yes, please drop in, and please, no surprises." Anita knew what I meant. She said she understood. Of course, "understood" can be a vague, elusive word. You can understand something all day long without agreeing to it.

"Oh, so you have feelings for her?" No point in responding. She interpreted my silence as "yes" anyway.

I called Carter and told him about my exchange with Anita. "Kindly talk to your aunt."

He called back the next day. "I tried Big Fella. Too late and it wouldn't have mattered." Maybe he's just busting my balls.

I called Anita. "She's coming, right?"

"Joe, this is good, now there's no surprise. It will be fine. You know, she's an accomplished woman with a lot of poise."

"OK, and I want to know what you did or what you and Carter did to sabotage me with DD. I cut it off, but you helped."

"Joe, you know Carter assisted. We didn't do anything. Now, if you didn't break up with her, we were prepared to say you were making a big mistake. Ask Liza. DD's family is dysfunctional, and her father is the kind of guy who would send a hit man after you if you upset his sweet little daughter. You know what? We don't need to upset your landlady's party. We'll see you separately."

"No, just come over. You might as well. She told me to invite people." I thought if she's ready to stop here, why discourage her? I want to be welcoming, don't I? As for Jen, I could always call her and suggest a separate get-together. No, let her come to the party. At some point, I need to think about her age. I'll be back soon enough to think about it. I shut out everything and went to work. Lisette turned this into a great day. I finally got to know her. A kicking, screaming, feeling human being.

After work that day, I took the train from Antibes to the tiny train station at Beaulieu-sur-Mer. From there, I went on a long, invigorating walk around Cap Ferrat, a gorgeous seascape of a peninsula with a pedestrian path and elegant homes. Cindy texted and asked how I was faring. She did use the word "faring," like I was a sea captain. When I daydream, I'm more like Starbucks, the shipmate, sitting on the masthead in *Moby Dick*. I didn't tell her I'm returning in a few weeks. Hold on to that card.

Of the women I met during my time away, Cindy seemed the most stable. I hate to agree with Carter. Stable is good, but it can border on boring. I don't know if there was enough to keep me entertained. She would be my top choice for a coach in the youth soccer league. Serious and disciplined. She provided practical bench strength. I held on to her to maintain my social life safety net. Did she hang on to me for the same reason? I needed a fluid personality to stay interested.

And Leslie, who I had all but forgotten, checked in. She wanted to know what I was doing (so did I) and asked if there was a midpoint like Milan to meet. Leslie was a great kid, just too scattered. That's who she was. In five years, she could be on terra firma, but I couldn't press the pause button for that long. At this time, Marie was the right mix of intelligence, beauty, sexual energy, and grounding. Hard to put all of those adjectives on the same line. And of course, she met the stature objective. They all did.

All right, should I invite Leslie or Cindy to Lisette's party? They are too far away so it probably doesn't matter. Bologna is closer than Basel, so I started with Leslie. She was surprised by the invitation and very thankful. Unfortunately, she was occupied with school. She was also strapped financially. That was enough for me. I wasn't flying her to Nice. And she didn't sound overly warm and fuzzy. Then I tried Cindy. She couldn't go either. She was getting ready to return to the States for her new position in New Jersey. She said it had a big upside potential three times. Two would have been fine. So, I won't be far away in the USA. I'm glad I reached out and sprinkled some goodwill. Maybe I'm still on her radar.

Finally, there were Margo and Patrice, the teachers from Kansas City. I called Margo, and she didn't recognize my voice. I mentioned the café in Nice. "Oh, Joe, that's right. How did you get my number? Oh yes, my card." She was excited about the chance to interact with real live locals. They were going home the day after the party.

I worked harder than ever the next ten days. The only break was a train ride to Monaco two days before the party. I was curious about the Casino. Ornate and decadent. Just the way it looked in the movie *Casino Royale*, minus the violence. A lavish facade and ostentatious interior ideal for losing money. As luck had it, the planets were aligned, and I left the roulette table more than three hundred euros ahead. Then I lost more than four hundred at blackjack.

Back in Antibes, I stopped at the Carrefour near Marché Provençal and bought Aperol, champagne, lemons, limes, mixers, and lottery tickets. And gin for the Brits. Lisette had unopened bottles of Absolut and French whiskey. I forgot the Picholine olives and ran back for them. Lisette was walking to her Fiat as I approached the house. I held up the bottle of champagne. She said, "Put it in the fridge, and we'll drink it when I am back. Merci."

I went inside, put ice, vodka, and fresh-squeezed lemon juice into a cocktail glass, and stirred vigorously. Can you drink like a writer if you're not one yet? You can act the part as long as you do the part. I took the drink and sat on a tulip chair on the patio. A moderate sea breeze was what the doctor ordered after a hot, humid afternoon. I finished the drink and topped it off. Lisette returned from the fish market. I heard the front door open. She called me. "I'm back here," I said, and opened the door to the kitchen. "Do you need help?"

"No, the post office needs help. I ordered two books, and it's been two weeks. One of them is the Peter Mayle book you were reading, *Hotel Pastis*. He's a bloke, you know. Well, let's have some champagne."

"I would have given you my copy. I'm almost done."

"If it doesn't come soon, I accept your offer."

I took the champagne from the fridge and found two champagne glasses. Through the kitchen, I saw the blinds were up in the living room. Even with bright sunlight streaming in, the room looked cold and unwelcoming. I joined her at the patio table.

Lisette changed from her gardening clothes. She wore a red and white shirt dress with an open collar. A classically pretty dress, slightly loose fitting and perfect for summer in a beach town. The top three buttonholes were unbuttoned. I poured the drinks. She leaned over to take a glass of champagne before I could hand it to her. It wasn't any effort to see she didn't wear a bra. Her breasts were floating in the air like small balloons. I wondered if this was intentional. Something was bothering her. Maybe the champagne would make it go away.

"Well, so here we are," she said nervously and sat back in her chair. "Bernard left this morning for Lyon. I think that's where he went. I don't know for sure. His ex-wife and children are there. I think he has a girlfriend there too. Or somewhere. I don't care. He's the biggest bore. When he's here, he's not here. Isn't that terrible? If you're alive, why not act it?"

"I'm sorry to hear that." I was sorry I had to listen too. She wanted to talk, and I'm the captive audience.

She perked up. "Well, we have champagne and we are celebrating, young man."

"Sure. What are we celebrating?"

"That Bernard left, and I feel better already. And the soirée can be the preview for your first book party ... I'm being silly." She looked away, then turned to me. "Now, Joseph, I must be serious for a moment." I didn't like her tone and thought about escaping to the bathroom. I waited too long. "Marie, your girlfriend."

"Yes, so? She went back to the States." I looked around the room. I don't want to talk about Marie.

"I saw how she looks at you. She lights up." I tried not to stare at Lisette's open dress. "Joseph, have you been told that you don't pay attention?"

"Yes, and I'm sorry. I don't mean to be rude. I think she sees me in a positive way."

She moved her chair closer to me. I don't know why, but I was concerned this could happen.

"So, you're not too serious yet?"

"We'll see."

"So, this is fine, so to speak?" She leaned over and kissed me. And then a longer kiss. She was just about in my lap. I was dumbfounded. Should I feel guilty?

"That was good?" she asked seriously, then smiled.

"Very good. Just surprised. Quite surprised."

"The best kind of surprise. I'm not too old, right?"

What do I say? "Right. You're fine." I'm glad I had a drink before this. I tried to relax.

"Now, for the next surprise.' She undid the next five buttons. Then she slipped out of the shirtdress. Yes, her breasts were on the small side, but nicely proportional to her thin frame. Not bad at all. Now, what should I do? I assume I know what she wants. If I get serious with Marie or Cindy, or even Jen, I don't want Lisette to complicate my life. Six months from now, it might not matter. But I don't know that. For peace of mind, I have to pass. I said, "I can't go ahead with this. You are very attractive, and it would be fun. I ..."

"No, don't say anything." She put her finger to her mouth. "You can have a rain check." She handed me an imaginary piece of paper. "I wanted to see how much you liked her." Lisette took my hand and held it tightly. "Oh, mon Dieu, Joseph, my little boy, you must care very much for her." It wasn't just that. I will be under Lisette's roof for another three weeks.

I'm glad I didn't proceed. I liked Lisette, but it's not worth the possible headaches, even for this one time. She was upset. I was caught in a buzzsaw of emotions. I awkwardly patted her on the back. She took a pillow from a tulip chair and knocked over a lamp in the living room. The bulb shattered. I hope she doesn't blame me for this. She breathed in and out. "That felt good. Well, the party has started." She smiled awkwardly. If it helped her bounce back, that's great. She said, "Let's have another drink."

We switched to vodka with lemon and soda. I put my arm around her, like a good friend providing support. She liked to be held and it was easy and comfortable given her slight frame. A little attention goes a long way. I suspect Bernard ignored her a long time.

After a few moments, she asked me to open the blinds. She was happy, as if nothing happened, and said, "Joseph, the late day sun, it's the brightest it's been all day." The light hit the dark wood hutch and coffee table in the living room. It was strange. The room no longer looked sad or empty. This unassuming townhouse, the charming Vieil Antibes, the bustling market, the coast, and the sea. It's too beautiful for sad thoughts to linger.

"Joseph, don't forget the rain check. I haven't."

CHAPTER THIRTY-ONE

> **You peel away the layers until you see something you like or not.**

The following day, Friday, we went into high gear for Saturday's party. Lisette put me in charge of the bar. She was in good spirits and didn't exhibit any resentment from yesterday. I got to know her more in the last twenty-four hours than I did the six weeks before.

Lisette's email invitation encouraged guests to bring a poem to read, either original or by someone else. Lisette took an American literature class at the University of Leeds and loved *Leaves of Grass*. She liked to read poetry while sipping Scotch. I had a dog-eared book of poems by E. E. Cummings, and read her one called, *In Just-* She loved it and told me to read it at the party. It was great to see her relaxed with so much energy.

"Joseph, I have old maps of Antibes and Nice on the walls. They're interesting, but they are too serious. I should have prints or posters that have splashy bold colors. Let's turn this place on its head. Bernard always told me he has a keen artistic sense. Then why did he decorate with gloomy-looking furniture and depressing old maps? Why didn't I say anything? But first, I'm buying a new outfit. Come with me. I'll look for a dress, and you go back to the market. One of the merchants sells red pepper and kalamata hummus. It's heaven with a drink."

"As long as you wait until four o'clock. Or go ahead. My work comes first."

"Yes sir. Or is it, captain, sir?" I laughed at her military-like response. We were almost pals. A woman friend can be a good sounding board. She can also be tricky. And after yesterday's events, well ... Let's just say, Lisette inspired me on the creative front. The words flowed. I rode an enormous wave that kept going.

We walked toward the market. She barely had time for one dress shop. There was a flower shop on Cours Masséna that stayed open until early evening. I picked a bouquet of tulips and roses. I met Lisette outside the shop, and we stopped at a crêperie on Rue Thuret, just off Cours Masséna, on the way back. We ordered crêpes with Nutella, strawberries, and bananas. Arno the cook placed a thin layer of batter on the round metal griddle, added the chocolate and fruit, and folded it to make the finished product. No extra charge for whipped cream. We sat outside and enjoyed it, while a steady stream of people walked by on this pedestrian-only street.

Lisette was eager to go back. She left, while I sat and savored every bite. I called Marie, hoping time and distance had not changed anything. It sounded like she was in an airport. I couldn't hear and called again. She was in the Austin, Texas terminal. "Joe, this is a great city for a work trip. The best Indian food. Thai and Middle Eastern too. And great barbecue. Do you know about Stubb's Bar-B-Q? I got indigestion last night, but it was worth it. Joe, it's a great country, isn't it?"

"Yes, a wonderful country."

"Joe, dear, I have to go through security for Chicago. Got to go. Love you. Bye." She was in a rush but had enough time to say the word. I was relieved there was no time to respond.

I ordered an espresso macchiato which bought me another half hour of people-watching at the crêperie. Across the street near the corner of Cours Masséna, a policewoman talked to a woman who didn't seem to be a local. The policewoman pointed in the direction of Lisette's house. The woman was confused and thought she was supposed to go in the other direction. The policewoman grew impatient, and the woman raised her voice. "I thought this is how people in Paris act, not here in the Cote d'Azur." The policewoman walked away. Another American who thinks you owe her something.

The woman turned. I looked, then looked again. I couldn't tell, and then she turned more. It was Jen. She looked different. Her dirty blonde hair was tied back, and the ponytail went through the back of her Boston Red Sox baseball cap. White slacks, blue polo, and a short red blazer. Blue sandals with a two-inch heel. "Joe, darling, how are you?"

I greeted her with a lukewarm embrace. Her touch was immediately familiar. "Well, well, the Red Sox have come to play."

"Joe, this is not a coincidence. I arrived today. I didn't want to trouble you. You told me you wander around late in the day after writing your opus. I know you like to shop and drink coffee or just drink, so I thought Cours Masséna was a good bet. I saw a perfume store on this street and stopped to look. I was disoriented, so I asked for help. This police lady has no manners." Just what I expect from Jen. She's the storm that blows in and lights up the sky. "Oh, I'm staying a half-mile from where you live. I wouldn't ask to stay."

I smiled as if to say, "I can't believe you."

"Now, Joe, I want a better hug than that." I complied. I smelled the familiar perfume. It was like being with her in New York. She went on. "I found the best bar in Antibes, the Absinthe Bar. It's at the corner of Cours Masséna and Rue Sade. Two streets over. Let's go. The bar is in the basement. The stairway creaks. It's very mysterious. Joe, I never tried absinthe. I heard it makes you a little crazy."

"I heard the same thing." No need to say I went there before the Lugano trip. I pointed to the cart. "Jen, I need to bring this stuff back to the house. Supplies for the party. I offered to help Lisette. We'll get a drink later. I promise." She puffed out her lower lip.

It was a month since I saw her in New York. Probably too soon to go into this, but … "Jen, help me out. I'm very fond of you. Ooh, that sounds so British, doesn't it? But you want this to last?"

"Why not?" She lowered the decibel level. "First, I wasn't sure. I thought so. You know, the age thing. Then again, who fucking cares?" She didn't ask me if I cared. "Jesus Christ, Joe, last time when you were climbing all over me and then under me, I thought, where does he get these ideas? His mind goes in multiple directions, and I guess his body follows. I couldn't wait for the next adventure. If this ends, I'll lose it." I looked around. I hope no one was listening. Between the expat Brits and the Americans, there are a lot of people who speak English here.

I prepared this line for the right moment. "When you're smaller, you're more versatile. Well, you can be. I got carried away. It's fun, isn't it?"

"No doubt about it. What about now?"

"Really, thank you, I have to get back. Lisette's expecting the food. Let's meet later at Absinthe Bar."

"Well, OK," she said grudgingly.

"Listen, Jen, just promise me you won't get too crazy when you're at Lisette's house. She's been very nice to me."

"You don't trust me."

"I don't."

"As well you shouldn't. Joe, I'm trying to stay calm. My husband hired a balls to the wall lawyer. Mine's better. Still …"

"Jen, breathe deeply, then exhale. You'll be fine. You're in good shape. All the way around."

"I'm getting there. He can't pay me enough for the great sex I gave him." I covered my ears. Can't some things remain unspoken?

"He'll never have it better. It's all a bunch of hubris. That's a good use of the word?"

"It's good enough. I get it."

"I'm so glad I'm here. I can breathe."

"Take a nap. We'll meet later."

"Yes."

Lisette was working in the kitchen when I returned. I felt a quiet calm. I need to stay detached in what could become a volatile situation with her and Jen. She looked at the roses and tulips. "Perfect, we'll put them out on the patio unless it gets too humid. Joseph, could you please pour me a drink. Vodka, soda, lime, just like before. You remember earlier today?"

"Yes, it's coming back now."

"He forgets already." She threw a wet dish towel at me.

I made the drinks, squeezed every drop from the lime slices into the glasses. We went to the patio, where it was more humid than yesterday. The sky turned dark. Scary dark. "Joseph, the olives, we need our Picholine olives."

"Yes, mum, I got them yesterday."

"Of course. Joseph, I hope you invited some people."

I needed a carefully crafted answer. "Two women, for now. One is my friend's aunt. She lives in New York. She runs high-end tours for high maintenance people. And the aunt has a friend. They're on their way to Venice for another tour."

"But no gentlemen?"

"Sorry, my café friends went back to the States. One of them is a serial philanderer. He would have made the evening entertaining but chaotic."

"Same thing with a couple of my friends. Maybe we need extra security?" she joked.

"No, I assume your friends are proper and well behaved," I said rather solemnly.

"Quite the contrary. They are very animated. Mostly English ladies who have a place in the south here. Three intact couples, as far as I know. The others left their husbands or vice versa. One of my newly single friends, you know what she said? 'I'm tired of taking care of men. Bunch of big babies. If I like a guy, let me sleep with him once a month, then he can go home and take care of himself. Come back next month for the old shagaroo. No tension, no rows. No responsibility' ... I get her point, but I think you need more. I need to talk. I need interaction."

"Makes sense. I do too."

"I mean, we're not fucking rabbits." I think she meant "rabbits fucking."

She asked me for another drink, which I diluted more than the last one. I excused myself, went out front, and texted Jen. I was ready to go to Absinthe Bar. She said the jet lag caught up with her. She knows I promised a drink, but she would rather get together in the morning.

Lisette was on the phone when I returned. The person she talked with was upset. Lisette tried to calm her down. I heard a voice say, "I'll kick his hairless arse out." And then, "Fucking wanker." Lisette invited the friend over for tea, but she was too upset. And then the coup de gras. Her friend said, "After he met me, he said I was a banger. Well, fuck him three ways up his arse ... I'll be alright. Cheers. See you Saturday."

Lisette hung up. "This woman is crazy. It's my old friend Kate. She gets too dramatic. I told her to stick with English blokes, even Americans. This François wanted a threesome, and she went ballistic. I think that's disgusting. Joseph, you are a one-woman man?"

"One at a time is plenty."

"Right. By the way, have you changed your mind?" I guess I didn't get much of a reprieve from Lisette. This still would lead to no good. It sounds funny, but I can't give in. I thought about difficult decisions I made as a young attorney. This one was tougher. Before I responded, she said, "Just kidding," then plopped herself in my lap and wrapped her arms around me. She said, "Don't you Yanks say heavy petting is OK for the second date? Emily Post says it's fine even if there's another woman in the picture. You haven't proposed to anyone, right?"

I just looked at her. We did what she proposed, and we stayed loosely within the set boundaries. This went on for a few minutes. You can use your imagination. Be assured, I made no effort to go for the home run. She got up quickly when she remembered to put the puff pastry with brie in the oven.

Lisette was pretty in a simple, unassuming way. And livelier than her modest appearance suggested. It's easy to mistake a reserved person for someone who is disinterested. One more reason you don't judge a woman by her cover. You peel away the layers until you see something you like or not.

The next morning, I met Jen at Bacchus. I watched the clock to keep to my writing schedule. She admired that. Still, she thought I was being a bit rigid and reminded me that she was only in Antibes for two days. Jen was the model for spontaneity and acted like she didn't give a shit about just about anything. I said, "Tell you what. Let's spend the rest of the morning doing what you would like to do. Picasso museum, the beach, a long walk on Cap Ferrat? It's captivating. I'll go to work this afternoon. Good?"

"How come fooling around wasn't on your list?" She looked at me like I was dumber than dirt.

"I thought it would be too forward and lack gravitas."

"You lost me. What's with you and gravitas, darling? Let's go." You can only apply a rational decision-making process to your love life for so long.

CHAPTER THIRTY-TWO

ʻʻ

It's people like you who obstruct progress in the world.

Lisette's long oak kitchen table was set with cold poached salmon, tomato caprese, ratatouille, salad niçoise, and five kinds of olives. A string of tiny blue lights ran over the back slide door to the patio. The booze and mixers were on the patio table that served as the bar. Lisette put blank name tags out for guests. I ran out and got some ice. One hour to showtime.

I drove up the wrong street and panicked for several minutes before I figured my way back. I think I could have walked to the store faster, given the one-way and pedestrian-only streets. Anyway, it's better to arrive later at the party. You have more control over who to mingle with. I parked and walked through the house to the patio and handed the twenty-something bartender the ice. I also gave him a ten euro note. He didn't expect it and lit up.

Lisette looked lovely with a dark-gray sleeveless cocktail dress. It was touching to see the effort she made to present herself. So far, fifteen or so people were here, mostly ladies, early middle-aged, and two older codgers. About half were single or people going solo. *Beast of Burden* played on Spotify. I'm being piggish, but the song reminds me of disgruntled women. Lisette waved to introduce me to some of her friends. I got a drink and came over. Anita and Jen were late, which was fine. It gave them a smaller window for anything dramatic.

Most of the people I met were Brits who lived here part of the year. There was a cacophony of English accents. To my American ear, they sounded delightful. Also, two French women who owned art galleries in Vieil Antibes. One of the galleries was on Cours Masséna, a few storefronts from Bacchus. The other one was off Cours Masséna, on Rue Georges Clémenceau, another lively street.

Lisette introduced me as a former U.S. government official who is working on a self-help book. I said, "It's an unconventional look at relationships." That got a lot of smiles, except from a perky little lady with two chipped teeth named Pam, who said, "You're just a lad. What do you know about relationships?"

"I don't. I made it up based on my limited experience."

"You're married?"

"No, but I've had significant others for very limited periods."

"Well, you're surely an expert then."

"I thought I had something to say," I said, with thoughtful reflection. She shook her head and went to the punch bowl.

One of Lisette's friends introduced herself as Jocelyn Montford. She was an accountant from Manchester and directed a nonprofit organization that dealt with climate change. I liked her enthusiasm. She was too anti-business for my taste, but if you spent all of your time in her world, you might think that way too. I told her not to bash industry. "They're the ones that come up with technology to reduce the carbon footprint. It's best to work together."

She liked that. "We should talk more. You might be good on our board of directors."

"Thanks. I'm occupied for now. Can you put me on your mailing list?"

"Absolutely. I'll stay in touch."

I went to the bar for another drink and waited behind a man. He turned around and said, "Terrence O'Neil. My wife dragged me here, what about you?"

"Joseph Fine. Nobody dragged me, but I know the hostess. She's my landlord."

"Do you know Felicity? She's the buxom one with long wavy brown hair and glittery dress." Terrence pointed to her in the back of the patio.

"No."

"She's a big pain in the arse. Fucking know-it-all. Her husband's my friend. He's not here. Lucky guy."

She was the same lady I heard when I brought in the ice. Anyone within thirty feet could hear her. She talked to four women who seemed to listen attentively as they held their martinis. "The little runt. Nigel, he broke up with my girlfriend Ivy. He was five-four, no, he was less than that. She was about five-one and very attractive. So, pretty close as height goes. He went off with another woman. She's four inches taller than him. You know, until he gained a few pounds in the old tum tum, he wore a boy's suit. He acts like a cad. Like some kind of a London playboy. What nerve." She laughed, a deep throaty laugh.

One of her friends reacted. "Well, is he accomplished? And what was her story ... You know, two sides of the story."

"That, Fiona, is beside the point. Little squirt."

The bartender handed me the vodka, lime, and extra olives. I walked by Felicity. She suddenly stopped talking. I thought about saying something and let it go.

"Is that him?" another lady whispered to Felicity, pointing to me.

"No, no, but he was about the same height as Ivy's ex-boyfriend."

Anita and Jen stood on the patio next to the kitchen slide door. I waved and called their names. Anita waved back and Jen walked toward me. She stopped and glared at Felicity. Within seconds, Jen erupted. "Who, the fuck, do you think you are insulting people who are short? Maybe you mean shorter than you and smarter than you?" I appreciated the sentiment but would have preferred to be a fly on the wall at that moment. "You know my friend Joseph here? He's a great guy, an accomplished attorney and writer, and ... And a better fuck than anything you'll ever get. And he's ..." She smiled deviously and looked at me to say something.

"Five feet three ... and one half," I said meekly.

"There you go. Now if this guy Nigel you're badmouthing was a douchebag or a wanker, just say that. But don't assume short guys are persona non grata, you self-righteous old bag." Jen had to catch her breath. "You ladies who aren't attached would do well to consider shorter guys, you know, include them in the mix." Felicity stood there and froze. Her friends were silent. The one named Fiona said under her breath, "Oh my God."

Lisette came out from the kitchen. "I heard somebody screaming. I couldn't tell what happened with the music playing. Is everybody OK?" she asked graciously. A number of guests faced her. Nobody said anything. One of the gentlemen said, "No, somebody dropped a drink and overreacted." That got a subdued laugh, but the patio stayed relatively quiet.

"OK, everyone," Lisette said. "I want to introduce our guests from far away. In case you haven't met him, this is Joseph Fine, he's been my tenant for almost two months. He's been a big help. And these are his friends from the States, Anita and Jen." I tapped Lisette on the arm and told her my friend Dennis was here too.

"Oh yes. Dennis Laporte, too," she said, and they put all their hands up. "Dennis is in Joseph's morning coffee group."

After that, the party became more sedate and no one asked about the poetry reading. Anita and Jen had plenty to drink. Jen talked to a guy who was with his significant other. I went to the bar, and she came over. I said, "That was ... well, you were awfully good."

"That's all you can say?" Jen winked. "Do you think I was a little strong?" She rubbed her hands together and laughed mischievously. "That bitch will think twice before she mouths off again." Jen was pleased with herself. I almost felt bad for Felicity, even though she deserved it.

Later in the evening, when the crowd started to thin, Felicity came up to me. "I'm sorry if I offended you. I must say, your friend is crazy," she said matter of factly. I thought she was about to say more, but she stopped.

I said, "Don't worry, it's OK." I was too nice. Yes, she offended me. And I don't like qualified apologies with 'IF I did this or that.'

"She must think you're something."

"I think so."

"Incredible." She shook her head like she couldn't understand what Jen saw in me.

I struggled to say something. "It's people like you who obstruct progress in the world." I walked away.

Jen stayed on an even keel for the rest of the evening. There was plenty to eat and drink and most of the guests were lively and engaging. Jen and Anita enjoyed talking to Lisette. Dennis flirted with Jocelyn. I could hear her ask him if the hair color he uses at the salons is biodegradable. I'm sure he was prepared.

At the end of the party, Lisette introduced me to a friend named Jon, who showed up late. "He's a good chap. We're leaving for another party." She didn't say if he was a friend or boyfriend. "Joe, you three are in charge," meaning Anita, Jen, and me. Jon and Lisette left.

I made coffee for her friends, Brooke and Vanessa, who drank too much. Brooke said, "Felicity isn't normally like that. She was quite the bitchy bitch. I wouldn't go out with a short guy either, but God bless you if that's what you want." It was too late for a confrontation. I walked outside with them just as Vanessa puked on the front walk.

That left Jen, Anita, and me. "One more for the road?" Jen asked. Anita and I had enough. "Oh, I hate to drink alone." We gave in and had a shot. The humidity disappeared. It was almost chilly outside.

Anita said Carter sent his regards and said I should behave myself. I imagined we were in New York at a rooftop bar waiting for Carter to show up. Anita went to the bathroom. Jen looked at me, "God, I am crazy about you. I was glad to help. Oh, and Joe, Lisette spoke highly of you. I bet you like her accent. She smiled when she said your name. You're not doing it with her, are you?"

"Well ..." I wanted a few seconds to pass. "Absolutely not." I was so pleased for anticipating this moment.

"You big liar. No, I believe you. I do." We laughed like two young children watching Donald Duck and Goofy cartoons. I gave her a quick kiss. She gave me one back.

Anita returned, and Jen said, "Anita, I think I'm going to stick around with Joe ... No, I don't want you to walk by yourself. Joe, you follow us." I cleaned up a few dishes, locked the house, and we left.

Anita was looking forward to the Venice trip. "You're fortunate enough if you can visit there once. I've been there twenty times, and each time I find something new." Jen wasn't listening. They say you're compatible when you share similar traits. Jen and I don't listen when we're not interested. So, we're compatible, right?

Out of the blue, Jen said like a nosy schoolgirl, "Anita's got a boyfriend, Anita's got a boyfriend."

"Can't you keep anything quiet?"

"You can't."

I said, "Who wants to tell me about him?"

Anita answered, "It's Fernando, and he's from Venice Mestra, it's the newer part of Venice. The little fucker was supposed to meet me here, and he pooped out at the last minute. How could I let him bullshit me with that phony accent?" We agreed it was a hazard of frequent international travel.

"Are you going to give him a second chance?" I asked.

"No, this isn't like you're out of jail, and you get a second shot. Fernando is history. Modern Venetian history."

Anita called Carter when we got to their hotel, and we talked on the speaker phone. Carter reported on a new woman, who he claimed he really liked. I thought, no way. He couldn't get her to leave Manhattan hotel bars, and she kept him up late on weekdays. We offered to provide Carter a second opinion. He suggested a rendezvous at Benoit, the French bistro bar on 55th Street. After France, I would prefer a place like Five Napkin Burger, but I went along.

While the four of us talked, everyone sensed it. No one wanted to say it. We enjoyed the camaraderie, and we didn't want it to stop. A special moment, indeed. I had developed a similar feeling with Lisette, and before that with Tammy and Brie, though I didn't know them as well. I liked women who were animated and dramatic. It didn't have to get physical, although that was a plus. And often a risk.

The question with Jen was whether a relationship could advance beyond the extracurriculars. Don't pin me down, but I think it could. I didn't want to have "the talk," but I thought it was coming. She and Anita were leaving for Venice tomorrow morning. Jen was taking an art class while Anita ran the tour. We sat in front of their Antibes hotel for a few more minutes until Anita went inside. I was left on this bright, starry, happy night with a woman who approached me at a bar on an obscure Venetian alley almost three months ago.

Jen read my mind. She said, "I don't want to talk about it."

"About what?"

"You know."

"You mean us?"

"Yep, us. I don't want to talk about it."

We stared ahead. Two teenage boys walked by and mimicked me, "About what, about what?" I shook my head and called them douchebags under my breath.

Jen lowered her voice. The universe stood still. "I'm glad we connected. Then I'll see you ... I wish I hadn't signed up for that class. Oh, fiddle fucking sticks. I want the best goodbye fuck you've got." Nothing to say after that but do what she says. Do you need more proof of a higher being?

I brought up "the talk" again later, and she still wouldn't say anything. I felt good about the two of us. Is there something she's afraid to tell me?

I returned to Lisette's house in the early morning. She sat in the kitchen and looked very tired. Jon must have dropped her off very late. She wasn't as friendly as usual. Lisette learned what happened with Felicity and Jen the next day from one of her friends. She said, "Felicity, she's not a close friend. More like a friend of a friend. Indeed, she can't see the big picture." Ditto on that. We agreed that the party was a great success even with the theatrics. She found my friends interesting and, well, different.

Alright, so what is the lay of the land, no pun intended? Jen was somewhere on the sliding scale between an enhanced one-night stand and something more enduring. I still viewed Marie as the leading candidate. Of course, I could touch down in the USA, make one call, and learn that, well, it was great while it lasted, and she's not sure ...

The good news. The last two weeks in Antibes were my most productive. Maybe it was the looming departure. I got so much done by three o'clock that there was plenty of time to explore or shop or drink.

Lisette reminded me that Bernard was returning Wednesday. Maybe it explained her mood change. She mentioned it again when I finished my work for the day. Was this a hint? Did the rain check expire? Lisette became more distant. I offered to help her shop, but she declined. I guess this was her way of transitioning without me there. Bernard was cordial and formal to the end. I was a renter to him. I never had an extended discussion with him. That's partly my fault. If something was intriguing about him, I would never learn it. Something sad about that.

A few days before I left, Lisette sprang to life, and asked me to take a walk around Cap D'Antibes, and then out for lunch. Bernard was playing tennis and having lunch with colleagues. It wasn't a warm day, but the light wind made it ideal for a walk. She was holding something back. Why can't she just say what's on her mind? We headed to Cours Masséna and then went south along the coast. She was quiet for a few minutes. "I'm leaving Bernard. I told him. He didn't show any emotion. It was depressing to see his indifference. It was like another day at the office."

"I'm sorry. That's what you wanted?"

"I thought it was coming. He took up space here. He didn't live here. It was like he waited for me to say something. He's moving to Lyon. I'll stay in the house."

"Maybe you need a change in scenery?"

"No, I like it here. He'll give me enough so I can stay put. That's not an issue. This is home."

"It's beautiful here."

"You're my long-lost friend. Where have you been? The party would have been boring without you and your friends. You have to come back. I'll throw a book party. I'll throw any kind of party."

"Yes, of course, a book tour. New York, Chicago, Antibes, more cities, for sure."

"I'll screen who comes to the Antibes party. No troublemakers." We laughed at that. "Joe, I know this is not my business. The woman who made a splash at the party when that idiot Felicity carried on. Your friend. Did you ever, you know …?"

Make an assumption and answer it. "No, no. She's a friend …, a crazy friend. That would not work. I need someone with imagination and balance." I thought about Cindy. She's too balanced. What about Marie? Or back to Jen, is she the one that's first on my bench? I was so mixed up.

"Can you stay another day? My daughter's coming Monday from London. I never mentioned her. I had her when I was twenty-one. Her father reminds me of you. You're more stable. And an inch taller. No, not the taller part. I'm glad your friend told Felicity off. Bloody hell, these women." Lisette had my back. It's the best feeling in the world.

"I appreciate that. Lisette, thank you for everything. I need to keep the flight. I have a bad habit of changing my mind." I wiped my eyes, hoping she wouldn't see. If she did, she didn't say anything. All a human being can ask for is attention and a fair shake. She gets it. She deserves attention too. We kept walking. A couple of minutes later, a young boy, maybe seven, chased after a soccer ball. It was headed for a small pond. I ran ahead, stopped the ball, kicked it back to him.

The boy yelled, "Merci, merci." His two front teeth were missing. He was all smiles.

"Je t'en prie."

"You're an athlete, too?" Lisette asked.

"I used to be good. I could kick the ball a mile ... and run. I played every day. Loved it. I played tackle football for fun, and we didn't wear pads." I had to add that.

"Joseph, there's no tackling in football."

"I mean American football. Hey, can we go for crêpes? It's something else I'll miss."

"Of course. Anything else you're going to miss?" What a softball.

"Let me think. You. Lisette, I'll miss you," I said with an apparent lack of conviction.

"You sound like you don't mean it."

"No, I mean it. You're a great landlord. A great lady."

"Do you have any idea what it's like not to sleep with a man for over a year?"

"No." I thought this was a trick question. So, change the subject. "Where are the crêpes? I'm hungry."

We had lunch at Le Rocher on Plage de la Garoupe. A low-key beach on a small inlet, with a colorful pier of bright yellow umbrellas. Lunch was delicious. I remembered the dessert crêpes. She insisted on picking up the bill.

On the walk back to Vieil Antibes, I got a knot in my stomach. The return to the corporate rat race. Life in the cage. I made a commitment to Richard and backing out now could wreak havoc on my career. Mentally, I wasn't ready. Sure, if I had another two weeks here, I could finish a bigger piece of the book. And another two weeks after that. I shouldn't do this, but I wondered. Did I ask the right questions? What would Fitzgerald do? What would Kerouac do? Stop right there. They can't guide me. Sure, they were literary giants. But role models? One was self-destructive, the other had a self-destructive spouse. And weren't they a tad narcissistic?

I also got a knot thinking about Marie. We connected briefly when she was in Austin. I sent three texts and she didn't respond. She had endless enthusiasm and was the most attractive woman I've met. That fact alone made me nervous. Still, I really liked her, and I felt good that the feeling was mutual. To their credit, she and Cindy and Jen (and Leslie early on) were in the special group of women willing to go out with a shorter guy. I can say I've had meaningful relationships with Marie and Jen. We connected on the requisite deeper level.

The next morning, I went to work like many days before. The routine worked. I maintained discipline. Could I continue when I have to play lawyer again? Nothing's perfect, but I am determined. And then, this happened. I was working on the patio when I saw an email from Marie. Say I'm old-fashioned, but if someone has something serious to say, I prefer the gravitas of a handwritten note. Or a phone call. I believe she meant well. That's what mattered.

Joseph,
It is breaking me up to write this. It took me a long time to figure out what to say. You should know that I adore you personally. Your self-confidence is contagious, and you really are very funny. I need to say the following loud and clear. This has nothing to do with your stature. Period. I always enjoyed being with you and loved to walk with you and was never self-conscious about any of that. Your agility in the bedroom is second to none.
I don't know how else to say this. I met a man in Chicago almost three weeks ago. Now for the record, he's taller than you but shorter than me. He's a psychology Ph.D. candidate. We started having coffee, and one thing led to another. I don't know where I'm headed, but for the time being, I'm happy with him. I admit when he talks about his thesis, I can't understand most of what he's talking about. I told my mom about you, and she was impressed with your intellect and wit. She thought there was a maturity issue, which I knew was a comment about your height, and I told her that was very unfair. Joe, please call me when you're in Chicago and good luck with your book. Stay with it, I know it will get attention.
Yours, Marie

I read it again in case I missed anything. Then walked in the kitchen and slammed my fist on the table. I told myself not to cry. Put one foot in front of the other and don't trip on anything. It was late morning, and I never drink before five o'clock. Well, hardly ever. I ran to Bacchus and had a shot of Glenlivet. A serious drink for a sobering moment. I was the only one at the bar. Charlotte could see I was agitated. "Tout va bien?" she asked. I looked at her and mildly shook my head. Three shots of Glenlivet later, I hobbled out and walked home. I thought I saw Marie's sister, but I kept walking.

You never know the whole story. So why analyze it? I dismissed family influence as a factor because I believe Marie thinks for herself. She's a strong confident woman. Was "the issue" festering in the back of her mind? I don't think so. I wanted to keep my options open, maybe that's how Marie thought too. What's good for the goose, as they say. I was sad because she was no longer an option. This really hurt.

Lisette returned from Marché Provençal and saw I was upset. I had to tell someone. Stumbling to speak. She showed an inordinate amount of understanding. I shouldn't put it this way, but this was the opening she needed. We sat, surrounded by a myriad of colorful flowers. An abundance of sympathy evolved into mid-afternoon sympathy sex. There's an implication that the sympathy part meant one of us felt obligated. I doubt Lisette felt obligated. I went along to be protected from the barmy world out there. Why don't I just call it non-obligatory opportunity sex? She was ready to carpe the diem, at this place, at this point in time. Ditto for me.

She was the oldest woman I've been with, and the first who needed hair color. Also, an inch or two taller, nothing novel about that.

Two days later, I closed the front door of Lisette's house and left. All was right with the world. Lisette wore the memorable shirt dress. She was buttoned up today. We had a few laughs and parted as friends.

CHAPTER THIRTY-THREE

"
I did you a big favor. I gave YOU a chance.

I flew from Nice to Newark Liberty with a connection in Paris-Charles de Gaulle Airport. On the flight from Paris to Newark, I had Seat 12F, a window seat. A dapper man in a pale golf shirt and dark blazer sat in the middle seat. His three noisy children were in the three seats behind us. After takeoff, his wife appeared and told their kids to calm down. I love children, but at that moment, I preferred quiet. She looked at me. "Excuse me sir, I'm in an aisle seat in row 17. It's 17D. Would you mind switching with me?" She was offering me a de facto upgrade.

"No, I don't mind," I said quietly to show this was not an easy decision. I got up to move.

"Thank you so much. Where are you from?"

"I've lived in North Jersey for three and a half years. I grew up farther south, on the Jersey Shore, near Asbury Park. How about you?"

"Altoona, Pennsylvania. Honey," she said to her husband, "he's from Joisey."

I politely said, "I've never talked like that. That's more of a North Jersey native thing." I think she felt bad. She thanked me again, and I quickly moved to seat 17D. Next to me was a striking flight attendant and a pilot. An older friend from prep school, Mikey Seltzer, met his wife, a flight attendant for Delta, on a trans-Atlantic flight. They called them stewardesses then. This flight attendant was pretty except for the brassy highlights in her blonde hair.

I fell asleep after takeoff. When I woke up, the flight attendant was sleeping. Antibes felt far away. No more Bacchus or Marché Provençal. Two weeks until the return to corporate America. Look, this is the deal. You worked and played in the sandbox, and now it's time to go back to school. Can somebody please rescue me? The Inner Voice correctly noted this is a long flight and no brooding.

The flight attendant, McKenzie, opened her eyes and asked if something was wrong. I told her I enjoyed southern France and had withdrawal symptoms, as much as I love the USA. She said, "Get a drink. Keep the party going."

"You're right, I'll do that. You want one too?"

"Not when I'm in uniform. It's an appearance thing."

"I get it." I ordered Dewar's with a separate cup of ice, and we talked. She was engaged, then broke it off. She wasn't bitter, it was time to move on, and all that rot, as Lisette would say. The banter was easy. Easy because I'm not interested in her. I said, "I'm an expert on relationships. No, really I've got my own issues." That got a laugh.

McKenzie asked if I had a girlfriend. She watched me as I reflected. "I think so. I'm not sure." She was disappointed. I told her about my friend who met his wife on a plane.

"Happens more than you think."

Good thing I started with Dewar's. Lunch was inedible stringy chicken and hard white rice. I needed to walk around. I got up and went to the back of the plane, which was full until the last five rows. Two very big dudes in the row 31 aisle seats spilled out into the aisle. The woman in aisle seat 32D got my attention. She looked vaguely familiar. I didn't recognize the glasses which were neon orange cat eyes. I stared a second longer, and she called out, "Hey, did you work at the Justice Department?"

It was hard to hear her over other chatter. "I'm sorry, what?"

"Didn't you work at Justice Department, DOJ?" I heard her this time. "I was a paralegal. I remember you. I should have said hi, but I didn't." Interesting. Another missed opportunity?

"If you said hi, I would have said hi and how it's going, I mean, how's it going? I worked at EPA. In headquarters." I loved to say headquarters. Sounded ominous like Joe Friday in old *Dragnet* episodes. "I had a six-month detail at DOJ. That's probably when you saw me. I shared an office with a smoker. Can you believe it? At the department where they enforce the environmental laws. Well, there's no more smoking. I'm Joseph."

"Hello, I'm Melissa."

She had a round, pretty face with high cheekbones. Reddish-brown medium-length teased hair and the ruddy freckled complexion of Thomas Hardy's Tess as she runs across an open field in Dorset. She took off her glasses, to reveal big, beautiful, brown eyes. The eyes of a happy, curious child. Hopefully, she will keep them off. She's too pretty to wear them. They do have good conversation value. Even more than my mermaid print shirt. I carefully walked around the big dudes and stopped.

"I remember the landfill that leaked in southern California," Melissa said. "You got a huge settlement. Other lawyers couldn't believe the amount. They said, 'Oh, what's the guy from EPA doing?' They looked down on the EPA lawyers, of course, that's the way Washington D.C. is. It's all about one-upmanship. Who can you look down on today?"

"Yes, it was a good result. And a lot of work. And I don't care what others think." I added some fluff for no extra cost. "My mantra was to work harder than the other side. I didn't like comments by defense attorneys about government attorneys. That got me motivated."

I remembered the case well. EPA spent big bucks cleaning up a very nasty landfill and sued three companies to recover the money it spent. The Regional EPA lawyer in San Francisco was about to retire. He didn't care. It wasn't a priority for the U.S. Attorneys' Office in Los Angeles either, which cared more about headlines in white collar criminal cases. Landfills normally don't get a lot of attention although they can be a mess. The case languished, EPA Headquarters took over, and I was assigned the case. The evidence had some holes, but we still collected millions. The U.S. Attorneys' Office took most of the credit. They offered me a job, but I didn't want to move to La La Land.

The dudes in Row 31 were getting impatient with me hovering in the aisle. I said to Melissa, "I should move."

I guess she didn't hear me. "You're still at EPA?"

"I left over three years ago. I went to the legal department of a big chemical company."

"I left DOJ last year ... Would you like to sit here?" She pointed to the empty middle seat. A man sat in the window seat, and I didn't want to bother him. When no one's in the middle seat, you think you own it.

"He's my brother," she said. "Andy, would you mind switching seats with Joseph? It's an aisle seat."

He gave her a look. Classic sibling response. I said to him, "It's 17D, an aisle seat. I'll buy you a drink. What would you like?"

No hesitation there. "Beefeater and tonic, piece of lime."

"Done. And I'm going to the bathroom."

When I returned, Andy had dutifully taken his new seat. The once-again bespectacled Melissa had moved to the middle seat, so I took her aisle seat. We could hear Andy laughing with the flight attendant. Everything has a purpose. He should buy me a drink.

"Now, where were we?" Melissa said. "Oh yeah, you went to the dark side." She smiled, knowing she was razzing me.

"Not at all, I call it the bright side. I help the company comply. We take it very seriously. We meet U.S. standards everywhere we operate." I felt like adding, "And I carry a badge."

I was trying too hard to impress her. "Anyway, I've been away three and a half months. They gave me an abbreviated sabbatical. I started a book. I'm maybe a third or so through a draft. A very rough draft."

"You did that? Wow."

"I thought seriously about leaving the Company altogether, but they lured me back. Did I do the right thing? We'll see."

"You thought about leaving, period?"

"I did. I'll see what happens. The big boss is letting me work part-time, so I have more time to write. He went out of his way to accommodate me."

She didn't like that. "You're too young." I wish she hadn't said this. No more second-guessing, please.

"I bet I'm older than you. I'm thirty-one."

"You are? I just turned twenty-eight. You look so young."

I shrugged. "Youthful genes. So why did you leave DOJ?"

"I wanted to do my art full-time. My plan was to work a few years and save some money." She pulled out a postcard. "I have a show in Chicago next month. Maybe you can come. You could meet my father. He's a big guy like you. We love short people in my family." I'm five-two, I don't think my dad is five-four. My mom's five-feet. Oh, Andy's five-five. He looks taller because he's thin. My sister is five-one." I was tempted to say my girlfriend is five-ten. Melissa's kind of cute. Please take the glasses off.

"So, you're five-two. That's almost five-three and a half."

She looked puzzled. "Why don't you just say five-four?"

"This is what I am. To quote Popeye, 'I yam what I yam.'" She liked that. A delayed laugh. I said, "Did you know that when you're shorter, you age more gracefully?" I know, I didn't make this up.

"Is that true?"

"Yep. There are other advantages. But you have to work harder. Well, you should work harder. You have to look like you mean it." She took off her glasses again. Thank you, Melissa. "Can I tell you something? Those glasses are something else." It's the best way I could put it.

"You like them?"

"Oh, yeah," I lied.

"No, you don't."

"Yes, you're right ... but as long as you like them." I didn't mean that either.

"I'm getting a new pair. Tortoiseshell. More like yours. Make me look smarter." Sounds like something I would say. I don't want her to look more like me, do I?

I learned about Melissa's family. Everything from her bipolar father Jerome to her ninety-nine-year-old great Uncle Morris. She suddenly switched subjects and asked if I liked baseball. I didn't hear the question and nodded like I did. My attention started to fade. I started to doze. She said, "What was my question?"

"You asked me where I grew up. No, sorry, I was in a daze."

"I told you I loved you and wanted to go away with you."

"Wow."

"No, I didn't say that. But I do like you. Now pay attention. Here's my card in case you forget my name."

"Melissa, I have a ..."

"I know. You have a girlfriend."

"Well ..."

"You talked in your sleep. You said, 'Who's going to win the race, Marie or Cindy? Both are ...' Then I couldn't hear what you said, and then you said, 'It's Cindy, that's right.' So, is it Cindy? Or Marie? You don't have to say who they are. And you kept repeating something with a 'J' sound. June, I think it was."

"What if I told you it was Melissa?"

"I wouldn't believe you." she laughed. "God, you're intense when you sleep. What's going on upstairs?" Her glasses sat on top of her book, and she was adorable. But her question gave me a tension headache. I second-guessed the seat trade with Andy.

Look, I don't owe her any explanation. The Inner Voice agreed. She said, "You just met her."

"I go out here and there, nothing serious." Which was arguably accurate considering the distances.

She whispered in my ear, "Well. I want to go out. So there." I think her lips touched my ear. Jesus H. Christ, is Melissa bashert, the one that's meant to be?

A lady in her late sixties sat across from me in the other aisle seat. She stood up. She had long gray hair tied back with lots of hairspray to keep it under control. She wore a green tweed pants suit that would have been stylish thirty or forty years ago. All buttoned up. She tapped me on the left shoulder. Something wrong?

"Hi, can I help you?"

"Yes, I'm ... Marjorie Sommers. I'm sorry to bother you."

"Not a problem."

"I wanted to tell you something."

I nodded. "Sure."

"I saw you two. If you don't mind me saying, you're so cute together. It's so sweet. I lost my husband last year. You two gave me a good feeling."

Melissa spoke up. "Actually Marjorie, he could be the one." Oh, my God.

"Well, you seem very happy, and I wish you the best. I know it's going to work out. I hope I wasn't too forward."

I wasn't yet over the shock. I said, "No, no, it's fine."

"Good luck," she said. She went toward the back of the plane. A few minutes later, a flight attendant delivered two small bottles of champagne and two wine glasses.

"This is from the lady across the aisle," she said indifferently.

"Thank you," we said.

Melissa nudged me. "Isn't that nice, honey?" She was ready to burst.

"So sweet." I was ready to gag.

I thanked Marjorie when she returned. Turns out, her husband was a real estate mogul from New Jersey. She said, "The media didn't like him. They said he slept around. Considering the corruption in that state, if he messed up once, I'd forgive him."

I was determined to get back to work. I politely told Marjorie that I needed to finish a couple of pages. As much as I wanted to talk, I said the same thing to Melissa. Consciously or not, she leaned against me much of the time. It was sweet and kind of make-believe. I made progress the next two hours. A couple times, I barked "yes" to announce minor breakthroughs. Marjorie tapped me and said that she had not met anyone so entertaining in a while.

I talked with Melissa here and there between work and naps. I learned that she was adopted from an orphanage in Northern Ireland. I had a feeling there was a sad story about the civil war and a birthparent, but I didn't ask. The adopting parents were a Jewish man from Chicago and a woman he met when he was in the Peace Corps. By the way, Melissa said her mom made incredible matzah ball soup.

"It's a great country, isn't it?" I thought about Marie when she said it. Anyway, I love stories like that.

"Yes. I am happy sitting here. My stepfather, he loves the USA." I guess her folks are divorced. There she was, my Irish American girl, who loved mom's matzah ball soup. I looked at her closely. She must have bought the cat eyes after I saw her at DOJ. Alright, enough with the glasses.

So, what's the next step? Melissa had a connection to Chicago, while I was stopping in New York to see family and friends on my way to Hoboken. We landed, and one of us had to say something. I hoped she would take the lead. We got up. She turned to me. "Joe, do you think you can come to my art show? I promise you'll like it. End of July."

"I'll try, but I have to focus on work. I like Chicago. I stayed at Palmer House when I was at EPA. We can have a drink in the lobby bar. It's ornate, like the Gilded Age with a French accent."

"Joe, my connection is tight. I need to run. See you at the show." We said goodbye with a half-hearted hug. She ran ahead, stopped, and turned around. "You'll call, right?"

"Yes, sure. See ya," I looked up. The sign said, "Welcome to the USA." I kneeled and kissed the carpet. I loved being away. I miss Vieil Antibes. And I love setting foot here although I'm edgy about work. God bless America.

Now Melissa walked toward me. What the hell? I said, "Are you OK?"

"Joe, I can wait until the next flight. They leave every hour to Chicago. I can change the flight. Or I'll say I missed it, which could happen anyway."

"Isn't your family expecting you? I mean, don't wait because of me." She must think the next connection will help our fledgling relationship.

"No, it's OK."

I liked Melissa, but I had a lot on my mind, like neutralizing the impulse to not return to StarColor. So on to passport control and plenty of waiting. Melissa asked about our official date. I said, "Can I get back to you? I need to get settled." A half-hour later, we were still in line. She stood close to me much of the time, which was nice, but was she the clingy type? I need room to move around.

"Did you give it any more thought?"

"Yes, the piano bar at Gibson's. The pianist is wonderful. Very classy."

"Wow. I've never been. I can get dressed up."

We finally approached the passport clerk. He was unusually nice. "Welcome home," he said.

"Thank you very much." I meant it. It's a thrill to walk through the door. It shuts behind you. You're free and clear in the terminal.

I had another hour with her. We found a Starbucks. Melissa said, "You're glad I picked the next flight?"

"Sure. Yes, it's a sign of good things to come. How's that?"

"Great." And they lived happily ever after. Until I said goodbye to Melissa for the third time and wondered if I created too much expectation. Forget it. She's very sweet. I headed to the car rental area.

I waded through a wall of limo and car service drivers with names of persons to be picked up. One sign read, "Joseph Fine." Is there another Joseph Fine? I told my mom I rented a car. She didn't mention a car service. I didn't recognize the driver. She wore a black pants suit with a white blouse, a black driver's hat, and round sunglasses. She had long brown hair and not much expression.

I got closer. She had a deep voice. It didn't sound real. "Mr. Fine, over here sir." I walked toward her. Uh oh. My pal Carter will be in a lot of trouble. She took off her sunglasses, then her cap. She walked up to me. I said, "What the ...?"

"Hi, Joe, how's my big guy? Hey, was your plane late?" DD planted a kiss on my chapped lips. "I counted the days until you came back. Carter told me when your flight left Paris. So here we are."

I struggled for words. "You look great in the uniform. I'm supposed to pick up a car. I don't know what to say." I didn't want to talk about my plans. I hesitated. "I thought we were ..."

"Done? No, no, give it a try. I'm here to rescue you. We're good, you and me. It makes sense."

I was still struggling. "Well, you came to the airport. OK, you want to get coffee? But I'm picking up a car, I'm flattered but ... We can sit down."

"I'll drive you to your family. Just drop you off."

My better judgment said not to do this. I have to get away from her. When I look into her eyes, I can't think straight. I thought for a moment. Another moment. The Inner Voice buzzed me. "Stay calm. Think clearly."

"No, thanks, DD, that's kind and nice, I don't think so. Please don't be upset with me."

She unloaded on me. My, how the weather changes. Look out. This was one angry, ranting limo driver. I don't need to relate the details but the other drivers in the area were amused. She hit me where it hurt. "You short fucking asswipe. You were lucky to find me. I did you a big favor. I gave YOU a chance. Get out there and see if other women will go out with you, you little dick." I thought I had tough skin. She pierced it. There was nothing comical about this.

I got closer to her and quietly said, "Well, sorry."

"That's it? And what's this writing you're doing. Something you can talk about to impress women. Well, you are so full of it, little man."

No reason to respond. I stepped back gingerly and waved. "See you."

Despite the tongue-lashing, I still felt a soft spot for DD. After all, she left a terrific first impression. I was taken with her. She was the smart, Vandy sorority girl who thought we were predestined. Needless to say, she was also a highly emotional creature. Which can be good at the right time and very bad at the wrong time.

I took the high road, the honorable approach. The Inner Voice winked, and said, "She'll send you a note in a couple of days and say she's sorry." I've been in some heated negotiations and mediations where the expletives and litigation threats fly, but you can't take it personally. OK, I did once or twice. But I couldn't remember when anyone attacked me like this. I was hurt and hoped someone with sympathy was around the corner.

I went to the Hertz counter, itching to get my car and drive to the Jersey Shore. The agent offered me a Mustang convertible. I needed a dose of the home area before returning to work. I wasn't ready to go to my Hoboken apartment. Cindy's back in Jersey. The boardwalk would be a good venue to catch up with her. But first, check in with Carter.

I heard clanging glasses and loud voices. "Hold on Joe. We're at McSorley's. Guys from work. Women too. You'd like one of them. I'll put her on."

Before I could tell Carter to wait, someone was talking. It was difficult to hear. "Hello?"

"Hi, this is Lucy."

"Hi, this is Joseph, and who are you? Carter's girlfriend?"

"Not officially. Unless knowing him a week counts."

"A lot can happen in a week. Hey Lucy, can I talk to Carter?"

"He can't. Someone spilled beer on him. Joe, he told me your criteria for a meaningful relationship. I thought it was cute. Carter told me you're looking."

"Carter has a problem with discretion. He does look after me, so I take the good with the ridiculous. We've been friends since prep school."

"My friend Carly and I just went to our fifth reunion at Leicester."

"You went there? He didn't tell me. Unbelievable. I went for three years. They went coed when I was there. Big Red, huh? I was a cheerleader."

"Wow, a cheerleader. It's funny. I bet kids are as full of shit now as they were when you went. I hope things haven't changed. Oh boy, Carly will want to meet you. She can shoot the shit like nobody's business."

"Well, that's what ties us together. The students are too serious now. And they're stressed out? Give me a fucking break. I had stress. I didn't moan about it. Lucy, can you put Carter on?"

"Sure."

"Isn't Lucy cool? She and Carly, too bad they're so young. So, Joseph Fine is back from his literary adventures." Then he whispered. "Carly's old man has more money than Moses."

"Carter, did you know DD met me as I left customs? It was ugly. She went nuts on me." I saw a call from Jen come in. I let it go. "It's done with DD. Just buy me a drink."

"I'm sorry Joe, I thought, well, give her one more shot. She kept bugging me about when you're coming back. I should have given you a heads up."

"Yes, please. She unloaded on me when I said we were done. She pulled out the height card. I'm thirty-one and she pulled out the height card. Short this. Little that. Fuck her. OK, the boobs were memorable. But they're replaceable ... That didn't sound right. I meant ..."

"I know what you mean. You'll find someone else's."

"Well, I had to move on. Hey, Jen is trying to reach me."

"Oh, Jen." Carter was impressed. "I'll stay on the sidelines while you do whatever you're going to do with her. By the way, DD's old man got his sentence shortened."

"I don't care."

"You better hide. Just kidding. Sorry, but don't you think the limo outfit was clever. Hey, come over later. Can you bring a bottle of Glenlivet? You know, to celebrate your return."

"Sure."

CHAPTER THIRTY-FOUR

I read about the four-percent factor.

If you're not used to it, driving from Newark Airport on the New Jersey Turnpike or the Garden State Parkway is intimidating. The regulars drive like they own the road. You merge when they say so. I've been away long enough to feel like an outsider. I dropped my stuff at my mom's house in Montclair and got back on the parkway. Mom wasn't home, she's a docent at the Metropolitan Museum of Art. I'm staying at Carter's for two days before I go to my place in Hoboken.

After a chaotic start, it was smooth sailing most of the ride. Heading south, I approached Exit 101 on the parkway. A small flatbed truck passed me on the right and pulled in front of me. The truck was filled with scrap. Two pieces of metal flew off, followed by hundreds of small pieces which hit the Mustang or went under it. I initially slowed down and was hit from behind. I veered around the truck to the right and was able to get to the shoulder. Car after car swerved to the shoulder. About sixty yards ahead, I saw two people get out of a car who looked hurt. I was lucky. Other than a few bruises, I felt fine.

I called the police. I was lucky I didn't get hit in the head. The back of the car was banged up pretty good. The truck driver ended up on the shoulder ahead of me. She walked toward me. "I'm so sorry. I didn't realize he loaded it like this." That didn't make it any better. The police said I should get checked and radioed for an ambulance. I called Hertz and started to feel a little dizzy.

One of the EMS persons was a short-haired redhead, all buttoned up for work, of course. The other one was a young guy who was new to the team. My right arm hurt, but I felt good enough to call Carter while I waited in the ER. I told him they wanted to keep me overnight to monitor any head injury. They were also taking x-rays.

The night nurse Marta gave me something to help me sleep. It must have worked pretty fast. When I woke up early the next morning, she looked at me as if I were the strangest thing she'd ever seen. Shouldn't she act professionally detached? She reminded me of creepy Nurse Ratched in *One Flew Over the Cuckoo's Nest*.

"Do you normally talk in your sleep?" She asked.

"I don't know. I know I dream a lot." I haven't slept enough with one woman to know if I talk a lot while sleeping.

"You told this woman Jen or Jenny to hurry up and get here before Marie gets here. And you said, 'Don't worry, Cindy's in Parsippany in the CEO's office.' You must have a busy social life."

I thought she was nosy. Maybe her job isn't normally this much fun. "You remembered I said all that?"

"You were very clear. And loud."

"Jesus, I'm sorry." I felt bad for my roommate, an older guy who was eating breakfast and couldn't stop clearing his throat.

"Oh, and the on-duty nurse said you were asleep by nine."

The nurse came by again and said, "Mr. Fine, you don't have a concussion and nothing's broken, so if nothing changes, we will discharge you this afternoon."

"Thank you for everything." She smiled, showing two large stained front teeth. She was now strictly professional. The creepiness was gone. I couldn't help noticing her uniform was a tad …, well you know, she wore it well. Very well. That sounds piggish, so forgive me. I felt better by midday. Then, the thought of reading and deleting hundreds of emails a day at work made me feel nauseous. Antibes looked awfully good.

I took a nap, then called Carter. I'll see him tomorrow.

"Joe, she misses you."

"Who?"

"Who do you think?"

"Carter, not now. I'm done with her. You're making my head hurt."

"Joe, she still acts like she's part of the family. Like this is a hiatus and you'll come back."

"No. Please don't engage her. I don't use the word psycho lightly, but she's getting close."

"And Cindy? What's the update?"

"You know, I met her in Venice. She has depth. She's pretty in a businesslike soccer mom kind of way. And very grounded. Maybe too grounded. She acts motherly like I'm one of her kids. I still like her a lot."

"Didn't I tell you she sounds boring? You don't need the motherly type. You need someone to take care of you without acting like that's what she's doing. You're grounded enough when you want to be. There has to be a woman to cope with the crazy shit that goes through your head."

"I'm hoping to see her later."

"It's your life."

It was almost noon, sunny and bright outside. Looked like a perfect beach day. I typed out some new chapter notes. Somebody knocked on the door. It's early for lunch. Jen rushed into the room. She held a big white plastic bag that she set in a corner. "Darling, darling, let me look at you. Anita told me you got hurt. What happened?"

"I'm fine, really I didn't want to bother you. It was a crazy accident but I'm OK. Oh my God, you didn't need to come down." I told her the details with a dramatic flair.

"I took the train from South Station early this morning. Almost missed it. And I caught my heel in a crack in the sidewalk. Fucking city can't fix the sidewalks. I picked up a car at Metropark Station." She went to touch my face.

I put my hand up to protect it. "Please be careful." She sat down.

"I'll save the kiss for later. The longer I wait, the longer the kiss."

"So, stay as long as you want. Thanks for coming. It means a lot." I took a closer look. I saw her in France a couple of weeks ago so she couldn't have aged that much. She looks awfully good for thirty-nine. Maybe she uses anti-aging cream. I've thought more about the age thing lately. She seems more vibrant than usual if that's possible.

"Joe, I can't get to Carter's this weekend. Sondra is coming home from Andover. I haven't seen her for a month. She needs to decompress. Hey, the summer's almost here, we'll go to the Cape. Darling, you must get better. ASAP."

"What's this decompress business? When I was in school, you finished your exams, you went home, you worked or sat around or slept. Nobody talked about stress. With these kids, it's a badge of honor to say how stressed they are. It's like, 'I'm more stressed than you.' 'No, you're not, I am.' If you're not stressed, something's wrong."

"I love it when you get excited. I would squeeze those cheeks if you felt better. Look, I can't tell my kid she's full of shit. This is how they act. You'll see for yourself someday. She's not self-indulgent. She's actually pretty normal considering the divorce and the happy horseshit that flows from it."

I lowered my voice. At some point, I had to have "the talk" with Jen. Not now and not on the phone. I thought about Anita's friend who only wanted a monthly sleepover. No deep discussions or baggage. That's not what I want for the long haul.

Jen tapped me to make sure I was listening. She said, "Here's something you might be interested in. I read about the four-percent factor."

"I have no idea what you're talking about." I think she was playing with me.

"Four percent of women will go out with a guy who is shorter than them. So, ninety-six percent won't. Women are really intolerant, aren't they? Not me. You're tolerant too." She winked and smiled. Like she was planning a prank. "Guys aren't as bad, more of them are willing to go out with a taller woman. I think it's twenty-three percent. Who cares? I'm here, you're here."

"Well, thank you for your support." That sounded like the end of a stump speech. I didn't know what statistics she was talking about, but it confirmed my instincts. And fortunately, I've been batting much higher. But why bring this up? So, I would appreciate her? I did. I'll try this. "Women don't tell you what they're really thinking. Here's what I think. You're high up within the four percent."

"Aw, shucks. Really?" she said, like the woman who walks into the saloon and nods to the cowboy. "One good thing with the four percent. I don't have as much competition. Look what these women are missing. Big slice of life left unexplored. Unexploited. Venice is a great city, isn't it? I could jump on you right now."

"No, please don't. My arm's sore."

"Not fair, but Ok."

She sat down. She looked unusually tired. "Joe, I can't stay, I have a dinner in Boston tonight at the Fine Arts Museum. Some kind of awards ceremony. It's a mutual backscratching society, these art-world types. I'll be late as it is ... I'll be back to New York or you come to Boston. We will catch up, right?" A gentle hug and a couple of light kisses, and she took off. "Bye, darling." I didn't have a chance to respond.

As quickly as she entered the room, she left, only to come back a few seconds later. She makes me dizzy. "I forgot to give you this. Carter told me you were a cheerleader at Leicester." She picked up the white bag in the corner. "For you." I opened it. It was a black megaphone with a big red "L" on it. "Don't ask me how I got it. Got to run."

I shouted, "Incredible," but she had already left. The megaphone meant a lot to me. It was pure bliss. I loved yelling through it at football games, in white jeans and a black sweater embossed with the red "L." It's one way of saying, "Here I am." My guess was that Carter got it from someone in Alumni Relations. I will officially forgive him for the airport limo incident.

Cindy called while Jen was in the hospital room. She was apartment hunting. I called her back while waiting to be discharged. Someone picked up and was screaming. I heard, "Look I've had enough. I have to focus on this new job, and I can't babysit you."

"Cindy?"

"Who is this? ... Oh my God, is that you Joe? I'm so sorry. I thought it was another guy. We went out three months ago. He keeps calling. You must think something's wrong with me. So, you're back. How does it feel?"

"I think I liked Lugano better. And it was tough leaving France. But here I am."

"Well, you left, and you're here."

We talked about Lugano and Lake Como. No question, it was exhilarating. "I'm glad we went to Villa Carlotta. The Romeo and Juliet painting. Just so special. I know you liked the big turtles. The artist on the top floor. What was her name, Leti... something?"

I acted like I didn't remember. "I think it was Livia or something." Her name was Livia.

"Joe, you were supposed to call me when you got in."

I mentioned the accident. Cindy didn't respond. Maybe she's doing something on her phone. "I don't know if you heard me. I was in a car accident. I'm fine. It was a bit traumatic."

"I'm sorry about that." She didn't seem interested. "This guy called again, and I blocked it. Where were we?" She cleared her throat like she was giving a graduation speech. "Yes, Joe, where we left off, you didn't know what you wanted. I thought about this. You have a great job. A lot of lawyers would love to have your job. It's important work." Does she have to be so serious? Some light conversation would be good. No such luck. "You need to be more decisive. I'm starting a new job. I need someone who knows what he wants, so I won't second-guess myself." Oh, fucknuts, is she crying? "Joe, wait a second." I could hear her blow her nose.

"Are you OK?"

"No."

"Nothing serious?"

"No, not like that ... I planned to break up, or stop going out, and I can't. You're an eclectic pain in the ass, in a good way." Try to decipher that. When you practice law, sometimes you have to read tea leaves. You're trying to figure out what the other side wants. This is harder. Figuring out what Cindy wants.

She paused, then said, "So, it's the status quo. Keep going out and then we'll see."

"We are still going out?"

"I think so. I don't know."

"We shouldn't meet until you figure it out."

"You'll go out if I want to go out?"

"Yes. I will. Then I feel wanted, accepted."

"Joe, I'm touched. I'm looking at an apartment right now. Can you wait?"

"I'll wait. You've been patient with me."

"I feel like you've been patient with me ... By the way, the Astros' best player is ..."

"I know. Altuve. He's listed as five-six. Sometimes, athletes add an inch for the stats."

"I know you wouldn't."

"I wouldn't. And check out Wee Willie Keeler. He was the real deal ... So, can you pick me up at the hospital?"

"Let me think." She hummed a line from the Jeopardy theme song. "Yes."

"We'll go to the boardwalk. Play Skee-Ball. Do you like Skee-Ball?"

"Yes. It's been a while."

Minutes after hanging up, Cindy called back. She thought things over, and she was finished dating me. She didn't use the word breakup. I choked up but kept a stiff upper lip. It wasn't the breakup that upset me as much as the fact that she gave me a chance and took me seriously. It wasn't gratuitous. As far as I know, her decision had nothing to do with my stature. I could have acted more decisively myself. I wasn't there yet, and she knew it. So, we didn't quite get to a meaningful relationship. I thought one more get-together might turn it around. I think I surprised her when I said, "You can still come down."

"Really, you want me to?"

"It's a beautiful day and Asbury Park is rocking. The boardwalk is alive. I don't want to play Skee-Ball by myself."

"I'm not good at it."

"It doesn't matter."

"Give me a couple hours." Is this a second bite at the apple with no downside?

When Cindy finally appeared, she looked like she threw on some clothes. I was an afterthought. She drove me to the boardwalk. Beautiful day, big crowds. My only consolation was beating her at Skee-Ball. She grew increasingly uncomfortable and wanted to leave. No time to play miniature golf, or buy a T-shirt at The Stone Pony, the band venue made famous by "the Boss."

Cindy dropped me off at the Metropark Station after a mostly conversation-free forty-five minutes and one final awkward kiss. I started to walk away, went back, quickly hugged her, and said, "Thank you." I walked away again and added, "Aperol Spritz" with a thumbs up. She waved back with a half-smile. It would have been better if she stayed home.

CHAPTER THIRTY-FIVE

> ***I told myself to grow up, but that will never happen.***

All of a sudden, I was down to Jen and maybe Melissa. I was anxious but did not panic. What good would that do? I have two good options. Two women who put me at ease. That was mostly true for Jen. When she gets crazy, I like that part too. The bigger point was that I was far enough along with Jen to say our relationship was meaningful, or close to it, and very much alive. Sure, I could use a number of other colorful adjectives as well.

If one of them bails, I have no bench. If both bail, look out. I couldn't be sure about Melissa, but I felt relaxed after our airplane introduction. It made me feel good that she remembered me from Washington. Maybe it was the English schoolmaster glasses, the slightly receding but nicely parted dark brown hair, thick sideburns, the heavily starched striped button-down shirt, or my enthusiasm that put me in a better position. You throw all of it in the mix and hope it helps. Is it worth the extra dollar for extra starch? Of course. You do what you can with the hand you're dealt.

It's nine days before I dive into the icy waters of the legal world. I sat in Bryant Park outside the New York Public Library with my laptop and a lingering thought. What happens when Carter and I have wives? Talk about distractions. Will Carter's wife be friendly with my wife? And vice versa? I hope so. She better be. We won't marry women who dictate our social calendars, will we? I took two Tylenol to preempt a headache. I'll talk to Carter in case he hasn't focused on this stuff. He tends to jump into relationships. Of course, he also tends to jump out. We both have to avoid the unintended consequences of a bad relationship.

It was too nice a day for gloomy thoughts. The Inner Voice put a lid on them. I felt happiness all around in Bryant Park. Adults and children playing. Soccer, a putting green, card games, chess games. Couples, families, and friends of all shapes, sizes, and colors. Two bars in the shade to accommodate the pre-happy hour crowd. No drinks for me until I spend four hours in the lion-flanked New York Public Library. The lions are great symbols for seriousness of purpose.

Melissa texted and asked me to call. A second text came two hours later, while I was deep in the creative process. Later, she was excited and nervous on the phone. Was I going to her exhibition? I was optimistic but noncommittal. Then the next subject. "Joe, I want to talk to you about something."

"Ok. Nothing's wrong, is it?" I thought about when I met her. Sweet, innocent, playful. Looking for something.

"No, no, no. See my stepdad is a congressman. Jack Golden. Remember when we were talking to the older lady on the plane? I thought about telling you my stepdad is a congressman, but then you were working. He's in a suburban district north of Chicago. That's where I'm from."

"A congressman, huh? You're from a distinguished political family?"

"Thanks, well, we're not the Kennedys. We live in Glencoe. It's very nice, but it's not Hyannis waterfront." I could see she took me seriously.

"Of course not."

"I hope you're not upset, but I told my dad about your background. I told him you're a great lawyer."

"Thank you. That's very kind of you." I knew where this was going. There is no way I will return to Washington. It's exciting to start a career there. For most, it's also a great place to be single. My life there was like a boat owner's two best days; the day she buys the boat and the day she sells it. For me, it was the excitement of starting a job at EPA and the relief when I left Washington and the government for the outside world.

"Well, he would like to meet you. He's chairman of one of the house environmental committees." This is one way to get me to Chicago.

The only thing is, it's way too early to meet her folks. I can't fall into that trap again. I've met parents of two women, and neither event was helpful. This is different, right? It's professional. It could advance my career, at some point anyway. But if her folks don't like me, I could lose an up-and-coming girlfriend.

"Melissa, I think I can do it ... Wait a minute. Jack Golden. I knew a John Golden. He sent letters to EPA. A lot of them. See, for a while, I wrote response letters for the EPA Administrator. He was one of the few congressmen who kept an eye on us. I admired him for that. Most of them don't pay attention, and they grandstand when something hits the fan. Not Golden. So that's your stepdad?"

She laughed. I'm happy to entertain her. I wonder how this story will play out ... or end. Just enjoy the attention and don't ask her how she got a job at the Justice Department. "He comes home twice a month. He will be at the exhibit unless an emergency in Washington comes up. Remember it's next weekend. Saturday. Not this weekend."

"Got it."

"We'll go on a real date too?" I guess in her mind that made it more official.

"Yes, we have to. We'll squeeze it in. It's ..."

"Bashert, it's meant to be." She has the sweetest voice. I thought I was in love for a moment, but it passed.

"Mclissa, this is a lot of pressure."

"Joe, I'm kidding with you. It's ok."

"Thanks. By the way, do you like Aperol Spritz?"

"What's that?"

"It's a drink with Aperol, which is an Italian aperitif ..."

"You say that very well."

"Thanks. It's equal parts Aperol, Prosecco, which is sparkling wine, and ..."

"I know Prosecco."

"And club soda. And then you float an orange slice in the drink."

"This is your favorite drink?"

"Not always, but it's festive. If I get to Chicago, we'll have one at the Drake Hotel. The bartender there knows what he's doing."

"I'm starting to think you're ... well, different."

"Thanks. I like different ..."

"Oh, Joe, I got new glasses. You'll like them better."

"Great." I hope she's right. "The other ones. They were OK." I said I had to go.

Like I said, Melissa's almost my height, a bit shorter. You might say we're such a cute couple. Of course, most women won't go out with a guy who's the same height, so I give her credit. And I have to admit, we could be a cute couple.

I researched Jack Golden. He's been a Congressman for eight years. Before that, he ran a real estate business that was started by his father. He grew up on the south side of Chicago when there was a Jewish community there. The family-owned rental properties throughout Chicagoland. Then he bought properties and built apartments in Boca Raton.

This guy must be good because he's a Republican in a more liberal district. Melissa showed me family pictures on the plane. The Congressman married Melissa's mom, Lisa, who is very attractive, almost striking. It's her second marriage. Melissa has two brothers who look like snotty prep school kids.

I'm good with political types. You stand up straight, you look the person in the eyes, and say, "Yes sir" or "yes ma'am." You wear a suit or a sport jacket that says you mean it. Solid tie or dark tie with bright stripes. And tuck your shirt in. When I meet a big shot, I prepare by imagining him or her as a five-year-old. One more thing. If he boasts about Chicago, I won't say the city has so much to offer, but can't hold a candle to the Big Apple.

Now, I'm excited. And each time I talk to Melissa, I get an inner calm. She's easygoing and friendly. She could have a new boyfriend by tomorrow. I called her back after I finished a chapter and before I headed to King Cole.

"Melissa, hi."

"Joe, hello, can you please wait a moment?" I heard paper rustling and pans clanging. A holiday I forgot about? "I'm making baklava with my mom. Do you like baklava?"

"I think I had it once. It was too sweet."

"You're sweet already?"

"Yes, that's it." That was easy. Now take the dive. "I'm coming."

"Coming where?"

"To your show. Your exhibit."

"You are?" More noise in the background. She asked me to hold. I heard her say, "Mom, he's really coming. Tell Jack." She came back to the phone. "I didn't think ... I didn't think you would ... You are."

"As long as we can go to the basement bar at the Drake Hotel. The guy plays while the lady swoons. It's very ..."

"Romantic?" I couldn't bring myself to say the word. Too nervous. Happy, but nervous. I told myself to grow up, but that will never happen.

"Well, it's cozy."

"Hey, I bet you know people at EPA at the Regional Office. The exhibit is close to the Federal Building on West Jackson. It's not far from the Downtown Club. Jack's a member. It's the club the Jews started when the others wouldn't let them in." I only know this, because a lawyer friend of mine, who is Catholic, explained the club culture in Chicago to me.

So, it looked like the weekend's all planned. Well, DD thought she had everything planned, and it didn't get us over the top. It got me on top, temporarily. Is Melissa different? "I'll stay at Palmer House. Old elegance. They have a good weekend rate."

"You can stay at my parents."

"Very kind, but please, it's not necessary. I'll stay there or I can stay with my aunt. She lives north of the Loop, near State and Division Streets."

"Look, if you're too busy getting ready for work, I understand. What did you call it, 'game day?'"

She listened.

"Every workday is game day. No, I want to go. I do."

My attention didn't last. There was a text from Jen. "Hi darling. I need to talk to you." I started to sweat. Everything feels so immediate.

"Melissa, can I call you back? It's noisy where I am."

"I miss you."

"Yes." You better say it. I don't know if I mean it, but OK. "I miss you too." Well, the lady on the plane thought we were an item. Horn rimmed and cat-eyes. She thought we looked good together. It's something. It's not everything.

CHAPTER THIRTY-SIX

❝
Joseph, I have a confession.

It could all come down to the X factor. The Jen factor. The variable in the pursuit of a meaningful relationship. And this was not just any meaningful relationship. In the beginning, I did not imagine words like soulmate or best friend. She was just a fling, right? I thought that's what she felt. I was wrong. She stayed interested. I woke up one day and started to take Jen seriously. The idea of something lasting with a woman eight years older couldn't work, or could it? You know, issues like kids and that malicious biological clock.

I went to Carter's and sat at his kitchen table. He was playing tennis and gave me a key. I'll see him later after another round at the library. I called Jen. She sounded distant and uncertain. Not her typical out-of-the-gate self. Her daughter Sondra got mono from a boy at Andover. Jen called the boy, Jason, a narcissistic prick. "They go to these fancy schools; they're supposed to get educated. But they don't grow up." She asked me to come to Boston. It sounded almost like a cry of desperation. "All of this miscellaneous quality time and I'm getting attached to you …"

Jen took a deep breath and there was silence. Before I could respond, she continued. "Joseph, I have a confession." She hardly ever says Joseph. This must be a big deal. She apparently can't wait to say it in person. I felt squeamish. I couldn't speak. OK, everybody, get your popcorn and Junior Mints and wait for the show to begin.

I stuttered, "Would you like to talk in person?"

"No, I have to tell you."

Jen cleared her throat. "Actually, I have two confessions. The second one isn't exactly a confession. It's more like a lie. Are you ready? The first is that I dated a guy while the divorce was pending, nothing serious, and I dumped him. It was about two weeks ago, in fact, it was right before I saw you in France. I had to come clean. It would have been unfair to you. I have come a long way, darling, I'm not used to thinking in unselfish terms, especially since I divorced the big douchebag."

"So, you dated somebody else. It happens." Now, what am I going to do with this information? "You're done with him now?"

"Yes." So far, I don't hear anything mind-blowing or life-changing. I'm still on edge. Next?

"And the other confession?"

"Well, you're going to wonder about me." Only now? I will never have a dull moment with this woman. "I lied about my age. Let me explain." So, Jen's an older, older woman? How much older? She took a long pause. "I told you I was thirty-nine, sure, a youthful thirty-nine, right? But thirty-nine, nonetheless. I'm really thirty-four. So, I had Sondra when I was almost nineteen."

I was tongue-tied. Women lie all of the time in the other direction, but she's younger? Jesus Christ, do I need to verify this? Should I ask for her birth certificate? I wasn't so much angry as incredulous. Finally, all I said was, "What?" The best thing to do was shut up and see if anything made sense.

"No, I mean it. Thirty-four. If you thought I was older, you would be less likely to want a serious relationship, and you would break it off before I was emotionally engaged. Before the fallout would be too much. And before I said my real age. I tried to stay detached. It didn't work. I got more attached ... More wrapped up in Joseph Fine. Does this make sense? I shouldn't tell you this, but Anita gave me the idea. She's had her share of men issues. I guess she's not the best source of advice." This is better than theater. "I'm sorry. I take full responsibility for my actions, and I'm not even a Republican ... So, what do you think?"

It's funny about age. On one level, it's a state of mind. On any given day, I can pretend to be eight, eighteen, or thirty-one. Jen could be thirty-four or thirty-nine. Or even a little older. She's in good shape. For that matter, she could be thirty, maybe even twenty-eight. Not less than that. Now that I think I know her real age, I'll look at her differently. Of course, all of a sudden, she will look younger. I have to admit, this made me more interested. Five years changes the analysis. Like I got some kind of discount. Makes it easier to look at the long term.

"So, Jen, you wanted it to work, but you made it more unlikely by changing a key piece of information. I need a drink to absorb this. I can't think clearly for the moment ... OK, I appreciate your interest, and I'd like to keep you and me going. I wasn't sure where you stood. Look, I'm not good at this kind of stuff."

"I understand. Getting laid, no strings attached, that was pretty good, huh?"

"Yeah, for a while. Well, at some point ... At some point, there has to be more to it. A lot more."

"You're right, it's a lot to digest. Darling, you need to have a chat with your invisible friends. What are their names?"

If I didn't know her, I would think she was condescending. "Huckie and Chuckie. They've been with me since I was five years old. Thanks, but I don't need a consultation." And I will not disclose The Inner Voice.

"OK and don't get mad at Anita. I thought she made no sense at first, but I went along. Then, I thought, 'Wow, why am I doing this? It can't help. It can only hurt.'" She forced a laugh. "It's a good surprise for you?"

"And you were saving it for the right moment?"

"I didn't think we would get to that point. Or you would."

"Jesus Christ, thirty-four? I just got another five years?"

"Pretty good, huh? How often does that happen? So, I'll see you in Beantown."

"I'll let you know. Boston looks good. By the way, I'm forty-one. I'm aging gracefully."

She ignored that. "Darling, I'm thinking about you."

"Me too."

Up to this point, no headaches, no pressure, no real decisions. I still don't know enough about Jen. There must be details I would rather not know. She's hot, she's smart, she's animated. She went to boarding school and never finished growing up. Like me. She's active in the nonprofit world. Money doesn't seem to be an issue. And kids? She has one. Would she like to have two or three more? That's what I'd like. We can get to that later, especially since I just got five more years. I think we covered enough in this conversation. Is it OK to lie about your age? It may have worked.

CHAPTER THIRTY-SEVEN

ff
So, you've had issues too? Interesting.

Thank God for friends and diversions. I lunched the next day with my friend Jim McCarty. We met at Westside Restaurant on Broadway and 69th Street. Jimmy and I worked together in EPA Enforcement. He left after I left and went to one of the top white-shoe New York law firms. We go to Westside for the best turkey clubs and matzah ball soup.

I hired Jim to represent StarColor when the DOJ sued the Company. They demanded the Company spend $60 million to clean up contamination at a former chemicals plant StarColor bought from a now deadbeat company. Fair or not, a company can still have liability as the current owner. The company scientists said we could do a cleanup for $9 million. We agreed to a few items that our folks didn't think were necessary and settled around $22 million. StarColor built a clean state-of-the-art paint plant on another part of the property and recycled ninety percent of its waste. You don't get brownie points for that.

Jimmy and I had a few laughs about the good old days at EPA. Aside from some peculiar habits like his aversion to green vegetables and fear of driving a car, Jimmy was a top-notch attorney. He was a tall, lanky guy with an understated demeanor that didn't fit the stereotype of a hard-charging attorney, but he sure was.

When we were in D.C. I occasionally stopped by his office around lunchtime to chew the fat. He sat at an old wooden desk in a windowless office and would neatly open a bag of Doritos with big scissors while discussing a new settlement. One was with a well-known company that falsified emissions reports, which is a major no-no and can land an executive in jail. The company paid a big penalty that resulted in a bulk load of bad publicity and a damaged bottom line.

"We weren't as smart as the guys and gals in the big fancy law firms," he said in his Arkansas drawl, "but we tried harder, and we knew the cases better and we got results. I had more fun at EPA than I have at this stuffy law firm. Casual day at the law firm means gray wool dress pants and a light blue Brooks Brothers dress shirt." It always came down to this. "Joe, how come we don't get the same results with women? We do occasionally, but there are too many dry spells."

"Hey, just have to keep at it." I'm with him on that despite my recent flurry of relatively good fortune with the fairer sex. Jimmy knows Carter through me and has wisely declined Carter's offers to meet women after work. Lunch with Jimmy was a great diversion from the oncoming corporate wave. When I see him, I wonder why we don't get together more often.

Corporate life has benefits, but I didn't want to learn stuff like new billing software which Richard bought when he got excited about vacuous corporate buzzwords like metrics. We laughed. I know how to manage costs. Hire the right attorneys and keep a close eye on them. Jimmy said the administrative hassles are worse at a law firm. Like the pressure to bill time, which can lead to unintended sanitary issues like phone calls in bathroom stalls. Disgusting.

I rarely drink at lunchtime, but we did shots of Dewar's a few blocks uptown at a dive bar on Amsterdam Avenue. Jimmy wished me luck on the work reset. I suggested a sabbatical for him too. He simply responded with, "What's wrong with you?" After that, I rambled north from the Boathouse at 72nd Street and Fifth Avenue through Central Park. A quiet, sunny, warm Friday afternoon. I ended up at the Met and walked back to 72nd. From the Boathouse bar, I watched the rowboat renters glide around the small pond. The sun hit the water creating endless streaks of light. I took out my blue notepad and jotted some notes. A tall, young woman with long, straight blonde hair asked me what I was doing.

"I'm getting warmed up."

"Oh, for what?" she asked.

"I'm scribbling, it's how I warm-up for writing. It helps get thoughts swirling."

"Really, a book?"

"One of these days."

"What's it about?"

Let me see. What's it about? "It's about the four-percent factor."

"What?"

"The four-percent factor. The four percent of women willing to date a guy who is shorter than them. I would like to see the percentage go up or at least improve my acceptance rate."

The guy next to her was tall and fit with cropped red hair and an Ivy League banker jock look. He said, "He's trying to get laid more often."

I said, "That too. But women could be more open-minded."

His wife turned to him. "Honey, what did you say?"

"I told this gentleman to jump in the pond."

"You guys are such liars."

"Thank you, honey."

"And …," she stared at me. "You're looking for an excuse. I've had a tough time too. Don't tell me about open-minded. I'm tall and thin. A lot of guys don't like that. This one did." She happily pointed to her husband.

I said, "I don't make excuses. So, you've had issues too. Interesting."

"Most people are stupid. They don't know what they want. Something's built in that tells you how to act. When I met Keith, I said, 'There's no way this guy is open-minded.' But he was. I'm Beth." Keith was pleased with the back-handed compliment.

"I'll drink to that. I'm Joseph." So, others feel they don't get a fair shake. Short guys and tall women have something in common. Are we kindred spirits? Well, not sure.

I left before the conversation got any deeper. There was a text from Jen. I should have shut the phone off, even for a few minutes.

"Well, are you coming?"

I texted. "You mean Boston?"

"No, Tahiti. Yes darling, Boston."

I called her. Less risky. "Jen, I've got one weekend after this and then I'm back to work. I was thinking of Boston two weeks after I start work.

"What about next weekend?" That's when I go to Chicago.

"I can't."

"You can't or you won't."

I was surprised by the challenge. I liked being around Jen because there was no pressure. I could be myself. And I'm having too much fun.

"Jen, please, bear with me."

"I think there's another woman, you little shit." Something upset her. I'll take the high road for now. I tried to respond. Before I could, I teared up and stayed quiet. Jen broke the silence. "I'm so sorry. I'm really, really sorry. I will never do that again. I wanted to see you. My ex got into my head." Blame the ex. It's part of basic training for disgruntled women.

"It's OK. Well, it's not OK. Please don't say stuff like that again. I'm still digesting our last conversation."

"I promise." She left it at that. I didn't get more questions about next weekend.

You don't know when a woman will turn on you. I thought Jen had a different attitude. I still do. In the past, I had trouble with women because I didn't pay attention and said "What?" too much.

Jen seemed to tolerate it, almost liked it, to a point. She liked to press her finger into my belly and say, "You're my Pillsbury Doughboy," which I could have resented, but I liked it. And I didn't want it to end. I started to panic. I thought about the efforts Jen made to see me. So far, in this relationship, I waited for her to show up. I had to reciprocate. I discarded anxiety about getting ready for work and took an impromptu two-day trip to Boston.

It was the right move to see my newly youthful friend on her home turf. She had a two-story brick house on a hilly gentrified street in Watertown, an old Boston suburb. She moved after they split up. In the den, there were pictures of a diminutive couple I guessed were her grandparents. They were her mother's parents. They immigrated from Krakow, their name was Cohen, and they changed it to Crane.

I met Sondra, who was a mix of smart and smart-ass. What helped me connect was when I told her that her mom got me the megaphone. "That is so fucking cool. When my mom gets it right ... well she gets it right." I couldn't help razzing her and told her that Leicester had better college matriculation than Andover, which prompted her to jump up and get a brochure on figures for the senior class. OK, it was pretty even.

As for sightseeing, Jen gave me an abbreviated tour of the Boston Museum of Fine Arts, where she's a professional fundraiser. We walked where Paul Revere rode, and I found an old tavern on Lexington Green where we had a drink and practiced our colonial English accents.

For a woman who moved easily around the world of major charity events, she acted edgy and seemed to want every detail of my trip to go right. I'm the fidgety one, but at one point during dinner in the North End, I politely suggested that she needed to relax.

The visit went off without any major glitch and we agreed that once I got settled at work, we'll connect again. As soon as I got on the train at South Station, I took a few deep breaths. Two prospects very much intact.

CHAPTER THIRTY-EIGHT

I promise, there will be no pressure.

I had a week to mentally prepare for work. Which meant there was nothing to prepare for, other than get a head start on skimming and deleting a majority of the hundreds of e mails that grow and fester like weeds. Wait until I have to respond to some of this stuff. The corporate world beckoned.

The Sunday night before my return, I ironed my khaki pants and had five heavily starched stain-free shirts ready to go. I wore a brown light-weight herringbone sport jacket and felt like a modern-day Mr. Chips. I had to look the part when I walked in the door. People remember. I also like the look. It's glued to me.

After all the machinations, the return was uneventful. Except for a couple of pals, I didn't receive the happy, welcoming faces a starting lawyer receives. I got mostly weak hellos in the hallway and in the legal department kitchen. I thought there would be more smiles. People quickly adapt to personnel changes. What is new quickly becomes familiar. I felt like I didn't belong. The biggest change was an office renovation to handle more staff that left me with a smaller office. I put the brakes on a latent bad attitude. Look, nobody made me come back.

My friend, colleague, and in-house comedian Freddie Bankhauser, an intellectual property attorney, took me aside and asked how many women I "shagged" in Southern France. I smiled and remembered what Richard said about office demeanor. I politely told him to get lost because I can't say fuck off in the office anymore.

Tara, my legal assistant, was polite and detached. She's in her mid-fifties and the best legal assistant I ever had. She was upset when I left for Italy because she got stuck with an attorney who had a bad attitude toward legal assistants. She was relieved to see me. "I got used to lawyers who could get a document done in two drafts. You're a perfectionist and a pain in the …, but I'm glad you're back. I can talk to you. I missed the free therapy." I missed talking to her too.

I quickly returned to my old breakfast routine, a soggy egg and cheese sandwich with a strong cup of dark roast. It didn't take long to spill some on my shirt. I missed the fresh morning baguettes in Antibes. Why can't I get them here?

I finished breakfast and strolled into Richard's office for an update. "It's great to see you," he said. He took a deep breath for dramatic effect like a crisis had been averted. This made me feel good. We bullshitted about my adventures and went through some cases. I knew there was a "but" coming. "Joe, I need to tell you. You created a little resentment when you took off. I'm OK. You did what you wanted to do, and we wanted to work with you. Keep it light with these folks," he said in a matter-of-fact way. "And welcome back. What a fucking relief."

He really liked me, notwithstanding the challenge I gave him. You would think professionals in a legal office wouldn't stoop to petty jealousy and resentment. Wrong. And most of my time away was unpaid. It's usually a select few who worry about what the other guy or gal is doing instead of just producing themselves. I said, "Thanks. Not to worry. You'll see results."

We reviewed a few minor settlements. There were no major new claims. Little fires that other attorneys put out for me. Three months isn't much in the life of an environmental matter. They can go on for years. Little changed on the big matters. If you're negotiating with the government, you know there's a hiatus before they get back to you.

Mid-morning, Tara knocked on my door and sat down. I missed the daily briefing on her personal life and office gossip. No new office romances, but someone got fired for inflating expense reports and inappropriate touching. Thankfully, her lively demeanor was intact.

"I bet you had fun," she said.

"Well, I worked mostly on my book and traveled to some great places."

She didn't seem interested in the details. "Well, I'd rather work for you than a couple of self-anointed young attorneys who think they're entitled. What happened to mutual respect and common courtesy?"

"I'm sorry you had to put up with that."

"Well, thanks for whatever. Joe, I'm sorry I forgot to tell you. I should have sent you an email. A woman called asking for you. I think it was about two months ago. She didn't leave a message. I think her name was Monica. No, it was Melissa. She didn't say how she knew you. I said you were away and didn't know when you would be back. She had a sweet voice. I didn't want to give her any details. This Melissa called again, I don't know, about a month later, and I told her the same thing."

I blushed. "Thanks. You did fine." So, Melissa tried to find me before the plane ride. That made me feel good.

"She left a number the second time. No message." Tara went to her desk, opened the top drawer, pulled out a sticky note, and brought it to me. "Here." I recognized the number.

"She's a ... friend. I met her when I was at the Justice Department. Over three years ago. Then she was on my plane back to Newark. I walked down the aisle ... The plane aisle. She stopped me. I didn't recognize her, she had funny red cat-eye glasses. They looked like a disguise."

"So, you're in love."

"Not quite. I ... I don't know."

"Wow. That's a good story."

I went to her Facebook page. "Here's her picture."

"She's a cutie pie. Oh my God, those glasses. How tall?"

"Five-two or three. Doesn't matter."

"Sorry. It's what's inside that matters, right? That's what I told you. Or did you tell me?"

"Yes, but most people are superficial." I didn't want to say women, but that's what I meant. Tara knew what I meant. She has a healthy disdain for women younger than her anyway. I was tempted but did not discuss my efforts to include taller women in my social life.

"You're not going to run off with her?"

"No, no, I'm here."

"I'm glad to see your social life is improving. What was her name? The one before?"

"I met someone called DD after I left."

"No, the one before you left. You know how you get excited and talk louder when you're on the phone."

"Oh, Susie. We went out twice and then she said something like 'no offense, I need a taller guy. You'll find a nice woman. For sure.' What patronizing bullshit. I was so angry. Something had to change." And it did. Now was not the time to explain.

She pushed my right arm and said. "Cut the self-pity. Just wasting your time."

"You're right. But it's not self-pity." Tara's like an older sister who helped me stay grounded.

"What's in Chicago?" She must have heard me on the phone.

"I'm not sure. Tara, I gotta go." I played the busy lawyer card. She didn't believe me. It wouldn't be the first time. "Please close the door."

What am I doing? With Melissa, so far, so good. There were blanks to fill in. I saw photos of her paintings. Definitely abstract. Is she a grounded free spirit? We'll see. She's in Chicago, I'm in North Jersey. Distance didn't stop me before. I hope I like her new glasses. It's not quite, "I love you just the way you are." Melissa's different, right? I was also intrigued by her stepfather's bio. As lawyers say, he's a separate issue. He could be a good contact for my career, and what career would that be?

And so, what am I doing about Jen? I love when she says, "Hello darling." I hear her voice, she's lurking behind me, waiting to make a smartass remark. What if she knew about Melissa and Chicago? One false move and she'll toss el niño out the door. I called and got Jen's voicemail. Maybe I'll cancel Chicago and ride off into the sunset with her. I stared at the computer screen. The thought of digesting new corporate policies was tiring. My mind drifted and I pictured Jen and I on horseback riding into an old Western town. We walk into the saloon. She wears a denim shirt, suede vest, and pointed orange cowboy boots. A cowboy is dumbfounded I am with a kick-ass woman. Jen senses a showdown and asks him if there is a problem. The cowboy says, "No ma'am" and sheepishly grins. Jen glares at him. He runs out of the saloon. We start to make out and I snap out of it.

I returned to the computer screen. After reading a fantasy demand against the Company, I typed out, "Are you fucking kidding me?" Since I was not in a movie, I quickly deleted it and put the email in the To Deal With pile. I called Melissa and hung up before she answered. Too late to cancel Chicago? Yes. I could be in Chicago for a number of reasons. If Jen asks, I can talk about Jack Golden.

Melissa called back. "Joe, did you call? I'm sorry. I was setting up in the gallery."

"No, it was an accidental call."

"A butt call." She laughed. What a sweet, cheerful laugh. "I'm glad you accidentally called. My mom and stepdad are excited to meet you. Jack thinks your background is so interesting."

"I appreciate that. Aren't we getting ahead of ourselves?"

"You're coming to Chicago. It's a big deal." She said it like I was the Prince of Wales making a royal visit. "I have to warn you. He smokes big fat cigars. He's gotten better about going outside to smoke but still …"

"Well, these are his simple pleasures. It's his castle. Well, your mom's, too."

"He'd love to hear you say that. He talks about having a cigar with his future son-in-law."

"I don't smoke."

"He'll still like you. When will you get here?"

"That's what I wanted to talk about. I think it's too early to go. You meet the folks, and there are expectations."

"I wanted to see you, see my work. They'll be at the reception. That's all. Is it something with me or them?"

"Honestly, I haven't fared well with parents. I meet them too early."

"I promise, there will be no pressure. Come to the gallery, drink some wine, or what's that drink? Ape something?"

"Aperol. Aperol Spritz."

"Jack likes Scotch."

"Now you're talking. I'll have one with him. We'll be fine." I looked around my office. That sealed the deal. "OK, I'm coming." Will Jack Golden have a new buddy?

CHAPTER THIRTY-NINE

❝

They made the wrong assumptions.

I flew to Chicago O'Hare on Friday night and taxied to Palmer House Hotel in the Loop. The art gallery was a mile and a half from the hotel. My room was small and warm. I had a bed, a rickety nightstand, and a desk.

The hotel had a distinct historical appeal, especially the inspiring ceiling murals, which were painted in the 1920s by a Frenchman with an Art Deco bent. It's two blocks to the Chicago Art Institute, which is worth a visit to see a painting called *Nighthawks* by Edward Hopper. I never want to be lonely in the wee hours of the night like the diner patron in the painting.

I couldn't fall asleep and went to the lobby bar. The bartender said it was closed, but she brought me a shot of Jameson. It felt good on this unseasonably cool early August night. We talked as she cleaned up. She told me about her micromanager boyfriend. I tried to be sympathetic but lost interest after she kept making excuses for living with him.

Next morning about seven, I got up. Bright light poured in through the small, sooty window. I typed eight pages of gratitude prose and fell back asleep. The phone rang.

"Hello."

"Joseph, hello, it's Jack Golden, Melissa's dad. How are you? Say, I wanted some time this weekend to talk."

"Very good, thanks, how are you, sir? I'm coming to the exhibit around eleven. Maybe after lunch?"

"Early afternoon, fine. We'll have a drink. I'll call you after lunch. You have an interesting background."

"Thank you." I meant to ask him what Scotch he likes.

"We'll talk then." Click.

I took the subway to Merchandise Mart and walked to Victoria Becker Gallery. The gallery is in a former warehouse in the River North area that was converted to art galleries, boutiques and restaurants. I wore my business casual uniform: dark jeans, a heavily starched button-down blue and white striped shirt, and round-toed dark brown cowboy boots. The plan with Melissa was simple; keep it friendly and stay positive. Don't snap at the artsy types who are more full of it than some members of my profession. The plan with the Congressman? Listen closely and don't commit.

Victoria Becker Gallery was one main room with rows of large pipes and ducts along an eighteen-foot ceiling. The walls and ceiling were bright white. There was a large desk with a Tiffany lamp in one corner away from the entrance. The gallery crowd included multi-generational artsy types, hipsters, and what I guessed were family friends and relatives. Against the back wall was a table with coffee and chocolate croissants.

Three artists were featured, including our own Melissa Spence. Her genre was splashy colorful abstract art with Jackson Pollock's legacy written all over it. The two other artists exhibited Lake Michigan watercolors and small group sculptures. What got my attention was the sculptor's clay relief of three elderly people sitting on a bench, each looking out in a different direction. Each one yearning for something. Nothing sums up the human condition better.

At first, I didn't see Melissa. A woman with long brown teased hair in a tight-fitting navy V-neck sweater, who kept saying "awesome" and "no worries," to guests, walked up to me. I made a mental note to assure her I'm not worried.

"Can I help you?" She giggled. Was it meant for me?

"What's so funny?"

"The way you're looking around. Like you're in the wrong city."

"Maybe I am. And who are you?"

"I'm Victoria Becker."

At that moment, Melissa walked in and greeted us. She didn't wear glasses, and her friendly brown eyes took over. I kissed her cheek and stopped short of a hug not knowing if her parents were there. She brought me back to a school friend, a happy girl on the playground, jumping rope in her blue paisley dress. Melissa turned to Victoria. "This is my friend, Joseph Fine. Victoria owns the gallery." Victoria is about fifty and tall, has a shit-eating grin like Carter, and emits an air of superiority, which I don't like. Jen has a devious smile but also shows class and decorum.

"Yes, we met."

Melissa asked me, "What do you think of the artwork?"

A half-lie would be required. "Oh, it's very interesting. The shapes, the lines. They go in all directions, but they don't meet up. Is that supposed to mean something?"

"OK, if that's how you see it. I didn't have a particular statement in mind."

Melissa pulled me aside. "Don't let Victoria bother you. She owns the gallery, and she thinks she is the show. You just have to humor her. Victoria is good at what she does. She manufactures buzz, and she gave me a show."

"I know the type. Not to worry."

I headed toward Victoria who was talking to an older gentleman. He stared at her chest which was also on display with the snug sweater. At a certain age, you get a pass for looking. She said, "Joseph, this is Mr. Davis, a friend of Mr. Golden."

He said, "Welcome to Chicago. Jack and I were in business together before he went to work in the swamp. Oh, and Victoria is a big deal here."

"Thank you, sir."

Mr. Davis left, and Victoria lowered her voice. She was within a foot of me. "The congressman's a bully. His family owns this building. He pressured me to give Melissa a show. Her paintings ..., well ... there's abstract and there's abstract. Her stuff is out there." She lowered her voice to a whisper. "Go meet Mr. Golden, then we can talk more." I just nodded. I did not like this woman, and I normally don't feel that way about anyone early on.

Across the room, the congressman talked with a young woman. She was upset about something. He was steamed and broke away, then saw me. He was my height and had big perfectly veneered white teeth. He reminded me of a younger version of my grandpa's friend, Irving Bluestone. Mr. Golden was bald with a round face, squinting eyes, a small nose, and a slight waddle. "Well, Mr. Fine. So nice to meet you," he said warmly like I was the only one in the room.

"Yes sir, it's my pleasure. This is quite a show."

"Yes, it is. If you ask me, it's ... Never mind." He smiled. "I'm told, Melissa has a few very good pieces. She is so happy you're here. I'm pleased because she normally goes for artists who think rent is a four-letter word and have a mañana thing about growing up. Anyway, Joseph, I want to talk with you about the Environment and Public Works Committee. I'm the chairman, and we need a staff counsel. You're the one that ghost wrote the responses to my EPA letters. They were very persuasive. You play golf?"

"No sir, I don't." I'm not surprised he knew I wrote the letters. There are few real secrets in that town.

"That's OK, we'll talk later. I gotta go now."

Melissa walked around, smiling and talking. For the first time, I saw the new glasses with dark squarish frames. An improvement over the cat-eyes, but these were too masculine.

Sometime later Victoria saw her opportunity. "Joseph let's go outside." I hesitated, then followed her to the door, and around the corner. "Great show, huh?" she said.

"Yes, it's fun." She seems like a backstabber, so I didn't want to give her much credit. I said something vanilla-like, "The people are more interesting than the artwork."

"I agree. Often the case." She put her hand on my shoulder. "I feel awkward saying this. You're a smart guy. You would find this out anyway. Melissa has problems." I wished she would stop right there. "She had to leave the Justice Department. Some kind of behavioral or anxiety thing. She started art as part of therapy. She has a few good pieces. I shouldn't have said anything."

"I wish you hadn't." This woman is awful. But is she helpful?

"She does have talent." I'm not sure she meant it.

I didn't appreciate what I considered Victoria's breach of trust. She's right, I would figure it out, sooner than later. I made a beeline to the bartender for a glass of pinot noir. It was wine and beer only. Ten minutes later, I had a second glass. I stayed with Melissa while she greeted a steady stream of visitors. A group of her high school friends showed up and then friends from University of Illinois. All smiles and bubbling over. I had a third glass. I better have a cup of coffee with lunch.

We stepped out for a quick bite. She looked naïve to the world. All goodness and sweet things. I could look at her all day as long as she takes off the thick-framed glasses. For the first time, I wondered if drugs affected her demeanor.

When we returned, Melissa's stepdad was ready to chat. She said to me, "He's a tough guy. Don't worry, it's your life."

"Thank you. I mean, Melissa, I just went back to the company. One thing for sure, we'll see eye to eye."

She thought. "Oh, I get it."

Mr. Golden wore madras pants, a crocodile belt, and a pale-yellow button-down shirt. The madras pants were red, white, blue, and yellow. He must be a real fashion plate on the golf course. "Congressman, it's nice to see you again." I poured on the charm.

With my cowboy boots, I was about an inch taller than him. It's not why I wore them.

We went to a pub named Fogarty's, which was around the corner from the gallery, and sat at a table in the back. The pub was dimly lit. It was early afternoon, and we were the only ones there except for a man at the front at the bar. You couldn't hear a peep. I felt like I was in a scene from an old gangster movie.

"The pub was started by my father. We own the property. He named it Fogarty's. 'Golden' wouldn't cut it for an Irish pub. The family was Goldwasser then."

The congressman wasn't as brash as he first appeared. He asked about my background. He liked the boarding school part. His children and stepchildren went to private day schools. "My kids don't realize what a great education I gave them." We had drinks. He was thrilled when I ordered Jameson. "It's the best antidote to a week in Congress where everybody shoots their mouths off. I'm amazed at how some of those folks got elected. They never did a fucking thing in their life, never played ball in the capitalist world before running."

He talked about the staff counsel position. "Joseph, the last person I had was very talented. She went to work for one of the big D.C. law firms. I think it was Covington. You'll be right in the middle of this climate change debate. I want a bipartisan bill and you can write it. We have to stop letting the other side take all the credit when it comes to environmental issues. We have to show we care. Pretty exciting, huh?"

"It really is." I loved talking politics and issues. "Congressman, when I was at EPA, I spent hours on legislation with congressional staffs. A year would pass with no results. And then another year. As a businessman, I'm sure it was frustrating to you. Fortunately, I had other work, cases that lead to big settlements."

I'm not sure he was listening. "Look," he said, "this position has nothing to do with my daughter. Whatever happens there, that's your business. And please, call me Jack."

"I will. Thanks, Jack."

The position sounded great, but the timing was not right. I would lose all credibility with the StarColor folks. How do you graciously say no to a feisty hard-ass short guy? I know. The stature adjective has nothing to do with it. "I very much appreciate the offer. Let me give it some thought. If it doesn't work, please keep me in mind in the future."

"That's fine. I know you just got back to Stanley Walker. I'll stay in touch. You know, Joe, I'm facing a tough race in November. I won last time because my opponent got caught in a scandal. If I lose this time, you would still be on the committee staff. But I'm not going to lose. It's a fucking swamp, D.C. Sometimes, to get away, I go to Montana for fly fishing. Maybe we'll go sometime." This wasn't a hobby I imagined for Jack Golden. He seemed like a canasta, blackjack, and shuffleboard guy.

So much for the interview part. The congressman rattled on about his premarital exploits, which were entertaining to a point. I felt uncomfortable, but I couldn't tell him to stop talking. He said, "When I was your age, I had to dare myself to ask a woman out. It was the only way I could do it. One rejection after another. I never gave up. You become a congressman, and the women are waiting for you at the Mayflower Hotel. Some guys spend more time there than their offices. They put on great dinners. And a lot more." He winked.

Then there was a touching part. "You won't believe this, but I met Melissa's mom on a volleyball court. She sat on a bench waiting to play. I was the shortest guy there. The other guys were a bunch of slugs. Lisa could see I was a good player and very serious. She went out with me. I was incredulous. She was taller too. Well, my teeth weren't as far apart as they are now, and I had nice thick dark hair. She turned out to be the right one. How did I know that? I didn't. You assume things and you know how often you're wrong? Well, a lot."

He wasn't finished. "All the women that wouldn't go out with me. They made the wrong assumptions. See what I mean?" He expelled a booming laugh. "You know what clinched it? Lisa's father had a variety store. They made egg and cheese sandwiches on the best hard rolls. I knew it was time to settle down."

"Jack, I love a good hard roll. I must say …" I couldn't keep from laughing. "You have a lot of wisdom."

"You're a good kid. You know where to find me if you're interested."

"Fogarty's, right?" He slapped me on the back. I felt a jolt.

"That's my local office. You're very intelligent."

"Thank you."

Back at the gallery, the crowd had thinned out and most of the pinot noir was gone. I took one more glass. Melissa was excited because she sold one of her paintings to a close family friend. Still, a sale is a sale. "Recognition is a great thing," I said to her, and I meant it.

The late afternoon was cool and bright. Not much wind in the Windy City. We walked down Orleans Street and over the Franklin Orleans Bridge to LaSalle, and on to the venerable Downtown Club. She wanted to buy me a drink. Which means it goes on Jack's tab. We entered the Club. The doormen, Charlie and Bert, greeted us. Charlie said, "Melissa, you're back from Washington? Shutting down the polluters? You saved the world already?"

"No, not yet. I'm an artist now."

They seemed confused. "Well, if that's what you want."

Melissa gave me a tour. I've been in a few clubs for legal seminars. They are staid, but calming, and sheltered from the unsettling world outside. The brown-stained wood paneling, Persian carpets, and small stained-glass windows exude warmth and refinement. We passed by the huge ballroom. Aside from an enormous French chandelier, it was cold and distant. I guessed she would get married here. She didn't say anything, and I took a deep breath.

We ended up in a small oak-paneled room that was the club's library. Bookshelves filled one wall from the floor to the ceiling. The coffee table had a large picture book of the Club's history dated 1951. We sat on the plush tan sofa and she showed me a picture of her stepfather's father, one of the club's founding members. I guess the drinks will wait. "You know the story," I said, "they started their own club because the others didn't want them." I'm not sure Melissa was listening. She got up and closed the door.

She moved closer to me, sat on my lap, and we started to kiss. I felt safe in this dreamworld where only good things can happen. Then came the surprising part when she said, "I love you." I froze and could not get the same words out. I think a lot of guys lie in this situation, but I couldn't. The reverie was over, and for a moment, I wondered what I was doing here.

Melissa saw me deep in thought. She got off my lap. "Are you OK?"

"I'm overwhelmed, sorry." She checked to see if the door had a lock. It didn't. Which meant we had to stop before second base? I didn't want to jeopardize the congressman's membership status or burn a bridge with him. "Melissa, it's been lots of fun, but I think we need to be careful in here." Suddenly, I was distracted by thoughts of Jen and how she took charge at Lisette's party.

"Don't worry, Joe, the staff knows me, they know my dad's a congressman. I always give them an extra bill even though you're not supposed to tip." I wondered if this was her go-to room, but of course, I didn't ask.

Melissa felt entitled, and I didn't like it. She acted like her stepdad would bail her out if she needed him. He was a tough guy, but I could tell he worked for it and didn't wear it on his sleeve. I still wondered if I was in the right place, but it was a moot point. She fell on top of me and we went to work. Her fairy-tale smile and the fresh, clean smell of her reddish-brown hair mattered more for the moment.

We took a break, and I asked, "Well, I guess you know how to take advantage of being the congressman's daughter?" As soon as I said it, I knew it came out wrong.

"What are you talking about?" She kept smiling. "You work with what you're given. You do, don't you?"

"I agree. You leverage what you're given. I mean what you're good at, not exploiting it." Why am I digging a bigger hole?

"I'm not exploiting anything. Not only that, but I was trying to help you. My stepdad likes you and well, I felt bad for you. You looked lost. Victoria said so."

I ignored the comment. And Victoria is a snake. "I had a great chat with your stepdad. Good man." As for others at the reception, her friends were flaky, and her art was ... thought-provoking?

She nodded. "Now, maybe we'll come back here after dinner. The club has a handful of rooms. They're a little outdated, but a bed's a bed, right?" So, there was a possibility to get laid. I mean sexual relations. Was there a downside? First things first.

We had a lovely dinner at an Italian restaurant in the Water Tower, thanks in part to two Dewar's with a lemon twist. Between the pinot and the booze, I was dragging after dinner. We ordered brandy for dessert. Melissa wanted to know how much I cared about her. I said, "I care, I do, it's early." That wasn't unambiguous enough to get me back to the club.

I suggested a nightcap at the Drake Hotel or the piano bar at Gibson's, the old Rush Street steakhouse. She said it was a long day, and she was ready to go home. You know what that means.

We left on a positive note. She was adorable when we parted. It was late, and she was a bit blurry or sedated. Was it fatigue or did she take something for whatever ailed her? I didn't ask and she didn't say anything. I said I would call her when I got home, and I was grateful for the trip and the attention. Maybe I grew up on this trip. My bench was in question, but it didn't bother me anymore. I don't know why, but I had a burst of energy and confidence.

Melissa drove back to Glencoe, and I walked the two miles to Gibson's. The cool air felt good. I liked this big, brash city. I sat next to a woman at the piano bar who wore a knee-length charcoal cocktail dress. She had layers of mascara and was inebriated. A Black gentleman in a tuxedo played piano and had a voice that was spiritual and moving. He had an electric smile and winked at me like he was giving me a heads-up about her. I think he was trying to warn me. I asked him to play *Corner of the Sky*. He graciously agreed. It's so uplifting.

> I've got to be where my spirit can run free
> Got to find my corner of the sky

The woman asked me to buy her a drink. I politely declined. She wanted to go to another piano bar a few blocks away. I declined that request too but was not ready to call it a night. I stayed for a few more songs. I imagined Jen sitting on the other side of the piano bar. She couldn't see me but ordered spritzes and brought one to me.

CHAPTER FORTY

""

Look how far you've come.

It felt great to be back in the Big Apple. I almost enjoyed the ride from LaGuardia through the orange cone obstacle course into Manhattan. The street congestion and noise were oddly comforting. I got back early enough Sunday afternoon for some quality writing time.

I stayed in touch with Melissa after the Chicago weekend. On the surface, she was the sweetest, most optimistic woman I ever met. It was hard to tell if there was a strong enough woman behind the blissful eyes and irresistible smile. A few weeks later, I went back to Chicago. The relationship, which began with sparks of light and magic, came crashing down. She lashed out, I mean really lashed out, during a walk on the lakeshore when I didn't make a strong enough commitment. The backstabber Victoria warned me. And yes, Melissa is almost my height, and no, height was not a factor.

The congressman's job offer was another matter. I knew her stepfather and I would get along well. It was hard to get around the timing. It might have worked after I left EPA. There was a practical side too. These congressional committee jobs can be seven days a week affairs, day and night, especially when a big hearing or bill deadline is coming. There is no way I could set aside enough time for the creative life. Jack and I continued to talk from time to time. He even invited me on a fly-fishing trip to Montana with a son from his first marriage and two of his old Chicago buddies. It was great fun, and something I never would have done on my own.

Naturally, to clear my head, I found myself in New York the following weekend. A shiny red Mazda Miata was parked in front of Carter's building. The car sat in a space marked for commercial vehicles only. I peeked inside and saw a Red Sox baseball hat and an unfolded laminated street map with "Venice" in bold letters. What are the chances? Wouldn't Jen tell me if she were in town? Is Jen looking for me? Did Carter borrow her car? I got closer and saw a Pennsylvania license plate. It wasn't her car.

I headed uptown to the Starbucks at 71st and Broadway and waited for Carter. All of the little round tables were occupied except one where someone spilled a drink which dripped on the floor. The chairs were dry, so I quickly sat down. Carter strolled in wearing a T-shirt that said, "I'm just here for the cheerleaders," in large capital letters. I couldn't help but smile.

He looked at the table. "Can't they do better than this? When I was in college, if we made a mess, it was a lot worse than this. Now, Joseph, my good man, I am here to give you a heads-up."

"Carter, I need a drink if I have to listen, and Starbucks doesn't serve alcohol the last time I checked."

"It'll just take a minute."

"Let me guess. A new girlfriend? An old girlfriend that wants you back?"

"Joe, you know what I was thinking about? Remember Bossley?" Bossley went to Leicester and was a slacker. "What an aimless jack ... He was drunk and sat in the common room in Harken House. He called you a dirty Jew. The putz was eating a powdered doughnut. He was pathetic with the powder all over his mouth. You grabbed him and screamed at the top of your lungs, 'Don't you ever talk to me like that, or I will fucking kill you. Got it?' A piece of doughnut fell out of his mouth, and you took it and rubbed it in his face."

"I was weightlifting then. Fucking Bossley. We became good friends. And he married a Jewish girl. He came full circle. People change. It's the second and last time anyone ever called me that. And why did you bring this up?"

"No reason. I just thought about it. You have a lot of balls. Or at least you used to. You've matured in your own unique way." Sounds like he needed something.

"Carter, I have to get something straight. How old is Jen?" It doesn't hurt to get additional confirmation.

"What? You know how old she is. She'll be forty soon. I think Anita told me. I didn't meet Jen that long ago either. "

"Well, it's not true. She said that originally and then told me she was thirty-four. She told me she was older, so I wouldn't view her as a serious prospect, and then she couldn't be hurt as much if I broke it off."

Carter's mouth dropped. "Holy shit. This makes no sense. Anita's known her for years. She never said anything."

"Carter, if I lose Jen, I'm down to no prospects. I built up a reserve and it's gone. Why I came back here, I'm still not clear. Well, the book is almost half done. I turned the *Unconventional Guide* … into a piece of fiction. The main character, a socially conscious guy, gets more women than I ever did."

"You have a vivid mind, but here's a pithy piece of advice. Keep the day job. It's looking better and better."

"I'm OK, for now. Just watch me."

"Unless … Joe. Does Jen talk much about her ex-husband?"

"He's not an official ex yet. She filed papers. She hasn't said much other than an expletive here and there."

"He's high up at Morgan Stanley."

"She mentioned something financial. I figured she had enough bucks to travel. I've never discussed money with her. I'll get to it. Right now, I want to run away, drive into the sunset. After that, get married. Have kids. A nice little dog. I like Cavapoos. Part cavalier, part poodle. They're the cutest. The kids will love him. Or her."

"I never heard you talk like that. According to my aunt, that's what Jen wants too, not in those exact words. I'm going out on a limb, but Anita doesn't think you'll go along. If my mom were alive, she would be rooting for a happy ending. She always liked you."

"Thanks. I liked your mom. She was so even-keeled, I couldn't figure how you were related. And your aunt? Jen's the best imperfect woman I've been with. We have a good back and forth. I think I'm OK with her new age. God, I better ask for more proof."

"You're a lawyer. You'll figure it out." Carter looked around the room. "Life's an adventure, huh?"

"I don't mind the drama. Keeps me interested."

"When we were backpacking around Europe after graduation, we were on a train, I think it was from Munich to Amsterdam. We talked to two women from Long Island, remember their accents? You were talking about the environmental movement and how it was the culmination of the industrial revolution, and this woman took you seriously. It was Tina, right? Who was the other one? I don't remember. Then they got off the train and we went on to Amsterdam. So, what happened?"

"Tina said I was cute. Once she said that, I thought she wouldn't take me seriously. She missed out. No, I blew it."

"You did. She liked you. You didn't pay attention. You let her go. Look how far you've come. Now, I found a new bar for your highness."

"Thanks, but I'm going to King Cole. I like fairy tales and nursery rhymes. Especially if they come true."

"Now, Joe, my good man, I gotta run."

"Thanks for mentioning Tina. My self-confidence was rocking, and you bring her up. I get it ... By the way, I signed up for a kickball league in Hudson County. I'm one of the captains."

"How did you do that?"

CHAPTER FORTY-ONE

" All I did was to feel empowered.

About a year after I came back from France, I had an early morning settlement meeting in midtown Manhattan. I walked past Grand Central Station on my way to a law firm in the MetLife Building. A woman ran down the street toward me. She got within ten feet, and I called out, "Wait a minute." She stopped abruptly. I said, "Is that you?"

"Is that me?" And then, "Oh my God, Joseph, it's you. I'm rushing. I have an appointment in ten minutes." She dressed professionally in a dark pantsuit and light silk top. A little heavier than when I last saw her. I've gained a few pounds too. I wore the same tortoiseshell horn-rimmed glasses. My hair was shorter, and a little darker from hair color.

"DD, what's going on?" She gave me a hug that I can only describe as significant. What happened to volatile DD? She looked happy and all grown up. Did I miss something?

"I wish I could talk. I'm meeting Henry at the doctor's. He's my husband. Joe, I hope you never have to go through this. We're going through in vitro. It's the second time. He's been so patient and supportive."

"I'm glad for you. You seem positive. I know you'll get there."

"Now Joe, don't be patronizing. I'm sorry, that wasn't necessary. I must run." She left, then turned around to face me. All lingering bitterness washed away. "Henry, he's a good guy. He's not Joseph Fine." Another big hug. I saw the bold lipstick smile that overwhelmed me when I met her in Venice. Seeing her made me emotional. She walked away, only to turn around one more time. "You were staring. They were yours ... Once."

"I know." Nothing more to say. She blew a kiss and ran off. At one time, her globes were part of my world. Upright, projecting, and proud. I was less mature then. Well, not by much. Did I do the right thing breaking it off? I think so. I choked up. I hope the in vitro works for them.

The months passed. Work and writing were progressing well. So, what happened? Where do things stand?

I decided a year and a half ago to expand the pool of potential dates, girlfriends, and/or soulmates by also seeking taller women. It didn't mean I would exclude those who were the same height or shorter, just that I would add more possibilities to the mix. I knew there were historical and cultural biases. Biases that were hard-wired into women and supported by men for a long, long time. Biases that I previously addressed by removing taller women from the chase. And they remain. The key was to connect with the subset of taller women who were open to someone like yours truly.

After all of the soul searching and overthinking, the results were a better social life and at least two meaningful relationships. Luck played a part, it always does, but you make your own luck by putting yourself in the right position. Sounds simple? It's the only way to get from here to there.

Now, what about the writing? Within a month of reentering the corporate rat race, I saw daylight. It was morning in the Garden State. Step by step, bit by bit, or as Annie Lamott says it in her book *Bird by Bird*, I made the writing work by going balls to the wall every weekend plus two to three evenings a week for a year. Maintaining a schedule was not difficult, except for a one-month period when I worked seven days a week on an acquisition. Even then, I squeezed in a couple of hours here and there to write.

Jen gave me tough love to get the writing done. She set targets before we would meet. I was rewarded for every eighteen pages. The number is supposed to be good luck because it's based on two Hebrew letters that spell "life." She gave me extra credit for twenty-four or more pages. No real symbolism there. This sounds crass and mechanical, but it worked. Especially the extra credit part. On long weekends, like the Fourth of July, she gave me a small reprieve.

Jen was certainly a mystery in the beginning. I didn't know what to think of her. There was no precedent, no frame of reference. And then, the question about her age, which I wondered about, and then she brought it up. The confession helped. Was it the difference? I verified her birthday for my own peace of mind. We understood each other since we were both adolescents at heart and played adults as needed. Yes, she was only three years and a few months older, and yet I needed to occasionally remind her that I was the more mature one.

Jen and I got together at least monthly, mostly in New Jersey and a few times in Boston. She exposed me to the nonprofit world and fundraising events at Children's Hospital and the Boston Museum of Fine Arts. Meanwhile, I continued to chase other women. I had to prove how many would find me datable. Nobody reached the point of meaningful. About eight months ago, I had the date from hell, which precipitated an epiphany to cut the shit and stick with Jen. It felt right. There was no more soul searching about keeping a bench after that.

Jen was especially supportive the last six months, when she moved to New Jersey, kept me focused, and simplified my social life. Love manifests itself in many ways, but when your partner supports your creative energies, it's the best. I threw a big party at my Hoboken apartment for her Jersey move. All the usual suspects were there, including Carter and Anita, my lawyer pals, and even Harry and Joanne.

Now for the good part. Through a friend at a literary agency, Jen located an editor who cleaned up the text and an agent who marketed the book to publishers looking for something new and different in the self-help category. It was featured as a book from the short-statured male perspective, but applicable to women and men looking to expand the pool of possible mates, by going beyond age-old self-imposed barriers. Take a leap and see what opens up.

Two months passed, and my agent called. A small outfit was interested. The sky opened up. It was sunny everywhere I went.

There were a number of good reviews and a share of uncomplimentary ones. Even some caustic folks who thought I had a lot of nerve. That's fine. Whenever you're trying to change the way people think or behave, some aren't going to like it. I had the toughest critics in New York City, where several women fumed this was really a book by a man telling women who they should date. One woman was particularly upset because her boyfriend, who had been loyal and attentive, started to ignore her, and then they broke up. She said I encouraged him to look for other women he hadn't considered. All I did was invite men and women to feel empowered.

My agent set up a series of book signings. I used my vacation days going to eleven cities. The events started and ended in New York. The last one was held at a large independent bookstore on the Upper East Side. The old wood floor creaked and the owner, Everett Parsons, played the part in a checkered sport jacket, white dress shirt with cufflinks, and a colorful bowtie. Jen helped Everett set up. Carter's job was to have enough pinot noir. He also found a lady friend to make Aperol Spritzes. Anita set up a large tray of cheese, thin crisp crackers, and Picholine olives from Zabar's.

My "team" got the word out, and we had a big crowd. There were more women than men, which I found interesting. I saw below-average height guys as well as women of various heights. The guys wore starched dress shirts, which I always recommend.

One of them told me he asked eight women out in three months, without regard to height, before he got a date. I told him to keep up the good work.

DD walked in and got in line. I was concerned she could cause a spat. She was remarkably restrained, even friendly. But she thought my book, which she hadn't read, was a self-serving piece. It created sympathy for guys who couldn't get a date, and women were the real victims. Yes, I wanted women to cut shorter guys more slack, but I didn't view the situation as a zero-sum game for men or women. "Open up the tent for both," I said. The point was to think broadly. She looked at me like I had a screw loose. I could only smile and say, "Thanks for coming." That disarmed her, and I blew her a kiss as she walked away.

She rushed back to my table and interrupted the next person. "Joe, I wanted to tell you. I'm pregnant."

I froze, stared into space, looked at her. "That's wonderful. I'm happy for you." I stood up and excused myself, asked Carter to cover for me, and walked outside for a couple of minutes. I took a deep breath. It hit me. No crying, please. I really was happy for her. I took another deep breath and returned to the table.

Later, Tammy and Brie showed up. I'm glad I left them a message. They waved and called to me from the back of the line. I waved back and said, "Holy shit" loud enough for others to look my way. I missed Brie's "Oh honey this" and "Oh honey that," and the excitement she generated when she walked into a room. And Tammy, there's a woman I can only wonder about. Well, what if …? They approached me. We had hugs all around. I introduced them to Carter.

Tammy said to me, "So you're a writer. I missed my opportunity ... Kidding."

I said, "Henry's Bar that was a great hangout."

"Loved it. I remember the happy little boy who raced by us, kicking the ball."

"I guess I missed that."

Marie sent best wishes. She was on another trip to Nice. I invited Cindy too. She didn't think she could make it from Parsippany in time. It sounded like her new position was demanding. When the event was nearly over, she came in huffing and puffing, carrying a large jar of jumbo green olives, with a blue ribbon wrapped around the top.

"Here's something to go with your next spritz," she said. "I'm on my way to a play, but I wanted to stop by and say congratulations. I brought these back from Milan." I barely had a chance to thank her. She left as quickly as she walked in. What mattered was she showed up.

Harry and Joanne came in just in time to help us clean up. Harry told Carter not to put the pinot noir away. He said, "I can't believe I know a real writer." Amazing what little it takes to impress someone. My lawyer friends Bill and Jimmy came after official hours. Each one said his social life was going well, no thanks to me. They sounded rehearsed. I told them that comment would get them a drink at the King Cole.

So, what to do when the book signings are over? No question there. It was time to re-exit the corporate world. Jen was the catalyst. She got me across the finish line. I guess everything was aligned that night in late April in that dimly lit Venetian bar.

Jen left the book signing before it was over to pick up a few things. She called after I said goodbye to all of the stragglers. I came outside. She was double-parked on the street down the block from the bookstore. "How did it go after I left?"

"Great. I recognized a few people. Some folks, well women, had opinions. Good and not so good. Some thought I was trying to tell them what to do. It's OK. Gets the conversation going."

"Well, you were, weren't you?"

"Well ... yes. I didn't tell them. I suggested and persuaded. You can't tell a woman she isn't tolerant or open-minded."

"You're so full of shit, but that's what I love about you. Yes, you have something to say."

I opened my arms, looked at her, kissed her. "Jen, thank you, here we are. At this point in time. On this street. You didn't want to say, but ... where are we going?"

"We're going West, young man. Interstate 80. Cleveland, Chicago, up to I90, Rapid City. You always talk about the Grand Tetons. On to the Pacific. I have the map that Kerouac drew when he crossed the country. Some of the roads aren't there anymore. We'll find our own roads. You told me Sal loved a little senorita in *On the Road.* He didn't meet her until California. I'll be your senorita. I'm here now."

"And OMG, you put out." That got me a light slap on the face. Well deserved. "Hey, Jen, love, before we hit the road, let's run up to the King Cole for one more drink?"

"Mr. Fine, we're out of here. You would never leave."

"Can we go to Denver too? I want to go to My Brother's Bar on 15th Street. Kerouac went there with Neal Cassady. Carter will meet us there. Let's get cowboy boots. And what else? I want to see you naked. I mean again."

"Yes, you big baby, we'll go to My Brother's Bar. The other two requests, can you be patient?"

"Not my best attribute. Oh, and I'm starting another book. A new biography about Wee Willie Keeler."

"Joseph, is this a joke? Who, pray tell, is Wee Willie Keeler?"

"I didn't tell you? One of the greatest baseball players of all time. Five feet four and one-half. He rarely struck out. He almost always got his bat on the ball. Do you know how hard that is to do? This is what he said, 'I hit'em where they ain't.'"

"Darling, you know what was easy? I fell in your lap. All you had to do was go along." I nodded. "Now, I know this is your Kerouac moment, and you want to hit the road. Can we stop and pick up something to eat? You know, with the baby coming, I get hungry more often."

"Sure. Let's go."

Made in the USA
Middletown, DE
11 June 2022

66852549R00205